The PASSAGE TO INDIA

ALLAN MALLINSON

BANTAM PRESS

LONDON • TORONTO • SYDNEY • AUCKLAND • JOHANNESBURG

TRANSWORLD PUBLISHERS
61–63 Uxbridge Road, London W5 5SA
www.penguin.co.uk

Transworld is part of the Penguin Random House group of companies
whose addresses can be found at global.penguinrandomhouse.com

First published in Great Britain in 2018 by Bantam Press
an imprint of Transworld Publishers

A CIP catalogue record for this book
is available from the British Library.

ISBN 9780593079133

Typeset in 11.25/15.75pt Sabon Next by Falcon Oast Graphic Art Ltd.
Printed and bound by Clays Ltd, Bungay, Suffolk.

Penguin Random House is committed to a sustainable
future for our business, our readers and our planet. This book
is made from Forest Stewardship Council® certified paper.

1 3 5 7 9 10 8 6 4 2

The PASSAGE TO INDIA

CONTENTS

PART THREE: A TIME OF WAR

Passage to India!
Struggles of many a captain – tales of many a sailor dead!

WALT WHITMAN, *Leaves of Grass*

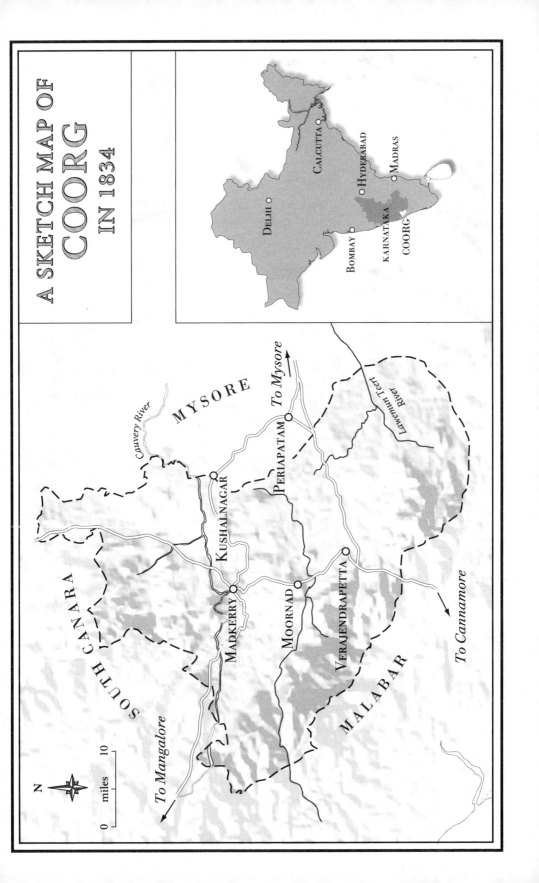

A SKETCH MAP OF
COORG
IN 1834

DELHI

CALCUTTA

BOMBAY

HYDERABAD

MADRAS

KARNATAKA

COORG

MYSORE

Cauvery River

Lawenun Teeri River

KUSHALNAGAR

PERIAPATAM

To Mysore

SOUTH CANARA

MADKERRY

MOORNAD

VERAJENDRAPETTA

MALABAR

To Mangalore

To Cannamore

N

miles

0   10

PART ONE

A TIME OF PEACE

It is an old observation, that a time of peace is always a time of prodigies; for as our news-writers must adorn their papers with that which the critics call, 'The Marvellous,' they are forced in a dead calm of affairs, to ransack every element for proper amusements, and either astonish their readers from time to time with a strange and wonderful sight, or be content to lose their custom.

JOSEPH ADDISON
(with Thomas Steele, founder of *The Spectator*, 1711)

I

The Words of the Preacher

The Cathedral Church of the Blessed Virgin Mary, Salisbury, Wiltshire,
Sunday before the Feast of All Saints, 30 October 1831

'I TAKE AS MY TEXT, the Book of Ecclesiastes, chapter three: "To every thing there is a season, and a time to every purpose under the heaven".'

Hervey settled a little lower into his pew. It was no church parade; there were no officers to whom he must give an impression of attentiveness, no serjeants to whom he must display an upright bearing; nor need he concern himself with what the regiment's chaplain was saying – what its consequence to the listening dragoons (or what the thoughts of the unlistening ones). Besides, from long experience of the pulpit in Horningsham he was certain that no great tumult or misunderstanding was likely to ensue from his father's homily. And the words of Ecclesiastes – 'The words of the Preacher, the son of David, king in Jerusalem' – he knew by heart; and their poetry at least was ever easy to the ear.

The Archdeacon of Salisbury, or Sarum as his father preferred, ever mindful of the time before the Reformation (that wretched word 'Reform' under another guise), looked up and over the lectern, the tallows in their glass sleeves lighting his face as well as his sermon book – a face of some age, now, but still one of distinction, and kindly – and glanced to left and right to the opposing choir stalls, where sat the major part of the congregation as well as the choristers and vicars choral; and, trusting to the *abat-voix* and the stones to magnify his words, began the roll call of every thing and purpose to which there was a season and a time.

'A time to be born, and a time to die; a time to plant, and a time to pluck up that which is planted . . .'

The first of the roll call had never given Hervey cause for contemplation, for the one was past, and the other was the prerogative of the Almighty. True, he himself might have been dead a dozen times and more – one dozen dozen – were it not for his own skill and address, but these he knew (in his better moments) to be a gift, a gift of the Almighty; and it was blasphemy to believe otherwise – as well as, perhaps, hubris.

'A time to kill, and a time to heal; a time to break down, and a time to build up . . .'

This, as a rule, did not disturb him either, for the one, literally speaking, was the soldier's profession – the killing and the breaking down – and the other was the thing of the settled life. His father, he knew, would say that the Preacher spoke figuratively also; but it did not serve the soldier to contemplate too keenly the figurative, for in him it was – in the words of the Bard – action that was eloquence, the eyes more learnèd than the ears.

'A time to weep, and a time to laugh; a time to mourn, and a time to dance . . .'

Perhaps tears and laughter were figures of speech too, though he'd known both very literally. And in truth he had never been able to shed entirely the mourning band – thirteen, rising fourteen years that it was since Henrietta perished (and so cruel a death, in the white wastes of Canada – terrifying, lonely, and on his account). True, it had not made him continent – Lady Katherine Greville remained a standing rebuke in that regard (there was no expiation of sin in old General Greville's being an absentee husband) – but did he let Henrietta's memory haunt him to excess, such that from the outset, and without his knowing, it had somehow stood between him and the second Mrs Hervey? Might Kezia's rejection of him, now, have just cause – rather than, as he supposed, arising from some deficiency in Kezia herself?

A 'time to dance' . . . He smiled to himself again, if ruefully. Certainly he did not now dance with much grace. Indeed he danced very little these days. There had been a time, very briefly . . . But there he was again, harking back: Henrietta – why did he torment himself so?

'A time to cast away stones, and a time to gather stones together; a time to embrace, and a time to refrain from embracing . . .'

Casting away stones, then gathering them? This his father had always said was wanting understanding. There were those who held that it was to mar an enemy's fields by casting stones upon them, as the Israelites had when they invaded Moab; but none could be sure. And the Preacher spoke not solely of conjugal embraces, but of parents embracing their children – as Jacob had his – and of one brother embracing another, as Esau had Jacob; and one friend another. Yet why should conjugal embrace be regulated by season? There were some, he knew (or, at least, he fancied he knew), who lived each day in warm embrace; why had his own seasons been so short?

'A time to get, and a time to lose; a time to keep, and a time to cast away . . .'

He sighed irreverently. Nothing was permanent, or so it seemed. In truth it were better not to get, so as to be spared the struggle to keep, and the pain of losing. Should he chide himself for so mean a thought?

'A time to rend, and a time to sew; a time to keep silence, and a time to speak . . .'

He sighed again, this time almost audibly – and then checked himself: he might be in a plain coat, with none of his dragoons behind him, but it would not serve for the family of the Succentor, and Vicar of the Close, which were Archdeacon Hervey's other preferments (how sudden these pluralities had come after so many years in that tumbledown parsonage at Horningsham), to appear in dissent. But this was indeed a time of rending. The country was in as divided a state of passion as any time he could recall. 'Reform!' – as if a single measure might right every ill of which its advocates complained. Reform had claimed already the best of men – the Duke of Wellington, no longer His Majesty's first minister because he had set his face against it. Yes, the system as it presently stood was imperfect, but yet it served. Who knew what injury might be done in some Jacobin-like amendment? Just half a league from where they sat now was a bare hill, 'the green mound' as the Reformers contemptuously called it – Old Sarum. Once it had been the city itself – castle, cathedral and all, the place in which that great and terrible king Henry Plantagenet had kept prisoner his queen – Eleanor of Aquitaine – for having incited her sons to rebel against their father. Since Edward the Second's time Old Sarum had returned two members to parliament. That it did so still when occupied by no other than sheep was, it was true, an anomaly; but no system could be raised to a state of perfection. That its two members were brothers who had made their fortune in India, come home and 'bought' the borough was an anomaly too; but ought a thing that had served the nation for four centuries now be cast aside by the demands of 'progress'? If the country's forefathers, who strove so manfully to make a parliament, chose to dispose the seats in this way, who now should gainsay them?

He smiled to himself. He recalled how he had put that very question to Cornet St Alban – Lieutenant and Adjutant now, and the best of men – during their Norfolk sojourn two winters ago. The younger son of the Earl of Bicester had asked as they passed Castle Rising (which also, like Old Sarum, the Reformists called a 'rotten borough'), 'Truly, Colonel, how can it serve that green mounds return a member – two members indeed – and a place such as Birmingham none?' And when Hervey had put his own question by way of reply, St Alban had countered very elegantly with 'Colonel, are not members of parliament meant to be lawmakers, not antiquarians?'

Few things had pleased Hervey more than the society of this new-come officer of light dragoons, though he supposed he would not have that pleasure for long. Officers with such connections and means were not much persuaded of the distinction of long service – unless the vainest, most empty-headed kind, like Brudenell in the Eighth, who'd bought his way from cornet to half-colonel in six years, and would doubtless have a regiment soon (without hearing a shot fired but at his own partridges).

His eyelids were growing heavy though. He'd posted through the night, nodding a deal of the way but waking at every change of horses, then stopping on the old Roman road just beyond Figsbury Ring – yet another 'green mound', though one at least that did not return a member to parliament – to watch as the last-but-one sunrise of October revealed the great cathedral below, which was to his mind the finest building in all the world (and he had seen and wondered at the Taj Mahal); and on arriving in the Close he had scarce had time to shave and breakfast before he dutifully attended Morning Prayer – 'Matins', as his father mischievously preferred – and afterwards walked with him a little in the cloisters to promote the circulation, walked next with his mother to the college of matrons to dispense alms and counsel, and then in the water meadows with the old spaniel who'd outlived his former master in the canonry. Evening Prayer – 'Evensong', as the arch-deacon also insisted – he would not as a rule have attended; once of a Sunday, these days, he found enough to be reminded of the eternity of damnation that followed from sin. And as the light faded in that glorious space, the nave and choir, he gave himself leave to close his eyes, for was it not said unto them 'The Sabbath was made for man, and not man for the Sabbath'?

But now came the most tumultuous of the Preacher's seasons, 'A time to love, and a time to hate', in which he thought his father's voice wonderfully conveyed first the sadness of the opposing passions, before, with a dramatic effect that he'd not formerly witnessed, the Venerable Thomas Hervey pronounced the concluding 'a time of war, and a time of peace'.

War: his (Matthew Hervey's) profession, one way or another, and pretty much all he knew. He'd been born into it. When he was but a babe in arms, the French had cut off the head of their king and broken down their neighbours' fences, setting alight all Europe and beyond, so that it smouldered still. As a boy he'd known the peril of invasion right enough, riding the Plain eager to see the beacons that stood ready to rouse the nation to arms. As a youth at Shrewsbury, all ink-fingered, he'd cheered when the tide turned against the would-be invader, when Nelson's 'wooden walls' had emptied the camp at Boulogne of the presumptuously named 'Armée d'Angleterre'. And then, as Britain found a lodgement at last on the continent, to become Bonaparte's 'Spanish ulcer', he had himself put on the King's coat, which he had with one brief interval worn ever since. Indeed, he had bloodied his sword with such regularity that he could think of it as nothing. It was as well that war was so terrible, otherwise he would grow too fond of it. But there was no avoiding war; it sought out the timid and the unprepared. It could be postponed only to the advantage of others.

Yet all was now determinedly peace, and soldiers in peace were like chimneys in summer. What therefore *was* his profession now?

* * *

IT WOULD BE A good night for glaziers. For carpenters and joiners too; likewise plumbers and bricklayers. For locksmiths, cabinetmakers, and any sort of handyman who could knock up a cot, a bench or a board. For drapers, upholsterers and sellers of china – even for wine merchants (that is, if their cellars had survived the tumult). Indeed, for any artisan or tradesman capable of securing or restoring the fabric, fittings or furnishings of the objects – civic and private alike – of the mob's destructive vigour.

But especially glaziers. No protest seized upon the attention of parliament, press, and public so much as the breaking of windows. In April, Apsley House, the residence of the duke himself, had been the mark for the London mob. Its illustrious owner had been too well accustomed to the fall of shot on the battlefield to care a rush for the fall of stones upon his floor (in regard of his own safety at least), but for reasons of public order – and no doubt, too, to damn their eyes – at the first lull of riot he had got himself iron shutters on every window, proof even against bullet and ball (whence he became to the more insolent of the press, 'the Iron Duke').

And for why? Because the *mobile vulgus*, the 'mob', bayed for 'The bill, the whole bill, and nothing but the bill.'

A Bill to amend the representation of the people in England and Wales. 'Reform.'

And in Bristol now there was many an Apsley House (Nottingham had faced the same but a fortnight before, the castle burned to a shell). The country felt tinder-dry, and whether or not fires began could turn randomly on the popularity or otherwise of a single man at the critical point of combustion. In the case of Bristol, that man was Sir Charles Wetherell, recorder of the city and member for Boroughbridge in the County of York, a seat which 'The Bill' would have seen extinguished; and thereby Sir Charles was an implacable opponent of Reform. Two days ago he had proceeded to the great port to open the assizes, in spite of warnings that his appearance would provoke disturbances. These warnings he had simply reported to Lord Melbourne, the home secretary, stating his intention to carry out his duty in the ordinary way, 'whatever risk to mine own person', and leaving the government to take precautions to protect the public peace. Indeed, it was almost with defiance that he entered the city – not privily but with a display of pomp befitting, to his mind, a judge of assize. The warnings were at once proved well founded; his carriage was received with yells, hootings, and stones, so that there was a considerable call on the constables to escort him to the Guildhall to open the commission of peace. Here he loudly threatened to commit to prison any person who could be pointed out to him as contributing to the disturbance, which though in law was proper, in prudence was lacking, not least because there was not the means to effect any arrest. Indeed, it was not so much a spark to the tinder, but a drenching of fuel to the flame of popular fury. By the time he reached the Mansion House, the mob had routed the constables and were attacking the building, so that he was only able to escape, and in disguise, by clambering over the roofs of neighbouring tenements. The mayor, himself a reformer (though little that served in trying to quell the tumult), remained in the Mansion House. Whether the mob knew it or not, they began now to tear up the iron palisades to use as levers against the brickwork of the adjoining walls to furnish themselves with missiles to hurl at every window, while others forced the entrance and brought in straw to set the place ablaze. Only the sudden appearance of the cavalry saved the situation.

The mayor's victory was short-lived, however. That Sunday morning, the last of October, the mob returned. Without firearms or other means of defence, all that his party could do now was follow the example of Sir Charles Wetherell by making their way out of the top of the house and hiding behind the parapets, then crawling along the roofs till they reached the Customs House, clambering in by a fortuitously open window, and quietly descending into a back street to make their way to the Guildhall.

In that party was an officer of the commander-in-chief's staff who had found himself in the city when trouble began and had volunteered his services. The mayor, much shaken by the escapade but now sufficiently recovered, turned to him and said, 'Major Mackworth, I was assured of the military to keep the peace, but there is evidently neither the men nor the will. I beg you, if you please, to do what you can in that regard. I know not how.'

Major Mackworth was not, however, a man merely to volunteer and then await orders; he had already resolved on his course. 'Mr Mayor, I would that you summon every constable, and as many others as may be sworn, and make this place safe as your headquarters. I myself shall go to the recruiting office to find what Colonel Brereton does. Meanwhile, I would that one of your men go to Reeves's hotel and present my compliments and ask Lieutenant St Alban of the Sixth Light Dragoons to come at once.'

II

Reform

The Close, later

IT WAS A HANDSOME canonry, the bounty of Queen Anne, perhaps, when that virtuous woman had appropriated the first fruits
and tenths for the relief of the clergy, which before the Reformation the bishop of Rome had enjoyed, and afterwards King Henry.
Or did he mistake his history? No matter; his people could now
at last live tolerably comfortable of a winter, for unlike the rectory at
Horningsham, here the roof did not leak, the windows fitted close, and
the chimney drew well.

But not merely live comfortable; live in a manner, at last, that was
their due, and proper to their riper years. Hervey's bedchamber, as
his mother had taken to calling the excellent sleeping arrangements,
enjoyed a prospect of the west front of the cathedral that Mr Constable
had lately made famous by his triumph at the Royal Academy, and
one which Mr Turner, a painter of whom Hervey now heard tell was
even greater than Constable, and long acquainted with these parts, had
already done so much to proclaim. The misty dusk of this last-but-one
day of October had however curtailed his pleasure in the west front,

and instead he had bent to one or two letters that were outstanding. He had then bathed, and after dressing for dinner at what was the fashionable hour of the Close, descended the noble staircase to pass a quiet evening in the company of family.

It was only his second visit to the new benefice. Two Easters had passed since his father had been installed in this his only preferment worthy of the name in all his long years of service to the Church of England. That, said his mother, was because he was too unbending a Laudian, though in fact his monograph on Laudian decorum was now in its third printing and had brought him approbation in some quarters, and a little money. (Taste in the re-ordering of services had of late been tending towards that which King Charles's faithful arch-bishop and martyr had endeavoured to impose.) The preferment may have come unjustly late, but come it had, and with it – *Laus Deo!* – three floors, eight bays, some serviceable attics and a garden both productive and pleasant (from which, indeed, the archdeacon could cast a fly on the tranquil water of the Avon). Hervey could only wish his parents long contentment here, and resolve to visit more often – which was the frequent request of his mother and the ever-repeated entreaty of his sister.

It was not as if the King's enemies detained him any longer. It was now almost two years since his appointment to command of the 6th Light Dragoons (Princess Augusta's Own), and but for apprehending common felons in various breaches of the King's peace, and a largely bloodless skirmish with a patrol of French cavalry on the border of Hainaut (quite remarkably near the place where in 1815 he had seen so many homicidal Frenchmen as he wished never to see again), his command had been a most peaceful one. Even when, in the lust for Reform – or simply for glass – the mob had broken the windows of Apsley House, the Sixth in their barracks at Hounslow had not been troubled. And, in truth, although there had scarce been a year in which his sword had not drawn blood before that promotion, and might

13

therefore be glad to rest a while in its scabbard (for who knew when the trumpet would call the regiment to arms in a foreign field?), he found the routine of Hounslow, with its alternating requirements of guard duty and ceremonial at Windsor and London, and acting from time to time as Mr Peel's auxiliaries, tedious – enervating, dispiriting even. Sometimes, especially when he dined alone, as increasingly he found himself, he would lay down his fork and his book or pen and wonder what had brought him to this state of alienation. It was not, however, a matter for contemplation this evening.

Lieutenant-Colonel (and Brevet Colonel) Matthew Hervey, despite the slowness with which command of his regiment had been won (there were men ten years his junior now commanding who had never been shot over, though they did possess the inestimable qualification of great wealth and an entry in Mr Burke's new *Peerage*), was still known to the Horse Guards as a coming man. The commander-in-chief himself, Lord Hill, was assiduous in pressing his cause and had personally authorized the brevet in recognition of his 'address and percipient judgement' in the affair of the 'French joust', as he rather archly called it. He had sent him to Brussels with half the regiment to mark with their former allies the decade and a half since the victory of Waterloo; but instead, Hervey had found himself in the middle of a revolution. The Belgae – *horum omnium fortissimi*, as Caesar had it: the bravest of the three peoples of Gaul – had risen in defiance of the Congress of Vienna, which had made of them a province of the United Kingdom of the Netherlands, and proclaimed their independence of the Dutch king. He, Hervey, had then, largely on his own initiative, kept the probing French patrols at arm's length, so that Monsieur Talleyrand could not make of *les Belges* a French province instead. He had, in the words of a letter home, gone to one country and left another without crossing any border – and received a star in the process (although, being but brevet rank, a star that must remain concealed).

He was content enough, though, for his original promotion to lieutenant-colonel had been without payment – reward for past service, contrived, it was said, by both Lords Hill and Wellington. If ever the time came to sell out, his fortune would be made (George Bingham – Lord Bingham – they said, had paid £20,000 for command of his regiment); and if promotion to general rank were to come, he could accept it without regret at losing his outlay (for on promotion to general rank, the lieutenant-colonelcy of a regiment reverted to the Horse Guards – the headquarters of the commander-in-chief – without recompense). So although he remained in command of his regiment to no great advantage in Hounslow, he held the rank of brevet colonel on the gradation list, at call to take command of a field force when the nation was next in peril. Or so ran the rule. He was most fortunately placed.

In truth, though, what he wished for was diversion. Even his particular friend Edward Fairbrother had deserted him (that is, taken leave of absence to visit with his people – on both sides of the blanket – in Jamaica). Command was a lonely business, it was said – at least, ultimately it was – and it therefore went hard with him each evening to return to a house (his residence at nearby Heston) that lacked the sort of intimacy that made command tolerable, indeed agreeable.

There was, of course, Lance-Corporal Johnson, who lived in adjoining quarters – very comfortably got up, too, in what had been one of the old coach-houses – and was on hand to attend him from reveille to retreat. Unless likely to enter within the field of vision of Regimental Serjeant-Major Armstrong, who had been a 'Hervey man' even longer than Johnson, his faithful groom enjoyed the status of plain clothes, and was more than glad of the life of quietude after so many escapades of recent years. But there was no mistress of the house, save for Mrs James, his house-serjeant's wife – an admirable housekeeper – for Kezia remained, as she had throughout his command, at her people's seat in Hertfordshire. Indeed he had not seen her since his unfortunate visit at Walden in the deep chill of winter the year before.

It had been a cold coming and a cold going. He could not account for their estrangement. It had begun almost at once, at the very outset of their marriage. True, he'd proposed in haste, wanting a wife and a mother for his daughter (for Georgiana had lived only with Elizabeth, his sister, and although it suited him, he could not in his heart believe it was best); but by that token, Kezia had accepted with equal haste. Why, he could not tell. Perhaps her status as widow troubled her, for she too had a child? Her late husband, his former commanding officer, had been the best of men. Perhaps having remarried in haste she then thought it dishonoured his memory, and now repented at leisure? How could he know? At Walden she had seemed so distant, so . . . distrait, that he feared she was . . . well, not altogether of sound mind. And yet her composure that day, while icy – her practice at the pianoforte, even, as he stood listening, unseen – suggested nothing of the sort. All he could conclude was that he had married a woman he did not know. He had done so in good faith, he told himself, although it was true that he had also desired her greatly and wanted to put away Kat from his thoughts, 'considering the causes for which Matrimony was ordained . . . for a remedy against sin, and to avoid fornication; that such persons as have not the gift of continence might marry, and keep themselves undefiled . . .' Now he must live with the consequences, 'forsaking all other . . . so long as ye both shall live'.

The vow troubled him of course. But he was of a mind to be so active always that it did not trouble him to distraction – certainly not (he trusted) in the exercise of his command. So despite there being for the most part nothing to do at Hounslow but, as he himself put it, the work of an accountant or storekeeper, which in peace gave copious employment to an army of quill-drivers to ensure that not a pound of beef was mis-eaten or a bushel of corn fed to an animal other than was on the strength, he filled his day as best he could without intruding too much on the business of his troop captains, and the evenings without claiming too much the company of his officers at mess, or indeed requiring them at his own table. Once or twice a week he would drive to London and dine at the United Service Club, sometimes with Fairbrother, whose comfortable arrangements at Hounslow he was also amply acquainted with, and from time to time there would be some sort of dinner of state requiring his presence, though not quite so many in these past twelve months with the fall of the Duke of Wellington's ministry. More often than not, though, he found himself enjoying a solitary supper, working on his translation of a lengthy treatise on war, which an officer of the Prussian general staff, an acquaintance from his late mission in the near Levant, had caused to be sent his way. It was not an easy work to render in English, not at all an easy work (not least for its being still in proof), but it contained much with which he found himself sympathetic, and when he was at work on it, all other thoughts were banished.

He wished that Elizabeth were here in Wiltshire now, with him and their parents at table. He could not have known that London would have call on her, though he might have been more prompt in writing, and more considerate in what her first duties (that is, of a wife) entailed, rather than supposing her to be at his own call, as ever she had been. He was now even more determined that, saving for the calls of duty, he would travel to Heytesbury before next summer's camp on the Downs was over, and stay a proper while with her and the baron. Her marriage had come late, and to a widower with children – and a wearer of the Waterloo Medal, a *Freiherr* ('von und zu'), of the King's German Legion. He liked the baron; how could he not? Though at first he'd been uncertain. He wished above all that Georgiana were here, for he supposed there was a good deal to talk about. She must be happy in so large a family and so well-found an establishment as at Heytesbury, but she was rising fourteen and must have her own mind in these matters.

He firmly resolved, there and then, to visit on her birthday – even, perhaps, to have her stay at Hounslow for a day or so. She might ride with him on the heath. It need not remind him too painfully of doing so with Henrietta.

*

The bell rang so loud that it carried to the dining room.

Soon afterwards the housekeeper appeared, uneasy. 'Please, sir, there is a Mr St Alban come to see the colonel.'

Hervey looked puzzled. He rose. 'I'll—'

'No,' said his father; 'Hill, please show in Mr St Alban.'

An officer of the Sixth, not yet twenty-five, upright and tall, in a plain coat which even in the candlelight showed evidence of galloping, entered and made his apologies.

Hervey explained: 'Father, Mama – this is Edward St Alban, my adjutant.'

The adjutant of the 6th Light Dragoons bowed again.

'Mr St Alban, you are wet through, sir,' said Mrs Hervey. 'Hill, take Mr St Alban's coat and hold it to the fire, and search out something suitable in its place.'

'Really, ma'am, I am tolerably comfortable, now that I am come in. The rain eased as we came to Wilton.'

'Then permit us to make you wholly rather than just tolerably comfortable.'

St Alban gave up his coat.

'Well, I am all eagerness to learn what brings you here,' said Hervey, 'but first, take a chair and some wine.'

St Alban gladly accepted both, although he looked more brightened by his exertions than fatigued.

'You've come alone?'

'With Serjeant Acton, Colonel.'

Hervey's mother glanced at the housekeeper, who went to find him, Hervey's covering serjeant.

'Very well. Manifestly there is something untoward in Bristol?'

St Alban nodded. 'Bristol is in such a tumult as I never saw in any place, and I fear the magistrates lose all control. The constabulary is in-effectual, and . . . I am sorry to say that the military is inadequate. That is, both its numbers and its management, which is why I am come.'

Hervey was at once transformed. Indeed his instinct was to ready himself at once, but as he could not make Bristol – fifty miles distant – in much less than five hours, it would not hurt to enquire a little more. Besides, a show of serenity never went amiss. 'Tell me of events since the beginning.'

In truth the regiment's sojourn to Bristol ought not to have been a thing of any moment. Certainly not an affair of any heat. In the great panoply accompanying the ancient assizes, there was supposed to be little for them to do but add lustre to the King's justice, the prospect of which had made for a pleasant change from the tedium of Hounslow. In any case, the city lay within an entirely different major-general's command – the Western, rather than the Home, district. It was only Hervey's brevet that had recommended him to the authorities of England's second city – as they were jealous to call it – and it had been but his own (very proper) pride that had made his presence the occasion for an escort. The adjutant, with the serjeant-major and their suite, had therefore proceeded to the city two days before and taken quarters in College Place.

'I ought first to say that I spoke with Major Mackworth, who sends his compliments and bids you hasten.'

'Lord Hill's aide-de-camp?'

St Alban nodded. 'He'd been in Clifton and came to the Mansion House on learning of the commotion.'

'Go on.'

'We hadn't long been in the city before it became apparent there was a very great objection to the recorder,' he began.

'Sir Charles Wetherell.'

'Indeed.'

Archdeacon Hervey's ears pricked. 'Wetherell? I don't doubt there is objection. He made the most intemperate speech in parliament against Reform, just before the dissolution. "Jacobinical and revolutionary" he called the bill. And his father as obliging a man as I ever knew – late dean of Hereford before going back to Oxford, and—'

He checked himself, not so old and cosseted in the cathedral close as not to recognize superfluity of detail.

'I can't comprehend what it should be to the people of Bristol, however,' said Hervey, frowning. 'As I understand it, the city returns two members – both of them Whigs – and stands to gain no more under the bill.'

As ever on the subject of reform, St Alban found himself in an awkward position. He was no Radical, but – to Hervey at least – his Whiggish views tended in that direction. But of all the subalterns, Hervey found him the most thoughtful. The Honourable Edward St Alban, though not long commissioned and only lately promoted from cornet, had shown much address the year before, both at Windsor and in what London was now pleased to call Belgium.

'The feeling for Reform as a principle is strong,' he said, not quite as if he were at a political meeting, 'but . . .' (There followed a discourse on the Bristol Political Union, the pertinence of which Hervey did not entirely see, though he thought it eloquent.) 'And it doesn't help that the bishop cast his vote against it too. And with the usual influx of roughs, the city was not a pleasant sight. I went to see the recorder's arrival yesterday. He came along the Bath road to the city boundary, where he was supposed to transfer to the sheriff's carriage for the processional entry, but there was a most violent welcoming committee, hurling stones at the coaches, which the constables could only get away with some difficulty. I followed – on foot – the entire way to the Guildhall, and I never saw so many people and such a tumult. Several constables suffered ill in the rain of brickbats.'

'And what of the military?' (There was no garrison in Bristol.)

'The mayor applied to the Home Office a fortnight before, and three troops of cavalry are at hand, if much under-strength – two of the Fourteenth, from Gloucester, and one of the Third heavies, from Trowbridge; fewer than a hundred in all. They're under the orders of the inspecting field officer of the district, and . . . with respect, I fear he has not the mettle for it.'

'With respect' was ever a convenient device for avoiding a charge of insubordination, but with adjutancy it was different. Hervey had told St Alban – as he had his predecessor – that it was no use his being adjutant unless he knew the mind of his commanding officer, and that he might always speak his own with absolute candour.

'His name?'

'Colonel Thomas Brereton.'

'*Brereton* . . . There was a Brereton at the Cape, as I recall, not long before I was there. Fairbrother knew him, I believe, from his time in the Royal Africans. I should have thought him capable, if it were he. *Lieutenant*-Colonel, I imagine?'

The point was of the essence: no matter what Brereton's seniority as a lieutenant-colonel – which must be considerable – Hervey's brevet would make him the superior officer.

'Yes. Though I don't know he is the Brereton you describe, Colonel, for he wore but a plain coat.'

'No, indeed. Father, do you have an Army List?'

'I'm afraid I do not,' replied the archdeacon. 'And I cannot imagine where to enquire after one at this hour. I could, perhaps, send to the chapter clerk.'

Hervey shook his head. 'No, let's not trouble him. I don't in any case recall the African Brereton's Christian name, but I'll proceed on the assumption they're one and the same. Carry on.'

St Alban told him of the mob's assault on the Guildhall and attempt to fire the Mansion House.

Hervey braced. 'That indeed gives matters a different aspect.'

Incendiarists, in his judgement – and to his certain knowledge that of the duke (though what sway the duke carried now he did not know) – could be dealt with but one way.

'Just so, Colonel. However, I believe Colonel Brereton thought the mere presence of the dragoons would have effect, which to begin with they did, but—'

'Had they drawn swords?'

'No. Colonel Brereton expressly forbade it, or pistols. Late last night I was able myself, with the sar'nt-major and Sar'nt Acton, to get into the Mansion House and announce ourselves, and soon afterwards Captain Gage of the Fourteenth came, much annoyed, for his troops had come under a great hail of stone and iron in the streets leading upon the square, and he wanted the mayor's leave to use carbines.'

'I know Gage somewhat, and to be a capable man. He must have had just cause.'

'The mayor thought so too, but then Colonel Brereton came and spoke strongly against the order, urging that if the mob were let alone, the hour being late, they would disperse of their own accord.'

Hervey shook his head, wondering by what precedent Brereton believed it might be so. More likely he was minded of another precedent. 'The shadow of Peterloo cast long, no doubt.'

St Alban raised an eyebrow. 'Peterloo' was before his time, a dozen years ago, but no officer of cavalry could be unaware of it. A great gathering of people – by various estimates fifty or sixty thousand – at St Peter's Field in Manchester, come to hear 'Orator' Hunt, with many banners proclaiming 'Reform', 'Universal Suffrage', 'Equal Represent-ation' (and even 'Love'). Fearful of revolution, however, the authorities had at hand two troops of cavalry – one regular, but the other yeomanry – and when the magistrates ordered the latter to arrest the speakers they had got themselves in such a disorder that the dragoons had to rescue them, with much damage to life and limb.

St Alban took another good measure of claret, as if to fortify himself. 'Matters only became worse, however, and much later – I believe at the urging of the mayor – the colonel cleared the square with the flat of the sword, and Gage's men shot one dead who'd assailed them. I should add that by this time Sir Charles Wetherell had left the city.'

'But we may take it, then, that the mayor is not a sort to quit his post.'

'No indeed. I observed him on several occasions and he showed much coolness. It was a little after the square had been cleared that Major Mackworth came to the Guildhall and at once took charge of the constables and arranged a watch and reliefs, and sent for me and asked that I present his compliments to you and request you come and take charge as soon as may be.'

Corporal Johnson now appeared, hastily got up in a tailcoat.

'Have Serjeant Wakefield bring the chaise, if you will,' said Hervey. 'We leave for Bristol this night.'

III

The Rash Fierce Blaze of Riot

Monday, 2 a.m.

'COLONEL, SIR, I THINK I'D best pull up and you have a see.'
Serjeant Wakefield's voice carried strong above the two-time of hooves and the growl of wheels on macadam, but it failed to wake his commanding officer. Having dictated a letter for the Horse Guards, which St Alban had been able to take down – and even correct – by the light of the carcel lamps brought back from Brussels, Hervey had closed his eyes just after Wylye and slept soundly through two changes of horses. ('When a soldier has no other duty to perform, it is his duty to sleep.')

St Alban put his head out of the window. 'What is it, Sar'nt Wakefield?'

Then he saw for himself. Had they been posting east, and some hours later, it might have been but the shepherd's warning, but a red sky in the west was a different matter.

'Colonel.'

The word and a hand to his arm was all that was needed. Hervey sat bolt upright. 'Bristol?'

'Yes, Colonel; and by the look of it, much in flame.'

Wakefield had brought the chariot to a halt atop the Pennyquick hill on the road out of Bath. Hervey climbed onto the roof. He hadn't his telescope with him, but there was no doubting what lay ahead. 'It's a great blaze, and doubtless soon unconfined. By God, I wish I'd even one troop with me.'

Wakefield was calmly checking the traces. 'Go to it, then, Colonel?'

Hervey jumped down. 'Are you sure of finding the lodgings? If we have to go a roundabout way?'

'Aye, Colonel. Hard by the cathedral. Shouldn't be no problem.'

Unless, of course, the whole quarter was in the hands of the mob. But Reeves's hotel, where St Alban said most of the military were billeted – the officers, at least – seemed to Hervey a better place to begin than the Guildhall. The sooner he heard from Armstrong his opinion, and met Mackworth, the better. The mayor and Brereton – if either of them were to be found – could wait.

'Very well, Sar'nt Wakefield. Reeves's, if you please. Give any crowd a wide berth, but have no scruple to drive hard if you can't.' He turned to Acton, who was riding a particularly disobliging post horse. 'Load your carbine.'

'Colonel.'

Acton took no chances. He jumped down rather than fiddle in the saddle with powder and shot. He could anyway better shield it from the persisting drizzle – and ease himself beside the road.

'Want me to hold them while you goes, Wakey?'

Wakefield had been the best rough-rider in the Sixth before the riding-master detailed him to the regimental chariot. He'd driven it to Norfolk the year before, on the mission for the Horse Guards, leaving Hounslow a corporal and returning with a third stripe, having pulled Hervey's old friend Peto from the sea at Blakeney. (Acton had likewise advanced by one stripe after duty as Hervey's covering man in the Levant.) He was more at home in the saddle than on his feet.

'Made water already, Fred.'

Acton had thought about it a while back, but not with a skittish mare. Wet through though he was, he'd no desire to ape an incontinent dragoon of a pay night. 'Per'aps we should be saving it for yonder.'

Hervey smiled to himself ruefully. The mayor of London had said as much – 'A woman could piss it out' – when they told him the fire in Pudding Lane looked bad. He could only trust that Bristol's mayor was of a more active bent, for the red glow looked much like the paintings of the Great Fire.

Nevertheless, they made it to Reeves's without a shot, though as they neared the worst of the tumult, off Queen Square, Acton had had to draw his sabre, sending more than one flying with the flat of it, drawing blood with the edge to another brandishing a halberd, and scattering the rest who saw he meant business. For, since drunk beyond sense they must be, he wasn't inclined to parley. Better to beg indulgence of a magistrate for wounding a few wretches than answer to a court martial for suffering his colonel to be assaulted. Besides, he had a lawful order from a superior officer, and that was all an NCO need ask.

It was a minute or so before three. Reeves's was a substantial mansion, with a handsome façade clear to see in the gaslight and the more distant incendiary glow.

'It has capability,' said Hervey – meaning that, properly shuttered, it would take only a few to defend it against aught but cannon.

A sentry stood at the door, cloaked and sabre drawn – one of his own dragoons.

'Carry on, Sar'nt Wakefield,' was all he said as he got out of the chaise – and all he needed to say.

Acton was already afoot. 'We've stables round the corner, Colonel – Leigh's bazaar.'

Wakefield was pulling away for them.

'Very well – a quarter of an hour, if you please, with new horses.'

St Alban handed him his sword, which he buckled on as they made for the door. Had there been any to see their arrival, whether honest citizen or felon, they could not but have been taken by the impression of purpose ('Action is eloquence' had indeed long been the Sixth's watchword).

The sentry was already at attention.

'Good morning, Spink. How long have you stood guard?'

'All night, Colonel.'

'Anything to report?'

'There were a lot of trouble earlier on, Colonel – a lot o' stone throwing – but the DGs chased 'em off and it's been quiet since, except a lot of noise from yonder, Colonel.' He nodded in the direction of the cathedral and the bishop's palace. 'And comings and goings all night in here, but no trouble.'

Private Spink was Armstrong's groom. He spoke as if it had been Hounslow of a band night.

'Who is in there now?'

'Of us, Colonel? Nobody.'

Hervey wondered why, with so many troops supposedly in the city, Spink alone stood guard here (except that there must be a deal of regimental baggage within), but it was not the time to enquire. No doubt Armstrong had first placed him there, and for good reason had not yet stood him down.

'Where is the sar'nt-major?'

'He went to the docks before midnight, Colonel, to muster the sailors. He thought as they'd answer to discipline.'

'And is there anyone else within?'

'Some of the magistrates came an hour ago, Colonel. They looked dead beat and proper frit.'

'Have you eaten?'

'Mr Reeves's sent me out plenty, Colonel.' He didn't add that the proprietor had given him a half-sovereign as well.

Inside, Hervey found half a dozen citizens of evident standing, who after turning anxiously to see who had come past the sentry looked intensely relieved.

'Upon my word, sir, you are come in deliverance,' said one, stepping forward with his hands clasped. 'I am Alderman Camplin.'

Even in the lamplight it was not difficult to make out the face of a man both anxious and at the same time exasperated – and who might give useful intelligence.

'I am Colonel Hervey. I am due here in connection with the assizes but am come on hearing of the tumult. You are a magistrate?'

'I am, Colonel.'

'Then what of the military here?'

Camplin hesitated a moment. 'They are too few, Colonel.'

'How many?'

'I think no more than thirty or so.'

'*Thirty?* After a day of riot?'

Camplin shifted awkwardly. 'There were more, Colonel, but they are gone away.'

'By whose orders?'

The man looked even more uncomfortable. 'I can't rightly say, Colonel. It was agreed, I think, between the mayor and the military.'

'Who is in command of the military?'

'Colonel Brereton. Of the recruiting office.'

'What does he do now? Where is he at this time?'

'I don't know, Colonel. That is the matter on which we were conferring when you arrived.'

'He is on the streets perhaps?'

'I think not, for the cavalry are returned to their billets, at the horse bazaar hard by.'

'Major Mackworth?'

'I am not acquainted with him, Colonel.'

'And the mayor – where is *he*?'

'He's taken refuge at the house of one of his aldermen. He was very much in fear of his life, and with good reason. He's been much about the city, but after the firing of the bishop's palace and the Mansion House, and—'

'The bishop's palace is fired?'

'Like a bonfire on Guy Fawkes's night. And the Bridewell, and its inmates let loose; and the new county prison and the governor's house – two hundred more felons running free.'

Hervey wondered why, in the first instance, Brereton hadn't made one at least of these places into a strongpoint. 'And constables?'

'Chased from the streets, I fear,' replied Alderman Camplin, warming now to his complaint that the military had deserted them. 'The mayor called for as many specials to be sworn as may be, but without support of the troops they lost heart.' He cleared his throat. 'Mr Goldney here, and Mr Harris, bear a letter from the mayor authorizing – nay, begging – Colonel Brereton to take action to restore the Queen's square, but they've been unable to speak with him.'

Hervey looked at the two of them.

Goldney, a surgeon, and evidently a man at the end of his tether, took it as licence to speak his mind. 'At about midnight, fearful that my house would soon be attacked – for two sides of the square were already alight and their contents strewn in the street and carried off – I went to seek out the mayor, or some magistrate capable of action, and found him at . . .'

He seemed to forget himself.

'Proceed,' said Hervey, and a shade peremptorily.

'The mayor gave me this letter for Colonel Brereton.'

31st Oct, 1831
Bristol, 1 o'clock, Monday Morning
Sir: I direct you, as commanding officer of His Majesty's troops, to take the most vigorous, effective and decisive means in your power to quell

the existing riot and prevent further destruction of property.
CHARLES PINNEY

To Col Brereton, or the Commanding
Officer of His Majesty's Troops.
Per MR GOLDNEY
MR W. HARRIS, Jun.

'I took it at once with Harris to Leigh's horse bazaar, where we found Captain Warrington, in charge of the Dragoons, and begged him in the absence of the Colonel – whose whereabouts he was unwilling to divulge – to read and act on it. However, on reading it – which I must say he was most reluctant to do, on account of its being addressed personally to Colonel Brereton – he said that he felt unable to act without the presence of a magistrate and asked if we knew where to find one, but we had given an undertaking to the mayor not to reveal his whereabouts, and so were unable to oblige, and so came here to consider our position.'

Hervey angrily pulled off his cap. 'In the name of God! Is there no one who will reveal *anything*? Where *is* the mayor?'

Surgeon Goldney, who only now appeared to realize the absurdity of the respective heads of the civil and military powers not knowing each other's whereabouts (let alone being side by side), swallowed hard. 'At Alderman Fripp's brother's in Berkeley Square.'

'Where is this square? I am strange to Bristol.'

'A furlong or so northwards, towards the park.'

'Very well. I desire that you bring the mayor here, and I shall have Colonel Brereton come here so that we can concert our action. Is there a high constable of the city?'

'No, Colonel, only chief constables of each ward.'

'And the fire companies?'

'I would say they have been largely ineffectual, on account of there being so many fires started, and the hostility of the onlookers.'

Hervey angered again. 'They'd do better to serve with their axes against the miscreants, then. See to it they're mustered and sworn.'

Alderman Camplin and his deputies thought it theirs to comply. This colonel of dragoons appeared to be in very sanguinary mood, and while they had no wish to subject themselves to the process of law that would follow when the riots were over – when the courts might be more concerned with the letter of the law than with the exigencies that had led to the suspension of it – they had no wish to dissuade him from the vigorous action necessary to preserve life, limb and property.

Hervey took their silence as agreement. 'Very well. Let us convene again as soon as may be.'

Armstrong now appeared, heated. 'Colonel, praise be you've got here. Can we 'ave words?'

St Alban turned away. Notwithstanding rank, customs of the service and pride, the greenest dragoon knew that Hervey and the serjeant-major had soldiered so long together that they enjoyed an intimacy not prescribed by King's Regulations. Armstrong was sparing with the privilege, but 'Can we 'ave words?' was the formula for claiming it.

They went into a small ante-room followed by a man in a tailcoat who announced himself as the night porter and offered to bring them coffee, which Hervey was glad of.

'Well, Mr Armstrong, quite an affair, it would seem.'

'Colonel, it's worse than aught I've ever seen – worse even than Brussels.'

Brussels had been shocking enough. They'd been at the theatre in some state – with their royal colonel-in-chief no less – when the city had lost its head: *Death to the Dutch!* (What an unhappy union of the two Netherlands the Congress of Vienna had made.) And 'Dutch' seemed to be anyone in authority – and uniform the mark of it. So they'd had to use their swords to clear a way through the mob, and watch the flames begin licking at the buildings.

Hervey's brow was deep furrowed: Armstrong was not given to excess when it came to these things.

'There's just no will to stop it, Colonel. Yon Colonel Brereton had four troops to hand last night – two of 'em already here, and some yeomanry come in at the mayor's calling – and Brereton sends away the Fourteenth, and the yeomanry clip-clop round for an hour and more trying to find somebody to tell 'em what to do – as if they needed anybody, for there're villains on every street – and then they takes themselves off 'ome, so all there is now is the Third and their captain, who's no more use than a bent nail. All the constables've scarpered – for all that Major Mackworth did his best to keep them. It's only the tars on them ships yonder who've any fight in 'em at all. There were word that the docks were to be fired, so we went down there with one of the magistrates and got them to muster, which they did good and proper – specially the blacks. Answered to discipline like a good troop. The harbourmaster's got them all mustered now, which is why I've come back – to try to find out what in God's name Brereton intends doing, for if he doesn't the place'll be naught but cinders tomorrow.'

Hervey said nothing for a moment or so, then called St Alban in. 'It's imperative we get every sabre we can into the city, and fast. We must get Brereton here, and the Third under arms again. Have their captain stand them to and come here for orders. I'm going to see for myself the state of things in Queen Square.'

Now it was St Alban's turn to exercise a privilege. 'Sar'nt-Major, might I speak alone with the colonel?'

'Sir!' Armstrong turned to Hervey; 'I'll go and get Acton, Colonel.'

The night porter came with coffee. St Alban waited for him to pour two cups and then closed the door after him. 'Colonel, I understand perfectly that it's imperative that order is restored, but afterwards there'll be no thanks for it. Of course you must act on your own account, but I do urge, at the very least, that you make plain in writing your reasons for assuming command – at once to London.'

Hervey frowned. 'I've said it before: an officer's choice is whether to risk being shot by a court martial for his forbearances, or hanged for his over-zeal by a jury. But I know where the sympathy would lie if it came to a jury here.'

St Alban wasn't so sure. He'd galloped to Salisbury to bring order to Bristol, but he didn't intend letting his commanding officer risk his neck unnecessarily. 'Colonel, the old order's changed. The duke is no longer prime minister. The temper of the government, the country . . . Any comparison with Peterloo would be . . . well, to your certain disadvantage.'

St Alban was not that long commissioned, but in him Hervey recognized both capability and judgement beyond his years – political judgement indeed, for that way, he knew, lay his ambition – which was why he'd made him his adjutant. (In many a regiment the appointment was filled by an officer from the ranks, a man who knew every trick through long years of 'undetected crime'.) Even so . . .

'Every minute that we're distracted from taking action will add at least a page to what I have to report. I'll write as soon as I have opportunity.'

'Colonel, with respect, we must get a letter away to Lord Melbourne immediately. I'll warrant that as we speak there are letters from others bound by coach or express. Let me get the Third stood-to, and Colonel Brereton here, and then let me draft the letter.'

Hervey frowned again, incredulous. 'To Melbourne himself? That would be to subvert the principles of military authority. It must go to the Horse Guards.'

'If it goes to the Horse Guards it will have to wait on Lord Hill's pleasure, which may not be prompt, for any number of reasons. Lord Melbourne will be apprised of the situation this day, if not already. You must so inform him that he sees you as the answer to the problem – as his man indeed – not later as one who must explain his action.'

There was something in the force with which his 'Pitt the Younger' of an adjutant made what was anyway a compelling argument that persuaded Hervey to take the straighter line. If in doing so it was 'Ware hole!' but too late – so be it. 'I would see the letter first, of course, *but* – if I am detained then you may send it "per pro". It should certainly go by the morning mail, if it's running still – or express.'

St Alban looked relieved. The new home secretary had so far shown himself suspicious of the military. Despite the trouble of the past twelve months – the rick-burning, machine-breaking and assaults on landlords (what some were pleased to call the 'Swing riots', on account of threatening letters signed by the mysterious 'Captain Swing') – Melbourne had refused to oblige the magistrates' alarmism, as he saw it. This affair in Bristol was of a wholly different order, but that wasn't to say the government would treat it so – not when to begin with the rioters had cloaked themselves in the mantle of Reform. St Alban was no Tory – his head and heart lay with the new administration – but he was not blinded to faults on either side.

They took their coffee quickly. Armstrong knocked and Hervey called him in.

'Sar'nt Acton's come with horses, Colonel, an' I've sent Spink for mine at the double.'

Hervey knew that by that he meant 'wait till I come with you', and if he said he wouldn't wait, Armstrong would only have taken Acton's horse; so he poured him a cup too, and then another for himself. 'Rash fierce blaze of riot cannot last / For violent fires soon burn out themselves.'

'Colonel?'

'Shakespeare, though here I can't believe he's right. Nor, I think, did he live to see his theatre burn down. The devil of all this here is that a few dozen peelers could have nipped it in the bud.'

'Oh, aye, Colonel. An' we'll get the blame – whichever way.'

'What do you suppose will happen, then, when daylight comes?'

'A good many of 'em'll fall down exhausted, but there'll be any number of low-life sorts coming in fresh, now that they've heard there's drink to be had, and more.' Armstrong spoke with the assurance of a man who'd weathered many a trial with both. 'There's all them prisoners let loose an' all.'

Hervey drained his cup, and nodded. 'That's what I'd feared, which is why we need the yeomen to return soonest – to picket the roads in.'

Spink was not long in running back with Armstrong's trooper. Out they went for the square.

'The owner's, Colonel,' said Acton as Hervey mounted the unfamiliar bay. 'It were the best by a mile. He says she's apt to drop her shoulder if she's held too tight on the bit, but nothing otherwise.'

There'd been no need to bring his own charger down from Hounslow, for there were no parades. As for dropping the shoulder, a horse without the odd vice was a horse without spirit.

'Will you lead, please, Sar'nt-Major.'

Armstrong put his mare straight into a trot. Up and across College Green – where a few dozen roughs skulked warily; past the recruiting office and then north along the towpath to the bridge across the floating basin; then south again along the quays to the back of the assembly rooms. A party in the charge of an elderly but redoubtable French-woman trying to remove waxworks from her travelling exhibition – *Le Cabinet de Figures de Cire de Madame Tussaud* – evidently fearful of the mob and the heat of the encroaching fires, brought them up sharp.

'Vous êtes de la police, monsieur?' she called as they picked their way through.

'Non, Madame,' answered Armstrong as he side-stepped a *portrait en cire* of Marie Antoinette. 'Nous sommes the army. Have no fear, but don't expose yourself to those ruffians.'

'Alors! I 'ad my own 'ead shaved for the guillotine. I am not frightened by these wretches!'

She reached under her skirts and produced a pair of pistols.

'I wish the constabulary showed as much fight,' said Hervey as he in turn tried to avoid collision with a *mannequin* – which looked remarkably like his mental image of Robespierre, and so *apropos* therefore that he shook his head. 'Bonne chance, Madame!' (He had to force himself not to say 'Tirez les premiers', though he supposed she hardly needed the advice).

A hundred yards on, where the street met the square, he saw for himself what they were up against. Hundreds of people – many hundreds – of all descriptions and states of sobriety: little groups of respectable-looking men and women, residents of the square, perhaps, staring on the scene in bewilderment; men and women that would have shamed a London rookery cavorting like fiends in a representation of Hell, and others carrying off all manner of plunder, some with handcarts. The noise was infernal: shouting, jeering, whistling, shrieking, howling, wailing, baying, roaring – legions of the lowest orders given leave to run riot. And above it somehow the sound of breaking glass – window panes, each followed by a full-throated cheer. And bottles, mirrors, table crystal – defenestrated without warning, hazard to fleeing quality, passing roughs and recumbent drunks alike; and all to a crackling, fiery continuo, as the whole of the west and north sides of the square were in various stages of flame, with here and there a sharp explosion – powder perhaps, or oil, even gas maybe; and then the sudden growl and rumble of falling masonry – chimney stacks pulled down with hawsers; roofs, floors, entire walls. And many a rough meeting his Maker in the rubble and the flames.

Queen Square, once the height of respectability, now a scene that Hogarth would have struggled to contain – Gin Lane and Beer Street a hundred times over, the contents of fine houses, of businesses in neighbouring streets, strewn about for the taking, or with coin for the felons who claimed custody of the piles. The grand equestrian statue of William III in the middle of the square stood festooned with red, the colour of defiance, and all around, Armstrong's 'low-life sorts' guzzled and chewed like Hogarth's wretches, or sat on looted chairs at looted tables to enjoy their provisions even more – just remembering occasionally to shout 'Reform and the King!', as if this somehow gave them just cause.

If Hervey had had any doubts where his duty lay, they were at once dispelled. Here was the nightmare that had haunted the authorities for a decade and more and set the Duke of Wellington's face against Reform; for if once conceded, there was no knowing the end of things. Or rather, there was: *Revolution*. All that was missing in this Hadean scene was that of which Madame Tussaud had spoken: the guillotine.

He set his jaw and turned about. 'This, Sar'nt-Major, we will sweep clear at first light of day.'

IV

The Edge of the Sword

Reeves's, later

Lieutenant-Colonel Thomas Brereton was ten or so years Hervey's senior, and in rank some five more, for Brereton had been promoted half-colonel in 1815 while Hervey had still been a cornet. But the brevet was the key: Hervey might wear the same lieutenant-colonel's crown on his epaulettes, but there was an invisible garter star too.

Brereton himself presented an unhappy picture. Handsome though he remained, with his spare, even sharp, features, his years in the tropics – the fevered Indies and then the Guinea coast – had thinned his hair, whitened it a good deal, dulled his eyes and weathered his complexion to a yellow-brown. Although roused from his bed, he had evidently slept little in the past days. He did not stoop, however, for he was by no means a broken man. Yet his nerves were evidently much shaken. His was a face that Hervey had seen before, in men whose self-belief was shot – at times in Spain, and at Waterloo; once or twice in India. There was no knowing what might overwhelm some men, and with others be impulse to great deeds. Nor was it always simple fear: he'd seen the look in men who stood their ground bravely through some paralysis of mind, rather than prudently withdraw. A seasoned soldier and man of Christian charity was inclined to pity, rather than anger; but the exigencies of the moment sometimes required harshness, or at least provoked it. There would be a time to treat kindly with one who had given so much service, but it was not now.

Brereton accepted Hervey's claim of authority at once, however, though at the same time began to defend his actions. 'I have been left in the most unenviable position, Colonel Hervey – betwixt an overpowering, infuriated mob and a magistracy from whom no essential aid can be procured.'

Such a situation would always claim the sympathy of a fellow officer, as here; but the question was – or rather, would no doubt be put at a later date – whether prompt action in the first instance would have prevented the mob from becoming overpowering. That was by the bye, however. They must now take whatever action they could to restore the peace. Hervey tried to get him to sit and take some coffee, but Brereton insisted on his *apologia*: 'Supposing we had shot a good many of them and dispersed them for the instant, they would have reassembled in considerably greater numbers – which I could not have prevented for I had not the force to occupy the many outlets of this city. Both men and horses would have been exhausted – *were* exhausted, indeed – and so exasperated were the mob previously that they determined to attack the houses for arms to destroy the dragoons in their quarters when they went to refresh. Would it have been right under such circumstances to hazard the troops being repulsed – for if they had been, the mob flushed with their victory would have had possession of the whole city and fired the shipping. Of this intent they made no secret, nor their plan to attack the banks – and then throw all the surrounding countryside into confusion.'

There was logic in these objections – where Brereton's semi-punctuated flow allowed him to see it – but Hervey was growing impatient of the counsel of despair. Indeed he had to check himself, for his instinct was 'Leave that consideration for the court martial'. (He would not humiliate such a man in front of those now pressing in the common rooms of Reeves's hotel.) There was also a substantial flaw in Brereton's logic: 'But my good fellow, the mob have possession of the city at this very moment. That is the material point.'

Brereton could give no answer. His mouth was open, but his face was blank.

Nor would Hervey have entertained an answer. Instead he turned to the officer in command of the dragoon guards. 'Captain Warrington, how many are you?'

'Thirty-two, Colonel.'

'And that is, as I requested, every one of your men?'

'Yes, Colonel, save for those wounded.'

'Very well, I desire that you form the troop in two divisions, and all to load with ball cartridge. I myself will address them presently.'

Warrington nodded warily. 'Shall there be a magistrate to accompany us, Colonel?'

'I cannot tell. Does that present you with any difficulty?' He said it with some asperity, having already concluded that Warrington was ignorant of the provisions of King's Regulations in respect of aid to the civil power.

'I understand that only a magistrate can authorize the use of firearms, Colonel.'

'Captain Warrington, I understand that Mr Surgeon Goldney delivered up to you a letter from the mayor for Colonel Brereton, and that he prevailed upon you to read it.'

Warrington looked awkward. 'Yes, indeed, he did, Colonel. But how may we avoid doing harm to the innocent?'

'My advice to innocent people when the Riot Act has been read is to get off the streets. Do you have any more questions?'

'No, Colonel.'

'To your duty, then.'

The mayor now arrived, with half a dozen others. Hervey was surprised to see a far younger man than he'd supposed. Charles Pinney was ten years his junior, perhaps – a good-looking man, with hair the colour of the Sixth's light chestnuts. But if Mayor Pinney were unburdened by experience, therefore, neither could he be fortified by it. (Only later would he discover that Pinney had been sworn in but a month before, which at that moment was as well.)

'Your worship, I am Colonel Hervey of His Majesty's Sixth Light Dragoons.' (There was, he knew from long practice, an advantage to be gained by punctiliousness in dealing with the civil power.) 'As the senior officer, it is my intention to take command of all troops in the city and direct them to the rapid restoration of order. I have the letter you addressed to Colonel Brereton some hours ago instructing him to take vigorous and effective action.'

Having expected civic objection, he was agreeably surprised by the reaction: a look of the greatest relief came over the mayor. 'You will send the troop of dragoons to Queen Square?'

Hervey frowned. 'No, I shall myself lead them.'

Pinney was even more delighted.

Hervey now set his jaw very decidedly. 'Regaining the square is but the first and most necessary thing – and I fear it can't now be done without a deal of bloodshed. Temporizing would be a dangerous and even cruel policy. Indeed, I'm of the opinion that exemplary violence is now necessary, else the mob is encouraged to return armed and in greater strength.'

The mayor suddenly looked less sure; but Hervey was in no mood to relent.

'Once the news is abroad that the square is held unassailably by the authorities, the heart should begin to go out of the riot. It's imperative therefore we have the greatest number of constables ready to take to the streets.'

41

Pinney seemed to recover his resolution. 'I signed the writ for the *Posse Comitatus* last evening. The sheriffs are posting bills as we speak. I regret it's an unduly lengthy business, for the law requires it be done by precept in every ward; but there'll be constables aplenty once they see the military means business. I intend going now to the Council House to assemble the magistrates.'

'Where is the Council House?'

'On Broad Street, at the junction with Corn Street – half a mile, no more.'

St Alban held up an old plan of the city he'd found in a frame in the smoking room.

Hervey nodded. 'Very well. I'll come there as soon as Queen Square is ours. You've sent for reinforcements, have you not – and regulars, I mean?'

'I have – to Gloucester for another troop of the Fourteenth – two if may be – as well as for the yeomanry. Major Mackworth went to Keynsham just after midnight to recall the Fourteenth's troop which Colonel Brereton sent away. And last night I sent word to Cardiff, for the infantry there.'

Hervey began to reckon. He might see the Keynsham troop at any minute, and those from Gloucester in an hour or so – the yeomanry much later, if at all. He was anyway uncertain of the yeomanry's discipline. Last year, in Norfolk, he'd seen much that had reassured him, but elsewhere reports were contrary. There had lately been mutiny in the Salisbury Troop of the Wiltshire Yeomanry – or rather, near mutiny – when their captain, Lord Arundel, voted against the Reform Bill; though it did not help perhaps that he was also a Catholic. And yet they were now the *Royal* Wiltshire Yeomanry, honoured this very year for their exertions in putting down the 'Swing' riots. There was just no telling.

As for the infantry . . . 'Have you sent a steamer to bring them from Cardiff?'

The mayor looked suddenly deflated. 'I'm afraid I have not. I confess it didn't occur to me. I suppose I imagined they'd have recourse to ample shipping of their own.'

Hervey frowned again. That was as may be, but a Bristol packet would have speeded matters – and they would need every bayonet they could find when the cavalry had done their work.

He looked at his watch. Ten minutes past six: first light in another quarter hour or so, though it was still overcast. 'Now, with your leave, Mr Mayor, I have Queen Square to reclaim.'

Pinney held out his hand. 'I pray your men will come to no harm, Colonel.'

Hervey took it, then pulled down his cap and gathered up his sword. If any of his men came to harm, it would not go unpunished – but he thought better of saying so.

Two minutes later he was surveying the troop of the 3rd Dragoon Guards from the saddle. All things considered, they showed well, the red of their tunics splendid even in the half-light, facings canary yellow, crossbelts well whitened. These were not men to be discouraged, he was sure. The horses were of a good stamp too, full sixteen hands or more. His own dragoons, and the Fourteenth, might be nimbler, but heavies might do the job by mere show. Just as were the horses, their troopers were sturdier too, and the great bearskin crest atop the helmet made them twice the height in the saddle. If only they were twice the number.

He need only be brief in his exhortation, though: 'You have been sorely tried these past days. It is now time to end the disorder that has befallen the city. We shall make a beginning with Queen Square. The Riot Act is read; the rioters are to be dispersed or apprehended. The troop shall form line at the west end of the square and proceed east at the trot, taking the statue of King William as the centre mark. The flat of the sword will be used to hasten, the edge only to check resistance. Carbines solely for return of fire. Captain Warrington, carry on!'

Warrington had them draw swords and turn to the right in threes, and led them across College Green at the trot, troop serjeant-major to the rear, Hervey and his party – Brereton, St Alban, Armstrong and Acton – following. They met neither brickbats nor abuse, which might have been auspicious had it not been for the fires on every side of them, testimony to the work of the mob and opportunism of the 'low-life sorts' drawn into the city like jackals to a great beast brought down. Here and there Hervey could see them in the shadows, out of range of a sabre-swipe, but he was determined their time would come. He could with confidence count on several hundred more sabres soon, and as many bayonets. He intended – as he was sure did Mayor Pinney – not simply to restore order, but to bring the perpetrators to justice, for there could otherwise be no true peace.

Having been so roughly handled by the mob, however, and then withdrawn – against the will, no doubt, of every one of their rank and file – the dragoons would be zealous in their work, perhaps even over-zealous, he reckoned; and despite the Riot Act, which in the event of death or injury indemnified anyone assisting with the dispersal of rioters, there would be a hue and cry in some quarters, no matter what the outcome – the corresponding societies, the Radical press, the houses of parliament. He would therefore make sure the Third did not exceed themselves . . . excessively. What that excess was, he could not yet judge – only once they'd begun their work.

Tricky business, aid to the civil power; but not impossible.

They surged across Clare Street bridge like the river bore, sweeping aside roughs and their plunder, trampling those who thought themselves faster runners and sending many leaping over the side. More than one who fancied himself a good swimmer forgot the weight of loot in his long pockets and fetched up downstream in a watery grave.

Wheeling right onto the quay, they overran half a dozen others scuttling from a lighter like rats, before coming on the rear of the assembly rooms and slowing to a walk to squeeze between the gutted

44

Excise Office and what little remained of the handsome houses beside it. They then turned left and right by divisions into line at the end of the north side of the square – Warrington leading the first, Brereton the second.

The scene was yet worse than before – steep banks of flame, great palls of smoke, tumbling walls, seared trees and jagged ruins which a Piranesi might have made picturesque had not the debris revealed what their interiors had recently been. As crept in the dawn, Hervey could scarce believe there were so many keeping the square still – hundreds, many hundreds. The noise was as bad as battle except there was no shot – yet; and as bad indeed was the smoke and the flame.

The dragoons took no pains to dress, inclining left and right as soon as they were extended, kicking straight into the trot. They would not be humiliated a second time. There would be no Brereton forbearance. There would indeed be no quarter.

Sabres began to swing – with the flat to begin with, but in a while there was no scruple, and in the middle of the square those who defied the Riot Act, whether stupefied or not, received the edge.

At the far side – a couple of hundred yards off, if that – a desperate pack of jackals now hurled themselves at one of the stouter houses, bursting the locks as if nothing at all, frantic to escape the retribution, but only to meet with an equally determined fight inside, led by a doughty negro. The troop serjeant-major drew his carbine, put his horse at the steps and fired into the narrow hall, then reined back hard to cuff the first of the pack as they bolted. Between servants and dragoons, none of the jackals escaped, and three were cut so badly that an hour later they were still immobile.

Brereton began trying to cool the dragoons' blood, but the square had only been ridden through, not cleared.

'Line about, Captain Warrington!' shouted Hervey, cantering the length of the south side signalling direction with his sword.

The dragoons needed no telling. Back they went with a will. Any man on his feet now was a defiant, a felon – and a good many felons there were still. Doubtless they'd thought the charge was over and not to be repeated. Sabres swung without restraint, with a savage ferocity indeed, and the sound of revelry and wrecking was now become that of terror. Scarcely a sabre reached the north side without new blood.

Brereton called on Warrington to hold – but Hervey wasn't done. This was the moment he must judge the margin between necessity and excess. They'd dispersed the riot in Queen Square, but the 'scum of the earth' – as the duke had called the class from which his army was drawn – once they'd tasted the pleasures of riot, could never be quelled entirely by bluff. Sanguinary though the dragoons had just been, they were small in number. If but a quarter of the 'scum' returned, armed perhaps with staves and iron railings – or, God forbid, a firearm or two – they'd be sorely pressed. They might even have to dismount and hold with the carbine, in which case a great many of their assailants would die – and even then it would be touch and go. When the Gloucester men arrived and those from Keynsham, he'd be able not just to hold the entire square but to proceed beyond; *exploit* – scatter the various rabble more effectually, in every direction and progressively until he reached the city limits. For then and only then might the constables be able to go to their work with confidence and result, restoring calm, arresting fugitives, recovering property. For the moment, though, all he could – and must – do was maintain a deceit: he must show that the military was in incontestable command of what his 'Prussian mentor' would call *der entscheidender Punkt* – the crucial point, the place of decision. And he could only do this by the application of such force as shocked the army of felons into believing that the forces of the Crown were many more, and overwhelming.

'Go again!' he cried. 'Don't give them opening to recoup. Not a man must be allowed to keep the square!'

He risked firing them up too much, but he couldn't risk the mob thinking they were blown. And the troop was under good regulation,

Armstrong making certain of it, cracking about as of old . . .

Back across they went, this time at a canter – and remarkably well in hand. He reckoned the Sixth themselves couldn't have done it better. At the far side he called Brereton and Warrington to him and said he wanted the troop now to patrol the roadway bounding the square, and at a good lick: they'd cleared the turf; now he wanted a display on the perimeter till there were none but lame singletons afoot. He rattled out the orders: videttes posted in pairs at each entrance – ten in all – with rosters to hold the square till the middle of the morning. And the reliefs to form reserve in case an entrance was forced, and ready to meet it with fire. He was sure the Fourteenth would be here from Keynsham soon, and perhaps even Gloucester.

That was supposing the whole of the square hadn't caught light by then. So far the drizzle had perhaps kept the flames from spreading, but now it was no more – and not a fire engine in sight. He certainly hadn't the men to spare, nor had he any notion how the fire companies might be got to help if they were not of a mind. That was for the civil power. He must hope that the householders – those who hadn't fled the mob – would now find mettle enough to tackle the flames (and that the dragoons would have the wit to distinguish them from the miscreants). He would stay until there was full daylight and calm, and then go to the Council House to concert the next moves.

St Alban offered him his flask.

Hervey took a good measure of brandy, though he would have preferred it mixed with strong coffee. 'I tell you, this is the worst business I saw. I doubt Gordon's men did greater destruction. I can't account it political.'

'No, Colonel. And no Radical, even, would seek to justify it.' (St Alban only hoped they would not condemn the manner of its overthrow either.)

'That, we shall see.' Hervey did not sound sure they would.

It was now just before eight o'clock, and St Alban thought it the moment. 'With your leave, I'll repair to Reeves's and get away the letter. The surgeon, Goldney, told me there's a mail leaves at ten.'

Hervey nodded, handing back the flask, conscious now of how prescient St Alban's advice had been, and wondering if his own powers were failing. He'd always reckoned he possessed the cavalryman's *jugement d'affaires* – the *coup d'oeil* both in the field and out. Perhaps it was arrogance – a disdain of having to explain himself as if a supplicant – but prudence demanded . . .

'Yes, go to it.'

Another letter for Lord Melbourne was already London-bound by the Bath coach:

> *My Lord, — I have the honour to represent to your lordship that in consequence of a requisition from the mayor of Bristol, between two and three o'clock yesterday, I collected my troop of Yeomanry with as little loss of time as was practicable. When your lordship considers that I had to send some miles in different directions, you will, I think, admit the alacrity of my men when I state that we were enabled to march from hence (Dodington), with scarce a man missing, by seven o'clock. Having, however, fifteen miles to go, and the night being very dark, we could not reach Bristol till after nine, when, I lament to say, we found the city on fire in many places, the gaols emptied, and the town in the greatest confusion. Having paraded through the principal parts of the city for more than two hours without being able to find a magistrate – hearing that they had, in fact, left the town, after withdrawing both his majesty's troops and the police – finding ourselves thus unsupported, and without a hope of being in any way serviceable – the city being actually in the uncontrolled power of the populace, I had no alternative but that of withdrawing also my men, and we returned home about five o'clock this morning.*
>
> *Feeling it my duty to make this statement to your lordship, I should ill perform it towards the brave men I am proud to have the honour*

*of commanding, if I did not further state that no men could have
come forward with more alacrity; and, although they might not have
acted with the discipline of his majesty's regular troops, they would
not have been exceeded by them in zeal, loyalty, or a determination
to have done their duty; and had they had an opportunity of acting,
they would have shown themselves not undeserving of his majesty's
approbation.*

I have the honour to be, my lord, your lordship's obedient servant,

C. W. CODRINGTON,
Captain of the Dodington and Marshfield
Yeomanry Cavalry.
Dodington, October 31st.

At the Council House – a handsome building, with a classical exterior
that spoke of the old wealth of England's second city, but which stood
now with most of its windows put out, the glass swept into piles in the
corners of its elegant rooms – Hervey found the mayor active, having
assembled the ward sheriffs and a dozen magistrates and aldermen,
telling him that several hundred special constables were mustering at
this moment in churches about the city, a good many of them out-
pensioners of the Chelsea Hospital (and therefore men of stout heart),
and a good few former officers of the army and marines. They were
eager to do their duty, said the mayor, and variously armed, some with
pistols, and would wear white armbands signifying their authority.
As soon as there were troops to furnish them a minimum of support, he would have them secure the gaols and begin rounding up the
absconders.

Hervey nodded. 'Is there sign of the Fourteenth yet?'

'Major Beckwith, their commanding officer, arrived from Gloucester
in advance not ten minutes ago. He has gone with his adjutant to the
recruiting office to arrange a depot. His squadron follows in about two
hours.'

Hervey frowned at the delay, though he would acknowledge that

Gloucester was some distance, and turned to Serjeant Acton standing exaggeratedly at attention two paces behind. 'My compliments to Major Beckwith, and would he attend on us at once.'

'Colonel!' barked Acton, turning to his right and saluting with a vigour that made the aldermen start. (It did no harm to remind them what a man was a serjeant of light dragoons.)

The mayor cleared his throat. 'I can't suppose the troop at Keynsham can be very long in returning.'

Not only was Hervey feeling the want of gallopers – he would not as a rule have sent his covering serjeant even as far as the recruiting office – he now chafed at the absence of men for videttes. There ought by now to be pickets on every one of the roads into the city, and dragoons for intercommunication. He would then know at once who entered and left, and be able to direct his reinforcements accordingly.

Instead he must wait, and while waiting discuss with the mayor what other means were available to extend the peace and order that he'd won – for the time being at least – about Queen Square.

In a quarter of an hour they'd made what he reckoned was a service-able plan – two plans, indeed, subject to when and in what strength the infantry arrived from Cardiff. It seemed unlikely, but if they were here by evening the cavalry could be rested ready for the morning, which, depending on the success they had today in breaking up any further assemblies – which in turn depended on what time the Fourteenth's troop arrived from Keynsham – would either be a day of renewed charges or one of pursuit of the subdued rioters. The mayor and his aldermen were unanimous that not to recapture escapees from the gaols, not to apprehend the readily identifiable perpetrators of the felonies in Queen Square and other public places, and not to recover stolen property (which at this moment could hardly be well concealed), would only give incentive to the underclass of citizenry to rise again and plague the city's honest rate-payers.

Having made his plans, Hervey now felt he could accept the mayor's offer of hospitality – excellent coffee, exemplary in its heat, and 'Bath bunns', a feast at any time.

A few minutes later, Major Beckwith came, and it was all hearty salutes, bows and hands.

'My dear Beckwith, how glad I was to hear it was you who came. It's been many years, has it not?'

'My dear Hervey – *Colonel* Hervey; forgive me – it has indeed. Had I known you were here I could have slept soundly in the chaise!'

'The charge against the Polish lancers, I think it must have been?'

'Yes, yes, indeed it was. My mare was wounded – not badly, but I was sorely grieved.'

'My gelding was killed,' said Hervey ruefully. 'Mr Mayor, Major Beckwith and I stood in adjacent brigades at Waterloo.'

The mayor looked ever more reassured.

Hervey began explaining his intention, and what he wanted of the squadron – five dozen sabres, said Beckwith. Before long, however, Major Mackworth arrived with the captain of the Bedminster troop – another dozen and a half sabres.

Again there was hearty greeting, as well as more formal exchange between Hervey and Captain Shute of the yeomanry. For there were now three officers in the mayor's chamber to whose names in Hart's the elaborate 'W' was attached – the Waterloo Medal: *Officers actually present in either of the actions of the 16th, 17th or 18th June, 1815.*

Hervey had first known Mackworth (then an ensign) at Talavera when he'd carried the 7th Fusiliers' colour and he himself had galloped for Lord Hill; and then again at Albuhera, that bloodiest of bloody Peninsular battles. Now he was in the personal service of that noble lord.

'The Keynsham troop's in the street behind,' he announced, as their captain came into the chamber and presented himself.

The mayor looked like a man delivered.

Hervey was exhilarated. He was certain he could now restore the peace. The only question was precisely when, and at what further price in blood. 'Captain Gage, I understand you to believe you have been ill-used. That is for a later date. For the moment you are to act under the orders of Major Mackworth.'

'With pleasure, Colonel.'

'Very well, gentlemen. Mackworth, you know the city: have the Third relieved as soon as may be. I'll send a note to their captain that they're to retire on the horse bazaar and await further orders. And Colonel Brereton may stand down also for the time being. I'll send him word too.'

'Shall we have a magistrate with us, or do I act on my own authority?'

Hervey looked at the mayor.

'I regret that my magistrates are not proficient, Colonel, when it comes to equitation. They would, I fear, be a hindrance, or worse. I shall give Major Mackworth the same instruction that I gave Colonel Brereton: to take the most vigorous, effective and decisive means in his power to quell the existing riot and prevent any further destruction of property.'

Mackworth looked pleased with the arrangement. He had no desire to nursemaid a magistrate in a mounted action.

Hervey was confident enough that Pinney could be relied on. He was assured nevertheless to see Mackworth making a careful note.

He turned to the Fourteenth's captain. 'Very well, Captain Gage, you are to act under the orders of Major Mackworth until such time as I am able to combine all the troops of the Fourteenth under Major Beckwith.'

'Yes, Colonel. We are all eagerness.'

Hervey glanced at Beckwith.

'I'll go myself to Queen Square till the squadron's come, with your leave.'

'Of course. And Mackworth, be so good as to send me word of the situation each hour. By all means extend into the surrounding parts if there is opportunity, but not risking the square.'

'Colonel.'

Hervey now looked to the yeomanry. Few though they were, as local men they might have a good instinct for the streets. It troubled him that they'd been inactive yesterday, standing in want of orders, and then quit the city; but yeomen were yeomen. They had a decidedly confined view of the world and its affairs, unlike the regulars, who considered themselves not to be bound by any territorial considerations, and their officers – the best of them, at least – willing and in most cases able to take whatever responsibility was demanded by the occasion. And regardless of rank, with none of the 'I am but a colonel, or major – or cornet even.' That was the essence with regulars. The liability of duty was unlimited, absence of orders no defence.

'Captain Shute, be so good as to take your troop to Mr Fisher's horse repository – you know its whereabouts? – and await orders. I understand you were awaiting them all of yesterday. They will not be long in coming today, I assure you.'

'Colonel.'

Hervey now pencilled scrips for Brereton and Warrington and handed them to Mackworth. 'So, gentlemen, to your duties.'

They left briskly and to warm expressions of appreciation by the aldermen – Whig and Tory alike.

St Alban came. 'The letter has just left by the mail, Colonel, and the same to Lord Hill. I impressed on the driver – and the guard – its imperative arrival this evening.' He handed him a fair copy:

My Lord, — I have the honour to inform you that, as the senior officer present in the city of Bristol, having proceeded to that place for ceremonial duty in connexion with the Assizes, I have assumed command of all troops and in concert with the Mayor, on whose authority I act, am taking the most vigorous action for suppression of the riot which has to this date done extensive damage to property in the City, both public and private, and occasioned certain loss of life to a degree yet to be determined. By the accounts given to me upon arrival in the early hours of this morning, the response of the Civil Power may at first have been uncertain, and that of the Military likewise hesitant, proceeding in part from a conviction that there were too few troops to impose order and that their presence only aggravated matters, which led to their most unfortunate withdrawal, leaving the major part of the City at the mercy of the rioters. I may assure Your Lordship that a large number of troops are now summoned to the City and their arrival expected this day, sufficient, I believe, to restore order on the streets and to enable the Posse Comitatus to apprehend the felons. I may further assure Your Lordship that I shall not hesitate to use any force as is available to me, and that that is the wish of the Civil Power also.

I am Your Lordship's humble servant,
Matthew Hervey,
Lieutenant-Colonel & Brevet,
His Majesty's 6th Light Dragoons.

'I think that will serve,' said Hervey thoughtfully. 'Mr Mayor, have you had any communication with London?'

'I have, sir. Beyond requests for assistance I sent a report – of no great length, I admit – by the first mail this morning.'

Hervey was now doubly pleased that St Alban had pressed him to write at once, and directly to the Home Office. 'Then I trust we shall have every assistance soon.'

Perhaps even a squadron from Hounslow . . . Though more likely it would first be a general officer, and his part in the proceedings ended. No matter: the business was his for the day, and almost certainly the night as well. It didn't do to be relieved of command while things were undecided; the officer who followed would claim any victory his and put the blame for any failure on the man who had gone before. (Poor Brereton: his handling of events was sure to bring about a court martial.)

If the Fourteenth did their duty now, he was sure the riot would be fatally weakened; and if the infantry were not too long in coming from Wales he was certain he would be handing to the general officer a *fait accompli*. Meanwhile he must depend on the special constables. 'I trust Lord Melbourne will send some inspectors.'

'I had not thought to ask for them, Colonel, but I should very much welcome such practised assistance to my sheriffs,' replied Pinney, as one of the aldermen handed him a note. 'Ah, I have word from the sheriff of the city that they've sworn three hundred military pensioners, and these are now mustered at the College Green – under a Major Arkle.'

'Arkle?'

'An officer of the half-pay, sir, resident here,' explained the alderman.

'Capital,' said Hervey, brightening further. 'I shall go to see them at once. You will permit me to have Arkle act under my orders?'

'I should be very glad of it,' said the mayor, and looking as if he would.

But there was one more application of force that Hervey knew he must consider, for if his plans failed he could not be left without reply. 'I intend then going to the docks to have one of the armed merchantmen brought up. I shall need your authority.'

The mayor blanched. 'Cannon, Colonel Hervey?'

'I have no intention of using them unless the troops are driven from the street, in which case the whole city will soon be ablaze. Meanwhile the mere sight of them – in broad daylight – gives warning; and overawes.'

Should overawe; but there was no cause to give the mayor any doubt, and therefore cause to refuse him.

'Very well, Colonel. I salute your resolution.'

'And I yours, Mr Mayor.'

'You may impress the *Earl of Liverpool*, just returned from Nevis. She is in my ownership. Her master is Joseph Bailey. I'll send for him.'

*

By the time Hervey got to Queen Square the Fourteenth had relieved the Third and dealt summary justice to a host of determined despoilers who had misjudged the strength of the squadron and tried to stand their ground at the southern end. He found Mackworth by the statue of King William, which, courtesy of the dragoons, was no longer festooned in drapery.

'You'll presently have two hundred special constables, all of them veterans, under a half-pay major – name of Arkle. They ought to be able to hold the square, so that you can begin cracking about the streets. I'll order Shute to take back the New Gaol – with veterans to assist – and when that's done we can begin restocking it, and then—'

His attention was suddenly drawn to a black-clad figure stepping out of the ruins on the west side. 'Who goes there?'

'I don't know,' said Mackworth, curious, 'but he hasn't the look of one we've just ridden over.'

'He appears to be making towards us – fuddled, or intelligence to impart perhaps? Let's do him the politeness.'

They trotted over.

The man raised his hat – a black, broad-brimmed shovel. And his black clad was plainly not a cloak but a cassock.

Hervey touched his cap in return. 'Reverend sir, these are evil parts this morning. You had better for your safety go back north towards King Street and beyond, but not yet to the cathedral. There are still ruffians to be rooted out nearby.'

'Thank you, sir, but I am not of the cathedral. I am the Catholic priest – Francis Edgeworth, sir, of St Joseph's chapel, in Trenchard Street. I come here to see if any of my charge have been caught up in this – as you say – evil.'

'It does you credit, Father, but I urge nevertheless that you quit the square. It wouldn't do for a dragoon to misjudge things, as may happen in business such as this.'

'I don't say that any of my charge would engage in riot, not of their free will, but some of them are barely in their teens and susceptible. I could not rest unless I saw to it that it was not so. "Dreadful are the wrongs of insolent and cruel prosperity."'

'Quite,' replied Hervey, suppressing a smile. 'Now, Father, it would be best that you retire to a safer—'

'When the mayor called for honest men as constables, I went to the Council House and said that I could raise two hundred, but the aldermen would not hear of it, on the grounds of their being Irish and therefore a prey to drink. But they are the King's honest subjects, sir, and would do their duty.'

'I don't doubt it,' said Hervey absently. He'd no wish to be distracted by questions of Catholic loyalty at such a time (Irish troops, under good regulation, had always done the duke well in Spain). 'But it is best that you quit the square without delay.'

Fr Edgeworth looked deeply disappointed.

'No, wait, Father. Where is Trenchard Street?'

'But a furlong north of College Green, sir.'

'Do you say you could assemble a hundred men and have them under good regulation?'

'I do. *Two* hundred indeed.'

'Very well. I am, by the bye, Colonel Hervey, the senior officer in the city at the present time. Upon my authority I would have you assemble these men ready to assist at the gaol.'

'It shall be done, Colonel. Two hours, perhaps three.'

'Then you may expect a summons for help soon thereafter. I thank you for your public spirit, sir.'

Fr Edgeworth raised his hat again and scurried off.

'I've no idea whether they'll be in the least useful,' said Hervey to St Alban; 'but it seems to me better to have two hundred Irish under regulation of their priest than trust to their sober habits.'

St Alban smiled.

'A learnèd priest, too, Colonel. You marked the Euripides – "insolent and cruel prosperity"?'

Hervey shook his head. 'Nor even what he meant by it, unless another advocate of Reform.'

'Do you know, Colonel, that is the first time I heard a Roman priest speak. I never supposed I would.'

Hervey looked at him in some surprise. 'We got on with them famously in Spain – and Portugal even better. The English sort are a different kettle of fish, I grant you. As for the Irish . . . Let's now go and see the yeomanry.'

He had no great hopes of finding a corps of any great serviceability. Most of the yeomanry had been disbanded when the French wars were done, and troops only very recently re-raised to deal with unrest in the countryside. The Bedminsters knew the open fields south of the Avon, not the streets to its north. They might very well be a liability. But they were at least under some regulation.

In fact he found them – if not exactly what he'd call soldierly – most business-like. They wore practical-looking shakos, nothing outlandish, and he had always observed that if a corps of men were sensibly topped, they were inclined to answer as a body. Indeed the Bedminsters, he knew, were part of the North Somerset Yeomanry, who'd never completely stood down after the Great Disturber sailed for St Helena, and the Somerset yeomen had not been idle in the years since – recalcitrant colliers in Radstock, machine-breaking weavers in Frome, and, only last year, rick-burners at Kenn.

Nor was Shute of the cast of men to shirk duty. Hervey had intended keeping his troop under cover till the rest of the Fourteenth were come, and all the constables paraded, but he decided he could risk sending them at once to take possession of what remained of the New Gaol, for there had to be somewhere to confine the sweepings of the streets.

A message came from the Council House: the troop from Gloucester had arrived.

Hervey gave Shute his orders, and hastened back – a gallop across College Green, on to the towpath, across the bridge where earlier they'd scattered a good few, up the Quay Head to keep clear of Corn Street, where ruffians still ranged, and into Broad Street from the north end.

He found a sight for the sorest eyes: a continuous line of dragoons between the Guildhall and the Council House. And cheering from every window in the street – the first sign of public approbation he'd had.

Now, at last, they'd make progress.

Inside he found the troop captain consulting with the mayor over a town plan.

'Ambrose Congreve, Colonel.'

He had the look of a man who knew what he was about. 'I am glad to see you, Captain Congreve. You had no difficulty on entering the city?'

'No, Colonel, but the road was crowded with roughs as we came to the turnpike gate; they took to the fields and ran in every direction. It was tempting to give chase, but my orders were to come here without delay. There were several handcarts abandoned, which must have been laden with plunder, but I could no more spare men to guard them than I could to chase their owners.'

'Just so. Be assured, though: as soon as there are troops to spare we'll pursue them.' He turned to the mayor. 'Where will they be bound?'

'Kingswood, for sure – pitmen. My constables'll roust them out – just as soon as you can furnish escorts.'

'Have you apprised Captain Congreve of the situation and our intention?'

'I have.'

Congreve nodded. 'I am quite clear as to what is required, Colonel.'

'I have given the captain the same written authority as before,' added the mayor. 'I would not have him in any doubt as to what discretion he has.'

'Admirable,' said Hervey. Whatever earlier neglect there had been, the mayor was displaying a very marked determination to make up lost ground. 'Your troop looks well found, Captain Congreve. My compliments. What is it from Gloucester to here – thirty miles?'

'Nearer forty, Colonel.'

Hervey looked surprised. That was a day's march as a rule. 'What time did you set out?'

'Two-thirty, Colonel. We received the express at two and paraded at once. We'd had rumour of call-out all day, and the men slept in their regimentals.'

It was now close to midday. Forty miles in nine hours, half of it at night with only a quarter moon . . . 'Then your horses are indeed in fine condition.'

'They are, Colonel.'

'Very well, as soon as they've caught their breath take them to Queen Square, where you'll find Major Beckwith, and act under his orders. Do you know the city?'

'But little, Colonel. The town plan is clear enough, though.'

'Good man. As for victuals, you shall have bread and meat presently. And corn. My sar'nt-major is quartermaster.'

'Very good, Colonel.' He made to leave.

Hervey's expression softened a little. 'Are you by any good fortune related to the Congreves of Waterford?'

The captain smiled. 'Indeed I am, Colonel. You know Mount Congreve?'

'It's fifteen years and more since I was there. To hunt – the Kilkenny.'

'They still run fast, John Power's hounds.'

To the mayor and aldermen it no doubt seemed strange to be speaking thus at such a time; but it never did ill to make some connection with a man suddenly placed under command. And it never did ill to remind those who were not under authority that those who were came ultimately of a different world. For not only might it avoid misunderstanding, it must reassure. These under authority might have their doubts and fears as well as the next man, but they could not take counsel of them.

The mayor was a man of discernment, however, as well as of business. As Congreve took his leave, he thanked him again – with civic dignity. He would not make too much of it with Hervey, though. A Congreve of Waterford, though the name meant nothing to him as such, was quite evidently of some standing, even within the superior society of dragoons. He himself, when all was said and done, was engaged in trade (though most successfully, which had brought him to his high office at the same age as Captain Congreve of Waterford had, he supposed, purchased command), and he was already acutely aware that Hervey bore the name of the family in which stood the marquessate of his own city (and so must presume a connection). He thought the Herveys were Whig; but the army was the King's device, and therefore Tory. Indeed, he was encompassed about by Tories, and so would confine himself to a modest expression of regard so as not to tempt any lofty response: 'I am confident we shall be delivered of this evil very soon, Colonel Hervey.'

He held out a handbill.

'I have had these circulated throughout the city.'

Council House, Bristol, Oct 31, 1831

The Posse Comitatus of this City and County having been called out to act in conjunction with the Military to endeavour to restore the Peace of the City, and as the most severe measures must be adopted to accomplish that object, the Magistrates earnestly caution all Persons not engaged in official duties as Constables to keep within their respective Dwellings as they will otherwise be exposed to the most imminent peril.

C. PINNEY,
Mayor

Hervey read it without comment, but for a nod. The citizens of Bristol had certainly been warned.

The mayor's expression turned more anxious. 'But I have had worrying intelligence of a threat to disrupt the supply of gas, which would plunge the main thoroughfares – and Queen Square – into darkness after sunset.'

Hervey braced. 'Where, and by what means?'

'I don't know. The intelligence was come by very indirectly.'

'You will, I take it, post constables at the gasworks?'

'Yes, at both the oil and coal works.'

'But there'll be other ways of disrupting the supply, no doubt. I think it best if you request that lights be placed in windows fronting the streets. That would have been the former practice, would it not?'

'I'll have handbills printed at once. With every shop and business house closed these past two days, however, I fear the results will be only very partial.'

'But a show of defiance will do no harm.'

He made to leave, but another reinforcement now presented himself, likewise brimming with resolution.

At first sight the bearskin crest looked that of the Dragoon Guards, but the cap was leather, not brass (and its wearer not quite the cut of a regular).

'Wilkins, sir, Charles Wilkins – Bath Troop, North Somerset Yeomanry Cavalry.'

Hervey bowed by return. His latest reinforcement looked an active man, though he'd seen faces less childlike wearing captain's lace. 'Not come alone, I trust? I am Colonel Hervey, commanding.'

'Colonel.' Wilkins saluted again. 'I have forty men. I regret I was not able to come sooner, but on receiving an express yesterday afternoon, I at once rode into Bath, but on going to my headquarters, the White Hart, the mob broke into the house and did much damage. In consequence of which the authorities were apprehensive of serious riots, and were obliged to keep the troop during the night.'

This was troubling news. Hervey looked at the mayor. Did the mob act in union?

'Bath is now quiet, we surmise, Captain Wilkins?' asked the mayor.

'It is.'

Nevertheless, Hervey decided he could take no chances. 'Captain Wilkins, I wish you to post a picket on the Bath road at the turnpike gate to prevent any but lawful entry – and, indeed, exit, for we'll be springing many a ne'er-do-well in the coming hours. The mayor believes they'll mostly fly west and north, but there's a chance that some will be homing to Bath. Use what force you must, but judiciously. The mayor will issue authority in writing. And dispose yourself, if you will, so as to maintain the picket until this time tomorrow, when I'll have fresh troops relieve you. My sar'nt-major will report as regards rations. I think that is all you have need of me?'

'Yes indeed, Colonel.'

'Very well, I shall visit the picket before last light. Depend on it, though: I mean to clamp down on the city tonight in such a manner that by this time tomorrow every law-abiding citizen may go about his business without hindrance.'

Wilkins saluted. 'We shall hold the Bath road, no matter what.'

The mayor was already writing yet another letter of authority.

Reinforcements continued to arrive – yeomanry from Gloucester-shire and Wiltshire, and more from North Somerset. By the middle of the afternoon Hervey was able to post videttes on every road. The Fourteenth had gained ascendancy in the main streets, though not without a deal of bloodshed, including, so rumour had it, the decapi-tation of at least one of the braggarts. Hervey was able then to send a number of dragoons to Kingswood and let the constables search for loot. Several of the coal owners were adamant their colliers were incapable of base conduct. ('We judge only as we find,' the cornet in command told them, proceeding to find plate and fine glass not usually associated with a miner's table.) Meanwhile, he himself went aboard the *Earl of Liverpool*, brought up to the Basin, and with the master sighted her four 2-pounder guns, and a long 6-pounder, to command the Quay. He could not give him precise orders, but the master he found to be a sensible man, and thought it better to give him the mayor's letter of authority and leave its application to his good judgement.

He then began a tour of every vidette and standing patrol of constables. The streets were so empty of their normal custom that it might have been seven o'clock of a Sunday morning, which he took as a promising sign. Certainly he was well pleased with what he found on his inspection – men both in uniform and out eager to do their duty, intent on putting an end to the anarchy. He drank a great deal of tea, each post with its fire and boiling pot, the sentries keen to offer him hospitality – a sure sign, he always reckoned, of *un bon état d'esprit*.

'I believe the city is yours, Colonel,' said St Alban as they left the last of the posts, on the bridge before the New Gaol. 'The most determined mob would not defy such a demonstration.'

Hervey might agree, but he wouldn't risk to. 'We hold the ring, so to speak, but if the mob wishes to brawl within, I couldn't vouch for the outcome. The dragoons are tired, and the yeomen soon will be. As for the constables, I've no idea of their resolution. Even the priest's Irish – a very motley company if ever I saw one. You may do much with cavalry, St Alban, but without infantry you cannot hold what you gain. Just pray we may have some soon. Or heavy rain.'

Beyond that, he would confide no more doubts, though he'd made up his mind that if they couldn't hold the centre, they'd hold the docks – at any price. The *Earl of Liverpool* (so appropriate a name, for Liverpool had been prime minister at the time of 'Peterloo') would be their underwriter, though he shuddered to think how the discharge of case shot would be viewed in the comfort of a London newspaper office

– or Parliament. (It would, of course, be preferred to the incineration of the docks, but the trouble was that if it succeeded, the alternative – their destruction – could not be proved. And who would be prepared to speak out and say that gambling on the consequences of inaction was unthinkable?)

He sighed to himself. That was his bond, his contract. 'We must trust the Cardiff men arrive sharp tomorrow morning – and that, meanwhile, word of the dragoons' bladework reaches every nook and cranny.'

They made yet another progress of Queen Square. It was dusk, and most of the horses were off-saddled, and many of the dragoons were sleeping – or at least lying on the ground. Hervey knew he must get them into stables before too long. He wanted them fresh if needs be.

He himself was beginning to feel the want of some respite – not least for the doughty little mare that had carried him all day – and a plate of something that would see him through the night.

'We shall repair for an hour to Reeves's.'

The streets remained empty, but as they neared College Green came the noise he'd feared: shouting, cheering, banging of drums – the sound of the mob as it gathered numbers and nerve. The whole of Park Street must be a tide of swagger and racket.

How, though? How had they overcome the pickets at the top of the hill? And why no report?

There were no troops to hand – just the vidette on Clare Street Bridge, and they must hold that defile come what may.

He drew his sword. There was nothing other he could do. 'Very well, gentlemen, we shall have to sell ourselves dearly.'

Out came the three other sabres, and not a word. Wakefield's was the third, and glad he was of it, but he sorely wished Armstrong's was a fourth.

Acton closed to his left side, St Alban the other, and then Wakefield.

Four abreast: they'd hardly span the street. The mob might just suppose them the front rank of many more, though. Ruse was the art of the practised soldier. There again . . .

He spurred into a canter towards the debouch onto College Green. If they didn't make the street before the mob began to come out they'd have no chance. At least the streetlights were lit.

Then rounding the corner he was never more astonished. Drums, cheering onlookers, even bugles – but wholly benign, the drumming regular, the tide in the street not ruffian but red-coated.

He sheathed his sword and sprang from the saddle. 'Love? Love – is that you?'

How the column came to so sharp a halt he couldn't imagine, but halt it did, and at attention. Their colonel stepped forward to exchange courtesies in the way of men who'd shared past dangers.

'Upon my word, but I'm deuced glad to see you,' said Hervey, taking off his cap to wipe his brow with his sleeve.

'And I you,' said the field officer of foot. 'I'd feared all we'd find was a bunch of frighted magistrates. But what do you do here?'

Hervey explained.

'Will you act under my orders?' he asked, as if laying a prospectus for sale before a doubtful buyer.

For in age, Lieutenant-Colonel Frederick Love, commanding the depot companies of the 11th (North Devonshire) Regiment of Foot, was three or four years his senior. He'd been brevet-major at Waterloo when Hervey was still a cornet (and most grievously wounded with Colborne's 52nd when they'd thrown back the Old Guard). These things were not lightly to be set aside.

'Hervey, I read the *Gazette* as closely as the next man. Of course I will – *must*. And with pleasure. Only I ask one thing: don't scatter us about the place in penny packets. We're two companies, each eighty strong. I'd not be averse to disposing them thus, though I'd prefer they be kept under my single command. They're good boys, but depot men, not yet fit for the line, and they're dog tired.'

Hervey nodded. 'I want you to hold the cockpit of the trouble so far – Queen Square, and as one, so that I may withdraw the dragoons and have them for a ready reserve.'

'Capital.'

'And nor am I surprised your men are dog tired. How the deuce did you get here so fast?'

'Hah! We'd have got here a damned sight faster if we hadn't had to fight our way onto a steamer at Newport – well, as good as. A damned crowd of insolent fellows stood in our way, and I had to threaten them with ball. I don't know what's going on, Hervey, but the word on the streets is evidently passed a deuced sight quicker than official channels.'

'It is so. There was the same trouble in Bath, it seems. But I'm sure now that we can quieten this place once and for all. I compliment you on your celerity nonetheless.'

'Well,' said Love, nodding to his adjutant to have the column ready to march again, 'we covered the fifteen miles to Newport in four hours. My old Light Bobs couldn't have done it much quicker. Just point the way to this square.'

Hervey shook his head. 'I'll march with you myself.'

The night passed quiet as a cloister – and as bright as the fullest moon. Not a gaslight failed, and in every other window an oil lamp or candles burned. Hervey made round after round, stopping at every post to enquire and encourage. He heard the midnight strike in company with Colonel Love beside a soldierly campfire in Queen Square, where they reminisced a little. *Were you at Waterloo? / 'Tis no matter what you do / If you were at Waterloo.* The old hands loved saying it, and with good reason. No sight, no sound – no sense of any kind – no sensation or sentiment, could compare with that day. A man might think his service nothing after Waterloo – and yet it must be, for what did the wretches who fired Bristol care of that day? Or those that broke the windows of the First Soldier of Europe? *Soldiers in peace are like chimneys in summer* . . . Oh yes, there was much on which to reminisce. Then as two o'clock chimed, and then three, with not a sound but the night noises of any peaceable place, Hervey decided at last to take some sleep.

At six, so that he could be booted and spurred and stood-to-arms at first light, Corporal Johnson brought him tea – very sweet (for this was Bristol, where sugar filled the wharves) – and soon after, he began his rounds of the waking city, breathing a silent sigh of relief that on his watch it had at last slept soundly.

At a quarter past eight a post chaise arrived at the Council House bearing none other than the Deputy Quartermaster-General, Sir Richard Downes Jackson. Sir Richard was not a Waterloo man but a Coldstreamer who had gained the respect of the Duke of Wellington, the whole army indeed, for his diligence on the staff in the Peninsula. Here was one of London's best men come to take command; and as perhaps with any officer assuming command from a more junior one, and at the moment when 'victory' had been achieved, there was a certain aloofness in his manner. There again, having heard reports of evasion and dereliction of duty, it was perhaps unsurprising. Hervey thought the way he demanded justification for the 'several hundred' rioters killed (and there was really no knowing the figure) was . . . un-friendly. But, again, this was England, and the rule of law might not be suspended simply because an adversary broke it. All the same, he was glad when the major-general at last pronounced himself ready to take command. (He'd learn soon enough what a trial they'd had.)

Leaving him to the happy mayor and corporation, Hervey withdrew to thank and say goodbye to the officers who had acted so readily under his orders – and to Colonel Brereton, who did indeed present a most dejected figure. He would confess that it was with considerable relief, as well as satisfaction, that he set off back for Hounslow.

*

Meanwhile, in the offices of the *Bristol Mercury*, the type was being composed for the day's editorial, secure in the knowledge that the King's peace was thoroughly restored:

> We are sorry to have to record another piece of folly – wanton cruelty we would call it – if it had not, as we believe, originated in the utter ignorance of the Magistrates of the state of the city. The shops remained unopened and the military were ordered to clear the streets – an order which was fulfilled to the letter by a party of the troops which had experienced some rough treatment and had in consequence fired upon the people the previous day. The sight of this useless piece of duty was peculiarly distressing; nothing was to be seen on every side but unoffending women and children running and screaming in every direction while several men, apparently on their way to work, were deliberately cut at, several seriously injured and some killed . . .

V

Good Order and Military Discipline

Hounslow, Wednesday, 2 November

WITH ONLY A TROOP IN barracks it was unusually quiet. The quarter guard turned out as Wakefield brought the chariot towards the gates at eleven o'clock, and Hervey returned the salute with a touch to the peak of his forage cap.

Hounslow: the epitome of order and civility; and never more so than after the sights and sounds of Bristol in the hands of the mob. He knew he'd done his duty, and he'd relished – if perhaps more in hindsight – the exhilaration of doing that duty. Bristol stood intact and calm because of that. Strange, was it not, that all the habits and practices of command learned in distant parts had never served King and Country more than in that place not thirty miles from where he was born.

He was entirely content.

They'd got back the previous day a little before midnight, having taken the northern turnpike through Marshfield, Chippenham and Marlborough, rather than the faster road through Bath, for he was still uncertain of its temper. St Alban had offered to take Wakefield's place in the saddle after Newbury, but Wakefield wouldn't hear of it. He'd therefore risen to the trot a full twelve hours, relieved only for a few minutes at the post-houses while they changed horses, and yet this morning he'd looked as fresh as a young chicken when he'd brought the chaise to Heston. Serjeant Acton had posted with them, and Armstrong had taken the Mail a few hours earlier – an expense that Hervey trusted he'd be able to recover from His Majesty – leaving Johnson, Spink and St Alban's groom to follow with the baggage in the fourgon.

He'd been surprised to find lights burning at Heston, for he'd given leave of a week to Serjeant James and his wife, and even more surprised to find Annie waiting. Armstrong had sent word that he was returning, she explained, but she hadn't known what time to expect him, and so she'd summoned the cook, but at eleven she'd sent her away again, but there was a ragout keeping warm, and soup, and blancmanges. Hervey had thanked her kindly. She'd certainly kept a good fire in his writing room, where he liked to sit of an evening after dinner if there was no one else dining, and she'd put by a decanter of best burgundy and another of brandy. In truth he would have liked to bathe, but he couldn't ask her to fill his bath – not without another of the housemaids to help – even if the copper were lit, which it probably wasn't. (He wished he'd had the money to put in pipes, as at the United Service Club, but he had only a short lease on the house, and there were other calls on his pocket.) He often smiled ruefully that he was better bathed in India, where bhistis and bearers never slept. And so he'd contented himself with a hand basin, and then a tray brought to his writing table rather than the dining room, though Annie said there was a good fire there too.

Annie had been a serving girl at the Berkeley Arms when Hervey and Fairbrother had lodged there before Lord Holderness, the former commanding officer, quit Heston. She'd served them well – friendly, without the least familiarity; honestly, diligently and with discretion. They'd lodged there many months, indeed, and it had been Fairbrother who said that if Hervey didn't engage her for Heston, then he would for his own modest establishment, an honest housemaid being a pearl of great price. Fairbrother had also observed in Annie a particular devotion to his friend, but if that were so, it seemed entirely to escape his friend's attention.

But for all their closeness, Fairbrother did not see everything. There was no man Hervey would trust more in the field, and no man he would confide in the same. But if he was able to confide his fears to his half-bred boon companion, he was entirely unable to confide his sins – even those committed only in the heart. In fact, Annie's presence was to him both a comfort and a trial. When she had brought him supper last night, she asked if the news she'd heard tell of was true, that Bristol was engulfed in tumult, with fire as great as that which had once levelled the better part of London.

An empty house was perhaps a wretched thing to return to after such an affair. 'Take a seat, Annie, and some wine', he'd wanted to say. It was reasonable enough to want a little company and an ear for what he'd seen and done – and thought, indeed, not all of which he could share with St Alban, even though they were meant to speak freely. But he'd not invited her to sit, let alone take wine with him. For one, it offended against all proper management of an establishment. That alone was enough. And yet in these peculiar circumstances it might not bring the collapse of social order. The truth, he knew, was that it courted graver sin. Annie was unread, unfinished, but she had the looks and simple refinement that was not associated as a rule with the class from which the nation's soldiery was drawn. As so often before at this hour, there was nothing now he wished for but companionship – the companionship of the pillow, the willing embrace, a few hours' consolation, and warmth on waking.

The struggle was not to be underestimated. He might be able to put from his mind that her brother had gone for a soldier, and that any impropriety would therefore be a sin not only against God's law but probably King's Regulations too. And as for adultery, how might any reasonable man – how might God, indeed – suppose he had a wife in any sense but that understood by the law of the land?

No; what kept him from improper companionship was simply that he did not wish to . . . spoil her. In that, of course, he made an assumption; so many girls in service were spoiled. With Annie, though, he felt sure. There were many things for which he would one day have to answer, but he would not add to that shameful list the spoiling of a simple and honest girl. And that resolution, indeed, was a powerful restorative to his self-respect.

So that evening – the early hours indeed – as many a time before, she'd stood before him listening attentively, and asked him questions – good questions – until he no longer felt able to speak to her on these terms, and so thanked her handsomely for her consideration in waiting on him, and said that he would himself douse the fires and draw the bolts, and that she should now retire and sleep, and that he would not rise before nine, and trusted there would be hands to bring him plenty of hot water in the morning. And Annie in her turn had thanked him for *his* consideration in telling her all that had happened in Bristol, and that she hoped all would now be well – and that she would go and run the warming pan through his bed once more, for it had been several hours since she'd done so first.

Then with her customary bob and looking him surely in the eye, she said with winning cheerfulness, 'Good night, sir.'

'Good night, Annie,' he replied, fixing himself in his chair with the remains of the brandy until he felt able to extinguish the fires, draw the bolts and go to his warmed bed.

He dressed next morning without the attention of Corporal Johnson. At first he'd thought to put on a plain coat, for he intended going to London in the afternoon to seek out Lord Hill, or if he were not at office, the Military Secretary, FitzRoy Somerset. Last night as he lay in bed, he'd had a premonition of confusion at the Horse Guards as letters arrived from the various 'parties'. In his experience it required fine judgement in order not to appear anxious to account for one's actions; but being forced to fight on ground not of one's choosing by waiting to be asked to give account was equally perilous, however much it might appear to reflect confidence.

In the end he'd put on undress. In the circumstances he thought it best to appear unequivocally 'on business' at the Horse Guards, and during the short drive to Hounslow had resolved on his course of action.

St Alban was waiting for him at orderly room; Armstrong and the chief clerk too.

'Would you have a fair copy made, please,' he said, handing the adjutant the report he'd spent from six o'clock till eight writing. 'I intend delivering it to the Horse Guards today, by hand.'

The chief clerk took it for his best copyist to begin on at once.

'What business is there?' he then asked as he sat ready at his desk and nodded to the question of coffee.

'Principally defaulters, Colonel,' said St Alban, handing him a sheet of paper. 'Rather a dispiriting number, I'm afraid. And too many sick as well.'

Hervey studied the list while one of the 'sable twins', as the regiment affectionately knew them – Abdel or Hassan (he was never entirely certain which, even with the supposedly distinguishing feather in the turban) – poured coffee from a silver pot. He'd made few changes to the room that Lord Holderness had bequeathed him. The prints of Wolfe at Quebec and Clive at Plassey, in their deep, gilded frames, still commanded the walls. The fine damask curtains that Lady Holderness had had put up in place of the heavy green velvet still hung smartly. The two gilt armchairs and sofa, silk-covered in blue and gold stripes, had not shifted an inch in the twenty-two months that the room had been his. In the fine Adam fireplace, with its eagle victrix moulding, coals burned cheerily, as they had on the first morning of his occupancy.

Indeed, the sole additions to the elegant taste of his predecessor – or more particularly, to that of his lady – were a silver inkstand, the present of the grateful ambassadress of the Emperor of All Russia for his mission in the Levant, and instead of the looking-glass over the fireplace, a likeness of the colonel-in-chief.

By custom at first orderly room of the day, the adjutant and serjeant-major stood. The parade was merely to report the 'states' – the numbers at duty, the numbers sick or absent (with and without leave), and the incidents since watch-setting the night before. But usually it was at ten o'clock, and there was comparatively little to report. With several days out of barracks, however, there was rather more on the adjutant's memorandum.

'Please sit, gentlemen,' he said, beckoning Abdel (or Hassan – he knew they switched feathers for mischief) to bring cups. 'I'll say nothing of the past days, save that I'm excessively obliged, as ever, for your service, and that I have commended you in my despatch to the Horse Guards.'

'Colonel,' said St Alban simply, and for both of them (Armstrong liked to remain formal whenever there were other eyes). Thanks were by no means rare, even if they were unnecessary, but, like an order, they required nothing more than acknowledgement.

Abdel's return with two cups saved any further awkwardness.

Hervey looked at the list again. 'Defaulters,' he began, with a sigh; 'It will not have escaped your attention that the list has been growing these past six months – not merely in number but in kind. Drink, quite evidently, is at the root of much of it . . . But Stokes – a bad business indeed. What is the supposition there?'

'He was taken by the police in a street near by the crime, Colonel,' said Armstrong, 'at the back of the Banqueting House. The body wasn't yet cold. Serjeant Bain, who was called to vouch for 'im, says there wasn't a drop of drink on his breath.'

'A common prostitute, was she, or did he know her?'

'Bain says she wasn't unknown to 'is troop, Colonel.'

'Mm.'

'I shall go an' see 'im, Colonel, as soon as the guard's changed at Windsor.'

Hervey nodded. 'Stokes is the feather-weight man, sandy hair, is he not?'

'He is, Colonel. Not a bad dragoon as a rule.'

'Well, we shall see what we shall see. And what is there to say about Corporal Owthwaite?'

'I'm sorely disappointed with 'im, Colonel. I gave 'im fair warning last time. He's the best rough-rider the RM has, but 'e just can't turn away from a pretty face and 'e can't see where these things lead – and on 'is pay.'

'Well, he's certainly going to have less of it in future. Pay, I mean.'

'Yes, and 'e knows it, and 'e's asking already if 'e can go to an Indian regiment.'

'Owthwaite's a rogue – don't we know – but a man to take on a tiger hunt. I'd be sorry to lose him, but on such a charge I can see no other course than to reduce him to the ranks. No doubt he thinks he'd regain his stripes quicker in another regiment – and India.' (The place had a way of making vacancies.)

'I think he's constitutionally more suited to its ways than 'ere, Colonel.'

Hervey agreed. Besides the extra pay and every pleasure a fraction the price, when a man had been through the breach at Bhurtpore, galloping between Windsor and Whitehall with a letter or two must be monstrous anticlimax. Little wonder he sought thrills at either end.

'You'll recollect how he fought that day at Bhurtpore, Sar'nt-Major.'

They'd never forget Bhurtpore: Kezia's husband dead before they even got out of the sap, Armstrong as good as when the mine caved in . . .

'Well I do, Colonel. But that was then, and this is now. Bhurtpore's no chit to stay out of gaol – with respect.'

Hervey wasn't quite sure for whom the respect was meant, but that was by the bye. It was good to be fortified in one's resolve when it came to cruel necessity – and losing Owthwaite as corporal would be cruel indeed. There'd been some who'd thought that Armstrong didn't possess the eye for discipline of a regimental serjeant-major – a doubt he himself had had to address. For Armstrong's own conduct sheet was not without entries, and his ready recourse to summary justice was well known. It was one thing for a serjeant-major of a troop, but with the crown atop the four chevrons it was another matter entirely. But not once had he had a moment's regret promoting him – and what relief that was, for he could never have borne the fall of the man who had been at his side since his cornet days (and been the last to see Henrietta alive – to die, almost, trying to save her).

'And four dragoons in Hounslow, no less, confined overnight and bailed by the justices; three more in arrest in barracks for insubordination . . . Seven others variously for making away with necessaries, or drunkenness on duty, or sleeping on post . . .'

The discipline of a regiment was the product of a good many variables, but the serjeant-major was its unvarying factor. Nevertheless, Armstrong knew his powers and influence were not unlimited. 'An' they're not all bad'ns, Colonel, though Roache and Eubank could do with a good 'iding.'

Or rather, something more emasculating, for he knew they'd had several barrack-room strappings.

'I know it,' Hervey conceded. Indeed it had been troubling him for some months. And they had not yet spoken of the sick list . . .

St Alban thought to say something consolatory. 'I have it from one of the Adjutant-General's men that one in every five on the Home establishment is confined in a public gaol.'

Hervey sighed, and drained his cup.

Armstrong said what he supposed Hervey was thinking: 'But the point is, Mr St Alban, sir, the Home establishment's *them*, an' we is *us*.'

Abdel poured more coffee during the silence.

Hervey put the memorandum to one side. 'Very well, let's be done with it. Orderly room tomorrow at ten, and then defaulters. I leave for the Horse Guards in a quarter of an hour – sooner, if the chief clerk's finished scribbling.'

VI

Post Mortem

The Horse Guards, later

'LORD MELBOURNE HELD A CONFERENCE this morning, and Lord Hill was called. There's to be an inquiry – a military inquiry – assembled with all haste. He's with the Secretary at War at present.'

Lord John Howard, lieutenant-colonel of Grenadiers, had in various ranks served an age at the Horse Guards. A succession of commanders-in-chief, including the Duke of Wellington himself, thought him indispensable. He was also an old friend.

'Who's to be its chairman?' asked Hervey.

'Dalbiac.'

He nodded. Major-General Sir Charles Dalbiac was Inspector General of Cavalry – a Peninsula hand, and India too. A better man it would have been hard to find. It was some relief.

'Lord FitzRoy has been asked to nominate four members,' added Howard.

Hervey nodded again. It would not matter greatly who they were. With Dalbiac in charge he should have no fear of the outcome.

Nevertheless he was anxious that his report was not overlooked at this time. 'I should like Lord Hill to read it, nevertheless,' he said, indicating the folio he'd just placed on Howard's desk.

'He will, I assure you.'

Which meant that first Howard himself would read it – as Hervey had very well known – and make sure that others would too.

'But the inquiry is most particular in its purpose,' added Howard, encouragingly; 'Lord Hill wishes that Colonel Brereton be afforded the fullest opportunity to meet and remove the unpleasant allegations set forth against him. It is only on account of those allegations, largely by the mayor, but also by sundry yeomanry officers, that the inquiry is called. Indeed, were there to have been no allegations there would, I believe, be no inquiry. Matters would proceed straight to law. You didn't suppose it to be an inquiry into your conduct?'

'Not expressly, no. But any inquiry would have to examine all that transpired. There are, besides, a considerable number of lives and limbs to account for.'

'Quite so, but that is first a matter for the coroner, I imagine.'

Hervey was content to imagine so too, though he was puzzled to imagine also how the Horse Guards thought that no inquiry would be necessary without the allegations of sundry officials and yeomen. But the Horse Guards had its ways . . . 'I suppose it's to be held in Bristol? There could be no more convenient place. When might it commence, for I suppose I shall be called to give evidence in addition to my deposition?'

'The seventeenth, I think it is,' replied Howard, looking into his order book. 'Yes, the seventeenth. Tomorrow fourteen days.'

'Mm.'

'See here; go and take your ease at the United Service and I'll send word as soon as Lord Hill is returned.'

Hervey rose. 'Capital idea. You'll dine with me this evening, perhaps?'

'I have to attend on his lordship at the French ambassador's. Come dine at White's with me tomorrow instead.'

'I thank you, yes. Until later, then. And Howard, would you be so good as to let me know if Lord Hill receives any separate communication from Colonel Brereton?'

'I shall.'

He left by the little door in the archway and looked in at the Light Horse stables, where all was predictably faultless – which it might have been in any case, but was certainly going to be after Serjeant Wakefield had suddenly appeared – and then walked to the United Service Club across the parade ground of the Horse Guards. It was perhaps a slightly longer route than up Whitehall, but although he liked to see the equestrian statue of King Charles, the works in King William's Square, a site of demolition yet, were unruly at the best of times. Besides, the Guards had their band beating quick time in the corner, by Downing Street – the Scots, he thought – and a company at drill, and it was ever a pleasure to step out to their music.

At the United Service there was the usual welcome from the hall porter, and the customary reference to the news or the weather – 'dreadful news from Bristol' (to which he would add nothing but 'Shocking, Dobbs'). In the smoking room it was the same: 'They need to feel a bit of cold steel, I reckon, Colonel.'

'No doubt, Prichard.'

'There's cannon on the way, I hears tell, sir.'

'And quickly, I trust. Coffee, please, good and strong.'

There were but a few others in the room, and none he knew, which he was glad of, for he'd no desire to discuss the news. Instead he would read what he could of it – or rather, read what was written of that which he knew already.

The Times lay on the bulletins table. He took it up and settled in a tub by one of the windows, full west. It was news two days old – 'From a

81

Correspondent. BRISTOL, Monday, 4 o'clock p.m.' – but it might tell him what to expect at the hands of 'the fourth estate', powerful and yet contrary as it was.

He was, though, gratified that it spared no detail of the destruction, for otherwise how could anyone form an impression of the urgent necessity under which the military acted:

> I concluded my dismal narrative to 11 o'clock last night, which, if I recollect right, was incorrect, in so far as the mob did not succeed further than breaking the windows at the White Lion and the Council House. They, up to that time, utterly destroyed by fire the three gaols, Bishop's palace, bridge toll-houses, and Mansion-house. They had unmolested possession of the city all night.

Indeed, it pleased him greatly: 'unmolested possession' – precisely the state he had found things early that Monday morning . . .

> After burning the Mansion-house they sacked the next house, then fired it, and so proceeded along that wing of Queen's-square to the Custom-house; thence to the end of the same wing, including the houses in King-street abutting behind on the same; thence to every house in the west wing, so that the entire of two wings is destroyed, including the Custom-house and Excise-office. The whole, or nearly the whole, of the square belongs to the corporation; there cannot be less than 10,000L. worth of building destroyed altogether in the city; and perhaps other property to a greater extent. I was on the spot the whole night, and it was a truly awful sight, comparable to no other conceivable thing than the infernal regions. The yells of the miscreant incendiaries were dreadful. Most of the inhabitants fled in time, but the loss of life was very great among the deluded victims themselves, who, after drinking all the spirits they could find, were unable to escape the flames in time, and so soon fell in with the floors of the houses. I saw seven persons meet their

just, though awful, retribution in this way, in the Custom-house alone. Besides the sacking which took place by the incendiaries, the property stolen by low women and boys was immense. There were no magistrates or constables; or military, seen in or near the scene the whole night; and this is so utterly inexplicable, that I will not attempt to surmise its cause, unless it be that they were panic-struck by this small mob, which, as actors, did not, after 10 o'clock, exceed 150 to 200!

This pleased him the more, for the only inference there could be was that any law-abiding citizen witnessing the events must desire the intervention of the military.

He read on with increasing approval, the words perfectly according with his own reports to the Horse Guards and the Home Office – 'the most wretched depravity', 'barbarism', 'drunkenness', 'devastation' et cetera – until he came to the account of the action by his own order, which, while faithful, somehow sounded ill:

At length the horrible transactions are arrested; the troops are acting, by scouring the streets and dispersing the mob by the gun, the pistol, and the sword.

For there followed, after much corroborative detail quoted from other correspondents, a statement which, no matter what the justification, he felt sure would be seized on in certain quarters as testament to the charge that His Majesty's Land Forces were the enemies of Reform:

The total number of killed and wounded, as far as we have been able to ascertain, is as follows: – 4 men and 1 woman, the latter in consequence of severe bruises received in one of the houses where she had been engaged in plunder: a little boy, also, who was shot through the bowels, is not expected to live; 51 other persons, including 4 women, have also received injuries, some of them very severe ones, principally sabre wounds; a few in consequence of the parties leaping from the burning houses. In this account we enumerate the cases taken to the public hospitals only. Many lives were lost in the flames, and several persons who received injury having been taken to their own homes, we have no means of acquiring the requisite information respecting them.

The numbers would be greater when all was counted, he was sure, but even so, Englishmen – English *women* – sabred on the streets . . .

Prichard brought his coffee. 'The duke was in this morning, Colonel. He's still not best pleased about all his windows.'

'Yes, I imagine so. Shameful business,' replied Hervey, lowering his paper on finding no other report. 'Is there a later edition of *The Times* to come?'

'Not as a rule, Colonel. But there's *The Courier* comes about five.'

'Very well, Prichard, thank you.'

He took a sip at his coffee and contemplated taking a bath, but although baths were very expeditiously arranged at the United Service – with hot water proceeding in quantity at the mere turn of a lever – he was sure the summons back to the Horse Guards would come before he could take its pleasure. And so instead he picked up *The Times* again and read the court circular:

A Cabinet Council was held at 3 o'clock yesterday afternoon, at the Foreign-office, which was attended by Earl Grey, Viscount Melbourne, Viscount Palmerston, Viscount Althorp, the Right Hon. Charles Grant, Viscount Goderich, Lord John Russell, and Sir James Graham. The Council sat in deliberation about two hours. Earl Grey came to town from his seat, at East Sheen, for the purpose of attending the meeting. The Russian, Austrian, and French Ambassadors, the Prussian Minister, and the Russian and Austrian Envoys Extraordinary, held a conference with Viscount Palmerston yesterday afternoon, at the Foreign-office. Sir Thomas

Cochrane, Lieutenant-Governor of Newfoundland, had an inter-view with Viscount Goderich, at the Colonial-office, yesterday. Letters from the Magistrates of Bristol, for Viscount Melbourne, were received yesterday at the Home-office. Despatches were forwarded by his Lordship yesterday to the King at Brighton.

Brighton. Forwarded by hand of his own dragoons, no less. They liked to post to Brighton, for as a rule they could stay overnight so as to bring back papers the following day – and they were always welcome at Mr Lincoln's establishment. The Sixth's quartermaster until lately (and before that, 'from time immemorial', the regimental serjeant-major), Lincoln had invested a lifetime's bachelor thrift, and, recently, wedded thrift, into 'a small hotel', which was already a place finding favour with the gentry for its economy and efficiency. Lincoln had married an infantry widow in India, and earlier in the year his stepdaughter, to the astonishment of all, had married one of the regiment's prize lieuten-ants. Lincoln himself had been wariest of the match, and was certain that Lieutenant Edward Pearce, Sir James Pearce's younger son (and Pearce the most respected Assistant Secretary at War), must transfer to another regiment, where the taint of marrying a daughter from the ranks could be washed out the sooner. He'd joined straight from Eton, where his learning, looks and graceful bat had by all accounts made him one of the most popular Oppidans of his day; he'd charmed Calcutta and the regiment alike, and fought like a wildcat at Bhurtpore. His future seemed assured; but then he'd married for 'love'.

As once he too had done . . .

Hervey drained his cup abruptly – and then spilled as much as he poured himself more.

But Lucy Lincoln was no Nan Clarges, old General Monck's un-polished duchess – the washerwoman who'd kept him comfort in the Tower, Cromwell's prisoner. At fifteen, the Lincolns had sent her to Eng-land to an academy for young ladies, and Lucy had emerged as pretty as the daughter of any earl and twice as clever. Pearce's fellow officers may have been astonished, but none but the dolts did but admire. The wedding party had filled the church in Brighton, and afterwards one of the great tents taken booty at Bhurtpore; and Hervey had found a catch in his throat more than once. Pearce and his bride had lately dined at Heston, affording yet more proof of the warmth that came of mutual affection. Heston had seemed much the colder for their leaving that night.

He shook his head – this wouldn't do – and took up *The Times* again.

The rest of the news amounted to nothing of substance. He read the money matters and thanked himself as ever that he wasn't in thrall to them, and then the private announcements, sometimes enlightening and invariably entertaining, called for more coffee (an hour had passed), and then exchanged *The Times* for the *London Gazette* of the previous day, under which a half-pay admiral had been soundly sleeping.

The *Gazette* was engaging, though he first had to turn many pages of 'rules and regulations proposed by the Board of Health'. There was, it seemed, an influx from foreign parts of Cholera Morbus, and 'a Committee of the Lords of His Majesty's Most Honourable Privy Council' were pleased to order that the symptoms and treatment be printed and published in the *Gazette* 'and circulated in all the principal ports, creeks and other stations of the said United Kingdom, with a view that all persons may be made acquainted therewith'. He read them, and found nothing that any man who'd served in the Honourable Company's domains would not know. There was advantage to being in England, he would freely admit, for the Cholera was infinitely the rarer; but was the Cholera in India not, after all, just another of the Grim Reaper's devices, the price perhaps for the brighter sun and easier ways? Death from the Cholera, too, though an undignified and stinking business, was at least quick by comparison with many a wasting sickness here.

There were not many promotions to read of, and these mostly restricted to subaltern officers, which was never of great moment. Only one, he noted – '59th Foot, Ensign James Mockler to be Lieutenant' – was without purchase. He wondered what had been Mockler's good fortune – bloody war or a sickly season? He smiled to himself at the macabre old toast they used to propose in Spain. Where *were* the Fifty-ninth now? They'd been at Bhurtpore; that, he knew well . . .

Then a name did catch his eye: the 7th Fusiliers had gained 'Second Lieutenant George Viscount Torrington, from the 60th Foot, to be Lieutenant, by purchase, vice Orr, promoted in the 88th Foot'. (It was queer how the Sixtieth called their cornets – or rather, ensigns – 'second lieutenants'.) It must mean that old Admiral Torrington was dead, the title passed to his son or whoever. That or he'd been advanced in grade, and young George had taken the courtesy title. He must hope the latter, for Sir Laughton Peto had always counted Torrington one of his supporters, and if his old and gallant friend were ever to be recalled from the 'Yellow Squadron' – Rear-Admiral without distinction of an active squadron (or as the army had it, the half-pay) – he must have his supporters. Perhaps, though, Torrington's death created a vacancy not just in the peerage? The system of admiralty was at best a secret, black and midnight one.

Thoughts of Peto were ever pleasing. That a man could be so grievously wounded and yet recover such mastery of shattered limbs as to persuade their lordships to reinstate him – promote him to titular admiralcy indeed – was witness to England's true glory. Witness also to the regard in which her sea captains were held, for the comforts of Houghton Hall in his native Norfolk, seat of the great Lords of Cholmondeley, had been placed at his disposal for as long as his convalescence required. There, of course, Peto had been nursed by Rebecca Codrington – now Lady Peto – and there was no knowing the power in that.

He couldn't help a sigh. He couldn't wish his old friend any greater happiness than this devotion – this love – of Rebecca Codrington's (and so young a woman at that), but ignoble though he knew it was, their mutual affection, as the Pearces', served only to magnify his own want of it.

But he smiled a few lines later on. Having so soon lost a viscount, the Sixtieth – who thought themselves always so superior – had replaced him with a knight: 'Sir Brodrick Hartwell, Bart, to be Second Lieutenant, by purchase, vice Lord Torrington, promoted in the 7th Foot.' In time of bloody war and sickly season, these things counted for far less, but in time of peace there was a strong financial interest. Regiments with a peer or two in their list, or failing that a baronet, could always command a higher price. When the wags spoke of a 'peerless regiment', it was not usually an expression of high regard. Sniff at these things though he was inclined to do occasionally, he could not deny that since his own assumption of command the value of his half-colonelcy had increased by the accretion of three sons of the peerage. That this owed nothing to his reputation as commanding officer, or to the Sixth's fighting record, but instead to their station at Hounslow and its proximity to London, was by the bye.

Having read the promotions and appointments, he then found a rather encouraging entry that suggested that when it came to affairs like Bristol, the authorities would indeed take whatever action was needed. Respecting the late disturbances in the Midland counties, His Majesty promised pardon 'to those who had forced open the prison at Derby and set at liberty the prisoners who shall discover his accomplice or accomplices therein, so that he, she, or they may be apprehended and convicted thereof', and with the offer 'as a further encouragement' of a reward of one hundred pounds 'to any person who shall discover the said offender or offenders, so that he, she, or they may be apprehended and convicted of the said offence'.

'Capital!' He said it so loud that several heads turned his way.

Indeed, he would have put down the *Gazette* had not turning the page allowed him to ignore the enquiring heads, thereby missing the most significant intelligence of the entire paper – from the East India House: 'the Court of Directors of the United Company of Merchants of England trading to the East Indies do hereby give notice that Sir Eyre Somervile KCH is appointed pro-Governor of the Presidency of Fort St George, vice Stephen Rumbold Lushington Esq on indefinite leave of absence'.

For here was ripe news indeed. The Somerviles were not long returned from Canada; he had not yet seen them, for they'd taken a house in Yorkshire for the summer. He'd supposed they would stay in London a year or two at least, for although Canada was the province of the War Office – the War and Colonial Office indeed – Somervile was a Company man to his fingertips. Madras was where they'd first met, when Somervile had been but a collector – and when he'd met his wife – and Hervey supposed the prospect of returning as governor must be delightful to both.

Delightful it was, of course, but with Fairbrother's sojourn in Jamaica, it now meant many months without the prospect of conversation on any terms of intimacy. He resolved to write at once. It was impossible that he should visit Yorkshire, but they were bound to come to London before sailing, and he must see as much of them as he might, for there was no knowing how long it would be until the next opportunity. There was a godchild, indeed. And Emma had been one of Henrietta's closest friends – perhaps the very closest.

He wondered, though, about this strange substitution of governors, *sine die*. What was it that compelled Stephen Rumbold Lushington Esq to indefinite leave of absence – or John Company to grant it? He supposed that among the occupants of the tub chairs there would be one who knew, but to enquire would invite a conversation – which might very well lead to Bristol, and he'd still no wish to speak of it before he'd seen the commander-in-chief.

The smoking-room waiter had already lit the gaslights, and the lamp trimmer was beginning his rounds, so he moved instead to one of the writing tables. But he'd scarcely taken up the pen before the hall porter appeared.

'Begging your pardon, Colonel, but a messenger has just come from the Horse Guards, and Lord Hill asks to see you now.'

Several heads turned, for it was never the practice of the club servants to announce messages with lowered voice. But they were looks of some regard – the hall porter had said 'asks to see you' – and Hervey took a certain pleasure in it, replacing the pen and folding the sheet of paper without undue haste.

As he rose and made to leave he was checked by the sudden appearance of the King's private secretary.

'Hervey, I understood you were in Bristol.'

'Good evening, General. You understood rightly.' Every head was again turned his way. 'I returned last night.'

They were well acquainted. Like John Howard, Lieutenant-General Sir Herbert Taylor had never been shot over – or not much (the siege of Antwerp, before Bonaparte's first exile, had not been much of an affair) – nor drawn his sword except on parade, but he possessed a great facility for counsel and discretion, having been private secretary variously to the late King George, and to his father and to Queen Charlotte, as well as, lately, Military Secretary and then Adjutant-General. It was not insignificant, Hervey reckoned, that he chose to announce to the room that he'd been in Bristol.

'You'll have read the report in *The Clarion*? Damnable. His Majesty's most grateful for your services.'

Well, there it was. The press – a Radical part of it at least – made trouble, and the King disapproved of it. Hervey didn't think he'd seen *The Clarion* on the bulletins table, but if His Majesty wasn't disturbed by the 'damnable report', why should he be? 'I'm about to see Lord Hill. There'll be a thorough inquiry.'

'Quite so. His Majesty's cancelled all levees for the time being. He'll await Lord Melbourne's report, of course, but he may wish to hear from you in person, at Windsor.'

'I shall inform Lord Hill.'

'And brace yourself for slings and arrows. The Radicals aren't above making mischief.'

Hervey thanked him. General Taylor was a courtier in uniform, but his occasional dealings with him at Windsor had been always agreeable, and any man favoured by the Duke of Wellington was a man whose own favour was worth preserving. *Slings and arrows* – what precisely did he mean? Lines in *The Clarion* and its like were hardly going to trouble him (he supposed).

At the Horse Guards he found John Howard still in uniform. It was the practice to wear a plain coat in the afternoon, which meant he'd taken no respite since seeing him earlier. Such, evidently, was the consternation that Bristol must be causing.

'Lord Hill returned but an hour ago. He's seen your memorandum, and a letter from Colonel Brereton – sent to the Military Secretary, for some reason. I've not myself seen it, and his lordship has not vouchsafed its contents. He seems, however, somewhat . . . preoccupied.'

'I don't doubt it,' replied Hervey, in some surprise. 'He must be wondering who'll attaint him first – the government for excessive force or the Tories for want of it.'

'That may be so, but I rather think that in the meantime he wonders how many will be the calls on the troops, and how if they're many he's to meet them. I gather it's taken every post-house from here to Bristol to get one troop of guns there.'

Were it not so serious Hervey would have smiled at the thought of the post-masters all along the Bristol road having suddenly to turn out horses for 6-pounders instead of mails or the occasional chaise.

'I beg pardon. I do him a disservice. I own that I substituted my own doubts, for I just saw Sir Herbert Taylor at the United Service, and he cautioned me against slings and arrows.'

Howard looked wry. 'I can't say, save that it would indeed be outrageous fortune. I should have thought the aldermen of Bristol are at this very moment considering the number of rubies to embed in the sword they'll present to you.'

'A sword with two edges, no doubt?'

'I shall tell Lord Hill you are come.'

The commander-in-chief of His Majesty's Land Forces, General the Right Honourable Rowland, Lord Hill – Baron Hill of Almaraz and of Hawkestone in the County of Salop – took off his spectacles as Hervey entered, and with them indicated the chair to the front and off-centre of his desk.

It was a good start, thought Hervey as he sat. That he was not 'marched' in was a good enough start, but to be greeted so familiarly – not with a word but a nod – spoke of the regard in which he was held by 'Daddy' Hill (as he was affectionately known by those who'd served under him in the Peninsula). It was a fact that a man who'd galloped for a general in a battle such as Talavera was never again a mere field officer to him.

'Well, a pretty kettle of fish, Hervey.'

'Indeed, General.'

'I have an account of it from Colonel Brereton. It seems very plausible, were it not for the fact that half of Bristol lies in ruins.'

'Well, half of civic Bristol, to be precise, my lord – and the major part of a rather fine square of houses. I don't of course know what Colonel Brereton writes, except that he gave me an account of events and reasons for his actions when I arrived.'

'You didn't hesitate in taking command from one so experienced? Brereton's seen a bit of the world, has he not, and knows the city?'

'No, I did not hesitate, General.' He didn't think he needed to add that his brevet gave him no option, or that Lord Hill's own man – Mackworth – had so urgently requested he do so. Nor did he feel it his place to comment on Colonel Brereton's service, whatever it was.

'No, I hadn't supposed that you would.'

Quite what point he made was unclear, but Hervey wasn't inclined to ask for clarification. There was always a certain . . . ambulation in Lord Hill's approach to questions touching on judgement.

He got up, beckoning Hervey to stay seated. 'Sherry?'

'Thank you, General.'

Lord Hill poured two glasses at a table under a rather gloomy portrait of the late Duke of York, returned to his chair and passed Hervey's glass across the desk. 'There'll be the devil to pay, of course – and rightly so. The second city of England in the hands of the mob for two full days, with more than enough soldiers at a moment's call . . . Melbourne's rattled, for sure. It wouldn't have happened with Peel at the Home department; that's what he's afeared of them saying.' He took a sip of his sherry. 'So "Aaron shall cast lots upon the two goats; one lot for the Lord, and the other lot for the scapegoat."'

Hervey took a sip of his, and raised his eyebrows. Since a boy he could recite much of the book of Leviticus by heart: '"But the goat, on which the lot fell to be the scapegoat, shall be presented alive before the Lord, to make an atonement with him, and to let him go for a scape-goat into the wilderness."'

'Or into the half-pay,' said Lord Hill, with an amiable smile. 'But it is no laughing matter, though you yourself have no cause for disquiet. It must be managed rightly, however, which is why a court of inquiry must be assembled with all haste.'

'General Dalbiac is to cast the lots, I understand.'

'He is, but Melbourne wants a lieutenant-general to be its figurehead. That way the press and the Radicals can't say the army's dealing with it too lightly.'

'This seems reasonable,' said Hervey, taking another sip of his sherry, and with rather more relish.

Lord Hill leaned back in his chair, glass in hand, and nodded.

'But now, elaborate a little, if you would, on the performance of the yeomanry . . .'

A quarter of an hour's elaboration was quite enough for the commander-in-chief. The situation of the yeomanry was something to be addressed once and for all, he said – 'When the hurly-burly's done.'

The clock struck six, and there was other business. 'And I've to put on levee dress for Monsieur Talleyrand's.' Lord Hill thanked him and bid him adieu without the formality of ringing for an aide-de-camp.

Hervey took his leave much encouraged.

In Howard's office again, where one of his own dragoons had just brought a despatch case from Brighton, he told his friend what had passed with Lord Hill. 'But now I'll bid you good night, for I know you're to the French, and evidently you have more reading first,' he added blithely, nodding to the despatches. 'Until tomorrow, then – White's.'

'Ah, yes . . . I'm afraid we must suspend that pleasure, for I must now attend on Lord Hill at Lord Melbourne's. It seems he expects there to be further business to discuss after tomorrow's Cabinet.'

'Very well. Send word as soon as you will.' He put on his cap, and then paused for a moment. 'Is all well, Howard? You seem . . . distracted.'

Howard frowned. 'Did Lord Hill say that the inquiry's now to be presided over by a lieutenant-general?'

'He did.'

Howard hesitated, then picked up a sheet of paper. 'A communication from Lord FitzRoy's office: Sir Peregrine Greville's to be the president.'

Hervey tried hard to keep his countenance. He'd never spoken of his connection with Lady Katherine Greville to anyone.

VII

The Barrack Round

Hounslow, next day

T HE WEATHER WAS ABOMINABLE. THE rain had begun again soon after he left the Horse Guards, and all night it had lashed the windows at Heston, but so irregularly with the gale that it was almost impossible to sleep. Besides, the thought of Lieutenant-General Sir Peregrine Greville presiding over the inquiry agitated his mind. The wind had now abated, and the rain fell vertically, which at least made less noise at the windows, but it fell in great quantity nevertheless. If only it had rained harder at Bristol . . .

It had been a wet year altogether. At the beginning of August there'd been a whole week of thunderstorms, and much hay lost. Yet Collins, the quartermaster, had saved the imprest account, and therefore the Treasury, a considerable sum by buying in June rather than after Michaelmas, as custom and regulation required – and getting far better hay into the bargain. Collins had been Hervey's covering-corporal in the Peninsula, when Lincoln had been serjeant-major and Armstrong his serjeant. He'd come through those years with scarcely a powder mark, only to lose an arm in 'the joust on the Brussels road' the year before. It had put paid to his prospects of being serjeant-major, but it also delivered Hervey from his dilemma in choosing between him and Armstrong. He'd not regretted the gamble in making him quartermaster. Even with his sword arm gone, Collins was a match for obstructive bureaucracy. Lincoln had tried many times, but the Commissary-General clerks wouldn't approve the buying of hay so early. Collins had simply decided on the expedient of not asking permission and buying on credit, telling the farmers that payment would be later than hitherto on account of losing his writing hand to a French dragoon. (He never actually said 'at Waterloo', but, being the consummate quartermaster, saw no reason to be exact if it meant getting his stores.)

But now he was bedded down a second time – in the first of the winter's barrack epidemics.

The surgeon was the same that had amputated his arm on the Brussels road. 'I confess he's the first limbless case of catarrhal fever I've treated, but if Lord FitzRoy Somerset can be Military Secretary without his right arm . . .'

He took a medicinal gulp from his coffee cup.

'Quite so,' said Hervey, though not entirely sure what Lord FitzRoy's case had to do with it, but adding for encouragement 'And Nelson.'

Then suddenly Surgeon Milne became briskly clinical again. 'It's a prodigious fever, and I've told Mrs Collins she must dose him with great care, and feed him determinedly. I've observed that it's the most generous diet that promotes recovery, but it's disagreeable on account of the cough.'

'Have you told Collins he must eat?' Discourteous as it seemed to enquire of a professional man, Hervey would take no chances – not even with the best regimental surgeon he'd known.

'I have.'

'Then he's as good as recovered, for he'll follow orders to the letter.'

'I pray so. He's an excellent specimen of manhood, but there's no knowing when it comes to catarrhal fever. The pulse is so peculiarly quick and irregular.'

'And the amputation: has it any bearing?'

Milne shook his head. 'He made an ample recovery. I've no reason to suppose it will be an aggravation.'

'And you now have thirteen in the sick-house.'

'Four more this morning.'

'What will be the best time for me to visit with them?'

'When they're recovered!'

Hervey looked dismayed. 'Some of my dragoons may very well die, and you would not have me see them?'

'No, Colonel; you asked what would be the best time to visit, and I gave you my opinion. You may visit with them when you please, for they're your dragoons, as you say, but you may very well contract the influenza, as it's vulgarly known, and then you too would be bedded down.' He did not add that nor would there be a Mrs Hervey to feed him determinedly (even if there were Annie to stand *in loco uxoris*).

Hervey always found Milne's gentle airs of Buchan reassuring. He was ten years his senior, perhaps, and *Medicinae Doctor Aberdonensis*. His wife had died some years before, his son was a flag lieutenant on the West Africa station, and seeing no cause to remain in those parts, he had left his practice in Golden Square and joined the 2nd Dragoons. What had then brought him to the Sixth was not entirely clear, but Lord Holderness had had a way of attracting capable men. Milne had proved deft with knife and ligature, and Hervey was not inclined to dismiss his opinion lightly.

'I shall think on it,' he said, sounding unusually uncertain. 'Anything more?'

'No, Colonel, only that I find myself deficient in understanding the significance of Michaelmas hay, which was all that Collins could talk of – having to see to the barns and such like. But I shall enquire of the RM.'

Hervey smiled. Even if it were the fever talking, it was Collins to a fault. 'Dine with me this evening and I'll tell you myself.'

Milne having exercised his right of first call at Commanding Officer's Orderly Room, 'Defaulters' now took its usual bracing course. Hervey's only consolation was knowing that in a regiment of Foot there'd be five times the number.

Owthwaite's, though, was a sorry affair. The adjutant read out the charge – and then silence.

Hervey eventually looked up and across his table at the delinquent NCO. 'Tell me, Corporal Owthwaite, why a non-commissioned officer of such experience and capability, one so highly prized by the riding-master, finds himself before his commanding officer on such a charge?'

Owthwaite stood ramrod straight, furnished and burnished as if about to stand before the King at Windsor, his eyes blue and bright, his face close-shaved, and his hair as sleek as a seal's. All the regiment knew his weakness, and the consequent 'trouble' that accompanied his looks.

'No excuse, Colonel, sir.'

'As you *were*, Corp'l!' barked Armstrong.

'Sir! Beg pardon, sir. No excuse, *sir.*'

Hervey sighed inwardly. It was hardly a point on which evidence turned, but, there again, the Orderly Serjeant had been drilling it into them for half an hour: Commanding Officer's Orderly Room was a parade; 'Sir' was the reply, not 'Colonel,' or even 'Colonel, sir.'

'I did not ask for an excuse, Corporal Owthwaite, but for an explanation.'

'Sir.'

Silence.

'Answer the commanding officer, Corp'l!'

Armstrong was becoming hoarse – or perhaps it was for effect. Either way, Owthwaite flinched. And Owthwaite was not a flincher.

'Sir!'

Silence again, but this time lawfully: Owthwaite had first to acknow-ledge the serjeant-major's order – 'Sir!' – and then to answer Hervey's question, and as it called for self-examination, his answer could hardly come at once.

But in truth, Hervey had meant the question to be rhetorical. He'd long believed that more men were flattered into virtue than were bullied out of vice.

'I couldn't help myself, sir.'

'You couldn't help yourself.'

'Sir.'

'You, uniquely among men, have not been granted free will by your Maker.'

Silence.

'Answer the commanding officer, Corp'l!'

'Sir!'

Silence again.

Hervey wondered for an instant if it were fair to expect a rough-rider to be conversant with the doctrine of the Fall, but Owthwaite had attended enough church parades in his time . . .

The procedure was, in any case, still novel, parliament having only lately amended the Mutiny Act. Hitherto, Owthwaite would have been tried by regimental court martial. Besides requiring seven officers to sit in judgement (or five overseas), which was an excessive inconvenience for a regiment of cavalry, dispersed over many miles as it usually was, it could lead to unedifying dispute, which might well linger. Now, at least, the district court martial, made up of officers of various regiments, dealt with matters at a healthy remove. Except that a district court martial could not be manipulated, and sometimes – such as in Owthwaite's case – it were better done 'within the family'. But Hervey had conceded that Armstrong was right to insist Owthwaite be tried 'by the book'; that is, that the proper charge be brought against him – even though because of its seriousness the commanding officer had no power to deal with the charge summarily and therefore must remand Owthwaite for court martial (unless he were to dismiss it for want of evidence; and in this case the evidence ran to many pages). The trouble was, reduction to the ranks was the only possible outcome (assuming the court martial were indeed to find him guilty), and Hervey had dearly hoped there might be another way. Whichever way, the formality of regimental orderly room was just that – a formality. Everyone knew it, including the prisoner.

And so all that he, Hervey, could now do was bring 'orders' to a close before there was a miscarriage not of justice but of dignity. 'Well, Corporal Owthwaite,' he began, in his best voice of disappointment, 'disagreeable though my duty is – especially when I myself witnessed your conduct in the breach at Bhurtpore, conduct of the highest order – I shall not hesitate to do it.'

Silence. He let it continue a good many heartbeats.

'Remanded for court martial. March out.'

Armstrong's words of command came in a split second. Owthwaite was fairly doubled out.

Lieutenant St Alban closed his order book and waited for the word.

Hervey signed the disposal and handed it to him. 'Deuced fool. He'd be serjeant in five years if he'd once learn to moderate his passions.'

'Indeed, Colonel.'

'Deuced trying, remanding a man for certain reduction who did what he did at Bhurtpore. It'll make a fine plea in mitigation, but it won't save him.'

'No, Colonel; on which point – Bhurtpore, I mean – will you see Corporal Stray now?'

Interviews customarily followed 'Defaulters', except on occasions when there was no one in arrest. Hervey found it helped restore the spirits. This morning there was just the one, however – the quartermaster-corporal – and the purpose of the interview was entirely agreeable.

Hervey smiled wryly. 'You are not, I imagine, well acquainted with Corp'l Stray's . . . broader reputation.'

'I regret not, Colonel – only that he pulled the sar'nt-major from a gallery that fell in.'

Stray had long been the fattest man in the regiment – in the army, some said. Yet there was not a man in the Sixth who was more at home in the field than he. His economy with stores was celebrated, and he could fashion any necessary from the most unpromising raw materials, and quickly too, but it was his soldier's solidness that the old hands admired above all. Stray was utterly imperturbable in the face of the enemy and superiors alike. Once, in Paris after Waterloo when he'd been a private dragoon, he was posted as a single sentry on a bridge which for retributive reasons the Prussians were intent on blowing up. After they'd laboured a good while to put the powder kegs in place, the officer of engineers asked him to quit the span and seek cover, to which Stray had replied, 'Not until properly relieved by the corporal, sir.' The Prussians had lit the fuses, but still Stray would not budge, standing on-guard with his sabre when they tried to remove him bodily, so that in the end the engineers had had to rush about frantically pulling the fuses from the kegs. Corporal Stray was not a man to have in the front rank at a review, but he was without doubt a man to have at hand on campaign – or even a tiger hunt.

Hervey leaned back in his chair, his smile widening. 'During the siege works at Bhurtpore – as well as pulling Serjeant Armstrong, as he then was, from the gallery – Corp'l Stray was attacked from nowhere by Jhauts as he drove his bullock cart from camp. They killed the bullocks one by one – six in all, I think it was, perhaps even eight – and then closed in to deal with him. But he just stood on the box as if he were at sword exercise and cut down half a dozen, until the rest took fright and galloped off. You'd scarcely credit it, would you?'

'No-o-o. Well, possibly.'

'Why uncertain?'

'Well, Colonel, I know him of course only by appearance, and his leave has evidently been . . . productive; or, I might even say, *reductive*.'

'Getting a wife – the promise of a wife – you mean?'

'That and new regimentals.'

Hervey looked intrigued. 'You allude to the red?'

'I think I should have him marched in, Colonel.'

'Very well; I love a mystery as much as the next man.'

It was one of the Sixth's happy customs that a man sought 'permission' before marriage. Permission for a private man was delegated to his troop captain, while an NCO had the privilege of hearing the commanding officer's will in person (an officer, as a courtesy, wrote to the colonel of the regiment). *Why* was uncertain, but Lincoln had attested to its being the practice before the regiment went to the Peninsula, and so the custom had returned with peace. Hervey imagined it possible that someone had thought it a way to emphasize the gravity of the undertaking – 'not by any to be enterprized, nor taken in hand unadvisedly, lightly, or wantonly, to satisfy men's carnal lusts, and appetites' – and, indeed, more than one dragoon had withdrawn from the promise on learning that he would have to march in front of his captain. On one occasion too, a dragoon had been refused permission – unlawfully, for there was nothing in King's Regulations or the Mutiny Act – his captain believing the man to be too young and callow; and being young and callow, the man had accepted the ruling without demur, and was seen whistling happily at stables an hour later, as if relieved ('Oh no, sweet maid, I cannot marry thee, for my captain won't let me on').

Dragoons for interview were not marched in, hatless, like defaulters. They entered without words of command, halting and saluting in their own time. Corporal Stray entered with unprecedented spring in his step. 'Good morning, Colonel.'

Hervey was momentarily speechless. 'Corporal Stray . . . how . . . very gratifying to see you looking so well.'

'Thank you, Colonel.'

'Is this transformation connected with your intention to commit matrimony? Stand at ease, man.'

'Colonel, I'll speak t'truth. When I went to buy a ticket for 'ome, t'carrier said I'd 'ave to pay excess, which vexed me; but then I said to meself, Mick, tha's only thiself to blame, and mebbe it's time to shrink a bit. An' I 'ave done.'

'You have indeed, Corporal Stray – in the course of which, it appears, you have found a woman consenting to be your wife.'

'I 'ave, Colonel, a right good'n.'

'From hereabouts?'

'From 'ome, Colonel – a widder. 'Er 'usband an' me were nippers together. 'E went for a marine, which were funny as there were no water for miles. Any'ow, 'e died a few years back, an' Olive – beggin' yer pardon, Colonel: Mrs Catchpole – went back to 'Ickleton and got work in t'big 'ouse there, an' then 'er uncle died – 'e were a farmer near there – an' left 'er a bit o' money – not a lot, mind, but so as t'ave nice things – an' I asked if she'd like to be wed again, an' she said she would.'

'Well, well; who'd have thought it?' said Hervey, shaking his head. That Stray, for countless years the doyen of the canteen, was to have the consolations of a good woman . . . Though it did beg an unhappy question: 'I imagine you will therefore be looking to your discharge, and going to live at Ickleton?'

''Ickleton it is, Colonel – with an aitch. No, I'll not be looking for me discharge. Olive – Mrs Catchpole, I mean – will come and live 'ere.'

'I'm delighted to hear it. And when shall the marriage be contracted?'

'With your leave, Colonel, just afore Christmas.'

'Admirable. Well, Corporal Stray, I give you leave to marry, and my hand in congratulation.' He stood up and reached across the writing table. 'And I look forward to meeting the future Mrs Stray as soon as may be.'

For what an excellent woman she must be to give up the comforts of this Hickleton to come to the rude quarters of a cavalry barracks, especially indeed if she had already seen those of the Marines. Stray came nowhere near him in rank, but in this measure he wholly surpassed him.

'Dismiss.'

At dinner that evening, Hervey found the surgeon unusually good company, though tired from his exertions in the sick-house – twenty-four hours in which he had had little sleep, though he would not own to it. The rain had continued, and Milne had come by hackney, and was thus already in good spirits instead of having first to be dried out in front of the fire, and the waiting glass of mulled punch served as a stimulant to conversation rather than just to warm. Hervey had spent the afternoon writing to the colonel of the regiment and sundry others about the events in Bristol – a somewhat repetitive exercise – and then on return to Heston had begun thinking rather too contingently on Sir Peregrine Greville's presidency of the inquiry. Milne was therefore especially welcome diversion, notwithstanding his reputation for the dryness of the granite city.

Annie and Corporal Johnson waited on them. White soup, steamed sole, and then beefsteaks fed their healthy appetites, but although conversation flowed freely, Hervey's guest sipped only moderately at the best burgundy.

'I have observed, doctor,' (he kept 'Surgeon' for the barracks) 'that as a rule you take little wine, but especially this evening.'

'I have nothing against the grape, Colonel, I assure you, only that it tends to induce drowsiness in me.' He did not add that he would be returning to the sick-house.

Nor did Hervey say that that was one of the properties he prized – an aid to sleep when unwelcome thoughts otherwise kept him awake. But it mattered not. This was an evening for easy talk.

'You have not by any chance had occasion to see Quartermaster-Corporal Stray since his return?'

'Indeed I have. He brought nitrous acid to the infirmary yesterday.'

'Nitrous acid?'

'A fumigant. Though I try to insist on the greatest circulation of free air.'

'Ah, yes.'

'I observed Stray's . . . reduced circumstances, and when I'd satisfied myself that he was not himself ill, as I'd first suspected, for such exceptional loss of weight is indicative of illness, but which from the brightness of his eye and general energy I concluded unlikely, I questioned him about his regimen. He told me he'd ceased taking all alcohol, in his case largely hops, and ate only vegetables and eggs. I shall take satisfaction in relating it at the next meeting of the Medical Society.'

Hervey nodded, and took a liberal sip of his wine. 'You are most assiduous in this – the Medical Society, I mean.'

'It is one of the attractions of practising in a regiment such as this, close by London. In truth there's not a great deal to detain me each day in barracks – several hundred men, by the nature of their calling and service active and in good health, and usually scattered about the country; and a couple of dozen wives. Not an exhausting practice ordinarily.'

'And the Medical Society – the meetings?'

'Papers are read, and there are questions, and then published in the weekly journal.'

'Have you yourself given a paper?'

'I have.'

Hervey drained his glass as Johnson removed their empty plates and then returned with another decanter. 'On some aspect of military surgery, I imagine?'

Milne frowned. 'I have to tell you, Colonel, that Collins's is only the second amputation I've performed, and the first was a poor fisher lad at Peterhead.'

'Then I should say that your skill with a knife is the more admirable for its being acquired by study rather than by practice. Did the fisher lad live too?'

'He did.'

'And may I ask, then, what *was* your paper?'

'Some aspects of post-partum morbidity.'

'Ah.'

'It is, I grant you, a subject somewhat on the periphery of military surgery, but I'd begun to make a study of it in my civil practice. You'll be aware no doubt that in the north of Scotland daylight is but seven hours at the winter solstice. My observations were to determine if the morbidity were in some way related to the attenuation of daylight.'

Medical matters had never been something in which Hervey interested himself, except to the extent that they affected his parade state (and women's medical matters had no bearing whatever on that). Nevertheless, a surgeon who took an enquiring interest in one aspect of his profession was likely to be receptive to new ideas in others. He'd known surgeons who appeared to have learned nothing since acquiring their licence – indeed, had forgotten a good deal of that in which they'd once been examined. But he'd no desire to discuss childbirth.

'What precisely is this catarrhal fever?'

Milne sipped a little water and said he would try to paraphrase the proceedings of a recent meeting of the Medical Society. When he'd done so, Hervey said he thought it amounted to a treatise on un-certainty, with which Milne agreed – complimenting Hervey, indeed, on his rapid grasp of the essentials, although he pointed out that in the realm of scientific enquiry it was as important to recognize that which could not with certainty be established as that which could. The material points, however – that it was not known whether the disease was infectious or 'merely' contagious, and that its cause and therefore treatment was unknown, but that its mortality was considerable – were, he explained, the reason for his anxiety for the sick-house. 'Which is why my professional advice was – remains – to visit once the fever has run its course. I acknowledge, however, that your going there this after-noon was probably better tonic than my sulphate of cornine, dissolved even as it was in best port.'

Hervey nodded. 'Collins, by the way, was sleeping when I called at his lodgings, so I didn't stay.'

'Perfectly reasonable.'

Annie now came with a dish of brandied peaches and jug of thick cream. 'Dr Milne's hackney has come, sir, but I've given the cabman some supper, and he's quite content.'

The surgeon looked at his watch. 'I hadn't realized the hour was so late, Colonel. Forgive me.'

'There's nothing in the least to forgive. I don't count it late before midnight. I hope you won't forgo the peaches.'

But the surgeon had engaged the hackney for ten, precisely so he could make a final round of the sick-house. He had at least the consolation of knowing the cabman was enjoying a bowl of some-thing pleasant in the kitchen. 'A very little, Annie, pleasing though it looks.'

Johnson poured more wine – for Hervey at least.

Over the peaches, Milne finished his discourse on the influenza, and then suddenly lapsed into thought. Hervey asked if something troubled him.

'There is one thing more, Colonel, which perhaps I should have mentioned at orderly room,' he said, laying down his spoon. 'The Philharmonic Society has invited me to be an honorary physician.'

Hervey rapped the table. 'Admirable. You play with them regularly still?'

'As a rule, each Thursday.'

'I recall one of their concerts two or three years ago. Most diverting.'

On the whole, he was not much appreciative of music, except, as his sister had it, 'drums and trumpets'.

'You have no objection to the appointment?'

'Not in the least. Why should I?'

Milne looked uncertain.

'*Should* I have reason?'

'No, Colonel, I . . . The benefit concert at Christmas . . .'

'Whose benefit?'

'The Royal Hospital.'

'Chelsea – the pensioners?'

'Just so . . . The duke is to conduct an overture . . . I had imagined you knew of it.'

'No, but I shall be sure to subscribe at once. The duke was always known for his music. And there's no nobler cause than the pensioners.'

Milne looked uncomfortable, however. 'I . . . I believe I have in my bag a handbill. I shall leave it with you.'

'Yes, if you would. Thank you. Another peach?'

'If you'll excuse me, no. I want to see how Fitch, my assistant, manages. He's diligent enough, but he's not nursed the epidemic fever before.'

'Of course,' said Hervey, putting down his glass. 'You'll report tomorrow morning?'

'I shall.'

They rose, and Annie went to fetch the surgeon's coat while Johnson roused the cabman. Hervey saw him off in the same rain as that in which he'd arrived – and hoped the cabman's oilskins were in good order – then repaired to the fire in his study, a glass of port and a page or two of *Vom Kriege*. Soon, however, he tired of the effort in the candlelight and instead took out the handbill that Milne had given him. It was as he'd said: the Duke of Wellington was to conduct an overture – which alone would be guarantee to sell every seat in the Hanover Square Rooms, regardless of the celebrity of the others whose names he began to read (names, in truth, he'd scarcely, if at all, heard of – nor their chosen pieces).

And then, towards the middle of the bill, he saw what must have discomfited the surgeon:

FANTASIA – PIANOFORTE – *La Violette* . . . . . . HENRI HERZ
MRS HERVEY

VIII

The Tribunal

Bristol, Thursday, 17 November

T HE 'INQUIRY TO INVESTIGATE THE conduct of the officer in command of the troops', as the convening order put it, had attracted many more spectators than could possibly be admitted to the Merchant Venturers' Hall. Hervey supposed it was only right that the public and gentlemen of the press be admitted, for although it was a military tribunal it touched on matters of public moment. Not that he supposed it would be very edifying, however. He was certainly pleased to observe two armed sentries at the entrance. Best to leave no one in any doubt as to who was in charge.

He took a seat in the front row reserved for the witnesses, and glanced in turn at the officers appointed to the inquiry, who sat one side of a long dining table, on the other side of which sat Brereton and his supporter, and at either end the clerks. They were as true a board as might be assembled: Colonels Sir Edward Miles of the 89th and James Fergusson of the 52nd Foot, Lord Loughborough commanding the 9th Lancers. None wore the Waterloo medal, but Hervey knew them to be men of experience and judgement nevertheless; and there was Major

Edmund Walcott of the Horse Artillery, who did wear the medal. He'd known him as a lieutenant with F Troop – and before that at Corunna, with C.

Brereton would certainly get a fair hearing.

But what a troubled appearance was the colonel's. He sat very upright at the table, with his supporter, Major Henry Ellard of the 65th Regiment, an officer on the half-pay, equally upright beside him, staring as if at some distant object and wholly oblivious to the rest of the assemblage. Hervey marked that he was smartly enough turned out, if without the 'edge' that might have presented a more commanding impression, and thought his expression ominously blank. When first he'd seen him that Sunday morning of the riot, brought from his bed and evidently having slept little, he'd observed a man whose nerves were clearly much shaken, but by no means broken. Now, he wondered if he weren't near that perilous point. He'd seen men bear themselves when drained of all resource – in the face of the enemy and after – through naught but habit, and then suddenly, without apparent cause, begin to sob. He hoped for Brereton's sake – and for that of the service – that he would not suffer the humiliation here, before civilians and scribblers.

Sitting somewhat aloof from the board, his chair to one side, was Lieutenant-General Sir Peregrine Greville. It was the first occasion Hervey had had to observe the 'other party' in Kat's *mariage de convenance* – a rather antique figure, not only considerably senior in years to Kat but with the distinct appearance of the old century. He did not actually wear a wig, but it looked somehow as if it were his custom to. His uniform was of the former pattern, the coat long and cutaway, revealing waistcoat and *embonpoint* like an old portrait of plenty. His breeches and court shoes served only to set him apart from the trousered field officers. He was portly, though not grossly so, his face was weather-beaten (which Hervey supposed was on account of his love of rod and stream, for he knew he had seen little service), and his hair like a cob's mane that had been ill hogged. What terrible prospect of Irish penury could have driven Kat, daughter of the Earl of Athleague, into such a contract? Sir Peregrine was by all accounts – or rather, by Kat's – a compliant sort of soul, undemanding, generous in most regards. He had for many years occupied the sinecure of lieutenant-governor of Alderney and Sark, where he had lived unaccompanied, occupying himself with sea fishing, before being appointed lately to an even better sinecure at Dublin. Three times a year he had occasion to journey to London, being also member for the 'close and decayed' parliamentary borough of St Felix in Suffolk (consisting of three houses and seven voters, most of the borough having long fallen into the sea); and three times a year he had hastened back to Alderney as soon as His Majesty's speech had been read, and would no doubt continue the practice in his present appointment. Hervey was at a loss to know to what talent, influence or corruption Sir Peregrine owed his promotion and sinecures, save sound Tory principles. High rank and honours had indeed flowed effortlessly his way – and the connection of one such as Lady Katherine. Yet he himself had no wish to emulate him – even for such a prize as Kat. For what did it profit a man to gain the world and lose his soldier's soul?

It soon became clear that Sir Peregrine intended to preside at a remove, as the position of his chair indicated. (Hervey supposed that he knew his presence to be mere window dressing.) It was General Dalbiac who began the proceedings.

'Gentlemen, I pray you, take note that this inquiry into the aid given by the Military to the Civil Power during the late disturbances hereabout is now open. The board acknowledges the receipt of written testimony by various parties, both military and civil, and these will form the basis of our proceedings. These notwithstanding, however, the board may require the officers and civic officials whence came these testimonies to give evidence orally.'

Hervey had expected as much, though he'd very much hoped it would not be so, since no good could come of trading accusations before the public. He perfectly understood that a man – principally Brereton – must know in full what had been laid before the board, and be able to question it or shape his own testimony to respond to it, but it would likely therefore be a matter of several days, and he had no wish to sit the while in the Merchants' Hall in any circumstances, least of all under the gaze of Sir Peregrine. As the senior officer to be examined by the tribunal (General Jackson was not to give evidence, apparently), he supposed he could claim the privilege of being called first . . .

A sudden murmur among the spectators made him look up. Kat was come to join her husband – to sit next to him indeed. Dalbiac's preliminaries were temporarily halted while the gallants rose and fussed until she was seated.

Hervey swallowed hard. She made a singular impression – green velvet coat with more frogging than a hussar's, a hat suggesting a Tarleton (or else something *auf der Jagd*), and a skirt that showed her ankles to any risking a look. Why had she come? Why had she dressed so?

General Dalbiac began reading the convening order – the last formality.

Familiar words brought Hervey back to the matter at hand, which in any case could hardly be far from his thoughts, even if he wished it so. For all that it was a fortnight since the untoward events, there was still outside the odour of riot – the smell of charred timbers, burnt paint and tar, and noisome substances liberated from flasks in numerous workshops. The board would have had ample evidence beyond that of their eyes of the cost of Colonel Brereton's hesitation – or else of Mayor Pinney's indecision. He told himself that he'd no cause for apprehension in the matter; though that was easier said than believed.

With the greatest show of courtesy, principally for the benefit of those who did not wear the King's coat, for otherwise there might seem to be no honour in the profession of arms, General Dalbiac invited the colonel to speak of events.

Brereton seemed suddenly to brighten. Hervey wondered what was the cause – what new consideration there might be. He was certainly keen to hear at last what Brereton considered his better judgement to have been, for the statements he had heard during those hours at Bristol, and read subsequently, were not to his mind those of an officer of experience in possession of his full faculties.

Brereton's testimony was, however, an unhappy business. He spoke from the extensive submission to which General Dalbiac had referred – and none too succinctly, which never, in Hervey's experience, went well with a tribunal, and in a tone of appeal rather than with the semi-contemptuous assurance that might have impressed the listener. Indeed, during the course of his long statement and the questions that followed, Hervey learned nothing new. Two hours they sat, before General Dalbiac, with an affirming nod from Sir Peregrine, spoke the welcome words: 'Gentlemen, we shall adjourn for one and one half of one hour for luncheon.'

Hervey himself had no great appetite after his breakfast at the post-house in Bath, where he'd rested a while having left Hounslow late the night before after a field day on the heath, and so instead of joining the procession of officers making for the inquiry's dining room, he thought to leave the hall and take a little air.

However, Sir Peregrine's somewhat fey voice carried all too clearly above the hubbub, staying him mid-stride. 'Colonel Hervey!'

He turned. 'General.'

'Have not had the pleasure. D'you do.'

Hervey bowed. Kat was nowhere to be seen (much relief).

'Will you dine with us this evening, Colonel? You and Lady Katherine are acquainted, I understand. It would be a kindness to her. She knows no others here.'

What choice did he have, unless he could claim some prior engagement, which in truth he could not, for he'd no very clear notion when he might give his evidence and have his *congé*. Dining would scarcely be agreeable – perhaps not even to Kat – but would it even be bearable? Once he had taken this man's wife for a mistress – no, not mistress; that demeaned them both, he and Kat; they had sought mutual consolation. Except, of course, that neither had the right to, and would answer therefore 'at the dreadful day of judgement, when the secrets of all hearts shall be disclosed'. And trouble him that did – *Memento Mori*; and one day, soon, he must make his peace, however that was done. For the moment, though, there was a more pressing day of judgement: did Sir Peregrine know more of their 'acquaintance' than he suggested? He and Kat had had no communication in over a year. He'd sought her once during that time – in truth, twice – but fortunately without success . . .

'Delighted, General. I thank you.'

'Capital! Clifton, then, at eight.'

The afternoon he found no more enlightening than the morning. Hervey gave his account of events as unadorned by comment as he thought possible. He was questioned on a few points of detail by members of the board, none of which points seemed to him materially significant; but not – to his considerable satisfaction – by Colonel Brereton, who remained impassive throughout. What penalty Brereton would suffer if the board considered his judgement to be defective to the point of negligence was not his concern. The man was done for, no matter what. The half-pay was the only future Brereton could reasonably expect (though he reminded himself that juries were strange things).

He began to gather himself for dismissal as General Dalbiac thanked him for his 'precision and dispassion'. Then to his dismay, he was asked to return the following morning.

'The board would deem it a favour, Colonel Hervey, if you were to hear Mayor Pinney's testimony and hold yourself ready to answer any matters arising which in the opinion of the board have not already been addressed.'

It was, he would concede, eminently reasonable, though he could hardly suppose it necessary. The facts were the facts. He wanted to return to Hounslow with all haste, for the regiment had buried three of its own this past week, and there were several more for whom the surgeon had little hope (Collins himself, though much better, was still weak). He wanted, also, to return via Heytesbury, and every hour he was delayed was an hour less that he could spend with Georgiana. It even occurred to him that he might not be dismissed for as long as the inquiry sat if General Dalbiac (perhaps at Sir Peregrine's bidding?) was minded to question his own handling of events.

'Of course, sir. But I would ask, respectfully, to be discharged at the earliest opportunity. We are much oppressed by sickness at Hounslow.'

Dalbiac nodded. 'Of course.'

At eight o'clock by the cathedral bell, which carried sharp in the still, cold air, Hervey presented himself at Sir Peregrine's lodgings in Clifton. That the bell sounded the hour was more than just expedient; it fortified him. It might so easily have been consumed by fire, like the bishop's palace, had it not been for a few stalwart parishioners and then his own determination to prevent a second night's incendiarism. Whatever the tribunal had in mind, he was assured that without his own address they would not have been deliberating on the matter in the Merchant Venturers' Hall, for that too would have been a pile of ash-cloaked rubble.

The lodgings were, he thought, rather grander than necessary for a stay of a few days, even for a lieutenant-general. Perhaps Sir Peregrine and his lady intended staying longer? Perhaps the member for St Felix intended making a visit to parliament, though he couldn't suppose his constituents gave him any cause (he chided himself at this sudden Radicalism)? Or perhaps Kat merely wished a home from home, the house in Holland Park being extensive, and likewise, he supposed, their lodgings in Dublin.

There was a corporal of Foot at the door, and clearly not for ceremony. Hervey acknowledged his salute and made his way into the hall, giving his cloak to a footman and ascending the stairs. At the top, another footman announced him, and Sir Peregrine, talking with a man in clericals at the door of his substantial anteroom, turned to greet him.

'Colonel Hervey, I am glad you are come. Bishop, may I present Colonel Hervey, whose action brought the disorders to a halt.'

A sad-eyed man of about his father's age returned Hervey's bow.

Hervey supposed there to be but one bishop who might receive Sir Peregrine's hospitality this evening, and, glad at least to have the favourable opinion of the president of the inquiry, felt he could express a measure of humility. 'Dr Gray, sir; I am only sorry that we were unable to save your library.'

It was not calculated to make the bishop's sad eyes brighter, but how might he not mention the most infamous, wanton destruction of the whole wretched affair?

'Because I had voted with my fellow bishops against Reform,' Dr Gray replied unhappily. 'Colonel Hervey, I say to you frankly that the loss of my library is but nothing to the loss of that confidence which I believed I had of the people in my cure.' (He did not mention in addition the loss, almost entire, of his more worldly goods.) 'I think they must have been incited by malign voices.'

Sir Peregrine had excused himself to attend on his other guests, and Hervey found himself in consolatory role. Bishop Gray, his father had frequently said, was a most amiable gentleman and scholarly divine. Hervey knew he had ignored all entreaties to leave the city that Sunday, instead insisting on the offices being said in the cathedral, and preaching a sermon of – by common consent – passing excellence.

'My lord, may I tell you that my sar'nt-major, who is from those parts, says that in the coalfields of the Tyne your name is spoken of with the greatest affection and regard.'

The words brought a faint smile. Before his translation to Bristol,

Dr Gray had had the living of Bishopwearmouth, and a stall in the cathedral at Durham, and some years earlier had invited Sir Humphry Davy to come to the coalfields to see what might be done to curb the explosions of firedamp. Hervey told him that Armstrong's own father and two brothers had been sent to their Maker in the same month as Nelson – not as heroes at Trafalgar, he was wont to say, but as unsung colliers at Hebburn (and it was at Hebburn Pit that Davy devised his miraculous lamp).

'I myself did no more than to suggest that Sir Humphry Davy turn his mind to it,' said the bishop, softly. 'There was no other of such eminence. But it is gratifying to learn of your serjeant-major's sentiments.' And then he appeared to rally. 'But you yourself, Colonel – your name, Hervey, is of some moment in the city?'

'I am only very distantly connected with the family. My father is Archdeacon of Sarum.'

The bishop brightened the more. 'Then you have the very best of men for a father. We were at Oxford together. I knew him then uncommonly well.'

Hervey thanked him, if more than a little uneasy, for what might 'the very best of men' think if he knew that across the room was Kat, with whom he had repeatedly broken the seventh commandment?

How, indeed, were they now to meet? Was he to present himself, or should he wait on Sir Peregrine? He could not anyway excuse himself from the present conversation; that was for the bishop. What should he say to her in any case? (He'd thought about little else since the invitation, but with no answer.) Would she even welcome words of his? He'd left matters unfinished in London in the haste to be in Brussels on the King's business. And then in his absence had come Sir Peregrine's appointment in Dublin . . . And there was the infant, Sir Peregrine's 'son and heir'.

He wished he were a mile hence, or fifty – a whole continent indeed.

'But you yourself, Colonel, have suffered calumnies in certain parts of the press, have you not?'

The question, disagreeable though it was, brought him back to safer ground.

'Yes, Bishop, I fear it is so, though I'm assured that the more fair-minded of the press have the ear in London.'

It was true, but in truth too, he'd begun increasingly to resent the accusations of excessive violence. He had no great confidence in the men of politics, who were perfectly able to change with the wind when it suited them, so that while they might be grateful for his address in saving the city, they might not feel it expedient to save him from Radical clamour if it all became too much.

The bishop now seemed to have regained his lordly resolution. 'Then let me say that if ever it were to be not so – that you were to find yourself the subject of official censure – then I should be obliged if you would let me speak on your behalf. There is no one in this city, perhaps, who witnessed the state into which it had fallen, yet who did not bear some responsibility under law to restore the peace, and who may thereby speak indifferently.'

Hervey expressed his gratitude.

Sir Peregrine returned. 'Bishop, I would detain you a moment before we proceed to dine. Colonel, would you excuse us?'

Hervey withdrew, and steeled himself to the task, for evidently Sir Peregrine was not going to present him to his hostess, and so he must do so himself.

He made first for a little knot halfway across the room – Shewell Bailward, Sheriff of Somerset, and his lady (though the city was not in the Somerset shrievalty); a squire of broad acres somewhere to the north of the city – an old friend of Sir Peregrine's, apparently, whose name he didn't catch, for his drawl verged on debility; and his wife, a woman of antique fashion and the assuredness of one who professed to reading only the *Baronetage*. Hervey prayed they would not be seated next to each other – as no doubt did Colonel Fergusson and Major Walcott of the board of inquiry, who were doing their best to be attentive to her opinion on Reform, which even the Duke of Wellington would have considered intemperate.

He was about to detach himself when Sir Peregrine brought the bishop to present to them, which gave him the opportunity, he thought, to complete the crossing of the room to where Kat stood.

However, Sir Peregrine anticipated him. 'Colonel Hervey, I must conduct you to Lady Katherine before we proceed to dine.'

It occurred to him as strange, suddenly, that having come most carefully upon his hour, he was the last to do so. Indeed, it troubled him.

'My dear, here is Colonel Hervey come.'

Kat turned. Candlelight was ever kind, but even so, she was exactly as he'd seen her last, the passing of eighteen months serving only to make her appearance even more pleasing. Her eyes shone quite remarkably bright, her complexion was as flawless as that of the woman he'd first met nearly fourteen years before, and her figure likewise, for she wore a dress he knew was no longer the fashion, Queen Adelaide having made known her disapproval of *décolleté*.

'Colonel Hervey, yes, I remember – Apsley House, was it not? Or Prince Lieven's?'

'Ma'am.' (Was it quite so necessary of Kat to affect such faint recollection?)

'Where is it you are stationed now, Colonel?'

Indeed, though her eyes were bright, they did not shine at him. He thought he saw . . . disdain.

'Hounslow, ma'am, still.'

And it pierced him. Kat had never possessed him body and soul, as Henrietta had (at least, he did not think she had). There were days, weeks, even perhaps whole months, when the thought of her was absent; but then, at no especial time – nothing demanding a bosom for solace – her face would come before him. But he had loved her – he thought he had loved her – and did still. How could it be otherwise when they'd shared such embraces, and laughed so much together? And there was issue, was there not, of those embraces? That is, Kat had told him so, and why should he doubt her? And he had sought out the news for himself on return from the Levant (the clerk at the office of *The Times* had been all consideration): 'The twelfth of March at Rocksavage, County Roscommon, to Lady Katherine Greville, a son and heir.'

'Hounslow,' she said flatly; and stood without another word as he himself struggled to find something by way of reply or explanation, or even to satisfy the conventions of polite society. But he too stood as mute as the tomb.

Hounslow: the last word she spoke to him that evening. For almost as if he had waited for the moment, one of Sir Peregrine's manservants announced dinner, and the twenty guests began making their way to the dining room, Kat taking the arm of Lord Loughborough, a man ten years his junior, and below him in rank too, and yet whose title claimed precedence.

And so it continued. She was merry at dinner, and Sir Peregrine all affability, while he himself had to endure the squiress and the bishop's chaplain. Afterwards there was no opportunity to speak with his hostess, who found herself paid unrelenting court to by those in regimentals (or did she arrange it thus?), and when he took his leave, at his earliest opportunity, she merely acknowledged unmoved.

By the time Hervey reached his lodgings, Corporal Johnson had long turned in – just as he'd told him to. The fire was low and the room unwelcoming but for a bottle of brandy. He wished devoutly he were at Heston – and Annie there to pour him a glass.

And then he thanked God he wasn't.

Next morning, when they assembled at ten o'clock, the inquiry was informed that Colonel Brereton was indisposed, and that Major Ellard would attend on his behalf. This caused no little consternation, but

General Dalbiac pronounced that, having heard at length Colonel Brereton's submission, he saw no occasion to adjourn the proceedings. So the dreary business of taking statement after statement continued until almost two o'clock, when Sir Peregrine himself announced that the inquiry would rise for one hour – but that before it did so, 'desirous as I am not to detain needlessly any officer or official of the city, I wish to hear the opinion of Colonel Hervey upon the matter before dismissing him to his duties'.

Hervey came to the table again.

'Colonel Hervey, on the evidence you have heard, is it your opinion that Colonel Brereton acted with all due address?' asked the president of the inquiry.

Hervey looked at General Dalbiac, by no means certain that it was proper for him to express an opinion – only to relate upon fact. Dalbiac gave him a somewhat quizzical look, but said nothing, evidently believing that Hervey's opinion was neither here nor there when it came to the board's deliberations, and therefore not worth the dispute with its titular president.

Hervey concluded likewise. In any case, a request by a superior officer was to be taken as an order; and a lawful order must be promptly obeyed. And since there was no legal counsel to pronounce on the law – this was, after all, merely an inquiry, not a court martial – he would answer promptly (though he would be circumspect too).

'Sir, my opinion on any matter occurring before I arrived in Bristol in the early hours of Monday morning would, I submit, be of no value, since it would be based on hearsay only. I think it right and proper for me to say this, however: that at that time of my arriving, when the city seemed to be threatened with total destruction, I was displeased that Colonel Brereton thought fit to retire to his quarters.'

His words caused something of a tumult, though it was not clear to him whether they proceeded from the revelation of Brereton's inaction or from his own denunciation of it.

The room now fell silent.

'Colonel Hervey,' continued Sir Peregrine; 'is that opinion formed by what you yourself did in taking command and putting down the riot?'

Hervey thought for as long as he dare. 'It is.'

'And so you conclude that if Colonel Brereton had acted with the same address, much of the destruction of the city would have been avoided?'

It was just as Hervey had feared. He was being asked to perform the work of the inquiry itself. He certainly didn't like the way Sir Peregrine put the question to him – sensing that he meant some mischief almost – but it was manifestly obvious that in adopting the opposite course with the rioters from that which Brereton took, he must believe that it was the superior one.

And he certainly didn't intend displaying any doubt or hesitation now.

'Yes.'

The clamour told him the line of questioning would serve him no good – that and the speed with which the writers for the press quit the room.

IX

The Verdict

Heston, Monday, 28 November

'Can they say that, Johnno?' Annie put down her sewing box and the shirt – one of Hervey's best lawn – which she'd taken from Corporal Johnson on account of his not repairing it with a neat enough stitch.

'They can say whatever they likes,' replied Johnson, smoothing the page of the *Poor Man's Guardian* on the tabletop in the servants' hall.

'Even when it's not true?'

'Well, a bit of it's true right enough. Colonel 'Ervey said 'e thought as Colonel Brereton 'adn't done what 'e should've done. But 'e didn't rightly say as it was 'im that stopped all t'rioting, though it were.'

'And will Colonel Brereton be in trouble now?'

Johnson took a noisy sip of his tea, which Annie had given him in a large cup, but which he'd decanted into the saucer. 'Well, Annie m'lass, when somebody's court-martialled, they're in a lot o' trouble, an' that's what t'inquiry said was to 'appen.'

Annie looked uncomfortable. 'It can't be pleasing for Colonel Hervey to say something and it mean that Colonel Brereton is court-martialled.

He sounds a good man, Colonel Brereton – as if he didn't want to hurt anybody.'

Johnson frowned. 'Tha should've seen the place when we got there. It were like nowt I'd ever set eyes on. Colonel 'Ervey won't give a fig about rank when it comes to court martials.'

'But will Colonel Hervey be in trouble too? I mean, all this about him, saying he was cruel – the women and children, I mean?'

'Nay, they dursn't. Colonel 'Ervey's a particular favourite o' t'Duke o' Wellington.'

Annie was not entirely convinced. She'd never had opportunity to read newspapers much, only when they were left in the Berkeley Arms sometimes, or, now, *The Times* in Hervey's study when he was out, but she knew they could make trouble. And this one – *The Poor Man's Guardian: A Weekly Newspaper for the People* – well, it wasn't very nice at all:

PETERLOO REDUX

It ought to be the gravest concern to all citizens that once again the Authorities have resorted to the employment of mounted soldiery on the streets of an English city for the purpose of suppressing protest against the opponents of Reform. We learn that at Bristol lately, although it is conceded that there were unruly elements of the sort that habitually attach themselves to any public gathering, a considerable force of cavalry, just as at St Peter's Fields in Manchester of very present memory, was sent against the people, including many women and children, and this in spite of the urgent appeal by the officer in command, Colonel Brereton, that the troops withdraw from the streets, but that instead one Colonel Hervey of His Majesty's Sixth Light Dragoons, by virtue of a brevet, did countermand the order and send the troopers very violently against the people, occasioning much loss to life and limb ...

'What does "Peterloo Redux" mean, Johnno?'
'Well, Peterloo's what they called the business at Manchester, on

account of it sounding like "Waterloo", but them were yeomanry that charged into the crowd, not proper soldiers. Most of 'em anyway.'

'And what does "Redux" mean?'

He shook his head.

Annie took up her sewing again. 'They were talking about it at the market this morning.'

'Who were?'

'Well, not all of them, but some of the people that sell things at the barracks. They said Colonel Hervey might have to go away.'

Johnson decanted more tea. 'No-o-o. I tell thee, Annie, lass, they'll be making Colonel 'Ervey a general. Tha'll see.'

Annie was content to be reassured for the time being, whether or not she felt she had a right to be. But Corporal Johnson was an old soldier – well, not old, but a soldier who'd seen service, who knew about things, and who had the ear of people because he was the colonel's man, and who in turn heard confidences. He seemed to know a lot about everything – a lot more even than Serjeant James. Whenever she asked Serjeant James about anything he would just say 'None of our business, Annie.'

Silence descended, Johnson intent on reading more of the *Poor Man's Guardian*, which he'd found lying in the yard at the post-house (somebody's lost pennyworth, but as there was no one about to take custody of it he'd thought to bring it back 'for safekeeping').

'Johnno,' said Annie at length, in a softer voice, not taking her eyes from the sewing this time; 'what's Mrs Hervey like?'

Some of Johnson's tea went down the wrong way. When he'd composed himself he answered matter of fact, 'She were Colonel Lankester's lady, but 'e were killed in India, and then Colonel 'Ervey married 'er.'

'Yes,' said Annie, her eyes on the sewing still, 'I knew that. I mean what sort of lady is she?'

Johnson's brow furrowed. Although he had very decided views, on this he would freely admit that he might not be an impartial observer

– and found himself unable to answer. 'I 'aven't really seen enough of 'er to tell.'

'But that's what I mean, really; why does she live away?'

He was now minded to say 'None of our business, Annie,' except that he thought better of her than that. Annie was like another dragoon, really; and she wasn't at all a tattler; and Colonel Hervey thought the world of her, and that was all that was important. He shook his head.

'I don't rightly know.'

And it was true. Hervey had never spoken of the matter – though Fairbrother had hinted once or twice – and he'd hardly been under the same roof as Kezia but for a day or so. He didn't think she liked him, though, but perhaps that was wrong; perhaps it was just her way – and everybody was different – and if she were here instead of away, perhaps she'd like him perfectly well. But it wasn't something to talk about, not even with Annie.

'Is she pretty?'

Now he felt on surer ground, though not ground he felt he should be venturing on. 'Well, all officers' wives are pretty, aren't they? That's why they're officers' wives.'

Annie said nothing.

'And ladies. They've got to be ladies as well.'

Annie continued to sew. 'Lord Nelson's wife wasn't a lady. Not born a lady, I mean. Her father was a blacksmith.'

Johnson thought a while. 'T'navy's different. Anyway, that wasn't Lord Nelson's wife, it were Lady 'Amilton. She were 'is mistress. You don't 'ave to be a lady to be a mistress. Just pretty.'

Annie reddened but continued the stitch.

Johnson, emboldened now to dispense more of his worldly wisdom, decanted the last of his tea and then drained the saucer. 'The first Mrs 'Ervey – she were right pretty. And nice. She always called me *Private* Johnson, not just "Johnson". It didn't make no odds to me what she called me, really, but I al'a's thought it were nice that . . . well, nice that she said it.'

'And the new Mrs Hervey doesn't?'

Johnson suddenly thought he'd said too much. 'She's very pretty an' all, Mrs 'Ervey, but diff'rent – pretty in a diff'rent way, I mean.'

More silence.

'What's Colonel Hervey's daughter like?'

Johnson smiled warmly. 'She's like 'er mother – looks like 'er mother, I mean. And full of fun – like 'er mother was.'

'And Mrs Hervey's daughter?'

'I've never really seen 'er. She's nobbut three or four. It were a real shame Colonel Lankester never saw 'er either.'

More silence.

'Johnno, this thing Mrs Hervey's going to be doing in London . . .'

'The benefit?'

'Yes. Would I be able to buy a ticket?'

Johnson looked at her, puzzled. 'Why'd you want a ticket?'

Annie had learned that when Johnson reverted to 'you' it was well to be wary. 'I just thought it would be a fine thing to do, to go and see it. All the officers and serjeants will be going, I suppose. And it's for the benefit of all those old men in Chelsea.'

Johnson shook his head again. 'T'tickets'll cost a fortune. They're for t'quality. Serjeants won't be going.'

She looked hurt, and he saw it. 'Why don't th'ask Colonel 'Ervey. 'E'd be able to get thee one.'

'Oh no, I couldn't do that.'

Johnson looked at her quizzically. But there was no point trying to fathom things, not now anyway. 'Annie, m'lass, I think we'll 'ave another mashin' o' tea.'

The Light Horse stables in Whitehall were the sweetest smelling that Hervey had ever known – or indeed thought possible. A generous allowance by the Treasury for oil of citronella kept the place like a Spanish lemon grove – and all so that His Majesty and his Queen-Consort might at any time visit without notice, and bring with them any of a foreign court without fear of offence. Why the Light Horse stables – but a dozen standing stalls at the Horse Guards – should have this benefit, and not those of the detachment of Household Cavalry next door, was a mystery, except that the Sixth furnished the 'War Office party', the NCO-gallopers who speeded the despatches between Whitehall and the royal palaces, and their horses were Tattersall bloods. The party was always hand-picked by the regimental serjeant-major, and known inevitably therefore as 'Armstrong's men'; and as a courtesy, Lord Hill was allowed one of the two loose boxes for his charger, which added further lustre to the stables. Hervey was never in doubt that here stood the reputation of the regiment, and in consequence these were probably the most inspected quarters in the Home District.

'In which stall did Owthwaite's offence take place?' he asked, almost wryly, as they were leaving.

Armstrong frowned. The offence itself he was not much concerned with; its place of commission he was. 'One of the boxes, Colonel.'

'Do we know which, precisely? Don't say it was the commander-in-chief's.'

'Colonel.'

'You mean it *was* Lord Hill's?'

'When he'd taken his charger to the park that afternoon.'

Hervey tried hard to suppress a smile. 'It must be the new red coat. What female heart could withstand it?'

'I always thought no good'd come of red coats. Well, Owthwaite's paying the price now.'

'Indeed.'

'But I'll say this for him, Colonel: he hasn't once let on who she is. An' I don't think it's because of any inducement from the lady. He's put in for India, just as we reckoned, an' a man wouldn't likely do that who'd been promised a small fortune.'

'No, perhaps not.' Owthwaite the gentleman, protective of a lady's honour: it was a fine notion (however improbable).

A dragoon in a blue coat stepped out from the forage store and saluted.

'Corporal Stray, is there something amiss? What brings you here?'

Armstrong explained that in the absence of the convalescing Collins, Stray had come with the Quartermaster-Serjeant for the inspection.

'Permission to speak, Colonel?'

'Proceed, Corp'l Stray.'

'Mrs Catchpole's 'ere, Colonel, and I wondered if you'd care to see 'er, Colonel.'

Armstrong took the whip from under his arm and began wagging it by his side. 'Corporal Stray, we're at the Horse Guards, not the Marquis o' Granby!'

But it was too late. Mrs Catchpole was already advancing on them – at the same time as the Field Officer in Brigade Waiting was coming out of the door in the arch that led to the parade ground (where a band was making a fair noise and several serjeants were exercising their lungs).

The future Mrs Stray was a comely woman, a fraction taller than her husband-to-be, about forty, and wore a brown cloak with a capacious hood. Had she carried a basket she might have been a flower seller from Covent Garden. She curtseyed when her husband presented her – or rather, when Hervey himself took charge to expedite things and greeted her as cheerily as the time and place allowed (at least here was a woman brought openly, he said to himself, unlike Owthwaite's evidently high-born paramour).

'We's to be wed a week on Saturday, Colonel,' said Stray with some gravity. 'By t'parson.'

By which Hervey presumed he meant the chaplain that His Majesty had seen fit to provide. 'Capital, Corp'l Stray.'

'Yes, Colonel,' added Mrs Catchpole. 'We were very particular in that regard.'

Armstrong's eyebrows rose, and then his eyes narrowed.

Stray didn't see, however, nodding solemnly. 'And we'd deem it a great favour and honour, Colonel, if you were to attend.'

Armstrong put his whip back under his arm – an emphatic signal that the interview was at an end.

Hervey just managed to reply that he would – duties permitting.

Armstrong cleared his throat noisily, and Hervey took his leave of the intending couple with all the gravity he could muster, which was not made easy by Mrs Catchpole's curtseys and Corporal Stray's unusually drill-book saluting.

As he made away, he saw the Field Officer in Brigade Waiting observing from the arch.

'Well, Hervey, quite a ceremony.'

'Good afternoon, Calthorp. I trust we have not offended against Good Order and Military Discipline too grievously?'

Lieutenant-Colonel Ralph Calthorp, commanding the Grenadier battalion at Windsor, and for the month of November the representative at Court of the general officer commanding the Home District, returned Hervey's salute – or rather, the customary touch of the cap peak. They had known each other since the hunting down of the incendiarists at Winkfield two years before, and Hervey had come to like his strict insistence on 'form' – but yet his evident amusement in it.

'I confess I find myself intrigued,' said the colonel: 'A corporal comes out of a stable and detains his commanding officer, whereupon a female joins them and quite overwhelms the sar'nt-major – Good afternoon to you, by the way, Mr Armstrong!'

Armstrong, already standing uncommonly rigid, saluted with something close to the precision of a Grenadier. 'Good afternoon, sir!'

'Just one of my corporals, Calthorp, come to present his wife-to-be. You have corporals, d'you know?'

Colonel Calthorp smiled warmly. 'I don't know how the discipline of the Light Horse works – I'm an old dog – but I do love its foibles.'

'We exist to garner intelligence,' replied Hervey, as archly as he could manage.

Calthorp nodded, and with a smile that conceded the game, before his expression turned more serious. 'You're come about Bristol, no doubt. Dreadful business. Vile things being said in the papers, too. You're not despondent, I trust?'

There were indeed vile things said in the papers, and more than one member had eyed him warily when he'd gone to the United Service Club that morning. But he hadn't imagined they'd claim the attention of the King's man at the Horse Guards.

'No, not despondent. Dismayed perhaps. The city was within an ace of self-immolation, which no one who saw it could have doubted – except, strangely, the man who was supposed to be in command.'

'Deuced lucky you were there.'

'I tell you frankly, it was – though lucky also that Mr Armstrong was there to send word for me in the first place.'

Calthorp turned to him. 'My compliments to you, Sar'nt-Major.'

'Sir!'

He turned to Hervey again. 'You're come to see Lord Hill?'

'No – a call only on Howard.' He smiled ruefully; 'As I said, we exist to garner intelligence.'

'Quite. Well, I myself have just seen the general, and all I'll say is that I've seen him in better humour.'

'On account of?'

'Lord Melbourne . . . the duke . . . the exigencies of the service.'

Hervey began to wonder if reconnaissance wasn't better deferred. But then, reconnaissance deferred was intelligence forgone – and did he not exist to garner intelligence?

They exchanged a few more pleasantries – and mutual invitations to dine – and then parted, Calthorp for the palace, Hervey for Lord John Howard's office.

'Sar'nt-Major, I can't suppose I'll be very long. Shall you come in?'

'I will, Colonel, yes. The chief clerk's always got good coffee, and a good ear for this and that.'

It was enough said. Hervey smiled to himself. He never ceased to wonder at his good fortune in having such a man as Armstrong at his side.

'My dear fellow.' Howard stood and held out his hand. 'It's good to see you. What a wretched business this inquiry evidently was.'

'Wretched? Well, tedious certainly.'

'That too, no doubt. Coffee?'

'Thank you, yes . . .'

'Madeira?'

Hervey shook his head as he took off his cloak and sat down.

'A man might think the inquiry singular for reading of it in the newspapers.'

'It would appear so. I own that I was tricked into giving my opinion.'

'Tricked? How so?'

But he could hardly say that he thought Sir Peregrine Greville had tried to lame him (after Kat had been induced to signal that their acquaintance was at an end). 'I meant that . . . in the interminable tedium of listening to people saying nothing but what might acquit them of responsibility, I allowed myself to speak my mind.'

Howard sighed. 'Well, it is done, and the inquiry's findings are unequivocal. Brereton's to stand court martial. Lord Hill wrote last evening to General Jackson instructing him to tell Brereton that he was to consider himself in arrest.'

Hervey nodded. There was no satisfaction in it, only pity – pity for an officer of Brereton's seniority, but who never should have found himself in the position of command. Perhaps it would be like poor old Admiral Byng, shot *pour encourager les autres*.

'Captain Warrington, too,' added Howard.

Hervey shook his head. 'I could no more understand Warrington's inactivity than I could Brereton's. He'd have let the whole city be destroyed for want of a magistrate by his side.'

A clerk brought coffee. Hervey took off his cap and stretched his legs as he took several sips.

'Colonel Hervey!'

He managed to spring to his feet without too much spillage. 'My lord.'

The commander-in-chief handed a sheet of paper to his trusted staff officer, looking far from happy with it. 'I believe I should wish to see it after the printer has set it up.'

'I'll take it at once, my lord.'

Lord Hill turned back to Hervey. '*Supplementary Instructions to Officers in Command of Troops in Aid to the Civil Power*. I should never have thought them necessary, but reading the inquiry made me doubt it.'

Hervey fancied he knew the commander-in-chief's mind in this. 'I am astonished there could have been confusion over the necessity for a magistrate. Or, indeed, that even had an officer earnestly believed there to be so, he could still stand by and see a felony committed.'

'We live in infamous times, Hervey,' replied Lord Hill, taking off his glasses to polish them. 'But I'm glad you're come. I would speak with you, though I fear it won't be much agreeable.'

Hervey felt his stomach tighten. He wasn't to face disciplinary action too?

Howard had already left with the draft. 'Come. Bring your coffee.'

That at least was encouraging. As the saying went, interviews with superior officers came in two kinds – with and without coffee.

The sun was already low across the parade ground, and the Guards

were marching back to barracks to the tune of *The Shrewsbury Lasses*.
Lord Hill settled behind his desk – the desk that the Duke of Wellington
himself had occupied only of late – and nodded to the adjacent chair.

'They play it because they suppose it pleases me – which it does, I
suppose.'

'It's a merry tune, General. My own band is fond of it.'

Lord Hill seemed unusually weary. Perhaps it was indeed the recent
'exigencies of the service', but whatever it was, Hervey did not now
think it could be anything too grave. The commander-in-chief did not
have the air of a man about to remand him for court martial.

'Hervey, some weeks ago I put your name before Lord Goderich
for promotion to major-general, as a formality before submitting it to
the King. I'm afraid to say, however, that in the present circumstances
he felt he couldn't countenance it – and I know that he canvassed
Melbourne's opinion and several others, perhaps even Lord Grey's.
He said that – of course – once the sea was calmer he would have
no objection whatsoever. I should, no doubt, have foreseen the present
objection, but it would not have made any difference to my decision.'

Hervey was at once of mixed mind – disappointed that promotion
was denied, but satisfaction that it had been proposed. He had certainly
not been expecting its mention any time soon. He placed his cup down,
trying to think what was the material point on which he should seek, if
not reassurance, then clarity.

'I am grateful, General. When do you suppose the sea might be
deemed sufficiently calm?'

Lord Hill nodded. 'I believe the Cabinet – if it were put to them –
would say "after the passage of the bill". Not immediately after, for that
might seem unprincipled, but a year or so.'

Hervey sighed. Two years; certainly no less. Would Lord Hill still be
commander-in-chief then? Might there also be other colonels – others
more agreeable to the government – to supersede him?

Lord Hill imagined his thoughts. 'The post, I should say, would not have been greatly to your liking – a district on the home establishment – but it would have placed you on the gradation list, which was my intent. As it is, my scheme is thwarted, but your brevet is some safeguard meanwhile. I only tell you this to put you on your guard, but principally because I wish you to know my esteem. I might add that Sir Henry Parnell was in complete agreement with me.'

Parnell: the Secretary *at* War, and Goderich *for* War – the peculiar terminology of a system that had grown like a cottage garden rather than laid out to a grand design. It was certainly reassuring to have Parnell's good opinion, for he was spoken of as a coming man (it had indeed been his motion on the civil list that had brought down the Duke of Wellington's administration the year before). But the Secretary at War's concern was administration; he was not in the Cabinet. There was no more he could usefully enquire, though, and he'd no desire to overstay the commander-in-chief's confidence.

'I'm excessively grateful to you, my lord.' He rose and made to leave, for there was a fine line in these things. A show of undue regret would have been unmanly. 'I shall at least have the satisfaction of commanding my regiment a good deal longer.'

That is, if his pockets were substantial enough.

Lord Hill rose and held out a hand – an uncommon gesture even for him. 'Speak softly, Hervey, and pray for better times.'

Hervey smiled. 'Or for a bloody war and sickly season?'

X

Acts of Charity

London, Tuesday, 20 December

HERVEY WOULD HAVE BEEN SURPRISED to learn of the lengths to which St Alban had gone. There was no end, however, to the duties of a good adjutant – only the limit of his powers of imagination and anticipation. The Sixth subscribed to the maxim that whatever could go wrong, would – Hervey had first heard it from his captain on his first day with the regiment – and as a consequence were rarely wrong-footed (or not for long). St Alban had been, so to speak, preparing the ground for the benefit concert since first learning of Kezia's part in it, knowing therefore that Hervey would attend – and all with the greatest discretion. To secure the best seats he'd offered the Philharmonic Society the services of six NCOs as ushers. Two of the in-pensioners at Chelsea were old 'Sixers', and there were countless out-pensioners. It was something he could arrange without rousing suspicion. He had also made sure that half a dozen officers whom Hervey held in particular regard would have seats in the row behind him, and that he would be flanked in the front row by Captain Worsley and his lady, and Captains Vanneck and Malet. Corporal Johnson would be there, too, for if anything untoward were to happen, Johnson was the man to have at hand. Serjeant Acton would also accompany – armed.

The reason he had made the arrangements without 'authority' was that he was sure Hervey would say they were excessive: a benefit concert, so close to Christmas – what was the probability of mishap? Yet the events at Bristol had been – continued to be – a licence to print every sort of calumny in the guise of 'news'. On the one hand, the name of Colonel Matthew Hervey of the 6th Light Dragoons stood for the violent suppression of Reform, while on the other his condemnation of Colonel Brereton was self-seeking. True, the more 'respectable' of the press denounced in no uncertain terms the dereliction of duty that had delivered the city into the hands of the mob, but there was simply no knowing whose voice was heard. St Alban, as much as Hervey himself, wished devoutly for the speedy publication of the findings of the military inquiry, as well as of the civil proceedings that had just begun.

But beyond these concerns, which were more than enough to occupy him, there were 'delicacies' to be addressed – Kezia's appearance in public. His professional duty required him to safeguard his colonel from insult and injury; his private regard compelled him further to employ every means possible to avoid embarrassment over the estrangement of which no one ever spoke. It was for this reason principally, therefore, that he had arranged the 'loyal party', reckoning that the presence of the officers would better allow Hervey to maintain his 'mask of command'.

He'd certainly taken great pains to make sure that all was well at Heston beforehand. Heston was the commanding officer's private residence, for all that there were blue coats there, and now red, for much of the time; but everything that happened in a regiment was an adjutant's concern, which was why the Sixth preferred 'regimental' officers in the appointment rather than those commissioned from the ranks, the more usual practice (for what was undoubtedly lost in efficiency by not employing a man who had risen from the ranks was more than made up for by the quality of gentlemanly discernment, besides enhancing the standing of the serjeant-major). At four o'clock, Serjeant and Mrs James, already at some pains to make Heston ready to keep a good Christmas, saw off the regimental chariot in good cheer and especially well provisioned.

St Alban's attempts at diverting conversation, however, were not entirely successful. 'Reform', on which he had always been ready to expound, was hardly appropriate; regimental business had been dealt with at orderly room that morning, and there was little more to say on those matters that hadn't been resolved – not least the increasing numbers at sick parade and the ever-falling sabre strength, the solution to both being better weather to banish the pernicious 'flu' and to allow recruiting parties to get out to the spring fairs. By the time they passed the Hounslow bar, Hervey had sunk into contemplation.

In truth, there was little that would have diverted him that afternoon. The deferral of promotion troubled him. The more he thought of it, the more he was convinced that the 'sea' would never be calm enough. He'd no wish to relinquish command, but he knew it must come, and when it did so there would be but one consolation, and that was the gradation list. So what should be his course: stay in command until he was ready to sell out, which would certainly bring him a small fortune, for regiments of cavalry were going at many times the regulation price (and all of it profit, for he'd been promoted without purchase), and set himself up with a small estate somewhere – and plant cabbages? The prospect appalled him. Or else he might convert his colonel's brevet to substantive rank and take some job on the staff, perhaps in a sunny clime – and wait. But wait for what? A bloody war and a sickly season? Five years was the Horse Guards' rule, and then either promotion to major-general or the half-pay. He'd lose his profit that way, for he'd have to sell out at regulation price (gift of command reverting to the commander-in-chief on promotion from lieutenant-colonel), and with no personal fortune, the half-pay would be a miserable existence. If he were lucky he might be made brigadier-general for some particular duty, but it wasn't permanent rank. He smiled to himself: perhaps he should take holy orders and find some fat parsonage – except that he'd find it difficult to convince even the most complaisant of examining chaplains that he subscribed sufficiently to the Thirty-Nine Articles.

'A bloody war and a sickly season.'

'Colonel?'

He shook his head. 'I was thinking aloud. Take no notice.'

Serjeant Wakefield paced the drive with his usual exactness. Serjeant Acton had to raise his voice at dilatory cabmen once or twice in Brook Street, but the procession in Hanover Square was marshalled with admirable efficiency by NCOs of the foot guards, and the regimental chariot pulled up to the west door of the concert rooms at twenty-five minutes to seven, where Corporal Johnson was waiting.

'Are we arrived before the duke?' asked Hervey as he got down.

''Aven't seen 'im, Colonel, an' I've been 'ere for t'best part of an hour.'

It was not necessary that they should arrive before the duke, but the customs of the military were ever the customs. While the Duke of Wellington was now a politician (a word he himself would have deplored, seeing it to be but an extension of that same duty with which he had served his country hitherto), he remained a field marshal.

'Very well.'

Johnson took his coat, and St Alban's. Hervey said he would take his seat at once, rather than a glass of punch (the gathering looking a deal too merry for his taste at that moment).

'I'll be sat just to yer right, Colonel.'

Hervey nodded. He was pleased his groom had a good seat, though how he'd got it, and quite why, was another matter. Or no matter; for Johnson always had a way.

They presented their tickets and entered the hall, which was already becoming full, the side benches especially. More comfortable benches, facing forward, filled the centre, with red plush chairs the front five rows. The surgeon had told him the hall could seat six hundred, and it looked as if it probably would. Hervey thought it gratifying that the quality turned out in such numbers for the benefit of the old men at Chelsea.

One of his NCOs, shako under left arm, bowed smartly. 'Colonel.'

He would not at any time have been inclined simply to return the compliment, but where others observed, he was always minded to make a particular show of regimental *fellowship* (as St Alban had perfectly understood).

'Corporal Ormerod, I have not seen you since you returned from the Martinmas recruiting. You brought some good men, I understand.'

'One or two, Colonel. And keen enough.'

'The red coat perhaps?'

'Tell the truth, Colonel, we took blue with us as well. Didn't want to be taken for heavies.'

'No, that would not do at all.' (He didn't suppose the King had thought of that exigency when deciding he didn't want his cavalry to look like sailors.) 'Have you received your bounty yet?'

'I have, Colonel.'

'Capital.'

He moved on. Days were when a recruiting party would bring two dozen men at least, but . . .

'Colonel Hervey!'

He turned to find a stout, rubicund squire smiling forcefully – Sir Watkin Williams Wynn, fifth baronet of Wynnstay, an improving landlord but a man of decidedly conventional opinion.

'My congratulations, sir. Such resolve, such address!' He spoke loudly (for he was at least half deaf).

Hervey nodded. Sir Watkin was member for Denbighshire, a friend of the Duke of Wellington's (or, at least, the duke tolerated his company, vigorous that it was), and had lately called out the yeomanry to deal with disturbances in the coalfields. 'I would not wish it again, Sir Watkin.'

'Eh?' He cupped his ear.

Heads had turned their way. 'I said I would not wish to have to do it again.'

'Aye, very true. Will you dine with me at Brooks's later? My brother Charles is to come.'

For a few months of Lord Grey's administration, Charles Williams Wynn had been secretary at war. Hervey had met him the once, at Windsor, and thought there might be advantage in a more intimate meeting (both brothers seemed to enjoy a measure of respect in both parties). 'I must return to Hounslow betimes, Sir Watkin, but a little wine before the journey perhaps.'

'Eh? Damned trouble in m'ear. Can barely catch a thing.'

Hervey was minded to say that he envied him, seeing how much Beethoven was to be played. With another effort and more pronounced mouthing he managed – he thought – to make himself understood, and then tried to withdraw to find his seat.

'The Grevilles'll be there, too. You can tell us more about Bristol!'

Sir Watkin's tongue was notoriously too big for his mouth, so that any utterance was a trial to both the speaker and the hearer. It was unfortunate, though, that his deafness made him raise his voice so high, for this time his tongue perfectly formed its way around 'Greville' and 'Bristol', so that none within a wide circle was left in any doubt.

Hervey supposed he imagined it, but the looks as he then proceeded towards the front seemed not entirely warm. He was glad to find the friendly faces that St Alban had arranged, and to find also that, if any of Kezia's people were come, they were not seated close by. He picked up his programme and made a pretence of studying it.

Just before the hour, the duke arrived. Those in the front and second rows, and on either side of the aisle, rose and bowed, which the late prime minister acknowledged with what for him might pass for affability. On coming to his honoured place just before the stage and noticing Hervey, however, his expression changed to one more grave; and he gave a distinctly approving nod of the head – a gesture made plain for all to see.

Hervey took his seat again with renewed assurance.

Shortly afterwards the band came on to the platform, fifty or so musicians – many more than he'd seen before, except massed on the Horse Guards perhaps. They were strings mainly, but he was pleased to see some trumpets as well – and horns, which he liked because they minded him of hunting.

The oboe sounded, and when the tuning evidently reached the point of satisfaction, the conductor himself – no lesser person than Sir George Smart, the foremost in the land – entered to great applause.

A long roll on the timpani brought the audience to its feet: *God Save the King* (Hervey was glad the custom was to hear it in silence). Then when all including the band were seated and settled once more, Sir George struck down with his baton to begin the first of the evening's pieces – Overture: *Der Freischütz*.

Hervey found it agreeable – a tune he might remember, if a little slow in coming, and rather a lot of portentous stuff to begin with. Ten minutes in all, though; not too bad.

Next a tenor came on stage, and sang something familiar by Rossini (he thought he'd probably heard it in Rome, when he'd gone there with his sister in that terrible year after Henrietta's death). Then some Beethoven – a violin piece – and then more Beethoven, and a lively march by Schubert to which he tapped his foot noiselessly.

Now the orchestra left the stage to great applause (when they returned it would be under the duke's baton – Beethoven again, but it promised to be stirring stuff: *Schlacht bei Vittoria*, or 'Wellington's Victory'), and it was the turn of the three soloists, of whom Kezia was first.

For the moment, though, Hervey resisted the temptation to look left or right, or to speak, and instead fixed his attention firmly on the piano, which had so far stood silent beside the conductor's desk. He knew there would be some who were studying him, who knew the talk of estrangement but were unsure of its truth; and he knew there'd be some who knew more, or believed they did – those of the highest *ton* perhaps, to whom Kat's 'friends' might have told 'confidences'. But no one could know for sure – certainly not the whole truth, for he had never spoken of Kat or Kezia with anyone. And he would give none the satisfaction this evening of revealing anything whatever. Besides, a commanding officer of cavalry ought anyway to maintain a pronounced reserve.

But the knot in his vitals tightened. He'd not seen Kezia in the best part of two years, and his chill dismissal from Walden Park (when he'd made his half-hearted attempt at rapprochement) he'd tried to put from his mind ever since. She was his wife, though. The priest in the church in this very square had pronounced it so. There was no escape: *Those whom God hath joined together let no man put asunder.*

He did not wish to escape, though – only from the condition he was in; and that, he had no idea how.

There was applause with Kezia's entrance. He turned his head to look; how could he not?

Sight of her tightened the knot even more. He made to rise – then saw that he shouldn't – and sank back into the plush like the rest, no more to her than were they. She wouldn't even know he was there. Why should she?

She was his wife. He should be by her side. Indeed, he wanted to be.

As perhaps would any man, for this evening she was beautiful – perfectly beautiful. When last he'd seen her, she wore a woollen shawl (Walden was bitter cold) and fustian that would have shamed a governess. Now she was in silk – deep blue, pinched to extreme at the waist as few could be, the form he'd so admired. In truth, desired. Why should he not? It fair took his breath away, still.

There was something to her beauty, though – remoteness, wanness even? – that belonged to a pedestal. He prayed she'd play more warmly, for her own sake – to win the applause her music deserved. Perhaps she practised to excess, to the exclusion of all else – he couldn't know – but on such an evening as this, how could he hold it against her? He hoped the piece she'd chosen wasn't too stern – not Beethoven-like. Who was this 'Herz'? Who indeed was *La Violette*? 'Variations brillantes avec introduction et finale alla militare' said the programme notes, but nothing else. *Alla militare*: it was auspicious. He suddenly began to will her all success – that *La Violette* would please every man and woman in the hall; that her playing would bring the greatest ovation of the evening – greater even than for the duke; and that, yes, she might at the moment of acclamation see him there . . . and be glad.

Kezia placed a hand to the piano and made a low curtsey, bowing her head also. Her smile was just sufficient. He wished it were as full as on occasion he'd seen, but her art was a serious business, and she must be utterly composed. Her look was anyway that of someone not entirely of the here and now. That, he knew – he supposed he knew – was indeed the composure of the artist. It was not unlike that he'd observed in men of war as they contemplated their task – had observed in the duke, indeed. Or was he fanciful? Did he take it to excess?

Kezia took the piano stool.

There was a long pause, as if for absolute silence, and then began *La Violette*. A threatening pair of chords made him start somewhat, then came a sombre arpeggio, repeated in what sounded like a different key, and then followed a descent of two octaves or so, and some tremulous progressions. He groaned inwardly: it was more Beethoven, but by another name.

And now a pause, strangely long, as if something *brillante* was to follow. But no – the last few bars were repeated (oddly, to his ear), and then a pause again; and then . . .

Nothing.

This was worse than Beethoven. Just chords, and gravid pauses . . .

But no, now he saw – as others had already: she was lost.

His grasped the arms of his chair, willing – praying – for her to find her way.

But she sat staring at the keys as if benumbed.

The murmur in the hall became loud. In an instant he was beside her. 'Kezia, are you unwell?'

She turned her head, but neither recognized him nor appeared even to see him.

St Alban was now at his side, and then the surgeon – and Worsley's wife.

'Help her up, Colonel,' said Milne, a gentle but insistent voice leaving no room for question or appeal.

Hervey took her forearms, which were still stretched out, and prayed she'd respond. Dorothea Worsley put an arm round her shoulders to reassure.

Kezia rose, her expression fixed, as if dazed by news of great tragedy. Hervey took her waist, intent on seeing her down before she collapsed entirely, as he feared she would for there was now no colour to her face.

There were helping hands as they reached the side of the platform, but unnecessary. Hervey was able to support her on his own, and she took his lead like one no longer able to see. Johnson cleared the way through the knot of musicians to the room where Kezia had dressed.

'What is it, doctor? What is wrong?' asked Hervey as they set her down.

Dorothea Worsley took out smelling salts, but Milne shook his head, lifting Kezia's arm to take her pulse.

'Not strong,' he said, laying it down again after a full minute. 'Nervous exhaustion, perhaps, if an extreme case . . . Catalepsy, it might be; there's no knowing until I observe more.'

He pulled up a chair, took one of the candles from the dressing table (the light was not so good, even with the large mirror), and held up his hand in front of her face.

'Mrs Hervey, I am a physician. Will you tell me how many fingers you see before you?'

Nothing came. She evidently heard no question, saw no hand.

Milne put his palm to her forehead. (He found no excessive heat.) 'We must get her to bed. Rest is what she needs directly. Thereafter . . . Who's her physician?'

Hervey shook his head.

'Where is her maid?' asked Dorothea Worsley.

'Indeed,' said Hervey. The little crowd in the room was entirely regimental. 'The Rumsey house is nearby. Perhaps she came unaccompanied.'

It would have been strange, certainly, but so was her condition.

'Then we should return with her there,' said Milne.

Hervey stiffened. 'I think . . . That is . . . I can't be sure there would be the necessary attention there.'

Milne was perfectly sensible of the difficulty, but duty overrode any other consideration (a problem not unknown to the occupation of military surgeon). 'We could but see. Or is there some alternative?'

'She may come to us at Richmond,' said Dorothea.

'You are very good,' said Hervey, knowing the Worsleys were about to leave for Yorkshire any day. 'But Heston's only a very little further.'

Milne looked doubtful; but he had no medical objection. 'I'd like to administer a sedative as soon as may be.'

'I could try to find a dormeuse, Colonel,' said St Alban.

Hervey shook his head. 'Too long. There are blankets in the chariot.'

'Let me take her to Heston in ours,' tried Dorothea. She didn't add that there might be things better done by a woman.

Hervey saw the sense in it, not least that he could drive ahead and rouse the household.

Milne opened his bag. He'd already decided on morphia. 'Corporal Johnson, be so good as to bring some lemonade.'

St Alban made to leave. 'I'll have the chariots brought to the rear door, Colonel.'

Hervey nodded. Nothing else mattered – not the dismay in the hall for sure; for here lay his wife, and he had vowed before God to 'love her, comfort her, honour, and keep her in sickness and in health'. He had vowed to do so 'forsaking all other', keeping himself 'only unto her'. And he had not – not in his heart; and now it had come to this.

XI

The Balance of the Mind

Heston, Saturday, 14 January 1832

EXPRESS FROM BRISTOL

THE TIMES-OFFICE, 2 o'Clock a.m.
DEATH OF LIEUT-COLONEL BRERETON.

Bristol, Jan. 13.

The Labours of the court-martial on Lieut.-Colonel Brereton have
been brought to a sudden and melancholy close. This morning the
ill-fated soldier, doubtless actuated by feelings the weight of which
the members of the military profession will readily conceive,
put a period to his mortal anxieties by his own hand. He shot
himself in his house at Redfield, near Bristol, about the hour of
3 o'clock.

*T*he *Times* had come to Heston a little after midday, rather late.
Hervey was not long returned from barracks (the exchange from
one duty to another was an opportunity to speak with troop captains

149

all together, though as a rule Saturday was the adjutant's parade). He could scarce believe what he read:

> Though the rumour of the event was current at 9 o'clock, it seemed so likely to be a fabrication of the time, that we did not lend any serious attention to it, and proceeded to the Merchants'-hall, expecting to witness the progress of the investigation. The Court presented the same appearance as heretofore, the same arrangements for the members, and the same crowded assemblage of well-dressed persons, male and female. At a few minutes before 10, the Deputy Judge-Advocate entered the Hall, and began to arrange his documents. The President (Sir Harry Fane), Sir Charles Dalbiac, and the officers composing the tribunal, soon afterwards took their places. After the roll of the Court had been read over, The President rose and addressed the members – Gentlemen, you probably have heard the most distressing report that is abroad respecting the prisoner, Colonel Brereton – a report which I fear, from his non-appearance here at this hour, is too true. I have sent the District Surgeon, and the officer acting as Assistant Adjutant-General in Bristol, to ascertain the facts. If you please, gentlemen, we will await the report of these individuals. The President then directed an orderly serjeant to attend the arrival of these two gentlemen in the ante-chamber. In less than five minutes, Major Mackworth, the Acting Assistant Adjutant-General to the officer in command of the district, appeared to make his report.
>
> President – Have you, Major Mackworth, in conformity with my orders, been at the house of Colonel Brereton?
>
> Major Mackworth – Yes.
>
> President – Have you seen the Colonel?
>
> Major Mackworth – Yes.
>
> President – Alive or dead?
>
> Major Mackworth – Dead.
>
> President – Gentlemen, under the unfortunate circumstances which have been laid before the Court, it only remains for me to

adjourn the sitting until I receive orders from His Excellency the Commander-in-Chief, to whom I shall forward a report.

Major Digby Mackworth, sworn by the Deputy Judge-Advocate, deposed that he (Major Mackworth) was Acting Assistant Adjutant-General in the Bristol district; that he had seen the body of Colonel Brereton, and that the Colonel was dead.

President – Sir Charles Dalbiac.

Sir Charles Dalbiac rose and addressed the Court. President, and Members of this hon. Court, I rise by permission of the President to address a few words to you. If the tragical event that has just been communicated to the Court, be a source of pain to you, gentlemen, how much more deeply must it not affect the individual on whom has devolved the duty of conducting the prosecution? I assure you, that I rise with a degree of distress and embarrassment such as I never experienced in all my previous life. (Sir Charles paused for a moment to master his emotions.) But I have one consolation, – and a great one, – I declared in my opening address, that I did not entertain the slightest feeling, save that of impartiality, towards the prisoner; and I now repeat that declaration as solemnly as if I were in presence of my God. I did not know, nor did I see Colonel Brereton until the 17th of November, when I was ordered to investigate the circumstances of the Bristol riots. I may add, that I was sent thither at the suit – I might say the command – of my King. I have borne the arms of my Sovereign, I have had the honour of serving him, and if Colonel Brereton had been my brother officer and my friend, instead of being altogether a stranger to me, I could not have departed from my duty, but must have held the same course towards that friend which I have held to the unfortunate prisoner now no more.

The President – I feel called upon to say for Sir Charles Dalbiac that no proceeding of the kind could have been conducted with less acrimony and more propriety than have been displayed by him.

The President then directed the members of the Court not to leave their respective addresses until he should have received a communication from the Commander-in-Chief.

The Court adjourned at 20 minutes past 10 o'clock. It is said that it will probably meet again on Monday. It is understood that a court-martial will be held upon Captain Warrington, of the 3rd Dragoon Guards, for alleged breach of duty during the riots.

He put down the paper for a moment, his thoughts confused. At the board of inquiry Brereton had looked near the perilous point – though he'd conducted himself with manly bearing during his statement to the board – but at the court martial Hervey had observed no deterioration. Yes, he'd seen men bear themselves when drained of all resource, and then suddenly lose all self-possession. His own colonel, Reynell, had blown out his brains at Corunna. (And – though it could hardly compare – he had the evidence of Hanover Square too.) But in quarters at Bristol, rather than on the battlefield . . . It was incomprehensible. Only that a decent man, asked to do more than he was capable of, in consequence of which disaster followed, might well think it the honourable course. He wished that he'd gone straight to Bristol as the assizes assembled, rather than to Salisbury, for then he would have had charge of things from the beginning, and Brereton would still be alive. Was there family? He hoped profoundly there was not.

He made himself read on:

PARTICULARS OF THE SUICIDE OF
LIEUT.-COLONEL BRERETON.

The report of this tragical event, as we have already stated, reached Bristol about 9 o'clock this morning, and, as may be imagined, it created an indescribable sensation throughout the city. It took place at Redfield-lodge, Lawrence-hill, an exceedingly neat and pretty cottage, the residence of the unfortunate deceased, and situate about a mile and a half from Bristol, in the upper Bath-road. Colonel Brereton, it appears, returned home there last night about

11 o'clock, from Reeve's Hotel, in this city, where he had been stopping during the progress of the court-martial. He came home in his gig, accompanied by his gardener. There was nothing unusual observed by the domestics in his manner or deportment on that occasion. He retired to his bed-chamber some time after 12 o'clock, but he must have remained up a considerable time in committing to writing the reasons which had induced him to perpetrate the fatal deed, for he left after him on the table a statement on the subject that occupied nearly half a quire of paper. His pistols had been as usual deposited on the table in his bed-room. He did not undress himself; but merely took off his coat and threw himself on the bed. About a quarter before 3 o'clock the housekeeper, hearing the report of a pistol in Colonel Brereton's bed-room, gave the alarm, and the Colonel's footman immediately proceeded thither. He there found his unfortunate master stretched on his bed, and life completely extinct. The ball had entered in the left side, directly in the region of the heart, which it must have penetrated, for instantaneous death was the result.

The pistol was lying on the floor, which as well as the bed, was inundated with blood, in consequence of the profuse haemorrhage from the wound. It was observed yesterday that the unfortunate deceased appeared more than usually affected by the evidence which was given towards the conclusion of the court-martial. In the written statement which he is reported to have left behind him, he is said to have attributed to some particular quarter the immediate cause of his untimely end. He was a widower, and has left two daughters of very tender years to mourn the fate of a good and kind-hearted parent.

Colonel Brereton was very respectably connected, and was about 52 years of age, 33 years of which had been spent in the army. Though never present in any remarkable engagement, he had acquired the reputation of being a trustworthy and meritorious officer. He served at the Cape of Good Hope during the government of Lord Charles Somerset. Appointed to the command of a regiment on the Caffre frontier (reported as being in a state of insubordination), he was intrusted by the Governor with the command of the whole frontier. The officers of his regiment (the 49th, we believe), presented him, through Sir Henry Torrens, with a sword, valued at 200 guineas. He was eight years Inspecting Field-officer of the Bristol district, where he succeeded Colonel Daniell, by exchange.

Two daughters of very tender years: he thought at once of Georgiana, and shuddered. There would be a subscription got up for them of course – and he himself would subscribe, as he did already to the Duke of York's fund for widows and orphans – but . . .

And that statement of Dalbiac's – 'I did not entertain the slightest feeling, save that of impartiality, towards the prisoner': could he himself declare the same, 'as solemnly as if I were in presence of my God'? He'd been exasperated by Brereton – dismayed, even – but it proceeded from professional observation, not any personal animus. That he knew, and could indeed declare as solemnly as if in the presence of his Maker. And if – God forbid – he had ever given Brereton cause to think otherwise (for sometimes men drew unwarranted conclusions), he begged forgiveness.

In truth, he was now doubly – many more times doubly – gratified that he'd been released from the court martial after the first day, and without cross-examination (he'd applied for early leave to the president because of Kezia's indisposition, and neither General Dalbiac, prosecuting, nor Colonel Brereton's counsel had objected, and Sir Harry Fane had discharged him with condolences). For besides being able to get back to Heston before the roads were deep with snow, he was spared the necessity of giving the opinion which, after the board of inquiry, had occasioned adverse comment. Even *The Times* might have been inclined to remark on it, making connection with the untoward outcome. At least he was spared that; but, more, the awful thought that however impartially he had given his opinion, it had, so to speak, been the finger on the trigger. *Two daughters of very tender years*: it was weighing heavily with him.

As indeed must the whole business of court martial have weighed with poor Brereton, 33 of whose 52 years had been given to the army, in which 'he had acquired the reputation of being a trustworthy and meritorious officer'. Hervey had himself suffered field court martial, but that was a very trifling affair compared with one for so senior an officer as Brereton: a lieutenant-general, four major-generals, six colonels and four lieutenant-colonels sitting as the military jury; Dalbiac prosecuting – and the whole proceedings open to the public and reported freely by the press. Little wonder Brereton had found it intolerable.

But to take his own life – a thing by common consent reserved for the final moment of capture by savages . . . Surely the balance of his mind had been greatly disturbed. Perhaps it had been so even before the riot began?

Hervey steeled himself to read the conclusion. He was sure it would be 'a calumny on a fine officer'; one 'made scapegoat by those in authority'; whose 'decency and moderation had been traduced by those who relieved him, for whatever motive'. It all boded very ill.

Yet he was all astonishment:

In the disastrous occurrences which led to the investigation into his conduct, the character of the officer suffered from the benevolence of the man. Deficient in the great military principle of decision, averse to the shedding of blood, and obliged to seek instructions from a magistracy anxious to shift the burden of responsibility for severe measures from their collective shoulders, he neither discerned with the requisite precision, nor acted with the promptitude which the exigency of the occasion demanded. The censure of those who were most bitter in their condemnation of him when living, extends no further, now that he has made his fearful and rash appeal from a tribunal of his fellow-creatures to the judgment-seat of God.

In his private relations, his conduct was unimpeachable. He was distinguished by invariable kind-heartedness to all; and when his death was made known in the neighbourhood of his dwelling, a crowd of women and children, many of whom wept him as a benefactor, gathered to his threshold to mourn his loss. His liberality was the more estimable, as, with respect to fortune, he possessed but a small private independence.

THE INQUEST.

The inquest is not expected to be held until to-morrow, as, the event having occurred in Glocester-shire, it will be necessary to send to Berkeley, about 20 miles distant from Bristol, for Mr. Ellis, the county coroner.

Deficient in the great military principle of decision, averse to the shedding of blood: could he have thought that any but a man under authority, having soldiers under him, might see it so simply, let alone state it so plainly? He shook his head, and sighed – and hoped that his sighing was not unworthy. He knew there'd be others breathing greater sighs of relief than he, for although no one might have wished it, it was a solution that many would quietly welcome. There would now be no appeals against verdict or sentence, no public campaigns one way or the other. Captain Warrington was to be court-martialled, yes; but that would be a straightforward enough affair. Brereton had both condemned himself and carried out sentence by his own action. It was all very neatly done.

But those two daughters of tender years, now made fully orphan – they came before him almost as his own. He made to find paper and pen. He must write a letter at once to condole with someone, and a respectful note to the colonel of the Forty-ninth . . .

'Is everything well, sir?'

He hadn't supposed he'd been observed. He certainly hoped his dismay hadn't been.

'Yes, Annie, perfectly well.'

But he thought a word or two in elaboration might convince her more that it was.

'Colonel Brereton, who was in command of the troops at Bristol before my arrival there, has taken his own life.'

'Oh, sir.'

'Dreadful, yes.'

'What about his family, sir?'

'He has none but two daughters, it seems. I'm sure there'll be arrangements made. There always are. But a great sadness, certainly.'

'Colonel Brereton was the man who you had to go to Bristol to speak for, wasn't he, sir?'

'Not so much *for*, Annie; I gave evidence to his court martial on what I saw.'

'Yes, sir. Serjeant James told me about it . . .'

She looked anxious suddenly.

'There's coffee, sir, just made, if you will. And I'll be taking a tray up to Mrs Hervey, as soon as the doctor's gone.'

Hervey nodded, thought for a moment, then put down his pen. 'Annie, I haven't thanked you sufficiently for all you've done these past weeks. The work must have been very tiring for you. Indeed, I don't think you have taken a full day's rest in a month. You must have some respite.'

He did not exaggerate. Annie had not had a day's rest since the fateful evening. She'd been nurse and lady's maid until Kezia's own had been brought from Walden, she'd continued as Mrs James's second, served at table, overseen the two other housemaids, and found a third when Elizabeth and Georgiana had visited. She'd been to see her mother in Osterley once, but only in the afternoon, and even then had been back by dark.

'That's not necessary, sir. I like to be at work.'

'Yes, I understand.' (He himself might have said the same.) 'How is your brother?' he added brightly, to divert things to happier matters.

'Oh, he's very well, sir. He wrote home and said that his regiment's bound for India. It set my mother's nerves into an agitation, but she's well about it now. We won't see him for many years, though, I don't suppose. I hope he'll have leave before he goes and can come and see us. Or perhaps we'll travel to Canterbury to see him. I'd like that.'

Hervey nodded.

'I'll go and take Mrs Hervey her tray, then, sir. The doctor said I should, after a quarter of an hour.'

'The doctor – I didn't hear him come.'

'Yes, sir, not long after you came in here. I'll take the tray then, sir?'

'Yes . . . yes, I'll join Mrs Hervey presently.'

His thoughts could now at least turn from Bristol, and happily. How that remarkable surgeon of his – physician, indeed; *Medicinae Doctor Aberdonensis* – was proved right. Or rather, had proved himself right, for not once had he let up in his regimen of daily observation, treatment and prescription. Kezia had gained strength and composure observable almost by the day, and, just as Milne had assured him it would – as much as any man of science might assure – her mind had regained equilibrium, so that there was about her now a calmness and equability that drew him to her more than mere duty.

For the moment, though, there was a good fire in his hearth, and he would content himself until the tray was ready by gazing at it and drawing strength from contemplating the happier events of the past month. For despite all, they had kept a good Christmas – a very good Christmas. At Hounslow the day itself had met with all the custom-ary observances – 'gunfire' at reveille brought to the barrack rooms in kettles by the serjeants; the troop horses turned away on the heath behind barracks until dusk; church parade – much abbreviated, at Hervey's insistence, but with hearty carolling; the dragoons' feast of roast pork in the riding school carved by the serjeant-majors and served by the officers; and evening stables with all ranks to the brush, followed by dinner at Heston with the half-dozen officers at duty still. Then there'd been three days of conviviality with Elizabeth and Georgiana, and a drive to Windsor, where they'd had the freedom of the park. He'd had a good morning's sport at Osterley by invitation of Lord Jersey; and in the evenings, when his guests were none, he'd done a little work with the German manuscript. Indeed, he'd not passed through the barrack gates at Hounslow until the second of the new year – and not once fretted over it.

'Ah, Milne: you come upon me by stealth. You'll stay and lunch?'

'Thank you, Colonel, but no. I thought that, since there's no one abed in the infirmary, I'd take the opportunity to dine with an old friend at St George's hospital. I've engaged a hackney.'

'Of course. And, it was so very good to see Collins back at duty this morning. My compliments.'

'In Collins's case, I believe it was more a business of amusing the patient while Nature took its course. He has a strong constitution and an even stronger will – and a wife for whom any man would fight for his life.'

Hervey blinked; Milne's forthrightness could sometimes be startling. 'Indeed. Quite.'

'But I've told him not to expect immediate recovery of all his powers. Two weeks, three perhaps.'

Hervey nodded. 'And how do you find *my* wife this morning?'

The surgeon looked thoughtful.

'Come, a glass of madeira.'

'Very well, thank you, Colonel.'

He took a chair, as Hervey poured him a glass of his best Blandy's.

'She is, I think, quite remarkably well. I hesitate only because I've rarely seen so promising a recovery, and there's always the chance of relapse. Her nursing has been exemplary; and the conditions could not have been better, save perhaps in some warmer clime.'

'And she has had the best of medical attention.'

'I cannot claim that.'

'The most diligent, then. Come, doctor, I am in your debt.'

Milne bowed ever so slightly and took a sip of his wine.

'I am only too content that she is restored a good measure to full health, but are you able yet to say what it was that ailed her – and what the reason for her . . . seizure?'

Milne shook his head. 'Not with any certainty, no.'

'Then with uncertainty?'

Milne looked reluctant, but Hervey's tone of encouragement tempted him to rehearse what he'd intended discussing with his 'old friend' at St George's. 'Postpartum disorders are perhaps the least understood of any generally occurring maladies. But—'

'Postpartum? But Kezia's birthing was four years ago – more.'

Milne nodded. 'As I said, these are among the least understood of disorders a physician in general practice encounters, if perhaps the most common. *Dolores post partum*, to give the condition its usual name, has been recognized for centuries – by Galen, even. I cannot be sure, for there is no clinical proof, but I believe Mrs Hervey to have been suffering from a chronic puerperal . . . melancholy. I was going to say "mania", but that is to excite an unnecessary fear.'

He took another sip of wine and settled a little more into his chair. It was the first they'd spoken in this way, and to his mind it was overdue.

'I believe I have told you, Colonel, that when I was in practice in Aberdeen, I had correspondence with Robert Gooch – he is the foremost authority on obstetric medicine; he lectured at St Bartholomew's hospital – for I'd begun to wonder if these cases of melancholy were not somehow connected with exterior factors, and had begun keeping a careful record. Gooch – who died recently, or else I would have consulted him in this case – was not of that opinion, and, indeed, over the course of years in which I made my records I myself was obliged to come to the same conclusion. There is evidence, however – which I myself could corroborate – that what he preferred to call puerperal mania is more common in the higher classes of society.'

Hervey still looked doubtful. 'And this puerperal mania can occur at so late a time as five years after childbirth?'

'I don't believe Mrs Hervey's . . . I should prefer to call it "prostration" rather than "seizure", can be characterized thus. It may be likened to the irruption you have told me of – with some delicacy I must say – of symptoms of melancholia much earlier.'

He did not add – for it would have been unkind as well as un-professional – that remarks by others (notably Fairbrother) had led him quite independently to that conclusion.

'Gooch believed that it might be connected with lactation, and the extended feeding of the infant, which leads to exhaustion. Mrs Hervey's regimen at the piano may have been an exacerbation – *the* exacerbation. As well, indeed, as a symptom. The prostration can be likened to the natural bursting of an abscess.'

Hervey struggled to grasp the import of the surgeon's diagnosis, for 'mania' was indeed a word that excited fear; but as ever when reaching the point of bewilderment, he fixed instead on the practical business of what to do.

'Your treatment – it has consisted almost wholly in sedatives, has it not?'

'It has. Gooch was against any depletion of blood, with which I am very ready to concur. My principal object has been gradually to relieve Mrs Hervey's exhaustion by procuring for her a good night's sleep – many good nights' sleep – but to do so without recourse to heavy opiates, upon which she might become reliant. In the most part, cases of puerperal mania, or whichever is the term, are resolved from within, or else not at all. The physician's function, essentially, is to facilitate rest in order to allow Nature to take its benevolent course – rather as with Collins. I remain of the view that Mrs Hervey will make a full recovery of her health – indeed, that she is close to that recovery now. Calmness is required hereon – a good diet, a little wine; and when the weather is better, exercise out of doors. Above all, perhaps, conversation.'

Hervey was for once content to let go all reserve. 'Doctor, there is nothing I should look forward to more.'

Milne, who was anyway not obliged to let rank stand between him and his professional opinion, now saw his chance. 'I can prescribe, Colonel, but I cannot make the patient respond. With respect, that is for you.'

XII

The Course of Nature

London, Wednesday, 25 January 1832

> *Bedford-square,*
> *24 January*

My dear Hervey,
Would you do me the honour of dining tomorrow at the Travellers
Club? I have intelligence that will be of the greatest interest and, I dare
say, much profit.

> *Ever yrs &c,*
> *Eyre Somervile*

IT HAD BEEN ONE OF Hervey's better days at Hounslow. His seat had not touched anything but the saddle. 'Evolutions on the Heath' were always pleasing, though with only two troops, the others seemingly permanently assigned every which way, he could scarcely take the head. In truth, too, with guard duties, fatigues and the usual 'sick, lame and lazy', even these two troops mustered between them fewer than eighty. There were times when he thought the Sixth would not so much disband as merely wither away. But observing a squadron at exercise, no matter what its strength, ever quickened his pulse and excited his thoughts.

And now he looked forward to dinner with his old friend Eyre Somervile, Knight of the Royal Guelphic Order and perpetual administrator of the King's distant settlements. They had first met in India and seen much adventure there, and then even more adventure at the Cape. They might yet have served in Canada together, where until lately Somervile had been minister, for at one time it looked as if Hervey would have to accept command of a regiment of Foot in lieu of the Sixth. He had even composed a letter to Kezia on the matter ('And now, my dearest wife, I return to the subject of the lieutenant-colonelcy of the 81st. Events here . . . have led me to the settled conclusion that I must take the commission. In doing so I know it to be contrary to your wish, and that you have every good reason to set your face against it, Canada being a place of some primitive society yet, and I therefore can neither insist upon your accompanying me nor even hope for a change of heart, for I see that such would be unconducive to your music and therefore to your happiness. I shall therefore bear the deprivation for as long as needs be, in the sure hope that it will not be excessively long, and that we shall soon be reunited in a station more agreeable to you.').

But in the end he had not had to send the letter; there had been no Canada, or a station more agreeable either (Gibraltar had been another in which there was a vacancy with the infantry). Instead he had gained his heart's desire, command of the regiment into which he had been commissioned. That it was so unfavourably stationed – except for social purposes – and duty there becoming daily more wearisome, was unfortunate, but could he really contemplate selling out?

For the moment, though, the prospect of good mutton, good burgundy and the best of company was enough to enliven a day already agreeably begun. Whether the promised 'intelligence' was of interest or profit was an altogether supplemental business.

*

'Eleven, then, Sar'nt Wakefield,' said Hervey as he got down outside the Travellers Club just before eight o'clock, giving him a half-crown's extra-duty pay and subsistence, though doubtless Wakefield would be able to find a free supper with the War Office Party (being so close to St James's Palace, they never went short of rations).

Inside he found Somervile standing by a good fire in conversation with the Portuguese Minister Plenipotentiary, and although he would have been glad to hear the latest news from that troubled place – for it was only a few years ago that he'd been there with the unfortunate force of intervention in the 'War of the Two Brothers' – he was glad that his host detached himself as rapidly as was polite and they went at once to the coffee room.

'It is a very agreeable club, this,' said Somervile, as they took the most secluded of tables, which evidently he had reserved with a good tip. 'There's no knowing the people who pass by – like Carreira there. And when we move to our new quarters later this year . . .'

The present ones were certainly remarkably shabby for an establishment so eminently favoured – an old inn, which Brooks's had once occupied, and now with every appearance of a Channel packet after a stormy crossing. It had been founded by Lord Palmerston and others after the French wars, when the Continent was no longer cut off from England, as a place where gentlemen whose interests extended beyond the shires might meet and offer hospitality to notable foreign visitors. The qualification for membership – that a candidate must have travelled out of the British islands to a distance of at least five hundred miles from London in a direct line – was not difficult to meet for soldiers such as Hervey, or administrative sojourners like Somervile, but it served to winnow.

'The United Service shall seem very provincial.'

Somervile smiled. 'That said, had I been of the committee, I might – indeed would – have urged an Indian palace rather than Italian.'

'No doubt, but it's a most handsome *palazzo*.' (It was scaffolded still, but its imminent grandeur was apparent enough.) 'I look forward to sampling the macaroni,' added Hervey, with a smile.

The Travellers' wine butler came with a bottle of champagne, uncorking it as deftly as a dragoon drawing sabre, and filling their glasses as promptly as the bubbles allowed. Somervile raised his and proposed 'To friendship.'

'To friendship,' replied Hervey.

Somervile drained his glass and let the butler refill it as a waiter came with a tray of oysters. 'Burnhams?'

'Yes, Sir Eyre.'

'Capital. I've taken the liberty of ordering our dinner, Hervey. There's excellent turbot today, says the *maître*, and thirty-day beef.'

Somervile was perhaps a little less stout than when he'd gone to Canada, but the battle with knife and fork was a never-ending one, in the course of which he'd learned many a martial art. Hervey was quite content to follow his lead when it came to the pleasures of the table.

'Delightful.'

'Wretched business, that – Brereton's suicide.'

Hervey shook his head.

'I trust you don't consider it should weigh on your conscience too oppressively.'

Hervey put down his glass, and sighed. 'No, the man was evidently placed in a position his temper was unsuited to, but not by me. What I regret is being asked – made – to give my opinion on his conduct, when that was the business of the board of inquiry. That damned old fool, Greville.'

Somervile had his own views on Sir Peregrine Greville – that it was sometimes useful for an idle but aspiring man to disguise himself as a booby – but he would keep them to himself.

'But that priest-fellow spoke well in your favour, I see. A most handsome testimony, his; and got up so full and well in *The Times*. I wonder when there'll be an end to these inquiries, though.'

'Just so. The civil trials continue, of course, which daily add to the population of what is pleased to be called "Australia" – those, that is, who escape the gibbet. But, yes, the priest's was a happy testimony. A good sort of man, not one to evade his responsibilities, though he got no great support in trying to carry them out. I've sent him my thanks.'

And then he told him what Lord Hill had said about promotion being deferred.

Somervile knew it already, however, for he prided himself in never making a move without first acquiring all necessary intelligence – though he kept this to himself too. He shook his head. 'It's as if when they consider making a major-general they look at what Cromwell did with *his* major-generals and therefore appoint someone not in the least capable of government – and frankly, therefore, the poorer for it.'

Hervey smiled thinly. 'Greville would be the last to ban Christmas, that's certain . . . But, now, what is this intelligence you have baited me to dinner with?'

'Of course, but first – how is Kezia?'

Hervey looked pained . . . and then quite content. They'd never spoken of matters, but the matters were now very public, and it was absurd he should think to deny anything before an old friend. 'She is well – very well, I think. Thank you.'

'Is she confined to her bed still?'

'No, no indeed. We've taken several drives, as far as Windsor, even. I believe she will be well enough to return to Walden soon.'

'And that is her intention?'

'Well . . . I had supposed . . . We have not yet spoken.'

'My dear fellow, you'll forgive my intrusion and my directness, but might she not be waiting for you to ask her to stay?'

Hervey suppressed (he hoped) both his surprise and a pitying smile. 'You are ever loyal.'

'I certainly trust so. Now, let's make a beginning with these oysters.'

'Is that, therefore, the interesting intelligence: you wished to know of Kezia's circumstances?'

'No, of course it isn't, but it's not unconnected – though that wasn't the reason I asked. Nor that it will be the second thing that Emma asks me when I return – the first being "What did he say to the idea?"'

'You will remember to tell me the idea, will you not?'

'At once.'

He beckoned the butler to refill their glasses, and took two more oysters.

'Yesterday I spent at East India House reading the latest despatches from Madras. There'll be trouble in Mysore – and there's been trouble enough already. Or rather, to begin with, in Coorg—'

Hervey inclined his head. 'Coorg . . .'

'To the south-west, touching on Malabar. Not very much bigger than your Wiltshire. Rather a charming place, a little like Scotland – well, the fairer parts of Scotland. Hilly. A fierce people, though, when roused – and their rajah capricious. Which, when you think of it, isn't unlike the Scotch again.'

Hervey's first footing in India had been the Madras presidency, but on the Coromandel, not the Malabar, coast. These little princedoms – kingdoms even – were many and distant, and as long as they didn't stand in the way of the Honourable East India Company's trade (which was, after all, the business of the Company), their rajahs were left to do as they pleased. He couldn't remember hearing of Coorg when first he was in Madras – and certainly not when, much later, he was in Bengal – but as he'd observed from his first entanglement in Chintal, the lesser the rajah, the greater seemed the way of disturbing the peace. He ascribed it to the heat, in the way that everything in India was far larger or more colourful, and as a rule more virulent, than anywhere else. The country had roused his passions more than once. It was not a place that admitted any sort of repose; certainly not for long.

'A strange name, though, is it not – "Coorg"? I don't think I've heard its like.'

'Oh, the usual thing, no doubt – a writer in Madras transcribes what he thinks he's heard. The native name's Kodagu, which in all probability I would surmise is from the Kanarese – "steep", "hilly"; that sort of thing.'

Hervey smiled. Somervile's delight in the native tongues – his facility indeed – was ever endearing. He himself had never even heard of Kanarese.

'I see. And what is our interest in this steep and hilly country – except, no doubt, gold?'

Somervile frowned. 'Hervey, you know full well that the Company seeks only fair trade in India. Its purpose is not plunder.'

'Of course.'

'Mysore invaded Coorg thirty years ago – when Hyder Ali was on the throne, just before Tippoo – but we put the rajah back in his palace and he signed a treaty bringing it under the Company's protection. So good an ally was he in fact, in the subsequent wars with Tippoo, the annual tribute was remitted. It had been considerable – 8,000 gold pagodas, as I recall. And since then it's been a single tributary elephant. But our good rajah died a few years later, and the place has since descended into all kinds of evil. It would appear the present rajah thinks he's Caligula. Coorg itself isn't, I believe, worth our regrets, but as a protectorate – a dependent ally indeed – we have no choice but to act. The resident also fears the trouble will spread to Mysore, which would of course be a peril for Madras.'

Hervey slurped another oyster. 'Your time at Fort St George will evidently be an interesting one. But you would not have it otherwise.'

Somervile managed two more oysters, and the rest of his glass. 'Certainly not. In any case, no matter what the outcome at Coorg, Mysore could pop its cork at any moment. The Company's hold over the place is by no means complete. Another regiment of cavalry's needed for that contingency alone, and one of Foot to strengthen the garrison at Bangalore. The Court of Directors have decided therefore to ask for two additional King's regiments.'

'This, I take it, is the profitable intelligence.'

'The position is yours.'

Hervey frowned, and swallowed the last oyster. 'I rather think that that prerogative is at least that of the commander-in-chief. In all probability, the secretary at war's.'

Somervile nodded to the *maître*.

'I know all that, of course,' said his old friend, dabbing at his mouth with a napkin as their plates were cleared, 'but he who pays the piper makes him play as he pleases – and the Company will be paying. Besides, I have it on good authority that Lord Hill considers he's in your debt and Parnell holds you in high regard.'

Hervey smiled. 'It would certainly be convenient for everyone if I were to be elsewhere but here.'

The butler brought white burgundy.

Somervile began eagerly on his glass. 'There, you see. You told me yourself 'twould be two years before promotion. How many more drawing rooms do you want to attend? Come and do something worthy of a soldier.'

The turbot arrived, a monstrous great fish. Somervile watched it being filleted, eagerly, while Hervey pondered.

When the waiter was gone, Hervey spoke his mind. 'Were the decision mine – I mean mine to make only for my own pleasure – I shouldn't hesitate. The saving to the pocket alone would induce all but a Bingham. But it isn't mine. The regiment's been home barely five years. Lord George Irvine – the colonel – would certainly have strong views on the matter. Armstrong wouldn't come; he has a family. Nor would Collins, for the same reason. Or St Alban, or Worsley – all my best officers; they'd all exchange. Even Johnson wouldn't want to go back.'

Somervile swallowed his first helping of turbot, and shook his head.

'You yourself told me the regiment was losing its edge, that it was turning into a company of constables and postboys.'

Hervey pondered again. 'And for myself, there is Kezia.'

Somervile narrowed his eyes. 'And you yourself have just told me that she will soon return to Walden.'

Hervey shook his head again. 'It is altogether too much.'

Somervile laid down his fork very deliberately, pushed his plate away, leaned back in his chair and folded his arms. 'Hervey, I never thought to see you defeated. What on earth has become of you?'

XIII

Who Goes There?

Hounslow, a fortnight later

AT A MINUTE BEFORE ELEVEN by the guardroom clock, the trumpet-major marched his calls party – with all but two troops out of barracks, just four trumpeters this morning – to the middle of the square, halted and then advanced them left. There were three well-found buildings at right angles to each other adjoining the parade ground, the central one – forming the orderly room and the offices of the regimental staff – built of London stock and topped by a pediment. The other two were plainer, longer blocks housing stables and barrack-rooms, and by using the regimental headquarters as a reflector, the calls could be sounded farther. Taking cue from the trumpet-major, up went the silver clarins for the regimental fanfare – day in, day out, save Sunday, come wind or weather.

Hervey, just come to office after morning exercise (his mare had taken some settling), turned from the window. The five made pleasing music, but there ought to have been twelve . . .

'What business is there?'

'Principally defaulters, Colonel,' replied St Alban, handing him the daily states. 'Rather a dispiriting number again, I'm afraid. And too many sick.'

It was always 'principally defaulters' – and the sick.

One of the 'sable twins' – Abdel, said his red turban feather – poured him coffee.

The regiment was losing its edge . . .

He would prefer that the first person he spoke of it to was Armstrong – twenty years was a singular time's acquaintance – but it wouldn't serve. If he didn't speak first to his adjutant, there was no helping it. 'I have news that will not be universally agreeable, though it is to me . . . The regiment is for India – Madras. In six months.'

St Alban's look of surprise was as he'd expected. But there was nothing to discuss, and so . . .

'Have the clerks make copies of this for despatch to the outlying troops,' (he handed him the Horse Guards Order) 'but first have the sar'nt-major come; and assemble the captains and staff.'

'Yes, Colonel . . . I . . .'

'Had not expected it.'

'No, no indeed.' St Alban looked as if he wanted to seek some sort of clarification, but evidently judged it best that he didn't. (News spread rapidly, and it was best that the news were as exact as he could make it.)

Armstrong appeared at the door almost at once.

'Come in, please, Sar'nt-Major, and close the door.'

Armstrong opened his order book, ready.

'The regiment's for India in six months. It won't be to your liking, I know, but it is to mine.' He didn't say 'I shall be greatly sorry to say "Goodbye"'. They'd served together far too long.

'Thank God for that, Colonel!' said Armstrong, snapping shut his book.

Hervey blinked. 'You mean it *is* to your liking?'

'Another twelve months here and there'd be no regiment worth the name.'

'But you yourself – your family and all.'

Armstrong looked as surprised as St Alban. 'I'm the serjeant-major; I go where the regiment goes, like it or not. But as it so 'appens, I like it very much. And as for Mrs Armstrong and the bairns, they knows the drill; they follows the drum.'

Hervey smiled. 'And as she is the patroness of the dames who follow the drum, with reverence let her name be spoken!'

'Colonel?'

'Something from a book the surgeon gave me – *Paul Jones*, quite a tale. You'd find it diverting.' He was not used to recommending reading to Armstrong, but he was scarcely able to contain the pleasure at finding his opinion of the regiment's morale confirmed. 'I read those very words last night just before blowing out the candle – read them twice, indeed, for they struck me so very aptly.'

'Well, Colonel, I'll tell our lass that she 'as a new title – "patroness of the dames". She'll be fair kittled.' He would not ask why the colonel's lady was not to have that honour.

'And she has a right to be. Now, we have the business of seeing how the rest of the regiment hears it.'

Hervey drove to Heston in the afternoon with fewer cares than he'd expected. Armstrong's adamant support would in any case have been enough to buoy his spirits, but the staff orderly room had been a business-like affair confined to the details of the posting: six troops, initially for five years, with the option then for *The Governor and Company of Merchants of London trading into the East Indies* to renew the contract.

The only note of disappointment voiced was by the riding-master, sorry that he would not now have opportunity to go to Yorkshire to buy remounts. (One day, Hervey told himself, he would go to see this Yorkshire, where horses – and the likes of Johnson and Stray – were so famously well raised.) For the rest, it seemed, sufficient was it to go and contemplate their future; and that of their subordinates. Six months was a short time to send in papers or arrange an exchange, but Messrs Greenwood, Cox and Hammersley had been the regimental agents for many years, and doubtless kept a ready list of officers wishing to transfer to an India-bound regiment.

Those officers would be a poor lot, of course – hardly impecunious, but clearly wishing to avail themselves of cheaper living – and therefore likely as not of humbler quality compared with joiners of late. That said, he (Hervey) himself had never had real means until lately through the legacy of a man who'd risen from humble beginnings to considerable wealth. Perhaps there'd be men of his mind exchanging, men bored with service as constables and postboys and in search of true military employment – or at least the sporting adventure – that India might promise. But he wagered they'd be a 'peerless' regiment that landed in Madras. St Alban had his eyes on parliament, and Malet intended committing matrimony with an heiress . . . Some would be losers, too, and resentful of it. The value of a commission in the Sixth stood high as long as they were at Hounslow. As soon as the news was out, its stock would plummet. Those who wanted to sell would be best off to apply for leave, or even for the half-pay, while those preferring to exchange would have to hope there were men in equally favoured regiments who wanted to go to India. What a business it was. But that ultimately was what it was – a business; or rather, something on which a man of not unlimited means must calculate his true best interests very carefully. There were days when he thought it the most pernicious system in the world, but others when he reckoned a man's loyalty was all the stronger for the investment. (And that, he knew, was the Duke of Wellington's opinion too, although the duke's concern was not so much with a man's stake in his regiment as his stake in the country.) *Winners and losers*; but it couldn't be helped, and he mustn't concern himself. That, indeed, was what Lord George Irvine had told him.

But 'patroness of the dames who follow the drum': he was pleased with that. Doubtless Armstrong was telling his wife this very moment. His loss had been a cruel one – his and five young children – but in Serjeant Ellis's widow this *treue Husar* had found a willing mother for his 'bairns', and 'the mutual society, help, and comfort, that the one ought to have of the other'. Jessie Ellis was no scholar, as Caithlin O'Mahoney had been – she would have been no more use in the regimental school than Corporal Johnson, except to instruct in common sense and hussifry – but she was a woman to go home to of an evening, and keenly. If she were to come to India as contentedly as her husband, then the battle was half won.

Now he would tell Kezia – and with feelings more mixed than he would have supposed even a month ago. He had of late begun to enjoy her presence at Heston, and not just as a salve to his conscience (much balm though that needed). There had been a distinct softening. They had not yet dined together – not in the usual sense – for she tired each day as the sun set, and took a tray in the warmth of her bedroom. Two evenings ago, however, he had sat with her and read Maria Edgeworth aloud for half an hour, until her eyelids were heavy and she asked for her maid to come. When he had gone down for his own dinner, and more of *Paul Jones* ('*He stood on the deck of his frigate in the dress which he wore during the battle, his pistols black with powder, and his cutlass stained with blood*' – splendid stuff, which brought to mind that first passage to India, when Peto had spoken of the thrill of frigate actions), Annie told him how pleased Kezia had been when she learned that a piano was to be brought tomorrow, and how she herself looked forward to hearing music, 'for it's so very quiet when the men are at barracks'.

Now, indeed, there *was* music. He took off his forage cap, laid it on the table and stood listening. Annie took his coat, for she was quicker to the hall than Johnson, who was taking his time with Hervey's new pelisse from the chariot – useless that that would be in India, though he himself was looking forward to India again, for there were always so many boys to run and fetch and do for him, and the women were always friendly – and clean. Why ever had Colonel 'Ervey thought he *wouldn't* want to come?

It was gentle music, too – a waltz. Hervey hadn't heard her play a waltz before.

Annie smiled at him. 'It came in the middle of the morning, sir. And Mrs Hervey came downstairs not long ago, but I haven't been in to see her. I didn't feel as I should.'

He returned the smile, with thanks. 'Will you bring in tea, then?'

'Yes, sir.'

'And is Serjeant James about?'

'He's not back yet, sir. Mrs James is.'

'No, I must first have words with the serjeant.'

He went to the drawing room. Kezia didn't see him at first, only when she looked up at the end of the piece. She smiled – a smile he'd not seen before (or didn't think he had). It was the expression of peace, contentment – perhaps of some appreciativeness even.

'It is a charming instrument. Thank you, Matthew.'

It was the first time she'd spoken his name in many a while. It caught him square. 'Broadwood's had only five octaves for hire, I'm afraid.'

She smiled again. 'They are more than enough . . . Shall I play a little more?'

'Oh, please do. Annie said how good it would be to hear music in the house.'

'Annie is a fine girl. Uncommonly obliging,' she said, leafing through the sheets on the rack.

'What was it you were playing?'

'Schubert. Broadwood's sent rather a lot of him. More Schubert then?'

He nodded. Schubert meant not a great deal to him, but it wasn't Beethoven. In fact it was the sort of music Elizabeth used to play (and, he hoped, what Georgiana was playing too) – tuneful, tender.

She began again – not in three-time, but in four-; a slow, simple melody, but a happy one.

And then to his surprise, she began to sing:

Still sitz' ich an des Hügels Hang,
der Himmel ist so klar,
das Lüftchen spielt im grünen Tal,
wo ich beim ersten Frühlingsstrahl
einst, ach so glücklich war.

Six verses – the joys of spring, and the pains of love, and the last verse wishing to prolong the joys throughout the summer, like the bird singing in a tree:

O wär ich doch ein Vöglein nur
dort an dem Wiesenhang!
Dann blieb ich auf den Zweigen hier,
und säng ein süsses Lied von ihr,
den ganzen Sommer lang.

He wondered: did she know the language? She certainly sang as if she did. He suddenly thought how ill it was that he didn't know. *Why* didn't he know?

'That was charming.'

Annie stood at the door with a tray, and a look of admiration touching on despair.

Hervey saw only the tray. 'Ah, Annie; you are very good. Please come in. Shall you pour the tea for us?'

'Yes, thank you, Annie,' added Kezia. 'Please pour tea for us. You are very good.' And then to Hervey, smiling the more, 'It is charming, yes. But this will be to your liking too.'

She began again: the beat of hooves – clip-clop, clip-clop, clip-clop, clip-clop, sounding them as she played, her face almost childlike, and then . . .

Ade! du muntre, du fröhliche Stadt, ade!
Schon scharret mein Rösslein mit lustigen Fuss;
Jetzt nimm noch den letzten, den scheidenden Gruss.
Du hast mich wohl niemals noch traurig gesehn,
So kann es auch jetzt nicht beim Abschied geschehn . . .

'But I can't remember all the verses – and the music isn't here. And besides,' (she smiled the more) 'it's all "Goodbye".'

Hervey swallowed; that indeed was the message he brought.

Kezia took her tea.

'Will that be all . . . ma'am?'

Hervey smiled to himself; Annie was indeed perceptive (she asked leave of the mistress).

But Kezia turned to him.

'Yes, thank you, Annie,' he said, and warmly; 'And do look to Corporal Johnson, if you will. He said he was fair famished.'

Propriety (where had she learned it so well?) forbade her smile fully by return, but she knew the confidence to which she'd been admitted at Heston. Johnson had told her that he'd been Hervey's groom for more years than she'd been out of swaddling (which wasn't true, but not perhaps by much), and endless stories . . .

'I will, sir.'

Kezia played a little more, and then they took a turn round the garden, and through the copse to the pond, where a few drab ducks made their haven. She seemed to take an extraordinary pleasure in it, though there was no colour but for snowdrops. He began wondering if he should ask about Allegra: should he send to Walden for her? She'd not spoken of her at all . . . and so he thought he ought not to either. Perhaps it was something he should ask Milne first?

He gazed at the ducks in their wintry plumage. In India, even in winter, no bird looked as dull as they. Or perhaps it was his imagining.

Kezia took his arm, a precaution, perhaps, as they stood by the water's edge.

But he did not speak of India. He'd intended to, but there was a fragility still, and she seemed to tremble from time to time, despite the coat he'd put on her and its fur.

Not that telling her could be any sort of peril. Milne had said her recovery to full health was close, in which case she would be able to return to Walden before too long – certainly long before they marched from barracks.

No, he did not speak of India, or of anything else. It was Kezia who broke the silence, and yet without consciousness of it. 'I did not say, but Georgiana was most charming when she came to see me, though I fear I was poor company.'

He laughed. 'She was very happy that you liked her hyacinths. They were hers she'd grown at Heytesbury, and she was anxious lest they die of cold on the way. Elizabeth said the carriage was heated like a forcing-house.'

'Elizabeth was all kindness too.'

'She ever was.'

Their visit had been but a few days, but he'd spent more time in the company of both of them than he could ever remember, and Georgiana's leaving he'd felt more than he'd come to expect. What was to be done about India he hadn't truly begun to think.

A squirrel crept along the low branch of an elm just in front of them, apparently heedless. They stood watching until a pair of squabbling jackdaws landed in the branches above, sending it scampering for safety – if indeed it had been in danger.

'Do you know the story of the jackdaw and the eagle, Matthew?'

'I . . . don't recall.'

'It is one of Aesop's stories, I think. An eagle swooped down and seized a lamb in its talons and made off with it. A jackdaw saw it and thought to do the same, but came down instead on the back of a ram, and when it tried to rise again it found it couldn't get away, for its claws were tangled in the wool. And the shepherd caught it and clipped its wings and gave it to his children. "What a queer bird is this!" they said laughing, "What do you call it, Father?" "It is a jackdaw, children. But if you should ask him, *he* would say he is an eagle."'

Hervey was puzzled. She said it with such sureness, as if its portent was of the utmost. 'A moral for all seasons, I think,' he said, though with nothing particular he could call to mind.

Kezia stooped to pick up an owl feather. 'And the jackdaw is supposed to be such a clever bird too.'

Hervey saw her shiver ever so slightly, but enough to make him concerned they should return to the house.

She twirled the feather, looking at it rather than him, but yet perfectly aware of his expression. 'But I suppose the jackdaw couldn't know that he mightn't imitate the eagle simply because he wished it – and *practised* so hard.'

He took her hand. 'Forgive me; I may mistake your meaning, and I don't know how else to be sure . . . Do you compare yourself to the jackdaw?'

She looked at him and smiled contentedly. 'I am done with striving to play the eagle.'

As she put her arm in his again to return to the house, Hervey steeled himself. 'There is something of which I must speak.'

At six o'clock he put down his pen. Letters to Salisbury, Heytesbury and Jamaica lay on his writing table. What they'd bring by return he'd no idea. He would, of course, see everyone in Wiltshire before he left for the East – but Fairbrother? He couldn't even be sure the letter would reach him this coming year. And then what? He'd sorely missed his strange friend of late.

He went to a side-table and poured himself a glass of sack, then returned to his chair to contemplate the easiest of his letters – to Peto.

He would of course – he hoped most dearly – see his good and brave old friend before the day came, but at this remove it was impossible to be certain. Meanwhile he would content himself with sending the heartiest congratulations on the news that the 'yellow admiral' was to become at last – like him – a father (and a better one, he didn't doubt). It had once seemed so impossible a proposition that . . .

'Yes, Annie?'

She had evidently been waiting for him to take his rest from the pen, and he hadn't noticed.

'Shall I put coal on the fire, sir?'

'No, Annie; there's no need. I threw on a shovel only half an hour ago. Besides, it's Rose's job.'

'Yes, sir, but I let her go into Hounslow to see her people.'

'Indeed? How will she return?'

'She said her brother would walk back with her, sir.'

He nodded. That seemed satisfactory. It was but two miles, though there wasn't much moon.

'Can I ask something, sir?'

There was just a note of anxiety in her voice.

'Yes, Annie, of course. There's nothing wrong, I hope?'

'Sir, Corporal Johnson's told me that the regiment is going to India.'

'Yes, that's the truth.'

He supposed he would have told her soon enough – perhaps he ought to have already – but the day had been . . .

'Well, sir, I was wondering if you'd be wanting any servants there. Corporal Johnson says "no" – that there's hundreds of Hindoo people all wanting jobs, and for hardly any money at all; but I was thinking that they wouldn't know how you liked things, not to begin with, and that I would, and that I wouldn't want any more money than them, because Corporal Johnson says everything costs next to nothing.'

Hervey leaned back in his chair. She seemed to be trying to remember what else it was that could recommend her . . .

'Oh, and as my brother's going to be there, sir, I thought it would be a very good and nice thing.'

Hervey stopped himself asking her 'A good thing for whom?', but instead asked equally impossibly where her brother was going to be.

'I don't rightly know, sir, yet, just that he's for India, and I thought . . .'

He smiled. 'Annie, I am most excessively obliged to you. I can't imagine there are many who would wish to leave their native homes for a place so distant and . . . alien. Doubtless, Corporal Johnson has told you a good deal about it already.'

'Oh, yes, sir.'

He raised his eyebrows; Johnson could paint hell rosy and heaven infernal as the case required.

'But I must sleep on it – and so must you, and for several nights probably. I'm by no means averse to the idea – quite the contrary – but we must be practical.'

'Oh, thank you, sir. I will sleep on it, but I'm sure I know how I'll wake on it too.'

Her smile was so full and innocent that if she'd pressed him to a decision there and then he'd have said 'yes'.

The doorbell rang.

'That will be the doctor,' he said.

'Yes, sir. I'll see him in.'

Milne was longer with Kezia than usual. It was nearly seven when he came down.

Hervey was not greatly anxious, for the evidence of the afternoon told him that Kezia's 'recovery to full health' continued apace. But all the same . . . 'How is my wife this evening, doctor?'

Milne put down his bag. 'Quite remarkably well, I should say.'

'Can I tempt you this time to a glass of something?' The answer was almost always 'no', because of duty or some prior appointment.

'I thank you, Colonel, yes. Is that sherry you drink?'

'It is.'

'Then sherry, please. May I sit?'

'Of course.' Hervey poured him a glass.

'You spoke with Mrs Hervey of India, I gather.'

'I did. This afternoon, after a pleasant turn around the garden.' He was suddenly uneasy. 'It hasn't excited any complaint, any relapse, I trust?'

Milne smiled. 'No, not at all. Quite the contrary. Indeed, I have now suspended all sedating. She tires still, she complains, but I am not at all surprised. I've instructed her maid to serve her beef tea of a late morning, and a glass of red grape of an evening. However, I would prescribe clement sea air by and by.'

Hervey was now distinctly puzzled.

Milne took a sip of his wine, looking as if he'd truly earned it. 'A prolonged sea voyage, tropical climes . . . sun.'

'Doctor, what is it exactly that you say?'

'Colonel, if you were to invite your wife to accompany you to India, I believe her reply would be "Aye". She asked my opinion of its healthiness of climate, and if her constitution would bear it – she has been there before, as I hardly need say – and though I am not expert regarding *tropicae salutem*, I pronounced that it would be of the greatest benefit. *Mens sana in corpore sano.*'

PART TWO

A TIME TO EMBRACE

Pray for a healthy mind in a healthy body.
Ask for a stout heart that has no fear of death,
And deems length of days the least of Nature's gifts
That can endure any kind of toil,
That knows neither wrath nor desire and thinks
The woes and hard labours of Hercules better than
The loves and banquets and downy cushions of Sardanapalus.
What I commend to you, you can give to yourself;
For assuredly, the only road to a life of peace is virtue.

JUVENAL, SATIRE X

XIV

Coromandel!

Madras, eleven months later

Will be dispatched on the 12th of July, Direct for MADRAS, the fast sailing ship PYRAMUS, burthen 800 tons, Joseph Harewood, R.N. Commander. Lying in the East India Export Dock. This ship has very superior accommodation for passengers, and carries an experienced surgeon. For freight or passage, apply to the Commander, at the Jerusalem Coffee House: or to JOHN PIRIE and Co. 3, Freeman's court, Cornhill.

The Oriental Herald Advertizer, June 1832

THE ACCOMMODATION WAS CERTAINLY SUPERIOR to many a packet, but 'very superior' might have deceived the inexperienced passenger into expecting a degree of comfort that only an admiral's state rooms might provide. Hervey was not to be thus deceived in this, his third passage to India, nor Kezia in her second. They were, however, considerably more comfortable than hitherto, having been able to take the round-house, in which there was much more air than in the lower cabins, if more noise, not least from the chorus of pigs, dogs, poultry, cats, sheep – and a cow – at sunrise.

They had put in at Madeira for two days and gone ashore, for although the crossing of the Bay of Biscay had been, according to Captain Harewood, one of the smoothest they might expect, once south of Cape St Vincent the swell had been a challenge to their sea legs, and both Hervey and Kezia – all the party, indeed – had wanted to eat figs and grapes in the warm calm of a *patio* (it had been quite cold at sea).

But the unexpected delight of the passage south, at the end of September, had been the sighting of Tristan da Cunha. This loneliest of islands seven miles wide and the same long, said Captain Harewood, was but an extinct volcano of 7,000 feet, five times as high as the Rock of Gibraltar. It had been claimed for His Majesty King George III, he said, by no less than an officer of cavalry – Josias Cloete of the 21st Light Dragoons. Hervey had known him in the Peninsula, when Cloete was with the Fifteenth, and then his family while at the Cape. They had extensive vineyards and a warm regard for the King, which was rare enough among the Cape Dutch. He told Kezia they might pay them a visit when they put in at Cape Town. But he'd not known of the connection with Tristan. Captain Harewood explained that sometime after Waterloo, Cloete had been sent with a party to take possession, on account of the Americans, who'd shown too much interest in the place during the late war. That, at least, was what they said at the Cape, but he reckoned it was because London was fearful the French might try to use Tristan to rescue Bonaparte from his exile on Saint Helena.

In saying this he'd laughed. 'Yet Helena's a thousand miles nor'-east. How this place'd be the least bit useful's beyond me. Winds and currents, Colonel Hervey: all wrong.'

But, he said, Cloete and his men had gone at it with a will, and soon there were a hundred souls – women and children too – living on what had thitherto been an empty island. Then, just a year on, when London must have looked at a few charts (he'd laughed again), Cloete's party was withdrawn – except for half a dozen families who'd asked to remain.

When, therefore, the *Pyramus* hove to off the island's only settlement, which clung to a tiny plateau at the north-west corner (Harewood said it was more a ledge), her passengers had been in keen anticipation of a walk ashore after so many weeks at sea. This, however, at first proved impossible, so treacherous were the waters. Instead, the 'Governor' – the corporal of artillery who'd elected to stay fifteen years ago – came out in a whaleboat.

The next day, though, the wind had dropped appreciably, and although Captain Harewood was yet reluctant, he eventually consented to lowering a boat. That evening, Hervey would add to his long letter home:

> *They looked very healthy and comfortable and cared not a jot for anything out of their island, and did not ask one question concerning anything outside their own little rock. The Captain gave the party which came out the first day a good supper and plenty of valuable presents, and everybody made up a parcel of clothes or some little oddments. They said what they most wanted was nails, as the wind had lately blown down their houses. They have fifty head of cattle and a hundred sheep; a little corn, twelve acres of potatoes, plenty of apples and pears, and I was curious to know whether old Corporal Glass, the 'Governor', was truly master, and whether the others minded him; but he said no one was master; that the men never quarrel, but the women do; that they have no laws nor rules, and are all very happy together; and that no one ever interferes with another.*
>
> *Old Glass does a great deal of extra work; he is schoolmaster to the children, and says many of his scholars can read the Bible 'quite pretty'. He is also chaplain, — buries and christens, and reads the service every Sunday, 'all according to the Church of England, Sir'. They had only Blair's Sermons, which they have read every Sunday for the last ten years, ever since they have possessed them; but he said, very innocently, 'We do not understand them yet: I suppose they are too good for us. Yet our faith is our strength'. Of course they were well supplied with books before they left us.*

They make all their own clothes out of canvas given them by the passing whalers; they sew them with twine, and they looked very respectable: but they said it was not so easy to dress the ladies, and they were exceedingly glad of any old clothes we could rummage out for them. Their shoes are made of seal-skin: they put their feet into the skin while it is moist, and let it dry to the shape of the foot, and it turns out a very tidy shoe.

At this, Kezia declared that she would like to visit with them if the sea permitted next day, which it did, though I confess I was fearful that it might suddenly change and we would be left marooned. I was much moved by her intrepidity, and also her generosity, for she gathered all the clothes she might, silks and all, to take to the ladies of the island, saying she could find more at the Cape and Madras and was sorry for several things she had left behind in England which would have been treasures to Mrs. Glass, especially worsted for knitting.

She is so wholly restored that I cannot begin to say how delightful is this passage . . .

They weighed anchor sharp the following morning. *Pyramus* gave the 'Governor' a salute of one gun and two rockets, which he returned by bonfire on the shore, and then beat north-east into the freshening trade.

It was indeed a good time to be making the passage, for the south-west monsoon blew from October to April, which they'd now be able to pick up soon after the Cape. After Madeira they'd run fast south to seaward of the Cape Verdes, then west almost to the coast of Brazil to get the south-east trades on the beam and pick up the westerlies. Indiamen put in at Saint Helena homebound, said Captain Harewood, but rarely on the passage out; and Tristan the same. With these winds, he reckoned, a fortnight should see them in Table Bay.

He reckoned accurately, too – and welcome it was. The winds had been fair, and *Pyramus* had run a hundred and fifty miles a day with sail to spare. The seas had been unfriendly, however – a constant rolling, day and night. Table Bay had come none too soon.

Hervey met old friends again, not least Colonel Harry Smith (and his wife), who told him there'd be more trouble with the Xhosa ere long, which made him envious, for the Cape colony was a fine place for campaigning. Hervey and Kezia hired horses each day and rode quite alone. The country was not so pretty as Madeira, perhaps, but they went by way of some fine views, as he best remembered, and Kezia was charmed by the white sand covered with flowers, which she said were those of the English hothouse, growing wild. They went to the English church on the Sunday, and then to the Cloete estates, where Kezia played a little. The following day they rode on Table Mountain, and in an hour more would have made the top had not the 'Table-cloth' descended. Hervey had then taken Kezia's reins to pick their way back, until they cleared the mist and, once more into the sunshine, they made a picnic by a stream.

And as they returned to their quarters in the Castle of Good Hope – such a heartening name – he was half-minded to cast aside all ambition and obligation and stay in this place, build a house, sow 'English hothouse' flowers; and plant cabbages.

In two days more, however, duty called him back to the *Pyramus*, and he turned his face to the east – yet this time with a wife at his side. As the tug steamed clear of Green Point and the wind began to fill the mains'l, Kezia slipped an arm through his. 'To a Calm Sea, and a Prosperous Voyage,' she whispered, leaning her head on his shoulder.

But as Hervey had supposed, a truly prosperous voyage could not come of a calm sea. The run to Madras was certainly prosperous – a succession of gales, often contrary, and a chopping sea pitching and tossing all aboard every which way. And Captain Harewood, whenever asked what prospect of change, would simply answer, 'There seems a fresh hand at the bellows.' But there were sudden calms too, when least expected, so that the captain concluded there'd been a hurricane somewhere which had 'upset all the winds'. Several of the passengers grew tired of one another and squabbled a little for amusement, as the captain said was always the case after rounding the Cape. Not, of course, that sea and weather discomposed the advance party of the 6th Light Dragoons, although Corporal Johnson sailed close to the wind one morning with an ensign of the Company's army whom he thought was getting above himself; and Serjeant Acton almost came to blows with one of the mates who objected to his practice with the sabre; and Allegra's govern-ess spoke her mind to some ladies who'd joined at the Cape and made disapproving remarks about her calisthenic exercises (they were poor specimens of their sex, she told them).

Two months was indeed a long time in a chopping sea. At the Cape, Hervey had wished they'd been bound for Fort William, for it was the northern presidency that had so beguiled him, but not long out he'd been glad to think their ordeal would end at Fort St George. In the event, however, once they'd broached the Bay of Bengal, the wind came offshore and they were able to beat up the coast of Coromandel so close that the scent of the land ran with them, part dust, part spice, and all tranquillity – Paradise, whether lost or regained . . .

> As when to them who sail
> Beyond the Cape of Hope, and now are past
> Mozambic, off at sea north-east winds blow
> Sabean odours from the spicey shore
> Of Araby the blest, with such delay
> Well pleased they slack their course, and many a league
> Cheered with the grateful smell old Ocean smiles.

And then came the best of days for landing – no surf to speak of. In England he'd several times bathed in a worse sea, and now thought his warning earlier to Kezia had been ill-judged, although how they would get ashore the Broadwood did not bear thinking.

That the Madras surf should as a rule be so formidable was curious. He'd seen Masoolah boats here as nearly as possible upset by waves that looked nothing – as the time when Jessye had seemed to falter, and he'd slipped from the boat to swim alongside her (at Corunna he'd seen strong horses drown in their panic). She'd settled at once, but he was not as fast through the water, and so a little abashed he'd had to grab hold of her mane. Once settled to the rhythm, though, they'd both enjoyed it – more, for sure, than the times they'd swum the half-frozen rivers of Spain – and in no time were amid the breakers, where Jessye had found her footing and he'd been able to get astride, and on to the strand to the acclamation of natives and sahibs alike.

Fifteen years – more – it had been. Kezia smiled; she wished he were bringing his charger now, to swim ashore as colonel of the coming regiment, for there was, she said, nothing he could not do.

And Hervey smiled too, for with Kezia's arm in his there was nothing he mightn't hazard. He pointed out the great fort of St George, where Robert Clive had begun his service, a beginning that had taken him to Plassey and immortality. Its massive walls enclosed buildings of such grace and proportion, he said, that Wren himself might have been here (the spire of St Mary's Church, standing proud of the fort, looked like any in the square mile of the City of London). And soon they could make out the *palazzos* along the shore, colonnaded, perfectly white, bespeaking a dignified wealth, a confident power – a mile and more of them. How strange he recalled it that first time: he'd expected a more 'native' picture – the jungle encroaching; domes and towers; 'Cholamandalam' – the realm of the ancient Cholas, which the Portuguese had turned into the dreamlike *Coromandel*. But this wasn't native India; this was John Company's India – the best of all possible worlds.

The coast of Coromandel was indeed highly favoured, for it lay in the shadow of the Western Ghats, the hills – mountains – which from January to October barred the south-west monsoons, so that far less rain fell here than in the rest of India, though in October, when for three months the monsoons came from the east, there were fearful hurricanes. Then, he said, it would be best to take a house in the interior.

Yet that would depend upon the Rajah of Coorg . . .

Coromandel! What a scene was the Madras Roads: Indiamen, boats of every size and shape, catamarans – three logs lashed together each morning, untied and left to dry when they came in again at evening – with crouching crew (three, two or sometimes just one), paddles digging at the water. Kezia was enchanted; as was Allegra too.

Then the big Masoolah boats were alongside – shallow draught, a dozen boatmen all singing a queer kind of howl to keep time with the oars, half naked. First Allegra and then Kezia edged cautiously along the gangplank, and into Hervey's arms. Kezia hesitated only momentarily, for she stepped not just for herself.

How did she know it; by what annunciation? If only the good Dr Milne had been with them, for the *Pyramus*'s 'experienced surgeon' had not looked a man much practised in such matters. But she knew. She knew because it had been thus with Allegra; it was not the 'chopping sea' that made her sick each morning, or the change of air that made the months pass without curse.

And she knew in her heart the moment of the passionate conception.

* * *

'BLOWN TO KINGDOM come, they were, Colonel – or to wherever it is these 'eathens go. I never saw anything its like. Nothing left of the four of 'em but scraps for the vultures 'n' jackals.'

The riding-master recounted the proceedings perfectly dispassionately, neither approving nor disapproving, merely in awe of the Company's powers of summary justice. Hanging – or, exceptionally, where the exigencies of a campaign required, a firing party – was the usual means of execution. But here the Mughals had begun the practice of fastening a condemned man to the muzzle of a cannon so as to strike holy fear into an adversary, for to be blown apart was to be denied the necessary funeral rites, and thus for believers – Hindoo and Mohammedan alike – the punishment extended beyond death.

'Heads flying straight in the air, arms left and right . . . and legs – what were left of 'em – just falling where they'd stood; and everything else just blown away altogether, not a vestige to be seen.'

'Yes, RM, I saw it once in Bengal. An unwholesome sight,' said Hervey, running his hands along the flank of yet another rough, trying to take in the measure of the remount party's work in the two months it had been here – and not greatly inclined to hear the riding-master's account of explosive dismemberment.

'And not a murmur in the ranks. They took it like good soldiers; I'll say that for 'em, Colonel. Mind, there were guns trained on 'em too, and the Thirteenth were ranked behind with their sabres drawn. Fine thing of a Christmas Eve.'

'I'm sure.' Hervey was trying hard to be congenial. Kewley had come to the Sixth full of the gospel of St John's Wood and delight in his new commission after twenty years in the ranks of the 7th Hussars. The Seventh stood only next in seniority in the line, but they might as well have been double-figured foot for the way they did things, and Kewley had yet to get the measure of his new regiment. He was able, of that there was no doubt, but not a man given to contemplation.

'How did you *find* the Thirteenth – their horses? All Deccanis?'

'Almost all of them, Colonel. Grand little things, but you'll know that.'

Indeed he did. The Maharattas' cavalry had out-marched the Company's many a time in the late wars – sixty miles in a day for weeks, even months, on end – and their horses had impressed him at Chintal. Since then, he'd learned, the Nizam had brought hundreds of Arabians to put to his native Deccan stock, so that now a Deccani re-mount had all the good points of the Arab – fine limbs, broad forehead, and docility – but without its thin skin, or its irritability when roughly handled (and the feet were generally better too). Besides endurance they also had a turn of speed: the commissary at Fort St George had told him a Deccani at the Guindy course had recently won over a straight half-mile in just 58 seconds – and that it would jump four feet carrying the same ten stone.

'Well, you did service by getting fifty of them, and I look forward to seeing them. But these Australians – New South Walers you call them? – they're truly admirable. I'd no notion. What a prodigious journey to make.'

The veterinary surgeon appeared, looking anxious. 'I beg pardon, Colonel. I only just got word you were in the lines. One of the governor's mares is foaling and—'

Hervey returned the awkward salute and smiled encouragingly. 'No need of explanation, Mr Gaskoin. A foaling mare takes precedence.'

It had taken some time to warm to the veterinarian, whose manners and appearance were not those of a gentleman, though this was only to be expected, for the occupation was not one that commended itself to a gentleman; except that of late years the Sixth had been fortunate in having men who had acquired the attributes (and even, at times, the appearance) of gentlemen. Thomas Gaskoin, on the other hand, had the air of the ostler's yard, or the corn-market, and looked more like an old-fashioned farrier than a modern practitioner of the 'science' imparted at the college in Camden. Yet Gaskoin had gained high marks there, and in all practical respects was as good a veterinarian as those who'd gone before. In some ways, indeed, he was in advance of their thinking. It was rather that he'd been slow to comprehend the practice – the prejudice – of the regiment. And yet, he'd been one of the first to declare for India – and Hervey was conscious of it.

'I was saying that these New South Walers are truly admirable.'

'Truly admirable, Colonel, yes. The cavalry board here wouldn't take those the Bengal studs were sending them, so they looked south instead. The trouble is, as I understand it – begging your leave, Colonel – horses bred here are small under the knee and deficient of bone and substance.'

'I don't doubt it, Mr Gaskoin, though the Marwari's a fine animal. Some defect in the breeding regimen perhaps?'

'Colonel Watercain's of the mind that it's vain to suppose an English blood can be reared in India – not one of equal bone and sinew as at home, that is. Or go well in crosses. There aren't the nutritious grasses. You can't grow lucerne in these climes. So any stud'll see a deterioration.'

'Indeed?' Hervey hadn't known the Veterinary Surgeon-General's opinion on the matter.

'Ah, I should say, Colonel, that I took the liberty of going to see him before we left.'

'Most commendable, Mr Gaskoin.' It was indeed. He just wished he could find Gaskoin more to his liking, for there was daily evidence of his attentiveness.

'Thank you, Colonel. Colonel Watercain gave it as his opinion that horses should be entire and at least half-bred, and up to seventeen stone, though I myself thought fifteen was enough for our dragoons, not being big men, and riding light as you have them.'

'Generally so, yes.'

'But these Australians all ride bigger than they look. They'll certainly carry seventeen. They're all four- to seven-year-olds, shipped last summer, and all broken, though the RM's men have still got work to do.'

'I don't doubt it, but they are indeed uncommon fine looking. Three hundred, you say?'

'Aye, Colonel – and ten to be precise. Six hundred rupees a head.'

'Admirable. Three months – once they're here – and the regiment'll be ready for the field. If the saddler and farriers look sharp, that is. I congratulate you, Mr Gaskoin, and you, RM – for both the Deccanis and these. The commissary told me you insisted on trying every one of the five hundred at the depot.'

It was their job to, but a job well done nevertheless (and the Duke of Wellington had once said he should himself have given more praise . . .).

'Colonel,' they replied, almost in unison.

'Very well. I'll take a turn out tomorrow. Carry on.'

They saluted sharply as he strode away.

'Well, Fred,' said Gaskoin when Hervey turned the corner of the horse lines, 'I fancy the colonel's rightly content. Not a fault found.'

The RM took his hat off and wiped his brow. 'They says it's India and the prospect of action that's cheered 'im so.'

'Aye, that it must be.'

XV

Words of Advice

Earlier

'THA SEES, ANNIE M'LASS, THERE are good snakes 'n' bad snakes. And the good'ns, when they bite thee, kill thee quick, and the bad'ns take days. One of 'em, what they call a Braminee cobra, it's so good it'll kill thee in a few hours.'

Annie looked increasingly uncomfortable. She'd seen adders on the heath at Hounslow, but they weren't a bother. These Indian snakes by all accounts (but principally Corporal Johnson's) were altogether different – evil things; cunning and spiteful. She'd searched her bedroom top to bottom that first night, fearful of what Johnson had told her, and slept fitfully under the mosquito net, though it wasn't the season for too much annoyance from that biting tribe – just hoping it would keep out anything 'slithersome' that might take a fancy to sharing her bed. Then when she'd got up that morning, when the dressing-boy brought her tea she had him beat about the room, for Johnson had told her that snakes couldn't abide noise, except for a flute, which he couldn't understand, because Indian flutes always made a terrible racket.

'What tha's got to do, Annie, is get a mongoose. They knows 'ow to catch snakes – well, 'ow to kill 'em. They don't 'alf go for 'em – back o' their necks, quick as owt tha's ever seen. I 'ad one when we were 'ere before. Well, I 'ad two, but t'first were frightened, so I got rid of it.'

He had indeed, and at a loss, which vexed him still – and the more so because, as Hervey then pointed out, a mongoose that was frightened of snakes was surely such a curiosity as to have commanded a high price among the snake-charmers. They were always keen to add novelty to their displays.

'But they're not as friendly as ferrets. Ferrets are better company.'

Annie was now confused; did she want a companion or a bodyguard? 'Mrs Hervey says that we shall be quite safe here in this house because of all the steps up to it, and that the chowkidar and the snake-catcher will be outside all the time.'

This put Johnson on the spot somewhat, for he didn't want to contradict the wife of the commanding officer, because that was like contradicting the commanding officer himself. Well, worse really, because you could always have your say with the commanding officer, if it was 'with respect, Colonel', but you couldn't really with the commanding officer's wife – or lady, as he was meant to say; and he was getting on so well with Mrs Hervey these days; she actually seemed to like him, whereas before, it always seemed as if she didn't. And this house they were in – the commanding officer's residence – a palace, really, wasn't like the sort they'd had in Bengal. It was all marble and fine things . . .

'Well, Annie, Mrs 'Ervey's right – course she is – she's been in India before an' all – but . . . What I mean is, what if one gets in when t'chowkidar's not looking – at night, say? It's just that it'd be better to be on t'safe side.'

Annie said she'd think about it, and perhaps ask Serjeant and Mrs Stray what they were going to do. 'Mr St Alban came this morning and said he'd seen six elephants already.'

'Oh, aye, tha'll see lots o' elephants, Annie. Best to go down t'river of an evenin' an' see 'em washing.'

'Mr St Alban said he'd arrange for me to have a ride on one.'

'Did 'e? 'E's a good man, Mr St Alban. 'E must've taken a fancy to thee, Annie.'

She blushed.

'But 'e's a good man, Mr St Alban. Colonel 'Ervey were right worried 'e'd not want to come to India, and'd go to another regiment instead. And Captain Worsley 'n' all – Colonel 'Ervey didn't think 'e'd want to come because 'e was just married, and Mrs Worsley wouldn't want to come, but Captain Worsley said 'e'd no more want to give up 'is troop just because they were going a long way away than 'e would if they were in a battle. Colonel 'Ervey liked that. An' Mrs Worsley – 'er people are right rich, th'knows – she said she 'adn't expected to marry an officer to take 'im from 'is duty. An' Colonel 'Ervey 'ad really liked that, especially cos it meant that Mrs 'Ervey'd 'ave somebody to talk to.'

'Mrs Hervey's very nice to talk to,' said Annie, wondering if she too would find someone to talk to – someone like her, for she couldn't expect Mrs Hervey to talk to her much, not when she was a servant.

Johnson nodded. 'An' it's not just Captain Worsley, but Captain Vanneck an' Malet an' all. There were only a few who didn't want to come, an' Colonel 'Ervey didn't think much o' them anyway and . . .' He checked himself, realizing he was going too far with his confidences, even with Annie, who was like his little sister – except that he didn't have a little sister; not one that he knew about at any rate. 'Th'knows, Annie, t'only one 'e were really worried about were t'serjeant-major. 'E didn't think 'e'd be able to come because of 'is children, an' them o' 'is wife. But Mr Collins – 'e's t'quartermaster, what's in charge o' all t'bed spaces, 'n' t'rations 'n' such like – well 'e's got t'serjeant-major a right good 'ouse wi' lots o' rooms. An' Colonel 'Ervey says that on 'is pay 'n' allowances 'ere 'e'll be able to 'ave plenty o' people to look after 'em.'

'That's good,' said Annie. She'd only seen the serjeant-major a few times, and only once to speak to, but she thought he was a good man, and deserved to be looked after properly after everything that had happened to him.

Johnson thought he'd said enough now, and that he'd better bring the conversation back to something less perilous. 'So, th'sees, Annie m'lass, th'can't be too careful wi' snakes.'

She nodded decidedly. However, she'd read a whole book about India during the passage, which she'd bought from her savings just before they sailed, but it said nothing at all about snakes. 'I'm going to ask Serjeant and Mrs Stray about them this very afternoon, Johnno.'

She really liked Serjeant Stray. She'd liked Serjeant James, too, but he could be a bit fierce. And she liked Mrs Stray just as much as Mrs James. It was funny that they hadn't wanted to come to India, but Serjeant James was a bit older than Mick (Serjeant Stray said she was to call him that whenever there wasn't anyone looking, but she didn't think she'd be able to), and he wanted to stay in Hounslow and keep a public house. But Serjeant Stray knew what he was about, right enough – and he'd only been a corporal six months ago. And Mrs Stray – well, she knew what she was about right enough too. They'd only been here a day, and already the servants were running round as if their lives depended on it (which, in a way, she supposed they did). Mrs Stray had never been to India before, but she knew exactly how to talk to them. She, on the other hand, had confused her poor ayah the first time she'd bid her do something (Yes: she, a servant, had her own servant, a very elegant lady in white muslin, and twice her age!): 'Ayah, bring me a glass of toast and water, if you please,' and the poor woman had crept to the door, and then come back again, looking anxious and confused, and begged, 'What mistress tell? I don't know,' and she'd replied, 'I said to bring me some toast and water, if you please, ayah.' 'Toast, water, I know very well, but mistress, tell "if you please"; I don't know "if you please".'

'You know, Johnno, I don't believe anyone has ever said "please" to her before. Isn't that shameful?'

Johnson nodded slowly. 'Annie, m'lass, the 'Indoos treat each other like muck, because it's their religion, because they all say that when they die they'll come back better off and can treat them as 'ave been bad to 'em in t'same way, so it doesn't matter to 'em.'

'But *we* shouldn't treat them like that, Johnno. I couldn't go to church of a Sunday if I treated them like that.'

Johnson felt a little chastened. 'No, I'm not saying we should, but th'doesn't 'ave to worry about what words th'uses so much. They'll know if th'doesn't think they're muck by t'tone o' thi' voice, an' if th'smiles. I 'ad some right good pals afore – syces, bhistis, all sorts. They knows when th'doesn't think tha's too much above 'em. An' they'll all know that soon wi' thee, Annie m'lass, because tha's as honest as ever there was.'

Annie lowered her eyes. 'Thank you, Johnno. I hope so.'

'Well then, p'rhaps we can get one o' these 'eathens to make us some more tea. There's nowt for me to do now for an hour or so, an' I'm going to take m'leisure 'ere.' For the servants' hall in the Hervey 'palace' was the best place he'd seen in many a year. *'Koi hai!'*

But he had to go and find the khitmagar for himself. It would take a day or so for him to discover – remember – that in Madras the language of the 'Indoo was Tamul, not what he'd learned in Bengal (Tamul and a lot of others as well, so that some couldn't speak to each other except with their hands, or in English – or in the strange words that the English used in Bengal. Which was sometimes useful, to pretend no understanding at all).

* * *

'Hervey!'

The voice ever boomed, but in the great entrance of Government House it was *fortissimo*. Sowars of the Bodyguard and ancient bearers alike stood frozen at attention.

Hervey stood hatless in his tropicals – blue jacket (the King had granted a grace period), crossbelt, sword, and white trousers strapped under the boot – and returned the salutation with a click of his spurs.

'Welcome, welcome!'

Somervile advanced with a broad smile and hand held out.

Hervey returned the smile, and with regard. His old friend had not reduced quite as much as Serjeant Stray, but his return to condition was marked nonetheless. The tropics ever suited him.

'How is Kezia? The passage not too tiring, I trust.'

'She is very well, thank you. The surgeon prescribed warm climes and sea air, and that is what we've had these past four months, save for the odd bit of weather. I believe she is quite restored.'

'Capital!'

'And Emma?'

'You must have passed her on the road, for she's gone to pay her first call on the station's new lady.'

'Ah, that will be most welcome.'

'We returned from Mysore late last night, else the carriage would have been sent for you to dine – as it will this evening. But come: there's much to talk about and I would have your opinion on Bangalore. I shrink from the word "mutiny", but mutiny it was.'

'I had account of its aftermath – the executions – from my riding-master.'

'Dreadful, dreadful. But cruel necessity.'

They went to Somervile's study, a high, airy room, facing north so that the governor could work at his papers without excessive intrusion of the sun. A huge punkah hung motionless, for although the thermometer stood at eighty-two, there was a light breeze off the sea, and the Guindy hills stood just high enough to catch it. Besides, eighty-two was not a temperature to trouble Somervile. It was not until ninety-five that he would consider removing his coat while at his desk; and at seventy he would have a fire in the grate. After months at sea, however, Hervey found his worsted a trifle hot, and looked forward to the visit of the tailor to knock up something in lighter twill for next morning (Collins said he'd engaged a contractor to make four hundred red cotton-duck jackets, and the same of white).

'*Nimbu pani?*'

'*Shukriya.*' He took the glass. 'I suppose, though, I should say "*Amaam, tandri*" instead.'

'"*Tandri*" is enough. But they all know bazaar lingua.'

'We tried to hire a munshee at the Cape, but none would come. They seemed to prefer the climate there.' He took a good sip of his lemon water, and nodded. 'I'd quite forgotten the delight of this.'

'So had I. I tell you, I'm uncommonly glad to be back here; Emma too.' He motioned to a chair. 'But now, Bangalore. It seems the plan was to strike at midnight – on the 28th – and to that very morning there were no suspicions whatever. The mutineers were all followers of the Prophet, and it appears that if this . . .' (he waved his hand, trying to find words of sufficient disdain) '*coup de théâtre* had been success-ful, others would have followed at half a dozen places – Hyderabad and Nagpore especially – and doubtless thereafter spread far and wide. However, that morning a jemadar of the Forty-eighth – the native infantry, that is – went to the major and told all. Inglis, the major, at once alerted the Dragoons, and the Sixty-second, and they rounded up the conspirators.'

Hervey nodded appreciatively.

'The instigator was a grandee, however, which makes the whole affair rather more serious than military mutiny – serious though that indeed is. It was evidently a plot against our whole administration in Mysore. The great panjandrum, it appears, had enlisted a host of discharged sepoys and Pindaris, and these lay ready to join when the signal was given, when the *gora log* were murdered in their beds, and he'd then proclaim himself Nawaub of Bangalore.' He shook his head despair-ingly. 'Really, the arrant conceit of these rascals!'

Hervey simply raised an eyebrow.

'Now, all that's been very efficiently dealt with, but it was also learned that the Rajah of Coorg's *vakeel* in Mysore had promised twelve thousand horse and seven of foot to be at Bangalore once he received word the mutiny had taken place. A great exaggeration of his strength, but . . .'

He stopped to take another long measure of his lemon water, and then waved a hand dismissively.

'All the details are in the report of the board of inquiry. I'll give you a copy. Suffice it to say that, by luck, the native artillery had left the city a day or so before for their practice ground, and so the two King's regiments were able to scotch the *coup* before it began. The ring-leaders we blew from the guns, as you know, and shot a good few, but I commuted many more to transportation. The whole affair's quite extraordinary. The sepoys had no grievance of any kind. Some of them had been years in the service – one of them nineteen – and several with fathers who'd died honourably in action. Now, you see what my next step must be?'

Hervey put down his glass. 'I imagine to arrest – or at least depose – the Rajah of Coorg. It seemed to me at our dinner in London you were of a mind to do that anyway.'

Somervile nodded. 'But in all truth, until this business I hadn't settled on it – until I was certain for myself. I'd hoped we might, as it were, *contain* this wretched fellow's excesses until Nature took its course. But as he's plotted against the Company – and the nabobs will know it, you may be sure – he'll now pay the price. It's not, of course, my decision alone to take. I shall have to submit to Fort William, but I'm sure Bentinck will see it as I do. He was first in Madras, after all.'

'And was recalled after the Vellore mutiny, was he not?'

'That is true. But he was young and knew nothing of India – or, for that matter, of Indians.'

Hervey smiled. 'The two are not the same?'

'Of course they're not the same.'

Hervey conceded. When first they'd met, Somervile had been Deputy Commissioner of Kistna and Collector of Guntoor district in the Northern Circars. There was no employee of the Honourable East India Company more respected by Indians of all classes than he; or indeed by the directors. Everyone said so. And yet no permanent governorship had been bestowed on him, for Somervile lacked political capital. It were better to be the son of a former prime minister and in possession of a courtesy title – as Bentinck in Calcutta – than to know the country, the languages and the ways of its people as well as did his old friend.

To Hervey's mind, Lord William Cavendish Bentinck hadn't been much of a soldier either. As a major-general, he'd failed in Madras, and then again in Italy in the higher rank. He'd made himself prominent, however, as member for King's Lynn in the Whig interest, and four years ago the Court of Directors in Leadenhall Street had suddenly imagined him useful. Anxious over renewal of the charter (due this very year), they'd appointed him to Bengal with instructions to put the Company's operations into profit, thereby to impress the government. And it was certainly the case that he was a reforming governor, but economies were unpopular with the Company's army, and it was not the best of times perhaps to be contemplating another campaign.

Then there was the question of Somervile's own tenure at Fort St George – a year, perhaps; two at most? Hervey raised his eyebrows conspiratorially. 'I fancy, in the circumstances, that you're in something of a hurry?'

Somervile was always in a hurry. That, he would freely admit. 'I could not allow the matter to rest until a successor's appointed. The word is, by the way, that it'll be Adam, once he's settled affairs in the Ionians. Not only would it be indecently unjust to him, there's no knowing the trouble this rajah will cause, not just in Mysore but further afield. John Clare at Bombay's in agreement too. Besides, it's why Leadenhall Street opened the coffers to send two more regiments here.'

'John Clare?'

'The Earl of Clare.'

'I confess I'd not given Bombay any consideration. I'd thought it was Malcolm still. Clare in Suffolk, or in Ireland?'

'Ireland. Is it of any moment?'

'Not in the least, I suppose, but I thought it better to know than not. I never heard of him.'

'Nor I, in truth, before he got Bombay. He was obliging in parliament of late.'

Hervey sighed.

'But that's of no concern to the present. We have to eject this usurping rajah, and as soon as may be – which, I'm assured, will be greeted with some relief in Coorg itself. A vile and loathsome creature he's become.'

Hervey put down his glass, looking as if something troubled him. 'You've said nothing of General O'Callaghan.'

Old friends that they were, the military proprieties must nevertheless be observed. There was a commander-in-chief at Fort St George – Lieutenant-General the Honourable Sir William O'Callaghan KCB – and the removal of the Rajah of Coorg by military means was first and foremost his business. He himself had yet to report to him, for the general was in the Northern Circars on a tour of inspection.

'No-o . . . But it can't be long before his return.' Somervile's look suggested that it wasn't his first consideration.

'Do you imply there's something you would have me do in the meantime?'

Somervile looked puzzled. 'Had I not made it plain? I shall wish you to command the field force when active operations begin.'

'No, you'd not made it in the least plain! But I'm all anticipation.'

Indeed he was. (Afterwards Somervile would tell his wife that their old friend had leapt like a hare sprung late from its form.)

'There'll be "difficulties" of course,' he added. 'I mean, it won't serve if there's a challenge to my seniority. The Company's officers don't count in that regard, as you well know, but how do things stand with the King's? It's just possible that one of them may have a brevet senior to mine. And there's a major-general at Bangalore, is there not?'

It was a troublesome regulation at times that a King's officer took seniority over one of the Company's no matter what the latter's rank, but in practice things were often as not sensibly arranged. A day's seniority between King's officers was, however, another business entirely. And when it came to generals . . .

'There is indeed a major-general at Bangalore, but I can't have him leave on an expedition to Coorg. It would only risk inviting trouble in Mysore again. As to seniority, I'll have the Fort look into it, but I have the authority to promote you brigadier-general for the duration.'

Hervey nodded. That would indeed address the proprieties – the 'niceties' as he sometimes thought them. 'Very well. Seems set fair. I should just say, however, on a point of strict military detail, I would be *appointed* brigadier-general, not promoted, since it isn't a substantive rank. That said,' he added, smiling, 'it will bring resentment enough.'

Somervile smiled too. He had a high regard for the profession of arms – indeed, Hervey always considered him a soldier manqué – but he did enjoy on occasions offending against King's Regulations. 'Mind, things proceed slowly in this country, as well you know, but then go off like a petard. Our advantage, at present at least, is that the rajah doesn't know that we know of his part in the plot at Bangalore. There's no reason to suppose therefore that he suspects our intention to remove him. That said, there's no possibility, to my mind, of having it done before the winter. That much I've learned already from Bentinck's people. Strictly speaking, I don't need his authority, since it's the business of Madras only, but as he's *primus inter pares*, it's only prudent therefore. It'd certainly be imprudent to begin any movement of troops in anticipation. When we make a beginning it must be as near to the end as may be, and therefore we must know when exactly is the beginning.'

It was not the way a soldier would have put it, but Hervey nodded. 'So we make ready for the spring.'

Somervile shook his head doubtfully. 'The monsoon in Coorg blows June to September. Even if Bentinck signals his intention soon, it seems to me unlikely you'd be able to have the business done before then – and the rain in June's especially heavy. If you were to assemble your force in October, therefore, you'd be able then to enter Coorg at the best time. The thermometer never falls below fifty-five even in December there. So even if this rajah eluded you to begin with, there'd be five months to hunt him out and quieten the place before the rains returned.'

Hervey nodded again. 'If he took to the forest we'd certainly need them.'

'I doubt by all accounts he's a likely *guerrillero*, but I agree you can't proceed on that as a supposition. The Coorgs are a warlike people, and if somehow he manages to rouse them . . . We must think how best to tempt him to give up the fight. What I wish you to do in the coming weeks is consider everything there is to consider and present me with a scheme of campaign that I can submit to Bentinck. He's more likely to agree if I can show it would be done expeditiously. You'll find the Fort has a good account of the place.'

'I'll begin as soon as may be. But in any plan of campaign it's best to make a reconnaissance first. I fancy you'll say it could not serve in this case.'

Somevile nodded gravely. 'I had thought it what you'd say, and I believe there may be opportunity. But I'll speak of it at dinner this evening if you're still so minded. Think on it first a little. Speak to the staff at the Fort if you wish – they work again from four at this season – but for now, let me not detain you. I know you've much to be about, and we can talk long this evening. When is it you expect the first of the regiment?'

'Within the month. Steamers to the Cape, and then on by whatever ships the Company have there.'

XVI

The Break of Day

Next morning

H ERVEY'S BEARER (HE DIDN'T MUCH like 'dressing-boy', as they called them in Madras) brought him tea at five-thirty under Corporal Johnson's close supervision. (Johnson thought it would be a week at least before he could trust him to do it right, though in fact the little Tamul – he was not much taller than Georgiana, reckoned Hervey – made exemplary tea and brought it with military promptness, and so would be entrusted with the sacred mission after only three days.) Then came hot water five minutes later, as Johnson had instructed, and at two minutes to six Hervey was shaved, booted and spurred – and outside on the hour exactly to take the reins of his new charger.

Minnie (her stable name; she was entered as Minenhle – in the language of the Zulu 'beautiful day') was a liver chestnut, three-quarter-bred at the Cape and brought to Madras as a three-year-old, turned away for eighteen months and then broken for one of the captains of the horse artillery. She was rising eight now and her owner was returning to England. Lieutenant (RM) Kewley had bagged her, and hoped his commanding officer would approve, though if not he was certain he could sell her on – and at a profit. Horses with plenty of blood were by no means common in the presidency.

At Hounslow, Hervey had begun to take his first exercise of the day alone. Though he was hardly obliged to converse with anyone, he felt freer to observe whatever took his fancy, and above all to think. At least to begin with, he'd decided he would make it his practice here too.

And glad he was to be doing so, for the sun was not long up, and the air still fresh. Later, the native quarter would reek of ditches and frying oil – or else the foulest ordure of God's Creation. For now, though, smoke was beginning to rise as the first fires of the day boiled up a little rice or whatever for the morning's labour, but no one abroad yet except for the odd bhisti, and here and there a dog standing contemplating. It was a good time to be thinking.

Dinner had indeed given him much to think on. They'd returned late and he'd sat with Kezia until her maid came, and then read the piece in *The Asiatic Journal* which Somervile had pressed on him. It was a masterly summary of recent history, and a necessary one, for although he'd read what he could on the passage out, it had tended to Bengal and the troublesome frontiers. He'd not quite realized the extent of the Company's advance of late beyond the Carnatic. He knew that after the defeat of the famous 'Tiger of Mysore' at Seringapatam – whose death, some thirty years ago, the young Arthur Wellesley had witnessed – a part of Tippoo's kingdom was seized and divided between the Company and the Nizam, and the remaining territory reduced to a princely state. He knew also that on the throne of this new polity the Company had placed the five-year-old Krishna Rajah, scion of the Wodeyar dynasty that had ruled Mysore before Hyder Ali's usurpation. As Krishna's *diwan* – chief minister – the Company appointed the able but low-born Purnaiah, who'd served both Tippoo and his father; and as resident, Fort St George had sent Colonel Barry Close, who had served long years in the presidency and was much admired for his humanity and good sense.

While Purnaiah ran Mysore's internal affairs, Close had charge of its external dealings, and the Company exacted an annual tribute and a subsidy for its standing force. On Krishna's sixteenth birthday in 1811, however, Purnaiah ceased being *diwan*, and died shortly afterwards – as did Barry Close, newly promoted to major-general. The cordial relations that Purnaiah and Close had forged between Mysore and Fort St George continued at first, but began to sour a dozen or so years later when the new resident alleged that the administration was corrupt. The then governor at Fort St George, General Thomas Munro, investigated the allegations and declared there was no substance to them; but the damage had been done, and the Company's influence began to wane. Krishna's government, however, corrupt or not, soon began to excite unrest, and in 1830 there was a revolt by the Nagar ryots. For the good of the health of Mysore and beyond, said the *Asiatic Journal*, the Company was obliged to take direct control of domestic administration as well as external affairs.

And this fragile but necessary annexation, Hervey now understood, was what lay behind the mutiny at Bangalore. The Rajah of Coorg must know that he tempted the same fate, therefore – and more – by giving succour to the insurgents?

An hour he rode out – more than enough to see how the cantonment began its day, but, more important, to think over Somervile's proposition to spy out the land of the Coorgs while waiting for the regiment to arrive. For although it was an idea that appealed to every military instinct, it did not appeal to his duty of command. The very reason he was here in advance was to make ready for the exercise of that command.

Except that all the material aspects of the regiment's reception seemed thoroughly well in hand. The admirable Collins had shown himself the best quartermaster since Moses, and the veterinarian and the RM that they were scarcely less exemplary practitioners of their trade. He supposed he might rely on his new major, who, after all, had command of the regiment during its passage. And Armstrong – and the captains of the troops. What, indeed, should necessitate his being here when they arrived – or, for that matter, for a month and more afterwards?

He would do it. It was irregular, but he would do it – to expedite the regiment's readiness to take to the field without delay. For, as the saying went, time spent in reconnaissance was seldom wasted. Did he not, though, require the express permission of the commander-in-chief? He might claim that because the general was in the Northern Circars he had to use his own judgement in this – and it was certainly the governor's wish – but it was not impossible that he should send by hircarrah to the general and await his reply. Except that the reply might be in the negative; and then where would he be? No, he would have to place his faith in the maxim that it was far easier to acquire pardon afterwards than it was to gain permission beforehand. His only true concern, indeed, was that he would have to leave Kezia for the best part of a month.

He turned for home, giving Minnie her head.

'Mistress not good, sahib,' jabbered the ayah as he made for Kezia's room. 'Please no go in. Mistress not good.'

'Not good? How not good?'

The ayah looked anxious, but it might have been concern that she didn't make herself understood. He knew these native servants were ever in fear of a sharp word, or worse.

'Mistress . . .' She clutched at her stomach and pretended to cast up.

Hervey pushed past her, knocked and opened the door. Kezia was sitting at the window, the shutters open, with a bowl on her knee covered with a piece of towel. She looked very pale.

'Dear heart! What is it?'

He put a hand to her forehead. There was no great temperature. But Somervile had told him there was a case of cholera in the civil lines. But it couldn't be so quick – surely?

'Do you have pain in your stomach?'

She managed a smile of sorts again, and told him it was nothing, but that she would like more tea, very sweet.

It was a surprising request, for as a rule she drank it with the least bit of sugar, if any. Hervey sent the ayah for Mrs Stray.

He felt her forehead again. He was sure there was no fever. He brought her shawl from the bed, for there was a breeze off the sea, though very faint.

Annie came. 'Begging your pardon, sir – ma'am – but Mrs Stray is gone into the market.'

Hervey asked her to bring tea, and to boil the water long, and first to filter it over the charcoal, as the surgeon aboard ship had told them. Annie, looking equally anxious now, hurried away to the kitchen.

'Such an obliging girl, Annie,' said Kezia, though her voice lacked strength. 'I hope she'll find kindred spirits here.'

'I'm sure,' said Hervey, trying to manipulate one of the shutters into a position that deflected the breeze from her face. 'But I wonder why Mrs Stray should go to the bazaar when every *dokan-awe* in Fort St George will be hawking their wares at her door before the day's out.'

Kezia smiled, if weakly. 'Mrs Stray wants to see everything for herself, as she puts it – and no doubt what the Indian pays for his mangoes and such, rather than what the shopkeeper asks of her.'

She put the bowl aside, pulled the shawl closer about her shoulders and rose to look out of the window. The soft lawn clutched her tight in the breeze. Hervey swallowed hard.

Annie returned with a plate. 'Excuse me, ma'am, but I'd just made some toast, and I thought it might serve for how you're feeling.'

Kezia smiled warmly. 'Oh, Annie, that is so very good of you, but I fear I couldn't eat so much as a crumb, but please leave it by, for I'm sure I'll feel well again very soon, and it would be a help.'

Johnson came not long afterwards, but Hervey said there was nothing to do, and would he wait on him in an hour.

Then in ten minutes more, Annie returned with tea. Johnson had carried the tray to the landing for her, but didn't wish to be seen; except that Annie thanked him as she took it, which both Hervey and Kezia heard.

'Please thank Corporal Johnson for me, Matthew. I'm sorry to be such an *invalide* so soon after our coming.'

There was colour returning to her cheeks. 'Shall I leave you to . . .'

'No, please: stay and have tea with me.' She sat down again. 'Annie, I think I should like to bathe in half an hour. I'm sure I shall. Would you ask the bearers?'

'Of course, ma'am.'

When she was gone, Hervey brought a chair to the window to sit beside her, and took his cup. 'You look quite remarkably better already.'

'I feel quite remarkably better. It was tiredness, that was all.'

'I confess I had a great fear it was . . . But you know this country.'

'Yes, I do, if only a very little. But it is intensely pleasing. Indeed, I am so enlivened by it, I shall take Allegra for a drive later. How was your ride?'

Hervey, relieved beyond measure at her recovery, was now in two minds about what in the saddle had appeared to be the right course. How could he leave his wife when she was not yet acclimated, and clearly suffering the change of air?

'It was peaceful. I came to a decision also – about that which Somervile and I spoke when you withdrew last night. But now, frankly, I think it wrong.'

'Not on my account, I trust?' said Kezia, sounding faintly alarmed. She put a hand on his and smiled. 'Matthew, you mustn't let a little thing like this stand in the way of your duty. I am not ill. I'm quite certain of it. What is it you decided?'

'To make a reconnaissance of Coorg as soon as may be.'

'Then should you not?'

'How could I do so, anxious for your condition?'

She squeezed his hand. 'There's no cause to be anxious, I assure you. And if you and Eyre Somervile believe it should be done with despatch then so it should be. What is the pretext, by the way?'

Hervey looked suddenly less convinced by the pretext than he'd earlier imagined. 'The rajah pays an annual tribute of an elephant, which is due at this time, and Somervile believes this to be the perfect pretext on which to spy out the capital. The beast is supposed to be brought to Mysore, but Somervile's design is to send the rajah word that this year the Company will do him the courtesy of sending a collecting party to his palace, with the present of a sword.'

'And you shall be the collecting party.'

'Just so. But I'd first thought you might accompany me to Bangalore. The country is very pleasant by all accounts, and would take seven or eight days, and you might have waited there at the residency while I spied out Coorg.'

Kezia turned her head to the window in thought, and then back again. 'Matthew, I should like that very much – very much indeed. But . . . Oh, I had not wished to speak of it until I was properly sure.' She took both his hands. 'I am with child. I *am* sure, but I've seen no physician yet, for it's such early days and . . .'

Hervey could barely speak, and shook his head gently to hush her, to save her the effort of words when none were needed. He gazed at her through moistening eyes, kissed her with the greatest tenderness, and then again with ardour.

XVII

Deccani Wallahs

A fortnight later

WHO SHOULD GO WITH HIM, and in what order of dress? Somervile had thought twenty sowars with lances and pennants – full parade dress. Twenty would be about the number to give due dignity to the representative of 'John Company', but not so many as to disturb the rajah – there must be no misunderstanding – and a few *feringhees*: ten of Hervey's dragoons perhaps?

Ten was impossible – or at least ill-advised. The advance party still had much to do. He would have Acton of course, and Johnson, and he could take a couple of rough-riders without greatly jeopardizing the RM's carefully laid plans. Serjeant Stray had asked to go, but Hervey couldn't risk leaving the household without a head (Mrs Stray and even Annie would be perfectly capable, he knew, but it was too much to expect them to know what an old soldier like Stray had acquired). St Alban, naturally, would come with him, although his work would have to be done by Collins. Collins himself would have been his choice, despite his one arm, but Collins was indispensible to the advance party. He wished that Fairbrother were here; and it went without saying that had Armstrong been, he wouldn't have given it a second thought (the senior troop serjeant-major would have stood duty in Madras). So instead, all they would be was six dragoons and a half-troop of native lancers. He was sure it was enough. Indeed, if things went wrong, ten times the number would be to no avail.

And the dragoons would wear blue, for Hervey was uneasy still about the 'redbreast'. He'd have preferred the yellow-brown colour that the bazaar-wallahs called *kani*, and which Collins was having run up as service jackets, but *kani* wouldn't impress the rajah. They'd wear them as far as Bangalore, therefore, then change into blue – the last time, in all probability, that he'd go to war (or at least, make reconnaissance for war) in that proud colour. It had been his for twenty-five years, from the Peninsula to the Low Countries, but it was the way of things, and the new king wished his soldiers to wear red, and his sailors blue.

He dined alone with Kezia the evening before they left. It was St Agnes' Eve, a Sunday – no parades, no calls, an altogether quiet day.

Kezia was now much better of a morning, although he'd gone alone to church that day, for it would have been asking too much of her to sit at attention for an hour and a half, even in that great and beautiful place (which Somervile said would be elevated to a cathedral soon). He'd promised her, as far as he was able, that he'd return by St Valentine's, when, he said with mock despair, he'd 'be another year older'; whereupon she'd said they would therefore mark his birthday on the fourteenth, or whenever it was he came home, 'for these things are, as you are fond of saying, subject to the exigencies of the service'.

She said it with such equanimity as he'd never have imagined even six months ago.

After dinner, he read aloud the Keats, as she asked. He'd not read it before, and was at once taken by the image of winter. So many times he'd shivered in the deadness it described – in Spain and Portugal, in France, in Canada, here in places; and not least, in England.

St Agnes' Eve—Ah, bitter chill it was!
The owl, for all his feathers, was a-cold;
The hare limp'd trembling through the frozen grass,
And silent was the flock in woolly fold.

She then played for him a little – gentle Schubert, *Rosamunde* – and afterwards they went early to bed, together, and slept a little. He'd said he would sleep in his room so as not to disturb her when it was time to go, but she'd insisted. So the Tamul bearer had brought them tea before dawn, and Kezia had been all of good cheer, and even teased him with the Keats – '*Awake! arise! my love, and fearless be.*' – and rose and watched him dress.

Never had he known it so hard to begin on adventure.

They rode on unusually light scales, especially for India – just half a dozen bat-horses, bearers and syces, for he intended making Bangalore in all haste. He'd studied the new Madras Road Book which Fort St George was preparing: dak bungalows stood every dozen miles or so along the presidency's principal highway, which was measured with bewildering precision at 229 miles and 3 furlongs, and in these staging-houses they would make their nightly refuge. What hazards and vexations they would encounter in between – or while at rest, even – he took no care of. This was India, not England; nothing but the monsoon was predictable. Indeed, when first they'd met, in the wake of the French wars, Somervile had said that in India one must expect the unexpected. And Hervey had found it sound advice – as well as the very delight of the country.

In the event, however, the country proved both easy and fine, and the heat merely warming rather than oppressive, especially after Chittoor and into the hills. The horses bore it well too – as well as any English troop horse on a route march in the shires. Hervey had at first thought to take the Marwaris, but they were only lately come from

Bangalore and he thought it best to allow them a little more time. So they'd taken the 'walers', which stood half a hand higher and covered the ground without tending to jog-trot, which he reckoned was one of the Marwari's few vices.

Everywhere, it was abundantly green – tall grasses, shoots of corn, sugar cane (how Fairbrother would have been intrigued at that), mango and linseed. The road itself was for the most part reddish-brown, and the people of the road, and of the fields and the villages, moved with a purposeful ease, confident, content – the grass-cutters, the tenders of the crops that would keep alive both man and beast for another season, the keepers of those beasts, which provided milk or the occasional meat (and fuel for the fire, and daub for the shelter), the carriers of water, mainly female, the makers of this and that, whether to eat or wear; and children playing, as they did in every country he'd ever been, except here perhaps they played with even less care. He saw no sullenness, no great indigence, no oppression, no fear. Here indeed was a country prospering – as was a great deal of India prospering under the Company's *Pax*. He took pride in that, and in the assurance that his mission in Coorg would extend the Company's *Pax* even further.

The dak bungalows were serviceable rather than affording true comfort, but, as the saying went in the regiment, a poor billet was better than a good bivouac. Each had a big dining room and verandah, and two or three bedrooms, with kitchen and servants' go-downs outside, the better of the bungalows with a khansamah to arrange their food and comforts. In the poorer ones there was merely a *durwan*, little more than a caretaker, in which case the bearers were put to foraging. In one of them, all the usual appurtenances appearing to have been mislaid – and since they had arrived in the dark they had no great desire to try to trouble the baggage – they ate off plantain leaves and slept on the floor. Hervey professed to enjoying it; it minded him of simpler times. Only next morning did they find they'd shared their quarters with a python. Johnson delighted to bloody his sabre for the first time in many a year, knowing that in Bangalore he would get a good few rupees for the skin.

The following night, however, they were able to make themselves comfortable in one of the larger bungalows, where the cook produced a fine dish of curried mutton, as they called most meat, which afterwards Johnson discovered was several parts crow. It didn't trouble him too much, for as a boy he'd often eaten rook, and the dish had been tasty, but he was able to negotiate a discount next morning when the khansamah presented the bill. In the early hours, though, a travelling lady – the wife of one of the missionaries in Bangalore – arrived, and Hervey's party, having spread themselves over all the rooms, and sleeping comfortably, had to rise and make way for her companions, after which, no doubt taking advantage of the minor confusion, two thieves made off with some of the bearers' clothes, which set them howling for the rest of the night despite the sharp edge of Johnson's tongue and a cuffing by one of the rough-riders.

That, however, was the sum total of vexation in what otherwise felt like a furlough, so agreeable was everything about their progress – not least the air, full of the scent of hay and flowers, despite the month, and even the villages for the most part free of the stench of night soil. But, oh, how he wished Kezia had been with him, or Georgiana, for the number and variety of birds was prodigious. He'd always taken delight in observing them, no matter where the place, though he considered himself no ornithologist. Hoopoes he counted among his favourites, and they delighted him almost every morning as the party took their breakfast; and orioles and blue jays, magpie-robins, barbets, koels and coucals – and all save the white egrets that speckled the fields seemingly more colourful, more active, more plentiful even than in Bengal.

By dint of good and early starts, an hour's rest in the early afternoon, and then marching until they reached the next-but-one bungalow before dusk, they made Bangalore on the Saturday morning – five days, six nights. Hervey soon saw why the city was so highly favoured by civil and military alike, for standing as it did at 3,000 feet on the Deccan Plain – though an ascent they'd scarcely noticed – it had more the feel of Malvern than Mysore. There were fireplaces in the houses, a very English-looking church, botanical gardens, ball-rooms, a dissenting meeting-house (not unlike that in Horningsham, only bigger), a circulating library, English shops – *very* English, and yet with Parsee merchants – but yet a Hindoo pagoda at the end of the main street; and elephants and horses walking together in pleasant company – English soldiers and sepoys likewise (and this despite the late trouble). Each evening, he learned, there was a promenade at a brisk English pace, and a sepoy band played 'God save the King' when the residency flag was hauled down.

But if parts of Bangalore brought to mind Malvern, the greater part remained as it had been in Tippoo's day. His old fort, though dilapidated, still stood square by the native town – the Pettah – which was crowded with the humanity of low caste, who bustled about and hummed like bees in a hive. Monkeys ran in all directions, jumping, chattering, climbing, scrambling – stealing. Children likewise ran – playing, laughing, quarrelling, rolling in the dust in imitation of the monkeys; and stealing too. The men stood smoking, chatting, spitting and bargaining, or else darting here and there as if life or fortune depended on it, while the women sold what they could – their labour, their talents, the produce of their skill, or else themselves. And the endless native music withal.

Here in the mud-walled Pettah was Tippoo Sultan's Mysore still. Hervey thought to write home of it, but also that words would fail him. He wished he had his paint box. St Alban was already sketching.

The hircarrahs that carried the official mails between Fort St George and the second garrison of the presidency had served them well. Although the commissioner was still travelling, his secretary kept the code book at Bangalore and had deciphered Somervile's instructions, which were to provide all necessary support for the collection of the tributary elephant, and to furnish a half-troop under command of a

British officer. Somervile had been quite particular in this: they were to be from the 2nd Lancers, Wellesley's old Hyderabad Contingent, and provisioned for seven days in rice, salt mutton and flour.

Hervey inspected them that same afternoon in his best blue, and he liked what he saw – Deccani Mussulmans, straight-backed but quick to smile, especially the rissaldar, the native captain. They wore green kurtas well cut, black turbans tied tight, and loose trousers strapped beneath the boot – the image of serviceability as well as show. It was the lances, however, eight feet of bamboo tipped with gleaming steel, and pennants, red and white, that truly made of them a corps that impressed by appearance. Exactly as he'd hoped, for to overawe was better than to overcome.

He liked their officer too, Neale, a youngish man who spoke four native languages as well as French and Persian, the best sort of Addiscombe seminarian, whom he'd have been glad to see in the Sixth. He asked no questions save the practical, and when Hervey told him he wished to leave at seven next morning, he conveyed his orders to the rissaldar with a fluency Hervey had rarely heard.

They dined that evening with the commander of the Mysore division, General Hawker. Hervey had met him in the Peninsula when he'd been a major in the 20th Light Dragoons, and he himself a cornet. By his enquiring smile, the general was evidently doubtful of the ostensible purpose of the mission, and Hervey thought it was as well that the Coorg resident was not here, or the commissioner, for between the three of them they might have been able to keep up an irresistible quest for information. Somervile had not exactly ordered him to withhold information, merely to use his discretion, but he had no intention of sharing confidences, for his experience was that senior officers were ever jealous of secret intelligence, and being jealous of it, once acquired, wished to share it further in order to demonstrate their standing. His march on Madkerry, when the time came, would be infinitely easier for giving the rajah no notice of it. Only St Alban knew their real purpose here, for as he'd told him when he became adjutant, he was of no use if he didn't know the commanding officer's mind on every matter touching the regiment. Besides, if anything ill should befall him, St Alban could at least take back the intelligence they'd gained to Madras.

In any case, General Hawker was evidently content to oblige him, if perhaps more out of fellow-feeling for a dragoon than professional judgement; or else in sympathy for what he said would not be a very agreeable visitation, for the most lurid reports of the rajah's depredations on the female sex reached Bangalore weekly.

Coorg itself, though, he assured them, they would find the most delightful of places – a green and pleasant land, the forests barely jungled, the finest of trees, 'hills as paintable as ever you'd wish for', rivers full of fish, tumbling streams, waterfalls, and game aplenty. 'It might be Argyleshire.'

But, he said, the country between Bangalore and Kushalnagar they'd find tedious. 'See a little of Seringapatam, though.'

Hervey certainly intended to. He fancied he'd never be able to speak to the Duke of Wellington again – if opportunity ever came his way – if he passed through that great scene of siege and slaughter without giving it thorough consideration. Besides, he wanted to see how it compared with Bhurtpore, the last siege he supposed he'd ever witness.

XVIII

Tigers of Mysore

Kushalnagar, Friday, 1 February

GENERAL HAWKER WASN'T WRONG: THEIR march to Coorg was tedious, the country unvarying and their progress altogether slower, for, there being no dak bungalows, they had to make and break camp each day and allow the sowars, the native cavalrymen, and camp followers (as many again) time to cook. Kushalnagar was not much more than half the distance that Bangalore was from Madras, but the march took them just as long.

They did, however, spend more time at Seringapatam than strictly necessary, though all were glad of it, since a good deal of the tentage had been drenched on fording the Cauvery. The river was higher than usual, for the south-west monsoon had continued into November.

They made camp inside the walls of the old fort, and Hervey explored the breach in the west curtain, a little to the right of the flank of the north-west bastion, which the Nizam's artillery had made, and through which General Baird's men had stormed. He'd been eight at the time, learning the rudiments of his trade – at least, to ride – on Salisbury Plain under the instruction of an old dragoon, but at Shrewsbury they'd had a porter who'd been a corporal with the Seventy-fourth, a Shropshire lad who'd found himself in a regiment of Glasgow men and who'd been with Baird's columns when they hacked their way in.

There'd been no quarter, the old corporal told them, especially after they'd found the English prisoners and how they'd been tortured. And there'd been no sparing the riches of the place either. He'd spent his prize money long before coming home, but he had a jewel still which he'd dashed from the hilt of a *jambya*, and which those he favoured were allowed to hold occasionally. And he'd seen 'Tippoo's Tiger' – the real one, not the dolls made up afterwards. Life-size, it was (Hervey could remember the description clearly), mauling a British soldier in his red coat, from whose mouth came a wailing noise made by bellows as his arm rose and fell in distress, and the tiger grunting. It was, he'd said, supposed to be Tippoo himself, 'The Tiger of Mysore' as once he'd been before the British began to get the better of him. 'An' us dashed it in pieces, an' us then shot 'is real tigers, which 'e 'ad in cages thick wi' jewels.'

Except that when one day years later Hervey had gone to Leadenhall Street to see Somervile, to his surprise he'd found the beast displayed in the little museum of curiosities there. Not only was it entirely without sign of once being dashed in pieces, it was much smaller than in the corporal's tales. By that time, though, he'd formed his own judgement in things, in particular old soldiers' memoirs; yet in these there was often, if not the perfect detail, then the essence of an affair – and here, now, it was just so. There were the dungeons where Tippoo had kept his prisoners – just as pictured in the corporal's telling – and the water gate, the place where Tippoo had fallen, sword in hand: 'Better to live two days like a tiger, than two hundred years like a sheep.'

But, he'd wondered, did the sowars think it a place of homage? Their lieutenant had reassured him that their loyalty was in no doubt, however – that their conduct in the late mutiny had been beyond reproach. And, in fact, they'd appeared to show no curiosity in the fort beyond what the hawkers at the gates could offer by way of fresh meat – preferably alive so they could slaughter it themselves in accordance with the rules of their religion.

In truth, the whole native people of Seringapatam, within and without the Pettah, showed them not the least interest beyond the commercial. As Somervile had often said, he supposed it mattered not a great deal to them who exacted the tolls and taxes, as long as they were exacted fairly – and in this the Company's collectors had a reasonable reputation. Besides, the storming and sack of Seringapatam was hardly in the lifetime of many of them. He came to the conclusion that if they were indeed to mount an offensive against Coorg, having Seringapatam to his rear, astride his communications with Bangalore, need not trouble him.

Thus he satisfied himself that they'd not tarried unduly in examining its walls. Time spent in reconnaissance was seldom wasted.

He had upped the pace to Kushalnagar nevertheless. They camped the first night at Gaadi Palya – 'the resting place of bullock carts', aptly – an unremarkable but pleasant enough spot astride the Lakshmana Tirtha, a tributary of the Cauvery. The forest – good teak, said the rissaldar, for they were nearing Coorg, and Coorg had the finest trees in the Carnatic – skirted the village, close, and Acton asked if he might look for game. Two sowars went with him, and an hour later they returned with a brace of pig carried by village boys who'd trailed them in the hope of an anna or two.

'*Bura janwar*,' Hervey had said with relish. 'Or what do they say here, Neale?'

'The sowars would say *handi*, Colonel, and the villagers any number of things – *mikka, jevadi*; or *kari-jati* perhaps. At Madras they'd say *pandi*.'

There was no conceit in it, as well as no hesitation. Hervey nodded approvingly.

'But your sowars won't eat it?'

'No, Colonel, but they'll barter it – and well.'

Indeed, there was a good feast that evening, dragoons and lancers messing together easily. The sowars relished the fowls exchanged for one pig, while Hervey's men ate the greater part of the other, though Neale too observed *haram*, and Hervey liked him the more for it.

But for all the feasting and fellowship, they were away not long after dawn, reaching Kushalnagar late in the afternoon and making camp in a grove of plum trees just short of the Cauvery. Hervey wrote up his journal and a brief report for Fort St George, but then decided that 'nothing to report' was not worth the effort of transmission, trusting instead to Somervile's (and indeed Kezia's) assumption that unless there were contrary news, all was proceeding to plan.

The political officer at Bangalore had told him what he could of Coorg, which was not much more than the political department at Fort St George had been able to tell him. The maps they'd been given at Madras were, as the chief engineer put it, somewhat conjectural, as no proper survey had ever been carried out. They were, he said, adequate enough for communicating with the rajah's seat at Madkerry, which lay roughly in the centre of the princedom, but not for exploration. In this, however, the political officer had been able to help a little, for he'd several times taken leave there, the sport being plentiful, and, after the monsoon, the climate reviving. The roads converging on Madkerry from the four points of the compass formed four quadrants, he explained, which each had its own charm and vexation in roughly equal measure . . .

Yet glad as he was to receive intelligence of the four quadrants, Hervey had a strong suspicion the political officer had every idea of his true mission. Any interest that he showed other than in the road directly from Kushalnagar to Madkerry might confirm that suspicion, and so he thought to make no notes or enquire too much. Indeed, he framed his questions in such a way as to suggest his only interest in the roads north and south from Madkerry was as an alternative if the Cauvery should be in flood and they could not therefore use the road west from Kushalnagar. The political officer doubted it would ever be necessary to seek an alternative route since although the Cauvery rose twenty or thirty feet when the rains came, there was a fine stone bridge that remained dry throughout.

What Hervey did learn to his advantage – or believed he learned – was that there was no speedier approach to Madkerry than by the four roads, which in turn suggested that if the rajah were to flee, as opposed merely to hiding, he would have no real alternative but to do so by the same roads. Therefore, when it came to his arrest – the word that Somervile preferred – control of the four roads would be of the essence. Yet for all practical purposes, communication between them could only be through Madkerry itself – or else by considerable circumnavigation – unless by some remarkably good fortune they were able to find guides. On the other hand, the rajah's men, if they were inclined to fight, would know the forest tracks and the mountain passes and be able to flit from one road to the other, and thereby able to concentrate a good deal more force locally than he himself would be likely to dispose. Both Madras and Bangalore reckoned the rajah could muster about five thousand, with a further three thousand from Mysore, fugitives from the late mutiny.

He'd wanted to ask more, but decided it best to hope that the perpetual vice of intelligence officers – to suggest their importance by revealing what others did not know – would come to his aid. And to an extent it did: the Coorgs, he learned, held their land by military tenure. All able-bodied men, who were anyway from an active and warlike peasantry skilled with the firelock and the *pichangatti*, the cleaving knife, were at notice therefore to answer the call to arms. The standing element, the bodyguard – the chowdigars – consisted of a small permanent cadre augmented by levies called up for a period of fifteen days at a time. Without regular discipline and organization, though, the rest of the army, should it be embodied, would be no match in the open for seasoned troops. However, in their stockades and *kadangas* – war trenches – they would take some dislodging. The political officer told Hervey of how at one place, the Heggala pass in the Periambati Ghat on the road north from Malabar, they'd thrown back a whole division of Tippoo's, who left twelve hundred dead and wounded choking the defiles.

Hervey had then chanced to ask – in a voice of simple curiosity – if there *were* any open ground in Coorg, to which the political officer had smiled wryly and said, 'Only upon reaching Madkerry.'

But what of Kushalnagar? Was it a safe place to leave his baggage rather than proceed encumbered on the climb to Madkerry? (He was able to put it, he thought, as merely a question of immediate practicality.)

At Kushalnagar, said the political officer, there was a customs post, as there was at the other three places of entry, at which he should expect the usual officials and a small detachment of chowdigars. Somervile's missive, he said, had been forwarded by hircarrah three weeks before, and they had had confirmation of its receipt into the rajah's hands. Hervey should therefore expect a conducting party at the frontier. As for their progress thence to Madkerry, it was but twenty miles, though the road was steep in places and it would therefore be the journey of a whole day. Nevertheless, when they reached Madkerry – for all the rajah's recent insolence – they could expect to be received courteously enough. There was, he said, a comfortable guesthouse, which the rajah's grandfather had built for the express purpose of entertaining his English visitors. They might even be invited to hunt – in which case, Hervey told himself, he would avail himself of every invitation, for the more he saw of the country the more he would be able to make plans.

Their reception at the customs post next morning came therefore as a surprise. And, indeed, he cursed himself for failing to heed Somervile's mantra 'expect the unexpected'. They had stood to horse (and therefore, but less noticeably, to arms) just before dawn, and then when it was full light they'd breakfasted, breaking camp immediately afterwards and mustering at eight o'clock. Leaving just a 'depot' in the plum grove, they then proceeded in parade to the bridge, where to his surprise, Hervey found the Cauvery here was no more than the Severn at Shrewsbury on a fine day – broad and steady. But unlike at Shrewsbury, the river was low enough to reveal a string of rocky outcrops across which they might be able to scramble if the bridge were contested in either direction. He didn't expect it, exactly – the political officer had given him no cause to; almost the opposite – but he could never ride a piece of country without wondering 'What if?'

He first suspected trouble when he saw the bullock carts drawn up on the eastern – Mysorean – side, though no sign of officials withholding their crossing. Hervey had made no secret of their camp the night before, and it was possible, he supposed, that the Coorgs were simply keeping the bridge clear to allow them passage. As he got close to the front of the queue of bullock carts, however, he saw at the far end, where began the Rajah of Coorg's dominion, the line of red-coated chowdigars across the road.

'A guard of honour, d'you think, gentlemen?'

St Alban deferred to Neale. 'They certainly wish to receive us with some sort of ceremony, Colonel. Beyond that I can't say until I speak with them.'

'And elephants, mind.' There were three drawn up behind the line of red. 'Well, gentlemen, we shall see what we shall see.'

They continued onto the bridge and across without let, but as they neared the further end, a tall, dignified man of middle years, in a *kupya*, the knee-length, half-sleeved coat with a broad red and gold sash, the *chale*, tied at the waist, distinctive to Coorgs of rank, advanced and bowed.

'Welcome to Kodagu, Colonel Hervey, envoy of the Honourable Company of East India. I am Pemma Virappa, vakeel of His Highness the Rajah.'

Despite the eccentric syntax characteristic of even the most fluent English speakers in India, the vakeel's was a voice of some refinement, and of rank.

Hervey returned the salute with equal formality. His instinct was to dismount, as courtesy would normally require, but Coorg, as Somervile had said repeatedly, was a dependent state, and he was the representative of the liege lord. So instead he spoke from the saddle, but in as modest a way as he could manage as envoy of the Company and atop such a fine mare.

'I thank you for the honour of receiving me here. I should be equally honoured if you would ride with me to the rajah's seat.'

'I am honoured, likewise, by your gracious invitation, Colonel Hervey. All is honour with the Company indeed. But it will not be necessary. To spare you the rigours of a journey through our arduous but exceedingly beautiful country, the rajah presents his compliments, and these three elephants so that you may choose as tribute which would best please the Honourable Company of East India.'

Hervey sighed inwardly. Why had he not anticipated such a ruse?

His right hand desired the sword; for in his salad days he would have charged at once, no matter the odds. For that was the way of great captains – surprise. But in India, Machiavelli was as apt ('The lion cannot protect himself from traps, and the fox cannot defend himself from wolves. One must therefore be a fox to recognize traps, and a lion to frighten wolves').

The affair before him now was of the fox not the wolf. 'I have with me for His Highness presents from the Governor of the Presidency of Fort St George, which I am in honour bound to place into his own hands and those of no other. I accept on behalf of the Honourable Company the tribute of an elephant, and place the choice of which one in your esteemed hands.'

The vakeel looked uncomfortable. Hervey could not be sure his discomfort was evidence of a trap – or rather, a ruse to keep him from

Madkerry – for if this rajah were as capricious as accounts suggested, the vakeel would be understandably anxious at any departure from the master's wishes; but it served to put him further on his guard.

A long silence followed while the vakeel thought how to save face in front of the rajah's men, and his own neck in Madkerry.

At length he bowed. 'It shall be as you wish, Colonel Hervey, although the rajah is not at his palace, and it is not known when he will return.'

But this, Hervey had anticipated. It was no concern of his to meet the rajah, only to spy out the approaches and the place itself, although to see the man whom he might be sent to 'arrest' would be a fine thing. Once at Madkerry he would have to await the rajah's return – which might be any number of days, weeks or even months – unless he could think of a plausible way of placing the presents in other hands without being in breach of his 'honour bound' and thereby raising suspicions. But he could think about that later.

He bowed. 'I should be obliged therefore if your lordship would choose the tributary elephant before we proceed.'

After a deal of confusion, during which Hervey noted one of the vakeel's men taking to the road (for it wouldn't do to find the rajah 'returned' to Madkerry), the chowdigars stood to one side and a mahout brought forward the larger of the two females.

'She is, in my considerable opinion, Colonel Hervey, the finest of these three fine animals.'

Hervey's mare was suddenly reluctant to stand her ground, though elephants had given them no trouble hitherto. Neale pressed his gelding forward, alongside, to settle her, and St Alban did the same on the nearside – when he'd settled his mare too.

'I have with me mahouts, who will take the elephant to Bangalore,' said Hervey, intent on pressing his advantage. 'I would ask therefore that you permit us to ride on, so that we clear the bridge, that they may receive her.'

The vakeel looked troubled again. 'Colonel Hervey, for favour of your honourable consideration, I ask that your escort remains here. Your safe conduct is our responsibility. To ride with an escort of lances might be thought insulting to the people of Kodagu – though, of course, I myself understand, as I am sure would the rajah, that the escort is to do honour to Kodagu as much as to represent the dignity of the envoy of the Honourable Company of East India.'

This was clever – an appeal to reason and propriety. Hervey almost smiled. 'I understand. I will take with me in addition to my dragoons, just two sowars as orderlies, and the remainder shall await my return here.'

He would be no more specific than that. He wanted Neale with him, and it was not a matter for negotiation.

Honour seemingly satisfied, however – or as close as may be (for in truth the vakeel had no more cards to play) – the vakeel bowed, and Hervey told Neale to make the arrangements: if they did not return by this time in five days, or he received a message to the contrary, the ris-saldar was to bring the troop to Madkerry with all haste.

And so they began their climb to the rajah's fastness – twenty miles of rutted red earth which twisted and turned through forest as green as any in Ireland, but cool and without the humidity the colour suggested.

They marched dismounted for at least half the way. Corporal Hanks, one of the rough-riders, forgetting his riding-school voice would carry long on the wooded slopes, complained that 'Nob'dy said we was goin' up the fookin' 'Imalaya.' Serjeant Acton sent him sprawling with a kick to the backside. 'Next time, Hanksy, Field Punishment Number One.'

The sowars smiled at each other.

St Alban made notes and drawings, which he was careful to show to the vakeel as if he were sketching in the manner of the grand tour. The vakeel himself, dressed more for ceremony than the field, impressed Hervey with his determination to walk at his side – whatever his motive

– but as it was impossible therefore to say anything to St Alban without being overheard, their exchanges were in veiled speech, which St Alban hoped he'd be able to clarify when reading back his notes at the end of the day. The gist of Hervey's observations, he believed, was that if a force had to march on Madkerry opposed, it had better have plenty of infantry, for the places to stockade were legion, and wherever the road was hewn away into some sort of cutting, the defiles were commanded from heights not easily scalable. In a fight, it was no place for cavalry. Though that wasn't the same as saying it was no place for the horse, for the answer to stockades was artillery – and foot batteries would find the going a sore trial. That, at least, was what he understood Hervey to say.

They stopped at midday by a waterfall. Johnson brewed tea, and they ate hard-boiled eggs and chuppattis, as the dragoons called them, made that morning in Kushalnagar, while the horses grazed on what looked like rye grass. The sowars chatted easily with the vakeel's men, which Neale kept an ear to, though nothing came of it but that the rajah's *jailu* was now so full that the excess prisoners – male and female – were being kept in a part of their own barracks.

After an hour's ease they resumed the march, and just after five o'clock, now mounted again, they reached the plateau of Madkerry.

'What a handsome prospect,' exclaimed St Alban, with as much exaggeration as he dare without inviting suspicion, taking out his sketch book again. The vakeel looked anxious, but evidently reckoned there was nothing he could do. Here, surely, was an Englishman, and they had their strange ways. Besides, who indeed would not wish to make a picture of this beautiful place? There was nothing in Mysore to compare, nor in Bombay, where he'd learned his English. The little hills that dotted the plateau, with their forts and pretty houses, their temples and their gardens; the river, the streams . . .

'There, distant, Colonel Hervey, is the rajah's guesthouse!' He shouted it, almost, as if to distract all attention, pointing to an elegant white *palazzo* at the foot of the hill on which stood Madkerry's principal fort.

'There you will be made very comfortable, and your men may build their tents on the maidan beside. Here you may wait on the rajah for as long as you please.'

'It is a fine prospect indeed, Pemma Virappa-sahib,' replied Hervey, and with sincerity. He looked forward to its comfort.

'But yet again I say, Colonel Hervey, there is no knowing when is the time of the rajah's coming.'

XIX

Time Spent in Reconnaissance

Madkerry, next day

THEY WERE INDEED MADE COMFORTABLE. Baths, bedclothes, roast fowls, brandied figs, mangoes, wine – the rajah's hospitality, if *in absentia*, was equal to any in Bengal.

Hervey wished it hadn't been. *The hand that mingled in the meal / At midnight drew the felon steel, / And gave the host's kind breast to feel / Meed for his hospitality!* Well did he remember first reading those lines – *On the Massacre of Glencoe* – and his disgust. They were a standing caution to all who did the King's business, as the Campbells merely claimed they did. *The winter wind that whistled shrill, / The snows that night that cloaked the hill, / Though wild and pitiless, had still / Far more than Southern clemency.*

What might be the Coorgs' reply, though, to the 'felon steel' and 'Southern clemency'? Would India's 'startled Scotland' demand 'revenge for blood and treachery'?

But that was not his business. Comprehending India was the business of a lifetime (and more). Besides, he'd no time for a ruler who schemed against the very power that had restored his own fortunes, nor one who abused his subjects the way he did. There was no need of scruple.

He reckoned their work here could be done in a day – two at most. There was of course advantage in seeing the rajah, but staying a 'guest' at Madkerry indefinitely would bring none worth the effort. He might send patrols along the roads north, west and south, but would they bring him any vital intelligence? All three, no doubt, had their defiles and defensible places. It was the last mile or so of each where the fighting, if it came to it, would be decisive. How did these debouch onto the plateau? Where would they be fortified – where indeed *were* they fortified – and how might they be overcome? These were not excessive questions. No, he wished to return to Madras as soon as may be, for the squadrons must arrive at any moment. In truth, too, there was Kezia.

He decided he'd have St Alban make a 'grand tour' of the city, sketching in the military fashion but with the addition of figures to give a harmless impression, while he himself reconnoitred the roads under pretext of ornithology (he had with him Pennant's *Indian Zoology*, which he supposed might be useful). Madkerry was no great size, the plateau not more than three miles north to south, and five east to west, and the hills – in the main, little more than enlarged mounds – were excellent points of vantage. As long as they were not delayed by 'hospitality', he thought it would be accomplished by evening.

In fact by four o'clock he was finished, having spied out the avians of all three approaches – north, west and finally south. He'd said nothing to Serjeant Acton of his purpose, but he hadn't needed to. An NCO did what he was bid, but one of Acton's acuity did so with an enquiring mind. All it had taken was the conditional – 'Sar'nt Acton, if . . . how would . . .'

Once back at the guesthouse, having fallen out Acton to swim, he'd washed away the day's dust and taken his ease outside in a cane chair to await St Alban's return. A khitmagar brought tea and sweetmeats, and Johnson appeared soon afterwards from the horse lines.

'She 'ad a nasty leech on 'er gash, Minnie, Colonel, but that Chelli's good. 'E 'ad it off sharp.'

Hervey had already marked out Chelli as a fine syce. But a leech? 'I can't think how that could be. I'm sure we stood by no water for long. A big leech, was it?'

'It'd 'ad a fair belly full, but Chelli put some pomegranate on, so it should be all right.'

'Permanganate, I hope. I'll come and see myself later.'

'She looks tired. Did you go far, Colonel? An' I'm sure 'e said it were pomegranate.'

'Ten miles or so, but at no pace. Permanganate – Mr Gaskoin began using it at Hounslow. You recall, surely?'

Johnson shook his head, as if it were entirely without consequence. 'I 'ad a good look round while you were gone.' He picked up Hervey's swordbelt and pulled out the sabre halfway. 'I'll run over t'blade afore stables.'

Hervey himself, as any officer, kept his side-arms clean in the field, but if there was to be ceremony tomorrow . . . 'Thank you. At what did you have a good look?'

'I went in t'bazaar. They'd some nice things.'

'Such as?'

'Nice ivory things, an' gold.'

'At a good price, d'ye think?'

'I reckon I could've 'ad a good 'aggle.'

'Perhaps tomorrow then. Except there mayn't be time.'

'An' I went in t'fort as well.'

'You went inside? There was no difficulty entering?'

'None at all. It's not like a real fort – well, it is really, but I mean there aren't soldiers and guns everywhere. T'rajah's 'ouse didn't look much. I wouldn't call it a palace. There's a bazaar there an' all.'

'Doubtless they can clear out the stalls when necessary. Was that all?'

Johnson smiled ever so slightly – the smile that Hervey knew portended some disclosure, if not necessarily of great remark. 'There were a door open in one o' t'buildings, an' so I 'ad a good look inside.'

Hervey raised an eyebrow, for although he'd many a time profited from Johnson's 'foraging', it did not always recognize the Articles of War. 'On the prog, were you, Corporal Johnson?'

(Feigned indignation): 'No, Colonel.'

'Carry on.'

'Well, it were a great big forge, but t'fire weren't lit an' there were nob'dy there. But it were full o' these – thousands of 'em.'

He handed over his find.

Hervey stiffened.

'An' there were another shed full of 'em an' all.'

He gave him one, twice the size.

Hervey shook his head. 'Caltrops – for foot *and* hoof. I suppose the obvious weapon.'

The Coorgs could scatter them, spring an ambush and then slip away. No infantry or cavalry would pursue hard through ground sown with caltrops. Any advance would be slowed to a crawl, since all the roads were but continuous defiles. They'd be days to Madkerry rather than hours.

'This is trouble indeed, Corp'l Johnson. But I'm glad to know of it. Well done.'

St Alban's field sketching was admirable too, and clever – ingeniously disguised, with annotations for colour and the like, as if preliminaries for the brush, and details which were of practical military use recorded in a very recondite Greek script. Together with his own notes they made for a very satisfactory reconnaissance.

'I see no reason, frankly, to visit here any longer. We have enough; any more would be speculative. And I confess I feel unease about being here on sufferance.'

'Break camp this evening, Colonel?'

'Tomorrow morning. I'll tell the vakeel it's not fitting to await indefinitely – that I take no offence but the Company's business compels me to leave. The presents shall be given into the rajah's hand at a later date.'

St Alban nodded. 'A warning order?'

Hervey shook his head. 'No, not till morning. I'd rather bear the delay than risk discovery . . . Tell me, did anything appear strange to you as you rode today?'

'No, Colonel; I found everything most unremarkable – like Bangalore and Kushalnagar, or any other place we've come.'

'Quite. I'd expected a certain . . . edge.'

'You think the stories of the rajah's excesses are unfounded?'

'No; they're from too many and different sources to dismiss.'

'Perhaps the rajah is careful in his excesses.'

'Yes, perhaps. But agreeable though this place is – very agreeable, a beautiful country to be sure – I find it stranger than it ought to be. I feel like Jack come up the beanstalk.'

St Alban smiled. 'The story has a happy ending, as I recall – well, a satisfactory one for Jack at least?'

Hervey laughed. 'Come; I want to take a turn round the camp.'

He spent a little time with the syces and bearers, as he took his turn, and with the two sowars, and his dragoons. They'd made themselves comfortable. There was good water nearby, and the horses had fed well on corn and pulses, but the sowars seemed unsettled. Afterwards Neale told him that some low-bred Mussulmans – Moplas, fisher folk from Malabar – had come earlier to sell salt cod, and that the women bared their legs to the knee.

Hervey had seen them all about the city. Their women appeared to cause no offence to the Coorgs (and, indeed, he found their lithe, clean limbs pleasing), but Neale said his Deccanis were most prudish in such matters, and thought themselves insulted.

'So they didn't buy the fish?'

Neale smiled. 'They did buy the fish, and found it very good indeed, and that is probably why they're discomposed. They're a contrary lot, the Deccani rissalah, Colonel, but I greatly esteem them nonetheless. In a fight there's none better. Though I wouldn't say that to the Jats, of course.'

Hervey smiled and shook his head. Comparison of the martial races was a perilous venture – especially with the martial races themselves. 'I thought to ask if the rissaldar would eat with us when we return to Bangalore.'

'That of course is most gracious, Colonel, but I venture to say he would find the honour too much.'

'But you mess with your native officers from time to time, do you not?'

'Yes, indeed. It's merely that he would feel it presumptuous to mess without the rissaldar-major.'

'Very well; perhaps the rissaldar-major too.'

Neale smiled apologetically. 'The rissaldar-major would feel discomposed without the commandant.'

'Then it will be something of a tamasha. I'll say no more of it now, though. By the bye, I'm obliged to you for taking duty today.'

Neale brought himself to attention. 'With your leave, then, Colonel, I'll attend on stables.'

'I too.'

St Alban was just finishing his own round of the horse lines as Hervey came up. 'All serviceable, Colonel. One of the bat-horses is colicky, but they've drenched him with turps.'

'Very well.' Hervey thought a little longer . . . 'St Alban, would you have Sar'nt Acton make the watch roster with the sowars taking the first and last.'

'Of course, Colonel. You have a concern?'

'Only a very little. It seems they've got themselves in a lather about the fish wives, and better that they take the easier watches than brood on it in the early hours. And I would wish for a fuller moon.'

'You have a concern for the fish folk too?'

Hervey shook his head. 'Not in the least.'

'I'll see that Acton arranges things – and torches.'

They messed together, the three of them, when all heat had gone from the day – not that it had been oppressive – and before unwelcome winged visitors became too troublesome. And they dined as if at Fort St George, with spotless-white table cloth, polished silver, fine china and glass, but every dish spiced, even the confections. Then again in the English manner, they rose to take their ease while khitmagars cleared the table and removed the cloth for the desserts – nuts, candied fruit, port much fortified, though Hervey drank only moderately, and Neale almost not at all.

'I have some letters to attend to,' he said, rising suddenly. 'Breakfast at seven, then, gentlemen, and we'll decide the day.'

The two rose and bid him good night, then took up a pack of cards.

They were still playing cribbage when just after midnight Corporal Johnson appeared.

'Mr St Alban, sir, there's two 'Indoos wants to see t'colonel. They says it's real serious, and they're proper people – grand, I mean. Speak English proper. One's a woman.'

Neale and St Alban were on their feet at once, reaching for their swordbelts.

'Just two – without attendants or any other?'

'As best I can make out, sir. Corporal White's with 'em. We was just 'avin' some tea. They sound worried.'

'Better receive them in here, I think,' suggested Neale.

St Alban nodded. 'Bring them in, if you please, Corporal Johnson. Then tell Corporal White to take a turn about the camp while you stand sentry.'

'Sir.'

'English-speaking: means nothing definite,' said Neale as Johnson scuttled out. 'They could be Bombay merchants even, though strange if the woman speaks it too. But no one would steal into our lines at midnight without pressing cause.'

St Alban couldn't help but marvel at the rich variety of his military life: incipient revolution in a great port of empire one minute, and in the next (with, true, the interval of a year) a midnight tryst the far side of the world. Parliament would be fearful anticlimax . . .

Johnson returned. 'The visitors, sir.'

'Thank you, Corporal.'

The light in the dining room wasn't strong, but it was evident at once that the visitors were high-born, not merchants.

'Good evening,' he said, bowing. He would give away as little as possible, but enough to satisfy the demands of courtesy. 'I am Lieutenant St Alban, adjutant to Colonel Hervey, whom I understand you wish to see.'

The man returned the bow. The woman stood still behind him, her head covered with the throw of her sari.

'Good evening, Mr St Alban. I am Chinnah Buswa, noble of Coorg and high official at the palace. This is my wife, Deewah Amajee, sister of the rajah.'

St Alban bowed again. If the rajah had but the one sister, then it must be she who had the claim to be the rightful ruler of Coorg, if her uncle had not claimed – usurped – the throne in his regency. 'This is Mr Neale, of the Honourable East India Company's army.'

The two acknowledged with an inclination of the head. The deewah evidently did understand English – or some at least – and she now un-covered her head to stand proud.

She was a striking woman of about thirty – tall for an Indian, slim and lighter skinned than most they'd seen here so far. Her husband was older – clean-shaven, darker skinned than she, and but an inch taller.

He had the bearing of nobility, but he too had the face of anxiety.

St Alban looked directly at the deewah. 'What may we do for you, your highness?'

She looked at her husband.

He nodded, as if acknowledging her permission to speak. 'We request an audience of Colonel Hervey, who is representative of His Majesty King William, is he not?'

St Alban decided that the finer points could be deferred. 'He is. May I ask the reason, huzoor . . . given the lateness of the hour?'

Chinnah looked at the deewah again . . . 'Mr St Alban, my wife's honour is in danger. Our lives are in danger. We seek the protection of His Majesty King William.'

St Alban was momentarily taken aback – until the instincts that had commended him to Hervey in the first place took rein. 'I assure you, you need have no fear. You are in our protection here. Some refreshment . . . ?'

Quite how effective that protection might be, if whoever it was that threatened honour and life were to challenge it, was another matter, but they expressed themselves grateful, while refusing the offer of refreshment.

'Sit, please, while I go and speak to Colonel Hervey. Mr Neale will give you every assistance.'

He went as quietly as he could, not wanting to rouse the guesthouse's servants.

Hervey had barred his door, however (and the windows, with their entry from the balcony), and St Alban had to knock louder than he'd have liked.

When the door opened he found Hervey still booted.

'Colonel, the rajah's sister and her husband are here. They want to claim our protection. They say their lives are in danger.'

'From whom?'

'I didn't ask, I'm afraid, Colonel.'

'Well, it can only be from the one man, else why ask *our* protection. You're sure they are who they say they are?'

St Alban shook his head. 'I've no way of knowing, but there's something in their bearing that suggests it. They're certainly dressed very well.'

'Wait a moment.'

He put on his jacket and fastened on his swordbelt, then nodded. 'Lead on.'

The two stood as he entered the room.

'Good evening, your highness . . . and—'

'I am Chinnah Buswa, Colonel.'

He spoke with dignity, and his features were those of an Indian of high caste.

Hervey bowed. 'These are my trusted officers. You may speak in front of them as you would to me. Now tell me, if you please, the cause of this alarm.'

The deewah spoke for the first time, and in a pleasing voice. 'Colonel Hervey, I thank you for receiving us. I am conscious that you take us on trust.' She removed a ring from her finger. 'This was the birth ring given me by my father, Linga Rajah. I would that you keep it until we are in His Majesty's dominions.'

She placed it in his hand. Even in the dull light of the oil lamps the brilliance of the diamond – bigger than he'd ever seen – spoke to her claim. He said that such a device was not necessary, however, and gave it back to her, but bid them sit.

The deewah bowed in evident appreciation.

Chinnah related their circumstances. The rajah had always been a boy, and then a man, of unchecked passions, he said, but of late these had become monstrous. He took unusual pleasure in killing – more than the sportsman's proper game – and this, like the tiger that acquired the taste of human flesh, had now become like that very tiger, satisfied only with the spilling of human blood. Indeed, he said, and with manifest distaste, the rajah baited his tiger hunts with village boys instead of goats. He knew, he said, that it was a practice not unknown in Bengal, but there at least the rajahs would pay the villagers well for a boy, and the tiger rarely got his bait. But here, this rajah demanded rather than bought – demanded with menaces. He would force himself upon a village woman, then threaten to do the same to a daughter if a son were not given for the hunt. And he would let the tiger maul the boy – frequently to death – before shooting. He had thirteen wives already, but his appetite was unquenchable, and no man's wife was safe, not even at court. He had murdered – there was no proof, but it could not be otherwise – every one of his cousins who might have claim on the throne.

'There is no one safe, Colonel Hervey. I refused him ingress last week, when he came for *my* wife. Our days are numbered therefore. I ought then and there to have drawn my sword and had done with it.'

Hervey remained silent for a while. 'Where is the rajah now?'

'At his hunting lodge at Virarajendrapet, about ten miles south of here, with his . . . wives. He went yesterday when he heard of your coming.'

'What then is to stop you making for Mysore?'

'I fear that in the unhappy state of affairs in Coorg, Colonel Hervey, my brother-in-law's men would not allow us to pass into Mysore. Even if we were to take the forest tracks, which few know of but the ryots, I fear there would be a price on our heads that none could resist.'

'You have made no preparations? You stand before me now intending to flee Coorg with but what you wear?'

'Two of our most trusted servants stand ready with horses and what little gold we can carry. Were you to reject our request, we should have ridden before daylight, even though it would avail us nothing, for what else might we do but wait to be taken like sheep?'

Hervey weighed their words for a little longer. 'Very well, wait here if you please . . . Mr Neale, stay with the deewah and her husband while I think on it.'

The khitmagars were now up, despite all the attempts at stealth (he supposed the chowkidar . . .). In a mish-mash of Urdu and Tamul he asked them to bring coffee to his room, which they seemed to understand.

'I suspect it will have to do instead of sleep tonight,' he said to St Alban.

Hervey was not unused to taking decisions at the witching hour, but it made it no less difficult. 'What are your thoughts?' he asked, opening the window onto the balcony just enough to see if there was anything to see (which there was not, only a dim moon).

'In general, Colonel, that if so insignificant a place as Coorg gives Leadenhall Street so great a concern, the omens for the Company aren't auspicious. But in the particular, honour demands we afford the deewah and her husband safe passage to Bangalore, else the word "Honourable" should be expunged from the Company's title.'

'A speech worthy of Mr Fox, for sure, but I was thinking more on how precisely we might proceed. I wish I had Neale in my confidence, but . . . Where's that damned coffee?'

St Alban looked somewhat penitent. 'I may inadvertently have taken Neale into that confidence, I'm afraid, Colonel, for I told the deewah she was now in our protection; and I should hardly have done so were we here on a merely tributary visit.'

Hervey nodded. He'd be glad if Neale had indeed put two and two together.

Coffee came, but with no sign that the khitmagar thought it unusual in the middle of the night. That much was promising.

'Colonel, if I may: as soon as the rajah learns his sister's fled to Mysore, which he surely will in but hours, he'll come raging back here. But we can't fold up our beds in the night. That will only signify deceit and put him even more on his guard, even if he makes no connection between her and us.'

Hervey drained his cup and poured more. 'That we agree. Go on.'

'The bearers and all can go at once, though, and the deewah, so that it's just you and the corporals tomorrow. If you make your call on the palace as early as is decent, then we might make Kushalnagar before the rajah hears of her.'

'Jack down the beanstalk.'

St Alban grimaced. 'Having taken a deal of gold.'

XX

Forests of the Night

Later

HERVEY HAD STRUCK CAMP MANY a time in the early hours, but he couldn't recall seeing it done with more despatch than this. The bearers, syces and grasscutters rose from their charpoys and bedrolls without complaint or question, with no noise but murmur and the occasional whinny from the bat-horses, and stowed and loaded every last piece brought up the hill from Kushalnagar. It was done in the space of an hour, so that by three o'clock, led on foot by Neale, all the impedimenta of the mission was marching east again, with, in their midst, the deewah and her husband and their two most trusted servants. When daylight came, Hervey walked across the abandoned ground and found nothing remaining but what might be consumed in the space of a few hours by ants and their collaborators. He would have St Alban pay the khansamah generously, in the way of one who stayed in another's house, trusting that he in turn would give the khitmagars, cooks and others of the household their due, and also the *mali* (or whatever in the Coorg language the gardener was called), in whose charge lay the campground. He intended leaving Madkerry having observed every politeness. It was only right; and if he was ever to return, it was only prudent.

After breakfast, which they ate together on the verandah, the party made ready for the palace: two officers and four non-commissioned officers of His Majesty's 6th Light Dragoons (Princess Augusta's Own) – in that moment and place the figurehead of the Honourable East India Company; indeed, of His Majesty's imperium. Just six dragoons – six sabres only, though as sharp as may be; four carbines and two pairs of pistols – all loaded, discreetly, before leaving. But as envoys of the greatest power on earth, what in truth was there to fear?

As they were mounting, however, the vakeel came. He looked disconcerted, whether because his horse, an arab, was unsettled, or the other way round, Hervey couldn't know. Either way it made for an awkward salutation, especially on an empty campground – which, overlooked from the fort, must have been the reason for his sudden appearance.

'His Highness is returned, Colonel Hervey. He wishes for no delay in receiving you.'

Hervey cursed beneath his breath: arabs were ever sensitive to anxious hands. What else might he do but answer boldly, however? 'Very good; we come at once, Pemma Virappa-sahib.'

In ten minutes, though (if they walked, not trotted), he'd have to think how to extricate himself. He cursed that he'd not anticipated the rajah's return – if, that is, he had ever been where the vakeel (and the deewah) had said he'd been.

'I fear I must decline any hospitality, vakeel-sahib. I am recalled to duty. The rajah will understand.'

He was averse to casual lies, lies of mere convenience; they had to stand judgement as *ruses de guerre*. Were they at war, though? If he didn't proceed on the assumption that in an instant they might be, then in that same instant they might be dead.

The vakeel could say nothing, which only confirmed his misgivings.

He turned to St Alban. 'At the palace, two to guard the horses and two to march at attention and present arms at my command. You understand?'

He did. '*Mais pas armes blanches?*'

It was a risk – French had once been spoken in the Carnatic – but in the circumstances . . .

'*Exactement.*' He could hardly unship his pistols from the saddle, but they would at least have two carbines – three with Acton's.

Johnson had reckoned it not much of a palace, and nor did Hervey. In Wiltshire it might have been a tithe barn, if a substantial one. Only the line of chowdigars in front marked it out as special.

The vakeel began explaining that this was but one of the rajah's palaces. 'They are many and elsewhere also. He would wish to receive you at Soamwar Pettah, his favoured, but he will understand that he cannot claim your presence, for you are commanded to return to Madras.'

The words seemed excessively formal even by the vakeel's standards. Doubtless they'd been composed with the rajah – if the rajah spoke English, that is – but at least it meant they would be not long detained.

He drew the party aside, and dismounted. 'Corporal Melia, muster yonder by that lower wall, not here. Keep a clear line to the gates, and sharp on your guard. We may have to make haste.'

'Colonel.'

His expression said he understood exactly. Melia was a pug. He'd have no trouble.

The others shouldered carbines and came to attention.

'Very well, vakeel-sahib,' he called.

The vakeel looked uneasy. Evidently he'd not expected an escort, but equally evidently he couldn't think how to bar them.

In they marched, St Alban bearing the gifts.

Through the arched entrance was a courtyard with a fountain and ornamental trees, and a gallery on three sides. Hervey supposed it served as an ante-chamber. But he didn't like being overlooked.

He removed his cap. It was better, he thought, to bow than salute – a courtesy rather than a gesture of subordination.

The vakeel shifted even more anxiously, in turn putting Acton on edge, who scanned the gallery like a hawk. The escorts remained at attention, while Hervey waited with studied unconcern for the next move. There was nothing else he could do.

Five minutes later the eruption of courtiers and attendants signalled the coming of the rajah.

The corporals presented arms. Acton stood at attention with his carbine at the port. It looked as if he were on parade, but his eyes continued to rove the dark places, and now the rajah's party. The carbine could be in the aim in an instant.

The rajah was a man of no great stature, about Hervey's age – perhaps younger – round-faced, with sallow skin, large dark eyes and soft features. This was not the image of a tyrant or of depravity, as Hervey had half expected, but it was not impossible to imagine indulgence taken to excess.

'Good morning to you, Colonel Hervey,' he said, his voice pleasing enough, without excessive modulation as was the case with many a native of India, and above all, measured. 'You are most welcome.'

Hervey bowed. 'Your highness, I have presents from the governor at Fort St George, Sir Eyre Somervile, small tokens of the Company's association with your highness's *raj*.'

St Alban advanced with the silver and sandalwood box in which were the tokens of 'association' – such a convenient word. And the ornamental sword. A servant took them from him.

'I understand that you must leave presently for your duties elsewhere, Colonel, but I would have you take some refreshment.'

Hervey thanked him.

Khitmagars came forward with trays of sherbet.

There followed a not entirely easy exchange of pleasantries – the rajah was reluctant to meet Hervey's gaze – but somehow ten minutes passed without mishap. Then the rajah put down his cup and stepped back, the signal for his assemblage to step back several additional paces too, so that there was once again a distinct separation between the parties.

Hervey put his heels together. Acton's hand tensed unseen on the carbine butt, ready for any treachery.

'And so, Colonel Hervey, you have had opportunity to see our country and our seat here, and our people. You will think, perhaps, that it is a place of welcome for those who are indeed welcome, as you. But not, perhaps, for those who wish us harm.'

Still the rajah's eyes did not meet his. It was, perhaps, unsurprising, for the rajah issued a warning, a threat indeed; and to do so to a representative of the Honourable Company was a perilous thing. Yet in not meeting Hervey's eyes, he revealed his uncertainty, whatever he said of his country's fastness. And that indeed was invaluable to know.

Then it was over, the rajah turning on his heels without farewell.

Hervey bowed.

What to make of it?

It wasn't the time.

They left the fort at a brisk trot, halting only as the road entered the forest, whence he watched for a good quarter of an hour to see if they were followed.

They were not. 'Very well, Edward. Let's away. I'll tell you what I think the rajah said.'

* * *

CRACK! CRACK! CRACK-CRACK!

Four bullets – one so close that it near kissed his cheek. A fifth made no pass. It struck Johnson in the arm, tumbling him from the saddle. Corporal Hanks sprang to his side. Acton had his carbine unshipped and in the aim in a split second. But where?

Hervey was trying to fathom it. Just a dozen more miles to the Cauvery. Why here?

Crack! Crack! Crack! Crack-crack!

A bullet struck Johnson's mare in the shoulder, and then another St Alban's boot.

Acton had closed up. 'Into the trees, Colonel!'

Hervey was making for them already.

Crack! Crack!

Two misses, but he saw the muzzle flash and jumped down.

Acton followed. And Corporal Melia – then St Alban, limping.

Crack!

Splinters from an ironwood tree bloodied Melia's cheek.

Crack! – but from behind. And a yelp a dozen yards in front.

'One's down, Colonel,' spat Acton, already reloading.

Hervey began weaving his way forward to down more. Pride came before an ambush, and he'd walked into it.

Crack! – uncertain from where.

He came on the half-dead, half-naked marksman, with Acton at his side.

Melia closed up, still tamping a new charge. 'I saw 'im fall, Colonel – just yonder,' nodding to their left.

Hervey thought they'd come far enough – too far, even. Fifty yards in forest like this and it could take all day to find the way back.

The man groaned and opened his eyes.

Melia picked up his rifle. 'By God, Colonel, this isn't country-made.'

'*Huli*,' sighed the Coorg.

'What?'

He groaned again. '*Huli*.'

Acton gathered up a handful of leaf mould and pressed it to the hole in his chest.

'Water?' said Hervey. (*Huli* – what else could he mean?)

Melia unslung his flask and put it to the Coorg's mouth. A drop or two went down but he coughed it up again at once.

'*Huli*.'

He lay staring, terror-struck almost. Hervey just couldn't tell.

'Water's no good with this wound, Colonel,' said Acton, blood covering his hands.

He was right. In a few seconds more the eyes fell shut, all life departed.

'Curse it! We need more than a single word. We'd better find the other, dead or no.'

Hervey could no more leave a wounded enemy than he could leave wounded game. And if they could get him to talk . . .

The forest here wasn't jungled – it hadn't been thinned, the light let in and a thick undergrowth therefore – but it still seemed an age to find him; and dead. His rifle wasn't country-made either.

How many had got away then? Three, certainly – the shots had come too quickly. Had they had two rifles apiece, perhaps? But no uniform like the chowdigars. A mistake maybe – a hunting party? Then why had they fired at them? Surely they'd seen? No; it was an ambush. That was why the rajah had summoned him – to be able to send his henchmen distant. Why, though? What would it profit him? It would surely bring down the wrath of the Company.

But now wasn't the time to be fathoming. He cursed again. 'Back,' he said simply. They'd given drink to the thirsty; there was no time for other corporal works of mercy, just a leafy shrouding. And – his stomach tightened – how was Johnson?

They picked up the rifles and cast about for signs of whence they'd come. It was remarkable how few there were in the forest, always, though doubtless to a native they made a trail as clear as would a plough.

It was several minutes, and it felt a lot more, but at last they picked up the paper trail – the cartridge paper. Still they moved cautiously, for to miss a sign would mean backtracking again.

In twenty yards – less – the trees formed a continuous screen, which was why they'd barely been able to fire an aimed shot. They stumbled onto the road eventually, rather than seeing it ahead.

Johnson was as white as any sheet, but more than conscious. 'Jesus, Colonel; I thought I'd never see thee again.'

Hervey, crouching, put a hand to his shoulder.

'Did yer get, 'em, Colonel? I 'ope so. Bastards, sneaking bastards!'

'Two, yes. I don't know how many more there were.'

Corporal Hanks staunched the bleeding with a wadding dressing. (Milne had had several hundred made up from cotton that the merchants of Bristol had given gratis.) The bullet remained, though, and there was no surgeon in fifty miles. Wounds in this climate . . .

But a step at a time. 'Into the saddle, Corporal Johnson,' said Hervey, trying hard not to sound anxious. 'A good pull of brandy should do it. And then to Kushalnagar. We can't dally here.'

'I wouldn't want to, Colonel. My mare's 'ad it, though. Bastards.'

Corporal Melia was already seeing to her. She couldn't put weight on the near-fore.

'My other pistol, Corporal Melia.'

Johnson sipped readily at the flask while Melia saw to the despatch.

It was never agreeable to a dragoon, not even in the heat of battle, but it was neatly done. A handful of bread from his haversack to distract her, the muzzle into the fossa above her left eye and towards the opposite ear.

Crack!

She dropped where she stood, kicked out, twitched for a few seconds, then lay still.

'Bastard Coorgs. She were a lovely little 'orse.'

'You'll take mine,' said Hervey.

The rissaldar greeted them with all the formalities. Beyond the lance guard in the middle of the bridge, however, was a business-like picket. No pursuers were going to be allowed across the Cauvery. Whether this was the rissaldar's doing or Neale's was no matter; Hervey was glad – relieved – to see it; and not least because by his own maxim (that of any light cavalry, indeed) he couldn't count the enterprise at Madkerry an entire success – 'Muzzle clean, mission thereby accomplished.'

But Neale's mission had been accomplished at least: the deewah and her husband were safely got away, he reported – and swearing perpetual allegiance to the Company. The tributary elephant was by now, he was sure, at Seringapatam. Did Hervey wish him to strike camp, and march at once?

Only then did he see Corporal Johnson. *'Rissaldar-huzoor: sarjana!'*

'You have a surgeon? I hadn't known.'

'He's called that, Colonel, out of courtesy.'

Hervey looked doubtful.

'He's very practised.'

Hanks and Melia had got Johnson down from the saddle and into the shade of a mango tree. He'd regained a little colour, for all the discomfort of the ride, but he was sweating more than the heat obliged.

When the 'surgeon' came – a daffadar with a beard that reached his chest – Johnson began sweating the more. 'I don't want physickin' wi' no 'Indoo stuff, Colonel.'

'You're in good hands. Mr Neale swears by him.'

The daffadar unrolled his canvas, to reveal the instruments of his unlicensed trade: knife, forceps, ligatures . . . Those, indeed, of any licentiate.

'Brandy?'

Johnson shook his head. 'No, Colonel; not in front o' these.'

Hervey felt chastened.

The daffadar eased the tunic from Johnson's shoulder, cut away the dressing, offered him a leather strop to bite on – which he refused – and took up a probe.

Johnson winced, but made no sound.

'Accha,' said the daffadar, putting down the probe and taking up a bullet-extractor. He spread the wound wide with his fingers, peered closely at it, prompting a sharp intake of breath from Johnson, and in less than a count of five had the ball out.

Johnson had made no other sound.

Next a pair of forceps, the wound spread wider still . . . and almost as fast, out came a tiny twist of blue and white.

Hervey nodded admiringly. It was one thing to remove a ball – a solid object, in one piece, unmistakable – and another to extract the debris with it, so that the wound mightn't fester.

'*Bahuta accha, daffadar-sahib!*'

The daffadar bowed, then took the brandy and poured it into the wound.

They bedded him down in the shade of a plum tree, wrapping him well and under a mosquito net, with Corporal Melia keeping watch. In a few minutes he was asleep. Hervey sighed: Johnson had gone through the French wars with barely a scratch, and now here of all places he'd had to submit to the surgeon's probe – a native surgeon at that (deft though he was). The Preacher – *A time to love, and a time to hate; a time of war, and a time of peace.* Was it so for Johnson too?

'Tell me, Neale,' he said afterwards, as they walked to the deewah's empty tent, 'how a Mussulman approves of brandy.'

Neale smiled. 'It is very simple, Colonel. The Koran does not forbid alcohol absolutely. It says only that in alcohol there is both harm and good, but that the harmful effects exceed the good. In this case, the daffadar saw no harm and only good.'

'Then I am all admiration, even more.'

'The rissaldar is having a *tanga* got up for Corporal Johnson. It won't have springs, I don't suppose, but filled with grass it should be comfortable enough. I am supposing we shall leave tomorrow morning, Colonel?'

'Yes. And extra vigilance tonight, please.'

They'd got down the beanstalk in one piece, but the beanstalk still stood, and the 'giant' might come down it – but it was a metaphor he preferred to keep to himself.

'By the bye, Neale, tell me: what is the Kanarese for "water" – "*huli*"?'

Neale looked at him quizzically. 'No, Colonel: "water" is "*niru*"; "*huli*" is "tiger".'

Hervey groaned.

PART THREE

A TIME OF WAR

For by wise counsel thou shalt make thy war: and in multitude of counsellors there is safety.

PROVERBS, 24:6

XXI

'To Your Duties'

12 July 1833

'PON MY WORD, HERVEY: AS fine a sight as ever I saw. Fine men, fine horses. I'd crowns resign to call them mine! Or even just a squadron. They do you great credit, sir!' There was ever a part of Somervile that was the soldier manqué.

Hervey had just ridden off parade, the first muster of the regiment complete. The last detail – fifty men of E Troop – had landed in the middle of March; and the RM had warranted the last remounts a month later. Hervey had given his captains time to work up their troops, and now it was time for regimental drill.

'Handsome is as handsome does, though,' he replied, yet certainly pleased with appearances too. 'We shall now put away the red for the season and put on something more workaday. Come and see us in a month in the hills yonder.'

'I shall. But it's a fine thing to be up betimes . . . What *is* the time, indeed?' (He took out his watch.) ''Pon my word – a quarter past seven! And your trumpeter sounded the first call at six. Where has the hour gone?'

Hervey had had a good look at each troop, purposely taking long to see how steady they could remain. Now, however, the heat would begin to try the horses, which was why he wanted them back to the shade of the stable and the relief the punkahs brought. 'I would ask you to breakfast with us, but I know you have an audience this morning.'

'Box wallahs, yes, for the Steam Fund. I tell you, Hervey, short that my time here may be, I'm determined we shall have steam to Suez.'

'Admirable.'

'But first, Mysore secured. I wouldn't have any successor take from me a sack of ferrets. That wretch at Coorg . . . By the bye, how does Kezia bear the heat? Emma thought her tired yesterday.'

'She's well, thank you. Very well. But next year I'll want to take the regiment to Vellore for these months. But . . .' (he smiled in somewhat bashful satisfaction) 'I believe she may be brought to bed even as we speak.'

''Pon my word, Hervey: ought not you to be with her?'

'To lend my considerable obstetric skill?'

His old friend recovered his senses. 'Quite. Besides, you have your parade.'

'Just so. Though I must say, I have at last a major in whom I can place the utmost trust. He's diligent without being excessively active.'

Somervile nodded. 'Yes, you have a good man there. You're fortunate; I've seen some rum exchanges in regiments come to India.'

Major Garratt, a bachelor four or five years older than Hervey, was an officer content with just a little soldiering and otherwise the pleasures of the table – including cards. He'd been a lieutenant at Waterloo, however – in the sand pits with the Ninety-fifth (or the Rifle Brigade, as now they must be known) – and a month ago had astonished all ranks by outshooting Serjeant Acton at the regimental sports. He too had been as unaccustomed to wearing a red coat as any in the Sixth, but was now as content as they were. Indeed, even Hervey had begun thinking the King might yet be right in demanding it of all his cavalry, not least that Kezia professed to liking it – all the ladies, indeed.

If, that is, they could have something more serviceable for the field.

'If you'll excuse me, Somervile – or "with your leave", I should say – I'd like to see them back.'

'Of course; of course. And you've much else to occupy you.'

Hervey smiled. 'You may tell Emma she need have no fear.'

'I shall indeed. But one last: when is your lancer coming?'

'I expect him any day.'

'Capital. I would meet him as soon as may be.'

Hervey frowned. 'After first he pays respects to General O'Callaghan.'

'Of course; of course. I don't wish to interfere in military affairs.'

That wasn't true, and both knew it. Somervile had a shrewd mind for campaign matters; it was just that his enthusiasm to see things for himself sometimes exceeded his capability. More than once in South Africa he'd nearly ended up 'vulture meat', as the dragoons liked to say.

Hervey did, though, look keenly to the arrival of Lieutenant Neale. As soon as Somervile told him the governor-general had approved in principle the annexation of Coorg – or something very much its like – he'd asked for him to be his major of brigade. As yet the Coorg Field Force was but a paper design, known only to a very few, but when the time came for its embodiment, Hervey wanted no delay on account of a deficient staff. At first he'd thought about St Alban too, as a supernumerary, but then thought better of it, for he was too valuable to the regiment, which Hervey intended should play the major part; and in any case, when the hurly-burly was done, he himself would return to command, and he didn't want the administration of the Sixth to have fallen off in the meantime.

In the bright sunshine, the red was undeniably impressive. The route to barracks was lined with Madrasis of every age, both male and female, and their looks – so far as the looks of any native of this land revealed the truth – were of esteem; even of awe. Hervey was as much concerned to observe them as he was the squadrons themselves. The major did have a tolerably good seat on parade, though, which he had indeed wondered about before. It would be the better for slightly less weight bearing down on his charger's back, but he wagered that was only a matter of time. The hot months in India had a way with excess flesh.

But it was good to be able to give the order 'To your duties, Dismiss!' and to know he could then turn his back, sure in the knowledge that there was such an eye – and an ear – as Garratt's abroad.

Half an hour later he sat in his office with his first cup of coffee of the morning. The punkah was not yet in motion, for it was better to bear the heat for as long as possible, to become accustomed to it, and it would be another hour before all but the half-naked sweepers found it a trial. In the distance a cuckoo called, not exactly as the English bird, but a cuckoo, distinctly, nevertheless. It was as well to be prompted to home thoughts from time to time – to Wiltshire, perhaps, where Georgiana too would be hearing the cuckoo (and in time, he hoped, here). *The cuckoo comes in April, / And sings her song in May. / In June she lays her eggs, / And July she flies away.*

Happy morning indeed. And as soon as orderly room was done he'd take a few *mozhams* of jasmine for Kezia, or for Annie to give her if she were in labour . . .

'Colonel, may I have a word?'

St Alban didn't usually presage business this way. Nor as a rule did he look uneasy.

'By all means,' said Hervey, putting down his coffee. 'Is something amiss?'

'Colonel, I regret to inform you that I intend sending in my papers.'

Hervey's spirits began to sink – and from such a high peak.

'Sit down, Edward.'

'I am in every way content in the regiment – and it goes without saying, I trust, that I'm equally so in being your adjutant; I'm honoured, indeed, to be your adjutant – but I'm troubled by what we're about to do at Coorg, I mean.'

'Indeed?'

'And with much else that goes with that. I'm sorry to tell you of it at this time, particularly, but I made up my mind some weeks ago, and I would have counted it a deception to continue without telling you.'

'I am grateful for that. But so that I might fully understand, what, precisely, is your objection to what is intended in Coorg? The man is a monster, is he not, and in breach of his treaty with the Company?'

'Undoubtedly, Colonel. My objection is to the whole situation of the Company in India, and we, in effect, but mercenaries. The search for a *casus belli* for Coorg only suggests that the enterprise is discreditable.'

Hervey might have bridled at the suggestion he was about to embark on something discreditable, but instead he nodded. He'd heard as much before, in many a place and many a time. Years ago he'd read Burke's speeches on the trial of Warren Hastings, which were enough to put off any man of sensibility. And yet, the world was as it was, and he reckoned its improvement was but a gradual thing at best, and that meanwhile there was many an 'accommodation' to make. He admired men like Wilberforce, but for the most part, the choice was between the lesser of two evils.

'For my part, Edward, I don't doubt that we aid corruption and help line the pockets of unworthy men, but I ask myself – as I did the first time I came to India – is our presence in the main beneficent? Would India without us be a better place – in particular for the poor devils who live on dust and whom we pass by without a word? I believe not.'

'I know that you believe that, Colonel. There were some at Hounslow – as you very well know – convinced that you saw only opportunity for glory in India, but I could never believe it. There is room for honour-able differences.'

Hervey knew perfectly well that there'd been dissent in Hounslow. There was nothing wrong with seeking glory; for a soldier, indeed, it was quite the reverse – though true glory did not come of dishonour. 'And your position is undoubtedly honourable, Edward. But I must say frankly, I shall count it a great personal loss. I've been most fortunate in both my adjutants; and I've taken much delight in your company.'

St Alban looked suddenly concerned. 'Colonel, I've not expressed myself well. With your leave, I don't intend sending in my papers until the business in Coorg is done. I couldn't send them in in the knowledge that the regiment is to see action. If one dragoon were killed – if any man, indeed – for want of something I might have done, especially after my time spent in reconnaissance there, I could not in conscience rest.'

If puzzled, rather, by what seemed excessive scrupulosity, Hervey was nevertheless gratified. 'For this relief, much thanks, Edward.'

He did not add that when, in due course, the Honourable Edward St Alban rose to speak in parliament, as one day – and sooner rather than later – he surely would, it would be with all the greater moral authority for such a decision.

St Alban stood up. 'With your leave, then, Colonel?'

Hervey opened the drawer of his desk – the old battle-scarred writing table that had come home from India with the regiment after Bhurtpore. Lord Holderness had replaced it with a fine French piece, but Lincoln, being of the school that believed 'disposals' were an affront to the quartermaster's art, had placed it in his stores, whence Collins had shipped it.

He took out a printed sheaf. 'Will you do me the favour of reading this, at your leisure?'

'Of course, Colonel.'

A Bill for effecting an arrangement with the India Company, and for the better government of His Majesty's Indian Territories.

'It's an early draft, by Somervile's account, but in essence that which will go before parliament – may indeed be already before it. I think you'll find it . . . encouraging.'

'Colonel.'

Hervey poured himself more coffee when the door closed, though managing to spill a deal of it in his disappointment. Who on earth might take St Alban's place when the time came?

The door opened again.

'Colonel, the surgeon . . .'

Hervey sprang up.

Milne came in, grave and saluting.

'What—'

'Colonel, Mrs Hervey is safely delivered of a healthy son at ten minutes before seven. May I offer my congratulations.'

And he smiled – so rare a thing that Hervey began to laugh.

'A son – at ten before seven, just as we got on parade!'

St Alban was just as relieved. Fearing the worst, he'd already sent for Armstrong.

'My dear Milne, take some coffee – brandy, whatever . . . I'll go at once. Kezia, she is well, you say.'

'I've never seen better, Colonel.'

Allegra, a child of rising seven, strong-willed and under regulation of a fine governess, had not yet been admitted to the happy parturiency. Sarah, Kezia's lady's maid, having bathed her mistress abed, was at work now with the hairbrush, and although the surgeon had been gone for half an hour, there was still much to-ing and fro-ing by the females of the household, including Allegra's governess, who had once been a nursery maid and whose assistance was therefore called on to supervise the newly engaged ayah. And Annie had been maid-of-all-work for two full hours while Mrs Stray endeavoured to keep some semblance of order in the residence of the commanding officer of the 6th Light Dragoons. Serjeant Stray himself had done his morning rounds of the outdoor servants – the chowkidar, the mali, and the syces who looked after the ponies and the *tanga* and the *chukree* – then sent away the houseboys on various errands, and retreated to what he preferred to call his 'store' (the silver room) to do the accounts. The receipt of babies was not something that had previously exercised him in his many years of quartermastering.

Allegra was determined to take full advantage of her release from the schoolroom, and of the sudden freedom of the house. There were sweet things to be had. But the cooks were about the kitchen yet, so she sneaked instead to the stillroom. It was always nice and cool there, for the air seemed to move of its own accord (the ventilator louvres set both high and low), and there might be *chikki*, which she liked best. She loved crunching the nuts, the almonds especially, and letting the jiggery melt in her mouth. No one would find her there.

She was right – about the *chikki* at least. There was a whole tray of it in the middle of the big table, in nice little pieces she could reach for easily – pink, green and golden brown. She filled her hands and sat under the table, just in case one of the *hubshis*, as Corporal Johnson called them (although she didn't think they had woolly heads at all), came in. She thought she might stay there all morning in fact, until it was time for her nap, when Miss Ames would come looking for her for sure.

It was so quiet.

And it stayed quiet all morning. In truth, 'all morning' was only about twenty minutes, but she'd had several handfuls of *chikki*, and given some to her doll, and it seemed like all morning . . .

And then Annie heard her – the plaintive little '*Ohhh* . . .'

She'd been taking the short cut to the dhobi house with a bucket of soiled bed linen, but she had a sharp ear, and the '*Ohhh* . . .' didn't sound right. She knew it was Allegra – or else a very clever myna bird. But how could a myna have got in the stillroom?

She put down the bucket and gently opened the door.

She gasped. 'Stay still, Miss Allegra. Stay still. Don't move. *Mick!*'

Serjeant Stray heard her distress. He could always move with speed even when the fattest corporal in the regiment. Now he was like lightning.

Long years of storemanship stood between him and his days in a troop, but not his skill with the sabre. It hung on the door, but was out of its scabbard before he was upright.

Seconds only to the stillroom, but . . . 'Christ!'

No word of warning, no 'Stay still!' No guard and no time to loft the blade. He just sprang.

The cobra – massive beyond any he'd seen in the bazaar – struck like a whiplash.

How had he known? How could his sabre move so fast? Neither cut nor thrust – no time, no space – just a flick of the wrist. The tip of the blade – two, three inches at most – barred its way.

The head fell at his feet, hood spread wide. What remained writhed so much that he struck at it twice – reflex.

He took a deep breath and pretended all was well – that all had *been* well. 'It's all right, Annie love. It's dead 'n' gone. You can come out now.'

Annie was shaking but trying not to, still crouching under the table, with Allegra beneath her. She hadn't been shaking before. Every muscle had been as taut as a wire.

'Is it a good snake or a bad one, Mick?'

She was stroking Allegra's hair now, to restore her own nerves as much as comfort the child.

'Not *is*, Annie love. *Was.*'

He'd heard Johnson prattle on often enough about good and bad – and every fakir in Bengal.

'An' it were a bastard.'

And then under the table he saw Allegra.

'Oh, bloody 'ell, Annie, you . . . Oh, I'm sorry, Miss Allegra, I didn't mean to . . . Good God, Annie, lass, what 'appened?'

Kezia lay upright when he came, her hair spread, shining gold, tumbling onto green silk pillows, her eyes bright, her complexion peaches and cream – the image of health, and of contentment. She'd smiled at him with such warmth, perhaps as only the bearer of a lover's child could, their son sleeping in a basket beside her, and the ayah with a look that said that all was well. Kezia said she was not at all tired, that she hoped to be out of her bed soon, and that she craved only to immerse herself in the great swimming bath.

They'd not spoken before of names. Hervey asked what was her wish. But she replied that that was for him to say, and with a completeness to her smile that made him unable to think for the moment. Then he'd taken up her prayer book and looked to see whose day this was, or nearest, but it was Swithun, which would not serve. Then Kezia said that since it was by Somervile's good offices that all this had come about, here, perhaps the child should be called Eyre. And he thought it an admirable idea, not least that it would be a fine reciprocation; and so it was settled.

Then she said she would like to see Allegra now that their son had a name, and also – she smiled again – because she now had her husband's assurance that she was fit to be seen, rather than just that of her looking glass. But first she asked for some hot milk sweetened with honey, and Hervey said he would ask Annie to bring it – or should he ask Sarah? 'Annie,' Kezia replied, so that she could thank her for all that she'd lately done: 'Such an obliging girl.'

Hervey said he would go himself and tell her, and then bring Allegra.

Annie was sitting in the servants' hall off the kitchen with a dish of tea, trembling still so that she could hardly sip without spilling it. She got up when he came in, but he insisted at once she sat down again.

Serjeant Stray caught his eye.

'Is there something untoward?'

Stray told him.

Hervey looked aghast. 'Annie . . . We must send for the surgeon.'

'It looked so evil, sir,' she said, shaking her head. 'Its eyes – it just stared at us, hating us, wanting us dead. And we . . . we'd done nothing to it, sir. Nothing to hurt it at all.'

Serjeant Stray put a hand to her shoulder. 'Annie, love, they don't mean it like that,' he tried again. 'It's just the way God made 'em.'

He turned to Hervey.

'It were nowt but a bit of a thing, Colonel. It gave 'er a bit of fright, but she'll be all right – won't you, Annie love?'

Annie nodded. 'Yes, sir, I'll be all right. But Miss Allegra's had a terrible fright. Miss Ames has taken her to see the ponies.'

'She'll be right as rain in no time, Annie,' said Stray, as avuncular as he could make himself sound. 'You'll see. Bairns – they don't think much o' these things.'

'Are you quite sure you don't want Mr Milne to come, Annie?'

She shook her head again. 'No, sir; thank you. I'll be all right.'

'Might it help take your mind off it if I asked you for some hot milk with honey? Mrs Hervey asks for it – and most particularly indeed that you bring it so she may thank you.'

Annie put down the dish and stood up, brushing her smock with her hands, though there was hardly need. 'Yes, sir, of course. I'd like to as well. I'm sorry, sir, I forgot myself: he's a lovely baby. I'm sure we're all very glad for you.'

Hervey smiled. 'Thank you, Annie. You are very good. Say nothing of this to Mrs Hervey, though, before I've had chance to speak of it with her.'

'Of course, sir. And it's not my place to.'

Hervey smiled again, appreciatively.

He nodded to Serjeant Stray to say he would have him follow, and went to the stillroom. One of the houseboys had begun mopping the floor. He took in the scene – the position of the table, the place where the snake met its end, the relative distances . . . and shook his head.

'A bit of a thing, Serjeant Stray?'

'Well, Colonel . . .'

'Where is it now?'

'I got the chowkidar to take it out.'

'I will see it.'

'No, Colonel, there's no need.'

Stray sighed, knowing well enough he couldn't conceal the fact any longer, even for right reason.

'It were a bloody big 'un. As big as I've seen. Well, perhaps not exactly – perhaps it just looked bigger in t'room, but it weren't a little bazaar thing. It were the big sort – hood as big as a saucer. Them that kill you in an hour.'

He paused, as if thinking whether he should say more.

'Colonel, that lass – Annie: as brave as a lion . . .'

'Oh, indeed: I see it all, Serjeant Stray – and you yourself.'

'Oh, I did nowt that anyone wouldn't've, Colonel.'

'Perhaps; but quicker, I'll warrant – and more effectively. Thank you.' He offered his hand.

Stray muttered inaudibly; he hoped Mrs Stray wouldn't make any fuss when she too heard.

'And now if you will, try and find a *sampera* to stop up any holes, and tell why such a snake came into the lines, let alone the house. What said the chowkidar when he saw it?'

'I don't know what he said, Colonel, but his eyes nearly popped out of 'is 'ead.'

Hervey went to find Allegra. It didn't do to think on what might have been – an inch in a miss was as good as an ell – but if the snake *had* struck . . .

Media vita in morte sumus. For so long he'd taken it for granted. It was his trade. But in the midst of life here, where death could lurk in a stillroom, where strange ills bred and where violent hands were for hire so cheap, it was well to buckle on as much armour as one might.

XXII

In the Midst of Life

19 December

THE MONSOON, WHEN IT BROKE in early October, had at first been welcome – as it always was, relief from the humidity that grew by the day and which in September seemed as if it could not be borne, when many of the *gora log* sought the relief of the hills. Not the Sixth; not this year at least. Hervey knew that if they were to endure a long posting in this station, they must work unceasingly this first season. Between them – he, Lieutenant (Quartermaster) Collins, Serjeant-Major Armstrong, and Surgeon Milne as their unflagging guardian – there was enough knowledge of India to make sure that unceasing work did not turn to exhaustion. They exercised the horses – with troop and squadron drill once a week – in the first hours of the day, or, when there was a good moon, at night. They laboured until the middle of the morning on camp comforts – making playing fields of all kinds; building a court for Wessex Fives, a game that one of the cornets come on exchange had brought with him; digging a fine swimming pool and new storm drains; getting going the regimental farm; and then at eleven they rested until three before parading for recreation or skill-at-arms, officers and men alike, and school for those who could not read or write.

The school had begun at Hounslow, but not without misgivings in some quarters, for there were officers of high rank in the army who were of the opinion that the fewer the men who read or wrote, the better behaved they were; and, indeed, it had met with no great success, for many a dragoon held the view that he'd enlisted for subsistence, not for self-improvement. Here in Madras, however, many an unschooled dragoon came to realize that a man might feel he were in less alien parts if he could read for himself a letter from home and write one in return, and also the periodicals and such like in the reading room. And while a dragoon might think it no shame to be unschooled at Hounslow, seeing 'darkie' here reading *his* language – English – was an affront to his pride. (It was curious, thought Hervey, how the children of the regimental school, who could all write the alphabet on their slates by the time they were six, were not a greater affront.)

They were better victualled than in Hounslow, certainly, and with cooks to make a good meal of it rather than the boiling pot in the corner of the barrack room. Collins's little army of bearers saw to *chota hazree* for every man when the sun came up – sweet tea and biscuit – and then bacon or the like when morning stables and exercise was done. There was a trencher of fruit at one o'clock (which they got to enjoy, for it kept them regular), with lime or lemon water; and then when the sun was down, a good mess of mutton and rice or some such, and, by common consent, excellent Indian coffee. The native sutlers were not bad either, was the opinion. Collins had them on a tight rein. The wet canteen opened earlier, but it also closed earlier; it had not taken long for the dragoons to realize that slaking a thirst with arrack and water, or the local millet beer, was a very temporary pleasure, the consequences next morning being more than unpleasant (only rarely did their pockets run to English porter, shipped in returning Indiamen). Charges of drunkenness were soon nothing to compare with Hounslow – to Armstrong's considerable satisfaction, for recalling his own youthful days he could become almost the abstinent on matters of 'barrack liquor'. There was even a temperance association begun from out the civil lines, though this troubled both Armstrong and Hervey, wary as they were of excess in any direction.

As many dragoons fell foul of *la grande vérole* here as at home, however – although it might have been more had Milne not addressed them regularly on the fearful consequences of the mercury treatment – tooth loss, ulcers of the mouth, throat, and skin; violent dementia; death – though this last to many seemed no more troubling a risk than was soldiery itself. In fact, so the chief medical officer at Fort St George reported, the Sixth's losses to the Grim Reaper by accident or disease honourably contracted (or at least, not dishonourably) in their first year in Madras were half the average for a comparable body of troops. Nevertheless, among these 'Indian mortalities' were one or two men whom Hervey had known for many a year. 'Shepherd' Stent, one of the Warminster men that he himself had 'listed, and who with Serjeant Stray had saved Armstrong at Bhurtpore when the tunnel collapsed, died of a fever in August. Two serjeants' wives had gone the same way – Milne found it hard to say by what exactly, though it wasn't cholera (that had steered clear of the lines) – leaving three orphans. Stent's funeral had been bad enough – he was popular, and after Bhurtpore a hero too – but those of the wives were particularly melancholy, with both widowers in despair of what would become of their 'bairns'. Had it been the serjeants themselves that had succumbed, their widows would have found a husband in but a few weeks, as was the custom in India, but despite the best efforts of Kezia and her ladies, there were no wives to be found.

As for 'the household', a new chowkidar and a long-toothed sampera – and a good carpenter – had prevented any repetition of the stillroom occurrence. Kezia had received the news without excessive alarm, though she was in no doubt of the peril in which Allegra had been, for in gratitude she'd had made a gold bracelet for Annie, with a sentiment inscribed. And when, a week or two later, Miss Ames – in truth the person who seemed to feel it the keenest, for she blamed herself for allowing Allegra to stray (although bidden to the birthing bed) – said she wished to resign her position and return to England, Kezia appointed Annie in her stead.

'She may be unread for a governess,' she told Hervey, 'but in every other respect I think her admirable.'

And he had had to agree. Indeed, he said that anyone who had struggled as she had during the passage out to read Mills's *History of British India* (with its strange ideas about the place) was not lacking in understanding. He'd even seen Hazlitt's *New and Improved Grammar of the English Tongue* in the servants' hall. So now she was promoted to 'Miss Gildea' and given new clothes and seated in the same pew as the family at church – where, indeed, she became the object of admiration (and no doubt even more of desire) by all ranks.

Hervey himself increasingly left the running of the regiment to Major Garratt and the adjutant and Armstrong, while he and Neale, who arrived in early September, just in time, he said, to enjoy his second monsoon of the season, spent their time in the maps room at the commander-in-chief's headquarters, consulting every document that seemed of relevance to the great object of Somervile's governorship. There was no shortage of accounts of battle with the Coorgs. Their rajahs' strategy in war with the lowland chieftains to the westward, or with the Mysoreans, had long been to let them enter the country, leading them on with the appearance of success, retiring to strongpoints in their mountain fastness and there letting them exhaust their provisions and patience. Then, attempting to retire with the glory of having penetrated so far, the invaders found the stockades they'd forced or turned so easily during their advance had been re-garrisoned. Checked in retreat, harassed on the flanks and now in rear by a pursuing, jubilant enemy secure in his knowledge of the jungle paths, too late the invaders recognized their perilous position – whereupon the Coorgs laughed at their confusion and spared neither sick nor wounded who fell into their hands. The general result of a small force entering Coorg was its utter extinction. Only once, it seemed, had the Coorgs been tempted from their highland stronghold – by Tippoo; and thereby been defeated. That, indeed, was the portent of the rajah's 'fraternal address' at Madkerry.

They had not, of course, faced an army of the Honourable East India Company. While, however, it was tempting to imagine that no native force could withstand the resources, both material and moral, of the Company, Hervey was not minded to believe that the same fate was impossible simply by nature of the coats they wore. It was certain that the rajah could not be tempted from his fastness; so there was no alternative but to enter the country. It followed that the size, composition and policy of his force must be such as to avoid the unhappy ends of those who had gone before. Time spent in reconnaissance was never wasted; and nor was time spent in gathering intelligence from the efforts of others, no matter how long ago.

Once a week Hervey held his commanding officer's conference, once a fortnight he attended a regimental parade, and from time to time he visited a troop drill; but orderly room he left to Garratt, whose views on discipline matched his own. As for St Alban, he regretted not seeing him every day, but if only to assure him there was no loss of regard for having announced his intention to leave, the adjutant found himself just as frequently invited to dine at Arcot House as before.

In Neale, however, he found a thinking officer whose knowledge and sense of the country was as good as he dare hope. In his twenty-something years – despite a third of them in India – there was a wisdom of the world that St Alban could not yet equal. And while St Alban descended from the earls of Bicester, Neale, like Hervey, was a son of the parsonage – and a poorish living at that, in the marches of Montgomeryshire. From a boy he had wanted to join the Twenty-third, the Royal Welch Regiment of Fusiliers, but the Reverend Mr Neale had not the means, and so at thirteen he had gone to the Company's Military Seminary at Addiscombe in Surrey, and four years later arrived in Madras a probationary cornet. Hervey reckoned that in the long hours in the saddle when they went once more to Bangalore to consult in as great secrecy as they might with General Hawker, he'd learned as much about the south of India as he knew of the north.

Indeed, he'd been contriving ever since how to make him adjutant when St Alban left. Neale wouldn't have the means, of course. He might have saved a little gold, for there were peculiar opportunities in India, but so too were there to spend it, even in the most wholesome way. Yet if he did have the means to purchase – and indeed the means to live thereafter (the Sixth were by no means the most expensive of regiments, but expensive enough) – why would he wish to? He was quite evidently in his element with native troops; what might attract him to change his coat? And so Hervey thought to say nothing of the idea at once, and let things take their course for a month or so longer. He would at least make him temporary captain when – and it was surely when and not if? – the Coorg Field Force was embodied, for Neale would be major of brigade. There was, however, still no indication when they might begin operations; and yet barely a week went by without more intelligence of outrages perpetrated by the rajah – even of late against the Christian community, little as it was, and papists all, though their priest, a Portugais, was spoken of highly in Bangalore. To Fort William, Coorg must seem a place of no account, and Fort St George a fussing presidency.

At any rate, as the year drew to a close, and with it the retreating eastern monsoon, Hervey had at last completed his appreciation of the situation and made his plan. He was greatly pleased when Somervile approved it in its political detail – though he insisted that on no account were the troops to fire first, believing there was reason to hope the ryots would join the Company against their ruler. Hervey was content: these things were settled quickly enough once campaigning began. He accepted, too, the logic of the ultimatum that would be delivered to the rajah once the force was assembled, for since it was hardly possible to assemble such a force in any secrecy, there was little chance of achieving surprise. Besides, an ultimatum would only add to the legitimacy of the undertaking.

He was equally gratified when General O'Callaghan approved the plan – indeed, commended it – in its military particulars. Only the intelligence of the caltrops was unresolved; and on this the general had no advice. For what might they do but bear it as best they could?

A SCHEME TO DEPOSE THE RAJAH OF COORG BY THE MOST EXPEDITIOUS MEANS.

OBJECT.

The object of Government is to secure the person of the Rajah of Coorg.

CONSIDERATION OF THE GROUND.

Coorg is a mountainous and woody state. The frontier rises in strength in some places nearly impracticable; in others, of comparatively easy access. Thus the mountain passes towards the sea are very strong, and wind through a forest country defensible at every step. The boundary toward Wainand, partly marked by the Bramagerry hills, is almost impracticable at any time, much more so with a hardy and active enemy in front. On the other hand, the south-eastern boundary of the country toward Mysore is comparatively open, while that part to the north is densely wooded and can be strongly stockaded. There are few good roads penetrating the country, which besides offering the best points of entry are also points of escape, as well as *pointes de sortie* for riposte (of the objects of riposte, it is considered that Mangalore is of greatest value). These must therefore be garrisoned whether or no the intention is to use them as points of entry. It is not considered likely that the rajah will try to escape through the jungle even by disguise, when he would have to abandon his women, which would dishonour him, fearing murder by his own subjects or being given up by them into our hands.

The roads are four in number from each compass point, which conjoin at Madkerry. Each rises by several hundred feet in course to Madkerry (the highest peak in Coorg is believed to lie more than 5000 feet above the level of the sea), in places by serpentine loops which, well garrisoned, might greatly hinder advance. The rivers which intersect these roads in a small number of places present no hindrance to movement save in the Monsoon between May and October. Intercommunication, which perforce must be exceedingly slow, is impracticable without local knowledge. Once committed to a route of advance, therefore, a force cannot come to the aid of another. Cavalry may maintain communications between the forces by relay, but the Coorga perimeter is in excess of 150 miles, which, with the distance travelled along each road in addition, does not permit of timely passage of information. Madkerry itself occupies a plateau favourable to the rapid movement of cavalry. There is a fortified residence, but otherwise the town presents no especial consideration. The weather is most favourable to campaigning between December and May. In other months the Monsoon rains will greatly favour the defender. It is considered that the latest that the campaign may begin is the first day of April.

CONSIDERATION OF THE ENEMY.

The Coorgs are counted a brave and hardy race. The Army of the Rajah is reckoned to consist of 8000 men, 3000 of them discharged Mysoreans. Their method is to avoid battle in the open and to fight from behind stockades, which the close country greatly favours. From the small extent of that country, and their knowledge of the jungle paths, information may be quickly conveyed, so that they might effect rapid junction with a view to mutual support. We may expect them to have had many months' notice of our invasion, and therefore to prepare for war, so that they defend a strong natural fortress amply stored. Their policy has been to oppose incursion with great vigour when the place of it is known beforehand and where the enemy force is small. Alternatively, when the situation is otherwise, the policy has been to permit of deep incursion to exhaust resolve and supplies, and then to counter-attack. On the other hand, the Rajah has forfeited the sympathy of many of his subjects, whose cooperation, active and passive, we might with judiciousness secure.

CONCLUSIONS.

It is not expedient to attempt to secure the person of the Rajah by ruse or before formal declaration of intent, since this might bring into question the legitimacy of the Government's actions and provoke a lasting resistance by arms. It will be necessary to take his capital, Madkerry, the command of which in turn commands the principal roads.

The largest force possible is required in order to blockade or advance along the four roads of access to Madkerry as early as possible, and to prevent an unnecessary effusion of blood, and a procrastinating warfare, which would cause severe suffering to the attacking force. These roads must be secured at one and the same time, or as near as may be. The force must include as many sappers and pioneers as may be to destroy those stockades and abbatis en route to Madkerry which it is not possible to garrison so that they may not be occupied in rear of us to harass our lines of communication. Supply must be contained amply within the elements of each force sufficient to sustain active operations for seven days (ten for the southern column), which in those elements at the furthest point of entry from Madkerry supposes an advance of 3–5 miles daily.

PLAN OF CAMPAIGN.

Without recourse to the more distant garrisons, which would impose a burden of supply and communication militating against rapid concentration of the forces on the border with Coorg, the General Officer Commanding the Bangalore District will furnish a force of some 7,500 from the garrisons in the neighbourhood of Coorg, who will assemble at their respective four points of entry and advance independently but simultaneously at the appointed hour (except for the Western Auxiliary Force, which is a corps of observation to cover Mangalore), with intercommunication by cavalry: –

BANGALORE

450 bayonets H.M. 39th Regt. and Head-Quarters	450
4th, 35th, 36th, 48th N.I.	2400
Rifle Company, 5th N.I.	60
Sappers and Miners	300
	3210

One Coy of Foot Artillery: 3 x 12-pounder howitzers
2 x 5½-inch heavy howitzers
2 x 5½-inch mortars
1 x 6-pounder gun

This force to be divided into two parts, viz.: –

Under Brevet Colonel Hervey, and termed the 'Head-Quarter Division'.

H.M. 6th L.D. (from Madras)	300
H.M. 39th	300
4th and 35th N.I.	1200
Sappers	230
Rifle Coy 5th N.I.	60
	2090

6 guns, with a proportion of Artillerymen.

Under Lieutenant-Colonel Steuart, the reserve,
and termed 'Eastern Column'.

H.M 39th	150
36th and 48th N.I.	1200
Sappers	70
	1420

2 guns and some Artillerymen.

CANNAMORE

Under Lieutenant-Colonel Fowlis, and termed
'Western Column'.

H.M. 48th	300
20th and 32nd N.I.	1200
Sappers	200
	1700

Half a Coy of Native Artillerymen: 4 x 6-pounders
2 x 5½-inch mortars

MANGALORE

Under Lieutenant-Colonel Jackson, and termed
'Western Auxiliary Force'.

H.M. 48th (from Cannamore)	150
40th N.I.	400
Sappers	35
	585

BELLARY

Under Colonel Waugh, and termed 'Northern Column'.

H.M. 55th	300
9th and 31st N.I.	1200
Rifles Coy 24th N.I.	60
Sappers	200
	——
	1760

6 x 6-pounder guns, and Artillerymen.

Hervey read over the letter to Lord Hill that was to accompany his appreciation and plan, and then added: 'I am confident of speedy success as long as there is no untoward delay in beginning active operations, and I have impressed upon the Government here that point.'

There was nothing more he could do to safeguard his reputation were the enterprise to fail on account of something that was not of his making. This was India, and the business of the Company. But London took an ever closer interest, to which the new Act bore witness. Besides, he was a King's officer. His promotion came from the Horse Guards, not Leadenhall Street.

He signed it 'Your Lordship's Most Obedient Servant &c &c . . .'

Later, when he'd played Fives with Neale, which he now thought was the perfect exercise for light horsemen, for not only did it agitate the respiratory system, it practised the eye and the sword arm as no other, he would write the same letter to the Duke of Wellington. He hated the business of advancing self, but when he was a cornet his old major, Joseph Edmonds, had once cautioned him that if he hid – or suffered to be hid – his light under a bushel, then he should not be surprised when lesser men made way with but a flicker of a flame.

Then, as it were, all venal concerns attended to, he would read over once more the letters from Georgiana which had come that morning after a month and more without, and then write the letter to her that he had long pondered on: 'Come this time and live with us in Madras . . .'

XXIII

Untoward Delays

Kushalnagar, 1 April 1834

Hervey had been booted and spurred since before first light, when the entire Head-Quarter Division had stood to arms against the possibility of a spoiling attack by the Coorgs. An hour later, just after seven, they'd stood down to make breakfast, and Hervey had done the rounds of the campfires. Now, just before nine, the air already heavy, his mare standing with sweated flanks but perfect composure, he sat still in the saddle, watch in hand.

'Well, Captain Neale, despite that we tell them the hour of our coming, and *"Tirez les premiers"*, by now we'll have stopped every earth and Madkerry shall be ours presently. I never saw men better found, black or white. Whether we find at Madkerry's another matter.'

Neale's hunting was more the Deccan plains than the English shires, however. 'That will depend on whether the rajah is more the fox than the jackal. The jackal never goes to earth.'

Hervey smiled. He was not yet accustomed to the quarry.

'Well, with luck, St Alban will find.'

'I'm sure of it, General.'

Hervey certainly hoped so – and a good more besides.

As long as there is no untoward delay in beginning active operations. They'd lost precious time, but perhaps that was his fault for giving Calcutta the option to delay. General O'Callaghan had concurred with him, and so had Somervile: April was the latest they could begin with any likelihood of complete success; and incomplete success in India, where the Company relied so much on its reputation for irresistible superiority, was tantamount to failure. January had passed without a word from Fort William, and then just days before his birthday, when he'd concluded that Calcutta – Bentinck – hadn't the stomach for the fight after all, the word had come. He was to vest himself as brigadier-general, proceed to Bangalore and assemble the 'Coorg Field Force'. Since then, the political officers at Mysore and the Coorg resident, under Somervile's very particular directions, had persisted in their attempts to get the rajah to yield. Towards the end of March, however, all persuasion having failed, the resident delivered the ultimatum. It had expired without answer on the last day of the month, and so now, at nine o'clock, on the first day of April – the latest day by which, as Hervey had advised, active operations must begin – the resident would be serving the formal declaration of war on the Rajah of Coorg (before being taken under escort, blindfold, to the western border).

'I'm sure of it, General.' It evidently gave Neale satisfaction, but 'General' was a temporary courtesy, and for that reason one that Hervey would have rejected had he not thought it would work to his advantage. Generalcy opened doors otherwise held shut, not least by those close in seniority – and, no doubt, superior in their own estimation. The attachment of the political agent to the field force was cause alone. Colonel Fraser was ten years his senior in age, and a Lovat Fraser, always a tricky clan; while Colonel Waugh, commanding the northern column, was likewise senior in years.

I'm sure of it, General. How could Neale be so sure, however? No matter how capable St Alban was, his task was as speculative as it was perilous.

289

The decision to send on a party to 'view', Hervey had made only lately. Three days ago, as they came to Kushalnagar, he'd formally handed command of the Sixth to Major Garratt, but had detached St Alban and six dragoons for what he called 'special duty', telling Garratt that he regretted taking his adjutant, but that he'd seen Madkerry and no one else had.

'If anyone's able to find where exactly the rajah's laid up, it's he. And with a half-decent guide St Alban and a few men'll be able to keep on his line until such time as one of the columns closes up.'

He did not say it, for he wanted no hesitation in the advance and had therefore made no mention of caltrops, but St Alban was to try also to make contact with the deewah's man at Madkerry to discover if Somervile's stratagem had worked. 'War in India is made with gold and bullock carts,' Somervile was fond of saying, and he'd sent a good many pagodas to the deewah to do just this. Or rather, to persuade as many at the court in Madkerry – she and her husband had their followers there still – not to make war. How they were to deprive the rajah of those fiendish devices he had no idea, but the promise of an even greater quantity of gold if they did had brought an assurance that they could do so. Somervile hadn't thought it very likely, but he'd been able to tell his old friend that action was in hand and that therefore he need not trouble his mind. It was no doubt a deception of sorts (just as, indeed, was Hervey's decision not to speak to his commanders of the threat), but some things were better dealt with by oblivion.

Garratt had been content enough with St Alban's reassignment. With Worsley's troop already detached to Hervey's column, and no more exacting a job than running a relay line – in which all the corporals had had plenty of practice at Hounslow – he'd said he thought he might bear the loss of a lieutenant without too great a difficulty, especially with Armstrong at his hand. And Hervey had smiled wryly, for Garratt might now wear a dragoon's red, rather than green, but he retained the infantryman's instinct not to allow a subaltern officer too great an opinion of his importance.

They were certainly paying well for the *dowras* (guides), though how decent these would prove, only time would tell. But the Company had undoubtedly been generous with its gold. By dint of hard riding (though not Minnie, who had bided her time at Kushalnagar), Hervey had been able to see two of the other columns at their assembly points, but Colonel Jackson's from Mangalore would have taken another day to reach, and his was the least to trouble over, for all he expected them to do was watch. One of the dowras, a Mopla fisherman (with salt fish to prove it), had been so certain of his knowledge that Hervey decided to send his reserve, Colonel Steuart's column, via a parallel road to his own, which the man said had been cut only last summer. It was a gamble, but with only a few miles between them it might be worth it. Besides, his own column was strong enough to fight its way through. He hadn't thought there'd be need for a true reserve until they reached Madkerry.

The very best of the dowras, as far as the deewah's agent at Kushalnagar was concerned (he certainly bore the scars of his story of torture at the hands of the rajah's men), Hervey had assigned to St Alban, and with the promise of more pagodas than he'd see in a whole year of plenty.

The larger hand was now perfectly at its highest point: nine o'clock. 'I think we may begin,' said Hervey, closing his watch and turning to the commanding officer of His Majesty's 39th (Dorsetshire) Regiment of Foot. 'Colonel Lindesay, your regiment bears the honour *Primus in Indus* on its colours. Proceed now to be *Primus in Coorg*, if you please.'

Lindesay was at least a dozen years older than Hervey, and an Irish peerage added distinction, but he was known by all to be so married to his regiment as to own no ambition – only an infinite pride in its long history, especially its rightful claim to be the first to have served in India. The regiment had fought at Plassey with Clive. Nothing could therefore dismay them now.

He returned the smile, saluted, reined about and trotted forward to lead his 'Dorsets' into another chapter of their history.

Hervey hoped he'd not expose himself too much.

For the time being, however, there was nothing he could do but let Lindesay make his way. Fourteen months it had been since he'd first come here, and but for the great *bandobast* – so many bullock carts, elephants and all the paraphernalia of a military town on the march – it was not in the least bit different, save that the river was higher. But so much . . . *impedimenta*; was this truly how to make war? Here were not so much its sinews, as Cicero had it ('The sinews of war are infinite money'), but a great bloated belly. Little rapid movement, and even less agility, could be expected from such a form as this. But he couldn't have it both ways at once: 'Supply must be contained amply within the elements of each force sufficient to sustain active operations for seven days.' And men could not fight on biscuit for a whole week.

There would certainly be no difficulty in crossing the river, at least, for the bridge stood well proud of the water still, and the company of artillery was arraigned in open view. He'd had a strong picket here, with guns, for several weeks, for it was possible that the rajah might try to demolish it. Now, though, with such a show of force – and King's troops, not just Native – no Coorg who valued his life would risk *tirer le premier*? Indeed, the more he thought about it, the more impossible the rajah's position seemed to be. Why, then, if he were a rational man – which he'd certainly thought the case during his audience – did he not now bow the knee to Fort St George? At Hervey's suggestion, Lindesay was to make a show of artillery as they proceeded, which ought to dissuade even the bravest of the Coorgs from discharging a single shot. Except that, as he very well knew, men under discipline did not answer to reason but to orders.

He took out his telescope to watch as the advance guard marched onto the bridge, skirmishers out. Halfway across there was a ragged volley from the barricade athwart the road where the customs post stood – much smoke and noise, but no effect. At once the 6-pounder in the embrasure on the approaches sent a round of common shell to the barricade. Three hundred yards, barrel elevation zero, sighted by the captain himself, the round struck fair in the middle just a foot from the top, gouging a cautionary hole and bursting with much noise and many fragments. The defenders fled, save two wounded, but the Thirty-ninth's skirmishers were over the barricade in seconds and gave a chasing volley. The Coorgs threw down their blades and dropped to their knees.

Hervey lowered his telescope. 'Nice work . . . nicely done. Come on, Neale, let's see if any of them have anything to say.'

Serjeant Acton unbound the firelock of his carbine. The Thirty-ninth might have secured the far bank, but that didn't mean he would take any risks.

By the time they made their way through the press of muskets, the Coorgs were having their wounds bound up. They'd live, said the Thirty-ninth's surgeon, who seemed uncommonly far in the van, as indeed was the commanding officer. Those who'd surrendered un-scathed were already enjoying the Dorsets' tobacco.

Lindesay handed him a *pichangatti*. 'By custom, as I recall it, the first trophy goes to the general officer commanding.'

Hervey thanked him. The *pichangatti* was more cleaver than knife – heavy, broad steel blade, with a single fuller on each side.

'Or an *ayagatti*, if you prefer.'

The *ayagatti* was like the Gorkhas' *kukri*, but longer. Both trophies were made of fine steel. 'Fearsome weapons, if handled fearlessly,' declared Hervey. 'But evidently not this day.'

He saw two of the guides talking to the captives, who seemed to be answering readily. Neale, by his side, caught the word *otteya'u*.

'He said "hostage", Colonel.'

'Indeed? Who is hostage? Go to it, Neale.'

The Coorg was willing enough to talk, and willing enough to talk slowly and clearly, and to repeat as much as was necessary until Neale was sure he understood. Hervey caught a few words, but not the sense.

It was scarcely necessary to pay a captive for information, but Neale gave him coin – and with some show – to encourage the others to think about it.

'Apparently the rajah's taken hostage a member of every family, and they'll be put to the sword if a *feringhee* so much as touches his person. An exaggeration, no doubt – every family – but I suppose a man doesn't know if it's his family or no.'

'Indeed; seven thousand hostages? Impossible. But if that's what they believe . . . Will he join us, though, and set free his family? Ask him.'

Neale put the question. The vigorous rocking of the head in reply needed no translation.

One of the other guides had been successful too. 'It seems there are a dozen stockades between here and Madkerry, though not all are occupied,' said Lindesay. 'Doubtless they'll fall back to each in turn.'

'Doubtless,' agreed Hervey. 'Some you must be able to enfilade from a flank, though. If only we can get these Coorgs to show us the forest tracks. Some of them must be from hereabout.'

But Colonel Lindesay's men needed no urging. The skirmishers were already moving on, with a guide and two of the captives.

'Green will find a way,' said Lindesay. 'A most pushing ensign.'

Hervey wished the guns were nimbler, though. If only he'd the Chestnuts with him. He'd seen them bring a team forward, the gun come out of action, limber up and be away in less time than it took to soft-boil an egg . . .

'Colonel?'

He turned. 'Mr Jenkinson?'

A face already flushed with the exertion of a good deal of galloping reddened further. 'I'm awfully sorry, Colonel, I meant "General".'

Lieutenant Jenkinson, the adopted son of the late prime minister – and then of the succeeding earl (of Liverpool), his brother – was always more than he first appeared. Indeed, Hervey had been much pleased when he'd learned that he'd not be exchanging but coming with them to Madras. 'Proceed, Mr Jenkinson.'

'Sir, I'm come from Colonel Jackson with this despatch.'

Hervey read it.

'Were you with Colonel Jackson from the outset?'

'I was, General.'

'Tell me what happened.'

For a moment, Jenkinson was puzzled. He'd read the despatch, and didn't think he could add much, but an order was an order . . . 'Sir, I joined Colonel Jackson's force on the 28th, at the border with Coorg. He had been there two days—'

'Why so early?'

'I don't know, Colonel – I mean, General. But he told me at once of his concern for Mangalore, which he'd had to leave with very few troops. He thought it "defenceless", he said, and it has much treasure – thirteen lakhs of rupees, he said – which might be the object of attack, either by the Coorgs or by discontented Moplas in that neighbourhood. So he'd decided on a spoiling attack, and before dawn on the 29th he struck camp and advanced on the interior, with his company of white troops leading, and yesterday they took the stockade at Coombla, about six or seven miles, and without loss, though several Coorgs were killed, and in the afternoon his scouts reported an abandoned stockade, whose garrison the local people said had withdrawn to Madkerry. And this morning he continues the advance but he asks for artillery, for he has none.'

'I am well aware of that, Jenkinson. His force was intended as one of observation only . . . Why did he not think to inform me of his going early?'

'I cannot tell.'

'Did you yourself not think it proper to report?'

'Only this latter day, General, which was when Colonel Jackson himself determined he would ask for guns. Hitherto, I confess I comprehended my task to be that of a galloper.'

Hervey nodded. It wasn't unreasonable. If a lieutenant-colonel considered it unnecessary to report, then so might an officer lately a cornet. But he couldn't welcome Jackson's advance if it required artillery, for he had none to spare. Indeed, he could scarcely welcome it even if it didn't need guns, for although clearly it put more distance between Mangalore and the Coorgs, it placed his force in the most perilous of positions if the worm turned, so to speak. And while Mangalore wasn't his responsibility, he'd have no option but to accept that it was if the place were overrun.

'What is your opinion?'

'*My* opinion, sir?'

Hervey waited. It didn't do to repeat himself.

'I could only concur with Colonel Jackson.'

'Why?'

'Because he is a colonel, sir, and I a lieutenant.'

'And I a brigadier-general.'

'Sir?'

'By your own logic, if I require something, then by the seniority of my rank I must be right in requiring it.'

Jenkinson hadn't doubted his own judgement, only his place to give it (he had a very proper view of these things). Hervey certainly didn't doubt his judgement; he'd seen it in the affair with the French three years before. On the other hand, he'd not had opportunity to meet Jackson, and couldn't therefore be certain of his temper.

'General, I believe that if Colonel Jackson were to garrison the stockade that he now has possession of, the Coorgs would not be able to take it without the greatest loss, and much time. I think that he needs no guns to do this, though they would of course be helpful. But he's advanced further – by now perhaps another ten miles – and may not be so securely placed were he to face an attack. The country in the west becomes tricky as soon as you reach the jungle – there are so many tracks which animals and forest people make, and which the Coorgs can move undetected by. But by all accounts they won't stand against artillery, and two guns – even one – would do great service. Whether or not it was right that Colonel Jackson advanced rather than merely observed, I can't say, General. It was a question of judgement, and he was infinitely better qualified to make and exercise that judgement than I.'

'Handsomely put, Jenkinson, but a question to be addressed when we've taken the rajah and Madkerry is ours. What matters now is your judgement of the need of guns.'

He turned to Neale.

'We'd better send a 12-pounder. Just the one, mind. We'll need every other here if Lindesay's men are to move at more than the snail's pace. And it had better have an escort of dragoons.'

'General.'

Hervey turned back to Jenkinson. 'Who took your place with Colonel Jackson?'

'Cornet Stubbs, General.'

'Who came with you?'

'My coverman only, sir. The change of horses would otherwise have been—'

'How long were you?'

'Five hours, sir, a little under.'

And some of that before dawn; Hervey nodded approvingly. 'Very well, I would that you conduct the gunners there as soon as may be, though I can't suppose it can be done in a single march. Tomorrow midday at the earliest.' He turned to Neale again. 'Better have the dragoons relay a note to Jackson telling him.'

'At once, General.'

'Jenkinson, take what refreshment you wish and then hustle the artillerists. My compliments to Colonel Jackson, but impress upon him that there's no honour for being first to Madkerry. Our business is to secure the person of the rajah, and the peace of the country, and I won't have it put in jeopardy.'

'Yes, General.'

He gathered his reins and saluted.

Hervey acknowledged with a touch to his peak. 'And Jenkinson . . .'

'General?'

'Good work.'

'Sir.'

Two hours later they'd gone but a couple of miles. Hervey had seen enough of the infantry in his time to know that at some things they couldn't be rushed. At this rate, however – and with scarcely a shot fired – the Coorgs would have leisure to turn Madkerry into a redoubt. He began wondering whether an inducement to be first at Madkerry might not have been a bad thing after all, though 'licence to loot', as at Seringapatam, wouldn't serve in these enlightened times.

He'd just got back into the saddle, intending to go up the column to see for himself what stayed them, when Colonel Lindesay rode back.

'The beggars've felled so many trees, my pioneers are sorely pressed cutting and hauling 'em clear; and they're harassing too – from a distance, and without effect, but a ball singing in the ears and no notion where from is trying for the skirmishers too.'

Hervey nodded, but they couldn't clear the whole way like this. He turned to Neale. 'Have Captain Worsley come at once.'

Neale detailed an orderly to take the message.

Worsley wasn't long in coming. 'What's the delay, General? I was about to come and ask if I could off-saddle.'

'Quite. The advance guard's having the deucedest job, it seems – trees felled and random shots. Do you feel able to take the lead for a while to hustle the shooters?'

'I don't see why not – at least up to the first stockade, or whatever it is. I'll take the whole troop. Luck might go with us.'

'Quite,' said Hervey, turning back to Lindesay. 'You'll keep your men well up, though, Colonel, if you please.'

'Of course. They're as eager for the fight as any.'

'I don't doubt it. So let's keep them for it, rather than this lumbering. Leave the rearmost company to do it.'

'I shall.'

Worsley was already cantering back to his troop, to the consternation of the Dorsets' baggage-train.

Hervey was glad that he'd put them second in the order of march, before the native infantry. He'd been uneasy about their churning up the ground, making it a trial for the foot-soldiers following, but the road was better going than expected. He took the risk because he intended loosing them as soon as resistance slackened, which he'd every reason to suppose would not be long. What he did now, though, was not in the drill book – cavalry helping infantry forward in close country – but he'd a notion that the sight of horsemen, and their red tunics, might actually discourage would-be marksmen.

And sharp they were about it. They were, so to speak, on parade, after all. Just ten minutes was all it took. Hervey nodded to the salute as they trotted past, scouts and dowra well forward, then the advance guard, and Worsley himself leading the main body – fifty sabres, with Troop Serjeant-Major Wainwright at the rear like the second whip at hound exercise. A commanding officer could not show favouritism; but none worth his salt could have *no* favourites. Wainwright was the best of men, and from so unpromising a place as they'd found him – in the biggest fencing crib twixt London and Bristol. In his less reverent moments, Hervey reckoned that Wainwright must have been born without Original Sin. And he'd so nearly gone to his Maker in the skirmish at the Cape those five years ago. But then another dragoon—

'Sar'nt-Major – what do you do here?'

Armstrong halted and saluted. 'Just wanting to keep an eye on young Wainwright, Colonel.'

It was none of Hervey's business, and he knew it, even though Armstrong persisted with the compliment of 'Colonel'. What happened in the Sixth at this moment was the major's affair. He'd known Armstrong long enough, though. 'You thought there might be opportunity to draw your sword, no doubt?'

'It's been a while, Colonel, except for the flat.'

'It has indeed. I shall accompany you.'

Serjeant Acton sighed to himself. It was trial enough covering a general officer commanding the field force, let alone one who still thought himself a colonel. The country was impossible.

Neale too looked uncertain, though the prospect of action – even just observing it – likewise lofted his spirits.

They didn't have to wait long. In five minutes there were shots – a fusillade; and then nothing. By the time they got up – taking several teak trunks in their stride – Worsley's men had sabred two and captured three.

Rough handling and then a canteen of water brought intelligence of a stockade a mile ahead, where the road turned back on itself to ascend a cliff.

The officer of the advance guard, Warde, a wheaten-haired cornet come from the Bays, asked Worsley if they could slip into the forest when they came a bit closer – it was clear of undergrowth here, the canopy complete – and try to work round the flank, for otherwise they'd only be seen without seeing.

Worsley agreed. He'd proceed with the main body, slowly, but enough to make the Coorgs think they were wary, masking Warde's party so that they could break away as close as possible to work round behind the stockade and open a harassing fire. Shots from an unexpected quarter, however light, could unnerve an unseasoned defender. They might well bolt the garrison, and if not, his dragoons could begin probing to test their resolve.

He didn't need to, but when he'd finished he looked at Hervey for assent. 'Leave to advance?'

'Kick on.'

The first of the Dorsets' light company were coming up, cursing the slope and the dragoons who could take it at their ease. Just behind were the lighter guns, and Hervey decided that once the stockade was behind them he'd give Worsley the 6-pounder. The 'whiff of grapeshot' could do wonders.

Meanwhile he thought it best to lighten his hands. 'Corporal Johnson, take these, if you will.' He passed him the knife-edged trophies, which he'd hung rather precariously on his saddle.

Johnson tried to cram them into his saddle bags, but admitted defeat and got down with muttered profanities to stow them in the panniers on the bat-horse.

'I've more blades now than t'bloody Master Cutler.'

But Armstrong heard – he always did, one way or the other – and it made no difference that Johnson was now groom to a temporary general officer.

'Then perhaps they'll be pleased to see you home in Sheffield at last, Corporal Johnson – which can be arranged if you wish.'

Johnson owed his survival over the years – and the affection in which he was generally held – to being able to judge how to turn away from the wind, having sailed too close. 'Beg yer pardon, sir,' was enough.

Decorum on parade, whether in the field or in barracks – Armstrong had himself offended against it in his greenery, and taken a few cuffings. Not that an outsider could have thought it of this paragon of serjeant-majory now. Hervey smiled to himself. Somehow these things were passed on, and there was no profit in asking exactly how. It was a mystery – like the apostolic succession, but without the laying on of hands.

'Let's see them go to it then, gentlemen. Do you propose to accompany, Mr Armstrong?'

'With your leave, General.'

Acton groaned quietly.

*

Hervey reckoned it was just short of a mile before they halted, but the road was twisty and the grade increasing. He'd checked his instinct to close up; Worsley didn't need him, and he didn't want any to think that he thought he did.

In sight now was the stockade – a furlong at most.

'Horse holders,' said Worsley quietly.

The order was passed down the column quietly too, and then 'Dismount.'

It was the lot of the junior dragoon, one in three, to hold the troopers while the other two, carbines unshipped, had their sport. None preferred it, but they supposed their time would come.

Warde's men were already in the forest, but there was no knowing their progress. They'd do well simply to keep direction.

Armstrong dismounted and gave the reins to his coverman. Worsley's was one of 'his' troops; he needed no leave to go forward.

In a minute or so Hervey followed. He was damned if he was going to ride to Madkerry at the back of a column of his own men.

He found Worsley studying the stockade.

'Not a sign of life,' he said, handing Hervey his telescope. 'But it's a deuced good position. Why would they *not* garrison it? I'll give Warde another five minutes and if there's nothing, we'll approach on foot.'

Hervey nodded, handing back the glass. 'You'll be careful of your flanks, will you. It's the very devil to see where the fire comes from.'

'I've put in flankers a dozen yards.'

'Capital.'

Two dozen dragoons in two ranks, and five unseen on either flank: it ought to make the defenders of the stockade think twice, for although theirs was indeed a commanding position, two dozen red-coated men could only mean many more behind.

But then, if they were fearful for the hostages . . .

Wainwright walked behind the line dispensing words of 'advice'. Few of the dragoons had ever been shot over – Bhurtpore had been the last time – and so many had joined since the skirmishing at the Cape. They might scoff at the Coorgs as "eathens', but it never did to underestimate an opponent, especially one who defended his country against an invader – and whose families' forfeit life was the stake.

Minutes passed, and Hervey began thinking it might have been better to bring up the 6-pounder, although the felled trees were even more an obstacle to the gunners than to the infantry.

Then came the shots, distant, muffled. Warde had obviously found a vantage. Worsley gave the word to load, and then advance.

In open order, the dragoons filled the road. To even a practised observer they would look like the infantry's leading troops, though in fact there was nothing behind them for half a mile at least. No matter; such was the game of war.

Hervey remounted, better to see ahead. Armstrong too.

But if the Coorgs were in the stockade yet, they kept their cover well – not even a sentry's shadow.

The dragoons advanced steadily, and silent once Wainwright had barked at them. It wasn't for stealth – they advanced in full view of the stockade and stood out like red berries on holly – but for discipline. 'What is discipline, Private?' was a regular of the drill parade; and woe betide the dragoon who couldn't answer at once: 'Discipline is that which animates a body of men with one mind, and impels them zealously to pursue the same end.' Some of them understood the actual words; all of them understood the consequences of not understanding the sentiment.

Wainwright's bark was not the threat of retribution, however. Zeal was never (certainly not in the Sixth) obtained by terror. Praise from a superior, or the regard, at least, of his fellows, was what animated even the reprobate. Those 'sweats' in the ranks who had gone at the Burmans at Rangoon, and then at Madho Singh's men at Bhurtpore, or even the savages at the Cape, knew it right enough. And those who now for the first time faced the King's enemies would understand it *soon* enough.

The shots continued, random, as if Warde were shooting snipe. Were they aimed shots – at fleeing figures or those who exposed themselves – or to flush the birds? Why were there none by return – or did the forest make no distinction? There was still no powder smoke above the parapets.

Hervey fretted for a mortar to drop a questing shell inside. It was no good; he'd have to arrange things better.

A hundred yards to go, and still no sign of life. If the Coorgs watched through loopholes they did it well, he conceded. But if they had muskets (and, God forbid, rifles), why did they not now begin their fire?

The sudden noise made even the seasoned dragoons blench. The sally port dropped like a stone. Out spilled a host whose like he'd never seen before. Not the numbers – a hundred? – but the baying and the blades, like ancient Gauls in the forests of the north.

No time even to think it. He drew his sabre. Acton just beat him to it, Armstrong a fraction slower; even Johnson.

With Neale, the RSM's coverman and two orderlies – seven.

Worsley ordered the front rank to its knees, carbines to the aim. Better a heavy volley from both ranks than two lighter ones. No time to reload.

Hervey shortened his reins. He shouldn't be here – but as well that he was. 'Ready, Sar'nt-Major?'

'Aye, Colonel.'

'Fire!' cried Worsley.

A perfect volley; much smoke; tumbling men; some still charging; others faltering.

'Clear the way!' Hervey pushed through and dug in his spurs.

Shots from Worsley's flankers tumbled several more.

Hervey made straight for the middle of them, sabre low, parting the mass and giving point to his right.

Acton took the man on the nearside before he could swing his knife at Hervey's mare.

Armstrong sabred two – impossible but for a man who'd practised on four continents.

Johnson parried and then cut so hard he severed a head.

Worsley's dragoons fell on what remained with barrel and butt.

No quarter.

Hervey galloped on – what use pulling up now?

There were scrambling figures atop the palisade, desperate to get away – and surely with intelligence worth having.

He spurred hard through the sally port, Acton hard on his heels.

And then—

He pulled up hard.

Women, children – corralled like so many cattle.

'What in God's name . . .'

* * *

SERJEANT ACTON HAD SAID nothing. It was not his place. He was not the colonel's keeper but his coverman. 'Whither thou goest, I will go.' That was his duty, his privilege, and – he trusted – his making.

Corporal Johnson had sworn a good deal, not least because it took him some time to recover the bat-horse, whose lead rein he'd had to drop as they took off, but otherwise he was enlivened by it. It would do him no harm in the estimation of the wet canteen.

Neale had confined himself to a quizzical 'quite a go, General'.

Armstrong was another matter. It was towards the end of the afternoon; the column had halted for the night and Hervey was sitting by himself under an atap roof in the second stockade of the day – taken without a shot, and without much sign that it had ever held a garrison worth the name – drinking tea sweetened with buffalo milk.

'A word, sir, please?'

Hervey knew what to expect. He'd first heard that request, probably, on the retreat to Corunna – or before that, even. It was the notice of displeasure – severe displeasure possibly. And Acton was nowhere to be seen, a sure sign he'd been told to make himself scarce.

'Of course, Sar'nt-Major. Tea?'

Armstrong shook his head. 'Charging like that, Colonel. It won't do.'

Hervey nodded. 'You're quite right, of course. Except that had we not done so, there'd be half a dozen and more dragoons in shallow graves.'

Armstrong sighed. 'I know that perfectly well, but it still won't do.'

'My mistake was to push Worsley's troop forward, rather than hastening the infantry, and the guns.'

He'd changed that straight afterwards, telling Worsley only to scout, that the light company of the Dorsets was advance guard, with the pioneers behind them to clear a way for the guns. It had worked well for the next three or four miles, and the taking of the second stockade.

'And getting between Colonel Lindesay and the enemy.'

He couldn't gainsay that either. It was a sound principle that a superior officer ought not to get forward of a subordinate. 'That I grant you too.'

'Not that it's done your stock with the troop any harm.'

'Nor yours, Sar'nt-Major. *Three* cuts, Johnson tells me.'

'I don't know how he saw anything, Colonel. He was going to it like we were at Sa'gun again.'

Hervey smiled. Happy memory, Sahagun, freezing though it was (he'd been monstrous young).

'And the women, Colonel. Can't we just send them down to Kushalnagar, or else let 'em high-tail it home? I don't like having women round something like this. Nor does the Dorsets' serjeant-major.'

'I had a mind that they might help us forward. Not a shield, but to discourage their menfolk – the rajah's men, I mean.'

For a good many of the women's menfolk were now dead.

Armstrong shook his head in disgust at the rajah's stratagem. 'Not even them Burmans did that – staking out women and bairns.'

It was true. In all his service, Hervey had never come across women and children 'staked out' in the fighting line. It had certainly not taken much interrogation to learn that their menfolk's charge – a forlorn hope if ever there was one – was ordered on pain of their women's execution. Indeed, when the dragoons learned of it, they swore to hang whoever had given the order, angered at having to kill men who charged just to save their kin from butchering.

'Some of them are sure to know a thing or two about what lies between here and Madkerry.'

He'd already discovered – if it were ever entirely possible to discover the negative – that they'd seen no caltrops.

'Aye, Colonel, true enough, but it's a slow enough business as it is.'

Hervey nodded. 'Yes, I believe you're right. Indeed, it's a deal slower business than I'd hoped. There are just too many men on too small a road.'

'That an' all.'

'So how do you suppose we'd get the women to Kushalnagar?'

Armstrong shook his head. It was a hopeless business either way. 'Why don't we put them under guard where they're at the village yonder, till all the column's passed? They'll be safe enough.'

Hervey thought on it for a moment or two. It seemed best. 'Very well. I'll have Captain Neale give the order. The NI's company, I think.'

Armstrong nodded. It had not been his place, he knew, but twenty-five years was a long time in the same uniform. And he'd every wish of seeing another five.

XXIV

The Culminating Point

Towards evening, four days later

THEIR POLICY HAS BEEN TO *oppose incursion with great vigour when the place of it is known beforehand and where the enemy force is small. Alternatively, when the situation is otherwise, the policy has been to permit of deep incursion to exhaust resolve and supplies, and then to counter-attack . . .*

He had gambled. He might not admit it – he preferred to think that first he'd reckoned, then risked, which was the art of generalcy – but he'd counted on the Coorgs losing heart as the columns converged. Progress had been damnably slow on all roads – almost continuous resistance: palisades and abbatis, cuddungs and breastworks, the closeness of the country affording no room for manoeuvre; and the sheer unwieldiness of the columns. His own, with the shortest distance to travel, was still a league and more from the plain of Madkerry, and before it, as the scouts reported, was a stockade larger than any so far (and who knew what lay beyond that?). Sickness, too, was thinning the ranks – of the Dorsets especially, on whom he depended most to maintain the momentum.

He began to wonder: did he have luck, that supreme and elusive quality which Bonaparte – mountebank that he was – said he prized most in his generals? He'd had his share in his rise from cornet to colonel; but was he a 'lucky general'?

They had but two days' rations left. The night before, as he contemplated the despatches from the other columns (including the death of the gallant Colonel Mill of the Fifty-fifth, who he thought must be the first commanding officer since Waterloo to die in battle), he began to think that no column would have the strength now to break through the stiffening defences as the Coorgs fell back 'to permit of deep incursion to exhaust resolve and supplies, and then to counter-attack' – his own words; his own cautionary words. Neale had suggested – urged, indeed – that the ration be cut by half, but Hervey had said no, for to do so would signify to the troops that the advance was faltering. Besides, to take away the source of strength to the fighting man at the very moment at which he might be called to a supreme effort would not serve.

So he'd gambled on breaking through this day – or on one of the other columns breaking through. The Coorgs could not prevail; not against an army of the Company. Not with him at its head. This was the culmination of twenty-five years practising the soldier's art. Failure was unthinkable; and therefore impossible. It was a question of time, and at what cost. That indeed would be the measure of his generalcy, not merely the achievement of his object.

He had one priceless advantage now, however – ripe intelligence. Of all the things he'd ever read before putting on the King's coat, nothing had made a deeper impression than what the great Duke of Marlborough had said: 'No war can ever be conducted without good and early intelligence.'

And having then put on the King's coat, he'd learned over the years how that good and early intelligence was obtained: by stealth, cunning, and daring; by extortion, enticement, gold – and chance. Recognizing the worth of chance intelligence was another matter, however.

The nautch girl had certainly chanced on them. She was, she'd told him – or rather, the dowra who'd brought her had – the wife of a high official of the court whom the rajah had sent towards the west to make sure there was no treachery in the ranks of the army there, as she believed he had also sent to north, south and east. The following day, she'd been hauled from their quarters by the chowdigars and sent east with the hostage wives, though they had largely shunned her, at least until she too was roughly corralled at the stockade.

And yet Neale had had his doubts at first. One of the wives had spat as she was led away, calling after her '*kottu*' – concubine (harlot, even) – and Hervey was anyway inclined to be wary, for she began with a litany of the rajah's crimes, just as would one who wished to ingratiate. On receiving word that the Company was assembling a force at Mysore, she said, the rajah, so as to be sure there would be no usurpation, no collusion, had murdered his mother and all his brothers and sisters – with his own sword indeed – and thrown them into a pit.

Had she seen this, Hervey asked. She had not, but neither had she seen the rajah's family in the days following; and it was spoken of freely in the palace at Soamwar Pettah. Pemma Virappa, the vakeel, was dead too – found hanged in the palace orchards, by his own hand or that of the rajah she didn't know. She said also that the rajah had begun to make free with any woman he chose, wed or not. That indeed, he had forced himself on her several times, and on others of her husband's family, which Hervey took to mean other of her husband's concubines. She wished only now for the rajah's death, she said, and would do whatever was in her power to assist him.

Hervey withdrew to speak with Neale, telling Johnson to attend on her as civilly as he could, and Acton to observe the dowra.

Then he sighed, and raised an eyebrow. 'And so, like Rahab before the fall of Jericho, to spare herself and her kin she now conspires with the enemy?'

Neale looked doubtful. Rahab had been a harlot too. '"And she said unto the men, I know that the Lord hath given you the land, and that your terror is fallen upon us, and that all the inhabitants of the land faint because of you."'

Hervey nodded. He was no Joshua, nor was Madkerry Jericho. His object was not to take the city, but its rajah. 'It is well said, but I have no task for this Rahab.'

Neale, however, could not quite bring himself to conclude that her words were merely honeyed. She'd borne herself well in being spat at. 'For the moment, General, I agree there is no task, but perhaps she might accompany in case of need. She would at least be able to identify the high officials, and those we might trust.'

Hervey wasn't inclined to dispute it. There was little mischief she could make under escort. 'Very well.'

They returned to find Corporal Johnson looking pleased.

'What is it?'

'Colonel – sorry, Colonel: Gen'ral – she knows 'ow t'rajah can get out o' t'fort if 'e 'as to.'

'What do you mean?' He glanced at Acton, who nodded.

''E'll tell yer, Gen'ral,' said Johnson, gesturing to the dowra.

Neale asked him.

'Sahib, it is true. She say there is secret way, to house of merchant.'

'Does she know which is the house?'

'Of course, sahib.'

'It might be useful,' Hervey conceded.

'There is more, sahib. She say rajah become angry when he learn all things taken from fort. All things to stop men.'

'What things?'

'*Gokharoo*, sahib – things hurt foot.'

'Take from fort – take where?'

'Rajah not know, sahib. They steal. That why angry.'

Hervey tried to conceal his satisfaction, for it wouldn't do to signal his earlier disquiet, even to Johnson. But relieved he most certainly was. He turned to Neale. 'I would know more.'

Neale was already looking as pleased as Johnson.

He had not long begun his despatch to Bangalore when one from St Alban arrived by hand of Private Owthwaite. Armstrong was at once at hand to observe – supervise – the novel experience of a private dragoon addressing a colonel, a brigadier-general even, on a matter other than a charge.

Hervey read it, and smiled. St Alban wrote that the prospect of Madkerry lay before them, and by tracks unused by the rajah's men. 'And you're able to return by these same tracks, Owthwaite?'

'I am, General. I 'ave a guide. They use the tracks to take stuff in and out without paying the dues.'

'Do they, indeed.' He supposed he ought to register some disapproval, given that he'd remanded Owthwaite for court martial for evading his dues – if it might be put that way. But St Alban had known his man. There were two real corporals with him – and good ones – but Owthwaite was the one for a job like this.

Neale came.

Hervey told him the news. 'We have our chance, now, of stopping the earth before our fox bolts. If our Rahab returns with Owthwaite, she can indicate the house.'

'Indeed so, General.'

Hervey dashed off a note for St Alban.

'Here, Private Owthwaite. I ought to send this by hand of an officer, but if you're true, there is no need. Just a sowar to accompany you back, I think, and the wife of a high officer of the rajah's court.'

Owthwaite took the note and saluted. 'General!'

'Read it and ask Captain Neale if there's anything to explain. But waste no time getting back.' There was but an hour's light left, at most. 'And watch the India woman like a hawk.'

'General!'

Armstrong frowned as Owthwaite doubled away.

'All is hazard in war, Sar'nt-Major, but I fancy not this time with Owthwaite.'

'I'd stake my pension on it, General. Well, some of it.'

The column had been at the halt for the better part of an hour. Even half-rations had to be cooked, water fetched and boiled, and sentries posted. They were to bed down *en position* that night again, as last night – no tents; weapons by their side, ready; and Hervey and his party with the Dorsets for safety. He must go forward and see Colonel Lindesay, though. There was now no reason not to run hard at Madkerry to-morrow, and early. Whatever barred their way – even another stockade – couldn't stand long, for without being able to salt the road with caltrops as they withdrew, the defenders risked being overrun. If the rajah stood his ground at the fort, the guns would make short work of it; and if he bolted via his secret way, they'd have him in the bag. He even contemplated resuming the march after dark, but moving at night in jungle, even on a road, was the devil's own business.

The brigade orderly officer came hurrying. 'General, a message from Colonel Lindesay: there are Coorgs approaching under a flag of truce.'

Hervey sprang up, letting fall the canteen of tea Johnson had just brought him. They'd off-saddled, but rather than wait, he set off at once on foot, telling Johnson to make ready and follow.

He moved rapidly through the Dorsets' battalion companies, Acton and Neale at his side, to where their light company, in the van again, were standing to arms in a small clearing. A subaltern pointed towards a bamboo hut.

Lindesay, speaking to the Coorg delegation (if delegates they were, or simply saviours of their own skins) – half a dozen, including two men-at-arms – saluted as he came up. Hervey touched his cap peak in return, taking as little notice of the 'delegation' as he could, reckoning that a show of indifference would strengthen his hand if they were here to negotiate.

The Coorgs braced. Their leader, a man of about fifty, in short *kupya* with a crimson and gold brocaded *chale*, bowed.

'Says he's chief minister and commander-in-chief, name of Konandera Apoo,' said Lindesay, showing no keener expectation.

Hervey acknowledged the bow, but curtly. He wondered in what capacity he came – as chief minister or commander-in-chief.

'What does he want?'

'To speak to you. He says he can't make a contract with any but his equal.'

'Contract?'

'If the interpreter has it right. Deuced difficult tongue. Rajender?'

'Sir, it is exactly right.'

Hervey turned to him. 'Did he say any more?'

'No, sir, only that he wished to speak to General Hervey.'

'He knew my name?'

'Yes, sir.'

Hervey tried not to look too surprised.

'Very well. Tell him who I am, and to state his business.'

Neale listened intently as Lindesay's dowra translated; and then nodded, content. His command of the language – if there was but a single one – was still elementary, but it served.

General Apoo stated his business, Neale's face revealing just a touch of relief as he did so.

The dowra spelled it out. 'He has at his command three hundred men, sahib, from the garrison at Madkerry. He wishes to place himself at your disposal in return for . . . *tappu, annassri.*'

'Amnesty,' said Neale.

'Ask him how many men the rajah now disposes at Madkerry.'

Just the guards at the fort, and his body-men, came the reply.

Hervey thought a little. Why would a high official about to deliver up three hundred men, and Madkerry and the rajah thereby, not ask for gold? Yet what ruse could it be?

'Where are his troops now?'

Camped where the road entered the forest, said the dowra.

'Tell him that I shall require that he returns at once to Madkerry accompanied by my troops. Tell him that I require him as soon as we reach Madkerry to send hircarrahs to all his detachments ordering them at once to lay down their arms and answer to the senior officer of the column before them. And to deliver up the rajah into my custody.'

Between Neale and Rajender the terms were dictated, and with few requests for clarification.

Then a simple *'Ate'* – 'Yes.'

Hervey studied the chief minister intently. He wanted to say that if he departed in the slightest from the undertaking, he would himself despatch him with his sabre as a common spy. But the eyes told him he didn't need to.

'Neale, send at once for Worsley's troop, and also to Colonel Fraser. His time is coming, I do believe.'

Colonel James Fraser, who would be the resident – in practice the governor – once they'd deposed the rajah, was at Kushalnagar still, at Hervey's express wish since he'd concerns enough without 'political' advice.

He turned next to Lindesay, at last with a look of triumph, if conditional. 'We march at once. We've an hour of light of sorts. We can make Madkerry before pitch darkness. Two miles only. We *must*.' The moon would not be up for a good few hours yet.

* * *

AN HOUR BEFORE first light, Hervey lay down at last, pulling his cloak about him. War took a strange course, he mused. Both sides would battle as if to the very last man, and then suddenly, inexplicably – except perhaps in hindsight – one side would yield. *Der Kulminationspunkt.* That was what the Prussian treatise called it. The greatest general might not see its coming, but must at once recognize when it did, so as to seize the opportunity. 'Go on, Maitland! Go on! They won't stand!' He'd heard the very words himself that day at Waterloo, and seen the duke wave his hat to have the whole line advance – the great turning of the tide of history.

It was absurd, presumptuous in the extreme, to make comparison with that greatest of battles. But just like the duke before Waterloo (and he himself had ridden with him), he'd miscalculated, misjudged, misapplied; and then last night he'd seized the moment. And yet it was not quite the irreversible moment that had been the duke's. He had only the word of a traitor to judge that the rajah's men would not stand.

After so many days, though, it was good to lie down under the stars rather than the forest's canopy. They'd not thrown all caution to the wind to get here – Worsley's men had gone at a brisk trot rather than a canter, for if it were a trick, it was sure to be one that anticipated a gallop – but as they passed one abandoned post after another, he'd begun to believe it true: Madkerry, as Jericho had been to Joshua, was indeed to be given up to him.

Only the inscrutable fort remained. Would that be given up also? Or would they have to lay tedious siege?

He'd decided not to conceal their sudden presence. Better to signal they were here, that they held the high ground and the road to Kushalnagar, and that more would therefore surely follow. He told Lindesay to build up the campfires therefore: make a show of force, sound the trumpet and bugle, tell the people of Madkerry that their deliverers were at hand, and the fort that their time was nigh.

Then St Alban had come. He knew where the rajah was – taken refuge in the fort after fleeing the palace – and Owthwaite's nautch girl had shown them the house where the secret passage emerged. He now had possession of it indeed, and for a very modest outlay of gold. But more: the fisher folk – whether or not the same they'd seen last year, he was unsure – had been willing accomplices for an even lesser amount. They professed a hatred for the rajah's men that counted more than any pagodas: licence to sell their fish could be bought only with the favours of their women. They'd told him of the priest at Madkerry, half *feringhee*, who was now in fear for his life and that of his flock after the murder of the rajah's family, for the rajah, Herod-like in his suspicion, might put anyone to the sword. St Alban had searched him out in the dead of night. He was of Portuguese descent, and inclined therefore towards them, and asked what he might do to help.

'None of this may be of any consequence,' St Alban had said, 'but we have at least men about the place on whom we may count for information.'

Hervey agreed. The chief minister was a windfall, and only time would tell what it was that had truly shaken the tree, but the rajah was not yet in their hands. Until he could make contact with the other columns he couldn't know if the minister's word was law.

For some time he'd turned over the options in his mind, mercifully few though there were, before deciding. When it was light, St Alban and his detachment would ride to the secret house, and even though it was theirs already, with great show would take possession. Meanwhile Worsley's troop would encircle the fort, and the weary regiments of foot and the artillery, the larger part of the force being still in the forest, would assemble on the plain. This, at least, should prevent Apoo's turncoats from any change of heart, he said. It was, however, though he possessed no secret weapon like Joshua's trumpets, a challenge to those inside the fort: 'Here, Chikka Virarajendra, Rajah of Coorg, are the means by which we shall lay siege.'

And when he'd arraigned his host before 'Jericho', he would send him the ultimatum. It would consist of few words.

*

Hervey woke just before dawn with Johnson's hand to his shoulder.

'Tea, Colonel.'

He sat up at once, dog-tired but enlivened by the prospect of the day. 'No brandy? No schnapps?'

'No Germans.'

Johnson had woken him thus at Waterloo. He'd said he'd tried to get drink from one of the King's Germans, but that the man had wanted gold for it. They'd joked of it many a time since.

Were you too at Waterloo? 'Tis no matter what you do, if you were at Waterloo.

'Deucedest luck, Corp'l Johnson, for our war chest's replete with coin still.'

The battle-bond never loosened, but it was more than simply the sharing of shot and shell that day. The rain had beaten down all night as the army lay in the flattening corn, yet somehow Johnson had found a flame to boil a pot. And all for a cornet. How many colonels had sipped hot tea that day?

When the sun was up he saw what a prodigious effort the Dorsets had made. Not only was their light company encamped outside the forest, but the battalion companies too – and all their baggage and sutlers, so that there was soon a great breakfast of coffee and bacon.

'Well, General, my compliments to you,' said Lindesay, enjoying his first cigar of the day. 'We have, it appears, the prize.'

Hervey smiled. 'Perhaps let us say that we know where is the prize and that it can go to no other but us,' he said, declining a cigar but accepting the coffee.

He told him his intention.

Lindesay nodded. 'We've left a couple of dozen sick behind us. I'd rather get 'em up as send 'em down to Kushalnagar. But all's well otherwise.'

Hervey thanked him. They would talk about what to do with the dead later.

Next he went to see Worsley. The farrier was busy, but otherwise the troop looked ready.

He told him his design: 'St Alban first, and once he's at the house, you may strike off. I've told Neale to have the guns drive forward onto that bluff yonder.' He pointed to a promontory above one of the streams a furlong away, a quarter of a mile from the fort and at about the same elevation. 'Just in case the rajah thinks we've come on light scales.'

Worsley understood. He'd already told off the three detachments – north, south, west – as Hervey had warned in the note sent with Owthwaite, their job to bring in the other columns. He was all eagerness – a gallop at last, even if not sword in hand.

'But six of your neatest men, if you will, to lend lustre as I take the rajah's sword.'

'Of course.'

He beckoned Johnson and the syces. Minnie looked eager too. He'd let her have her head a little as they made for where St Alban had set up camp half a mile along the jungle edge.

There was no hiding their satisfaction. 'Coffee, Colonel?' asked a dragoon well known to the serjeant-major (as the saying went), especially after a pay-night.

Hervey took it, more out of duty than desire. 'There'll be a little prize money, no doubt, Dixon. Best spend it on coffee, though, think you not?'

Dixon smiled dutifully. 'Colonel.'

He walked aside a little with St Alban. 'Edward, no exploring officer in Spain had more success, I fancy. Smart work. Smart work indeed.'

'Thank you, Colonel. Though it deprived me of a charge, I understand.'

'A trifling affair, not worth your regrets.'

'That's not what Serjeant Acton said.'

Hervey shook his head knowingly. 'What is the essence of *éclairage*, Edward?'

St Alban smiled. 'A clean blade.'

'Quite.'

'Ready in half an hour?'

They were. And sharply away, and in ten minutes were signalling from the roof of the house that it was theirs.

Then Worsley's troop, followed by the artillery at a purposeful trot – less one of the 12-pounders, which Hervey decided he would take with him directly. The Dorsets were already disposing their red coats the length of the ridge – a sight to behold, exactly as he'd intended – and the native infantry stolidly filing onto the plain from their woody bivouacs.

Hervey had not long taken post on a bluff with a clear sight of the fort – and the fort thereby with a clear sight of him – when Colonel Fraser came.

'''Pon my word, you've made admirable haste, Colonel. I'm glad to see you.'

'I set off as soon as word reached me. The moon was up by then.'

'Even so . . .'

Fraser was a spare, intense-looking man, resembling more a minister of the Kirk than a soldier. He was a man nevertheless who possessed Somervile's every confidence. Hervey told him all that had happened, although all that mattered was what they now beheld.

'Do you wish to accompany me to take the rajah's surrender? That is, if he's not inclined to play the antique Roman.'

Fraser said he would indeed wish to accompany him, but that he was certain the last thing this rajah would do was fall on his sword. Nor, by all accounts, was he prepared to wield it against any who carried one.

With an escort of six dragoons, and the gleaming 12-pounder, the general officer commanding the Coorg Field Force left his vantage point for the fort, to call out the last Rajah of Coorg.

He was in good spirits. 'Neale, you might have found yourself a red coat for the occasion. You are quite the odd bird in the flock. They'll take you for a footman!'

Neale was in equal spirits. 'In green, General? Foot's the very last thing I should be taken for. India's yet to see a rifleman.'

They laughed. He liked Neale more by the day. He was determined – by hook or by crook – to have him in the Sixth.

He glanced over his shoulder again. Fraser and his party looked serviceable, and Worsley's men had somehow turned themselves into a creditable escort, some feat given that they'd fought and slept in their jackets for days. It was a moment to savour, long in conception, and accomplished, he supposed, at not too great a price.

Their progress gathered other admirers. Or rather, they were watched in silence by the people of Madkerry, high and low caste alike, for what were they to make of the invader? Except the children, who watched with acclamation, as anywhere when soldiers passed. No doubt, too, but unseen, they were closely observed by what sentinels were left on the parapets of the fort. Acton, certainly, was not inclined to slacken the rein.

They proceeded not with a flag of truce, however, but as victors, an orderly carrying Hervey's pennant. Halting three hundred yards from the fort to have the rajah walk, or ride, a suitably humbling distance, he sent the ultimatum forward under escort of two dragoons. It was in both English and Kanarese so that whoever opened it could be in no doubt – written very exactly by his dowra under Neale's sternest supervision, with a second translating back into English to be sure that there was no possibility of misunderstanding – and borne by the dowra so that there might be no confusion at the gate. He took with him, too, a sealed letter from Somervile, which Hervey had carried throughout in an oilskin. It was, his old friend said, a letter assuring the rajah of safe conduct: the seal of the governor when facing men of war might be a powerful comfort. Hervey had not gainsaid him, but he was inclined to believe that the threat of oblivion was the more powerful persuader.

The gunners began unlimbering the 12-pounder.

'Have it lay on the gates.'

Neale nodded to one of the orderlies, who took the order to the bombardier.

Now it was merely a time of waiting. 'Very well,' said Hervey, 'we shall see what we shall see. But I'll not wait long for it.'

He dismounted nevertheless. His mare had borne him well these past days, but he saw no reason to weigh upon her back when there was no need, and besides, the sun was gaining heat, and there was shade nearby. The rest followed suit, save the dragoons, who remained mounted in line, but at ease.

He took up his telescope as the dowra delivered the ultimatum to the captain of the guard. It was done quickly, as if the captain understood exactly what was afoot – as indeed was the purpose of the entire spectacle.

Hervey took out his watch. 'Fifteen minutes, and then I shall knock loudly on the gates.'

'A whiff of roundshot,' said Neale.

Hervey smiled grimly. 'A lesser charge made Bonaparte's reputation, did it not?'

Neale smiled too. 'Just so, General.'

And in truth, a bombardment of even a single round would have been pleasing to all who stood with him, save perhaps Colonel Fraser, who if all proceeded rightly would remain here many months – years – after Hervey and his field force had returned to their stations.

But no powder, it seemed, would be necessary. Not five minutes later the gates were opened wide, and out walked – walked, not rode, exactly as prescribed in the ultimatum – an assemblage of evident importance.

'Is it he, General?' asked Neale, glass to his eye.

'He or someone vested very much like.'

Colonel Fraser was surer. 'It is he, or very remarkably like. He walks in that way the rajah has.'

Hervey was not inclined to enquire how exactly. He didn't himself recall any peculiarity – though in truth he'd barely observed him walk ten paces during his audience. 'Very well; stay here in the shade, if you please. Better that your hands are clean.'

Fraser might well indeed find things easier later if he were distanced from the actual 'regicide'. Anyway, this was his, Hervey's, moment.

He walked with Neale back to where the dragoons stood, Acton following within a sabre's cut (he trusted no one, despite the overwhelming force standing on the hills behind them).

'Can you be sure it's he?' asked Neale. 'He's made an art of perfidy.'

There were six in the party, two female and one who might have been a body-man (there were several knives at his *chale*), and three in silk, though the rajah – if it were indeed he – more richly brocaded.

At fifty yards, Hervey felt almost certain. 'A year ago, and not long in his company, but I would say it was.'

'He'll not speak to you till I'm certain,' said Neale sharply.

'How do you propose to be?'

'I'll know, General. I'll know.'

He went forward to stay their advance – or to greet them, as perhaps it seemed to them, and for all the world as if he were on parade at Bangalore. His orderly had shone his boots and got out his dress crossbelt and kurta – green, 'like a footman', against a background of red.

But to a Coorg – to any 'Hindoo' – while red was revered for its purity, green was the colour of singular significance. Om, the Sun, drove across the sky each day in a chariot drawn by a green horse with seven heads, preceded by Aruna – Dawn. Neale, his youth concealed beneath his braided forage cap (like those worn by British officers), was thereby to all save perhaps the rajah, who might indeed recollect his visitor of a year before, the most important of the assemblage that awaited them –

the English general who sent the ultimatum, the insult, and to whom they must all now submit.

Hervey followed as close as seemed dignified, keen to hear the exchange, whether he understood it or not.

The rajah made a grand if obviously uneasy show of greeting. Hervey knew it was he – the round face, the sallow skin, the large dark eyes yet soft features – features indeed that betrayed both depravity and terror.

Neale bowed to acknowledge.

Then—

'Feringhee!' cried the body-man, pistol out from nowhere.

The ball struck like David's stone.

Neale tumbled back.

Hervey leapt, sword drawn, thrusting vengefully.

The man was dead before he fell.

Then as quickly again he lunged at the rajah, sabre lofting for *Cut Two* – Upper Left to Lower Right – but Acton's blade stayed it as the terrified prince fell to his knees.

The dragoons surged forward, trampling the women and the silks.

Colonel Fraser ran to them, sword in hand. 'Hervey!'

XXV

A Time to Mourn

Later

. . . And, my dearest wife, the rest has been most dreadful melancholy. My dragoons, who had all seen Neale's murder – for murder it was – would have hanged the rajah from a gibbet with their own hands. Except that it had not been by his hand, nor could it conceivably have been by his design or desire, for he is a man by all accounts fearful of death, and death would surely have followed, and indeed did almost follow but for the address of my covering serjeant (Acton), who has thereby preserved me from a fate that might have been worse than any injury . . .

ST ALBAN HAD QUIETLY TAKEN Neale's place. In the afternoon, to Hervey's relief, Armstrong appeared and soon afterwards Major Garratt and many of the communicating troop. Hervey struggled hard to keep up the mask of command as the field force now closed on Madkerry from all directions. He greeted them with a hale salute and a congratulatory word or two, but the returns shocked him: fourteen King's officers killed or wounded, 139 rank and file; two native officers and 144 rank and file. It was nothing, perhaps, compared with a battle in Spain, no matter that the forces there had been far larger; and certainly not with that great battle that ended the 'never-ending war'; but a butcher's bill – a wretched term, but one they all spoke grimly of – was not paid without pain.

Native rank and file: somehow the words were more dismissive even than those the duke had famously used of his own men – 'the scum of the earth'. Anonymous words, too; yet they were men known well enough in their villages. He would not differentiate in his despatch to Fort St George (and yet he knew that at some point he would have to, for the book-keepers would have to know). Two hundred and ninety-nine, and with Neale, three hundred – a most convenient figure, for somehow it sounded less, being shorter, than 'two hundred and ninety-nine'. He would have to include the names of the officers, of course, and one of the names was Jenkinson – whose greatest friend, Cornet Agar, had also perished under his command, in the Levant.

Nothing but a battle lost could be half so melancholy as a battle won. The duke had said it, and now he himself might, for it was *his* battle won – his entirely.

He rode to Bangalore a week later in much despondency still (though he trusted he concealed it), turning over in his mind the letters he'd write to Neale's and Jenkinson's people, as well as to those whose sons or husbands were not directly under his command but on whose conduct his laurels had depended. He had handed command of the little force of occupation – a native battalion, a King's company and three guns – to Colonel Fraser as soon as he thought able, which in any case was not until the proper obsequies were carried out. The priest at Madkerry had come at once on hearing of the *feringhee* who'd been shot, and although finding him quite lifeless, had without any concern as to creed pronounced him *in periculo mortis* and anointed him with holy oil: '*Per istam sanctam Unctionem et suam piissimam misericordiam, indulgeat tibi Dominus quidquid . . .*'[*]

And then in the days that followed, as practicably as could be had, the bodies of those *feringhees* who had been killed outside Madkerry were brought to his church, and he conducted the burial service for each or severally. So Neale and Jenkinson had at least a proper committal, and a final resting place in hallowed ground, which Hervey thought also must be comfort to their families. Poor Mill of the Fifty-fifth, however, would remain in his lonely forest grave. His officers had, they said, buried him as he would have wished – with those he had commanded – though they vowed to raise a memorial in Madras.

On the last night, Fr Rodrigues had dined with as many of the officers as could assemble before they began the march back to their regular stations, and Hervey had presented him with a goodly sum for the repair and beautification of his church. It mattered not that he was a priest of Rome; had he been a Baptist they'd not have minded, for all a man wished for was that someone of religion would read the words over him if he were to fall. But if Fr Rodrigues had made no converts, said Hervey later, he'd done much to mitigate the Englishman's natural distaste for the odour of popery. For himself, he'd have appointed him the regiment's chaplain there and then, and brought him back to Madras. Except that Fr Rodrigues would never have consented to leave his little flock. That was the trouble with holy men.

---

[*] 'By this holy unction and his own most gracious mercy, may the Lord pardon you whatever sin you have committed . . .'

XXVI

A Time To . . .

Madras, 6 May

IT WAS THE CUSTOM ON St George's Day to have a great *tamasha* for all ranks – in England they called it a levee – to mark the raising of the regiment in 1759, the *Annus Mirabilis*, the year of victories against the French; but as they'd not all returned by the 23rd, the celebration was postponed for a fortnight. It would serve also to celebrate the victory at Coorg. They'd honoured the dead, and now it was time to honour the living.

For victory it most certainly was, as the laurels were already promising. On arriving home, or rather, on reporting to Fort St George, Hervey had found not just the commander-in-chief but Somervile, and when General O'Callaghan presented him with the ribbon of the Most Honourable Military Order of the Bath sent by London for his 'services in the late United Kingdom of the Netherlands', Somervile had pronounced himself certain that this signified also approval of his services in Bristol: 'Depend upon it, sir: the prime minister would no more consent to such an honour otherwise, than he would pin a medal on a Frenchman', adding that when Earl Grey heard of his actions at Coorg, 'He's sure to put a "K" before it.'

He'd certainly left Fort St George in a happier spirit. *We do but row, we're steer'd by Fate, / Which in success oft disinherits, / For spurious causes, noblest merits.* And thus it seemed; he was indeed a 'lucky general'. He was, though, surprised to discover just how much gold Somervile had secretly dispensed – to the deewah and her people, and thence to all manner of men at Coorg, not least to Chinnah Buswa and Konandera Apoo; and even, in the promissory letter that he himself had carried, to the rajah himself. 'War in India is made with gold and bullock carts.' In truth, it had been the same in the war with France: 'the cavalry of St George' – the gold sovereigns stamped with the very image of England – had done as much to hasten Bonaparte's end as the cavalry of the Duke of Wellington. But no matter; it was his good fortune – his luck – to serve one such as Somervile, without whom his victory could not have been so efficient. It was not money that would be talked of in the clubs in London, and the places that power resided, but his victory in the field. Generalcy would be his. He was now certain of it.

But for now, he would be glad to relinquish the temporary rank and return to command of the Sixth, with all its rewards and vexations. There were men whose services must be written up and commended (Owthwaite being just one; he would restore his stripes tomorrow) but, first, there was the *tamasha*, and the church parade and the games, the outward and visible signs of the inward and spiritual grace that was the discipline and morale of a King's regiment. A regiment was, he'd said more than once to St Alban – as Burke himself had said of 'Society' – a contract, a partnership, 'not only between those who are living, but between those who are living, those who are dead, and those who are to be born'. What else, indeed, was the point of exalting the founding day and the battle honours emblazoned on the guidons?

So he'd gone thence to the regimental lines, like the leopard to mark its territory. There he'd found things exactly as he'd left them – better, indeed, for the new white paint – for in his absence Lieutenant

(Quartermaster) Collins, whom he'd known as a corporal, serjeant and troop serjeant-major, had carried on 'in the best traditions'.

Armstrong was there, too, already harrying all and sundry in the time-honoured fashion, as if to say 'The rear party's stood down; it's the regiment now'.

'Coffee, Colonel-sahib?'

Hervey brightened the more. 'Sammy, *mikka nanri*' (thank you); '*Nalamaa?*'

The little Tamul beamed as he always did. No one could understand why he smiled so readily, for he'd no family and slept in a lean-to at the quartermaster's. 'I very good, Colonel-sahib; thank you, Colonel-sahib.'

Sammy swept the floors, ran errands, made tea and coffee. The quartermaster gave him a few rupees from time to time, to buy a little rice. The dragoons called him all the names under the sun – and then gave him a few annas of their own, for a little old Tamul who smiled when he'd nothing but their company was comfort in a hard world. One day, no doubt, they'd find him dead, with a smile on his face, and they'd give him a 'regimental' funeral, for as far as they were concerned Sammy was on the strength.

He came back at once with coffee in a silver pot. How he kept it hot, yet tasting fresh, was always a wonder to the orderly room. 'Is anything more, Colonel-sahib?'

Hervey shook his head, still reading over the first of his letters – to Lord Liverpool. The official notice of the death of his adoptive son was already at sea.

'Colonel-sahib, permissy speak?'

Hervey smiled. 'Of course, Sammy: permissy speak.'

'Colonel-sahib: Mr Jenkinson-sahib – I sorry for him. I like say he very fine gentiman.'

Hervey swallowed hard. 'Yes, a very fine gentleman.'

'I dismiss now, Colonel-sahib?'

Hervey smiled again and picked up his pen. 'Yes, Sammy; you may dismiss. And . . . thank you for speaking of Mr Jenkinson. I write his father. I write you say he was fine gentleman.'

Sammy, smiling ever more broadly, saluted.

When he was gone, Hervey rewrote a page of the letter, adding with the assurance of literal truth, 'He was held in the utmost regard, by even the lowest native bearer.'

A man could not wish to read better of a son than that.

And now he must add a little more to that to the Rector of Llanfihangel.

'Colonel, might I intrude?'

Hervey looked up.

'Oh, I beg pardon. I should have seen, you are writing.' St Alban imagined he knew to whom.

'Is it a matter for the moment?'

'No, Colonel, it was just that . . . No, there is no pressing need.'

'Then come to Arcot House at seven. The hock should be tolerably warm by then.'

St Alban was not unused to Hervey's humour, though he was not always certain of it. 'Thank you, Colonel.'

'Is all well for the morrow?'

'It is.'

He nodded and took up his pen again. 'Half an hour more, Edward, and then I'll ride for Arcot House.'

And tomorrow he'd write to Messrs Greenwood, Cox and Hammersley to have them send out Edward Pearce somehow.

He got to Arcot House a little after two, the hour when all but the chowkidar had leave to take their ease, but the household were expecting him.

Serjeant Stray, never given to great ceremony, however, confined himself to 'All present and correct, Colonel, and I'm sorry about Mr Jenkinson – and Captain Neale.'

Hervey thanked him. 'Mrs Hervey, the children – all are well?'

'They are, Colonel. Right as ninepence.'

He'd reckoned that word would have reached him otherwise, but India was a place of sudden events and imperfect communications.

'Have you eaten, Colonel?'

He was peculiarly glad to be returned, but he wasn't hungry. 'Lemonade, I think, Sar'nt Stray. As cold as may be.'

'Very good, Colonel. And I've placed all t'letters for you on your desk.'

Hervey nodded. 'And all has been well here?'

'They've been fine, Colonel. Not a snake or a *jogee*'s come near,' he said, with the old twinkle. 'Mrs Hervey's ridden out a lot – and Annie. Oh, Miss Gildea, I ought to say,' (Hervey smiled) 'with Miss Allegra on a leading rein.'

'Whose leading rein, Mrs Hervey's or Annie's?'

'Mrs Hervey, Colonel, with one o' t'RM's men, and a syce. But Annie's seat's coming along nice as well.'

'Capital.'

'And there've been ladies' gatherings an' what 'ave you. There were an 'Indoo princess at one of 'em. An' a bishop.'

'Admirable . . . I take it Mrs Hervey's resting now?'

'She is, Colonel. Johnson said you'd not be back for a couple of hours more.'

'That's the price of having so efficient a quartermaster. By the bye, the adjutant will come at seven, and also the major. And now, if you please, I'll sit outside and look over my letters. A bath in half an hour?'

'Colonel.'

He went to the south-facing verandah (there were three), looked through his letters for familiar hands, and at once opened two. They told him the same, and so doubled his pleasure: Georgiana would by now be taking passage in the company of a major and his wife bound for Madras. But as he read Elizabeth's letter he realized there was no mention of a governess. How was he supposed to manage, therefore?

'Oh, I'm sorry, sir, I didn't—'

He rose without thinking – a female voice. 'There's no need of regret, Annie. I was just taking my ease. You are well?'

The question was mere formality: she looked in the best of health.

'Very well, thank you, sir. And you? We have heard much of what the regiment has done.'

Her voice had changed. It was more measured. She'd never spoken with a pronounced accent, but it could now pass for a drawing room – which, he supposed, was only to be expected in her new position. Her appearance had always been pleasing, but in her cotton white and her broad-brimmed hat, there was now no telling her from a lady.

He smiled. 'The regiment – such as was of it – did very well, yes. But you'll have heard, perhaps, that Captain Neale and Mr Jenkinson are dead.'

She lowered her eyes. 'I did, sir, yes. How dreadful it will go with their families.'

'Just so. How is Miss Allegra?'

She smiled warmly. 'She is very well indeed. And in such spirit.'

'Serjeant Stray informs me that there've been no more untoward visitors since the cobra.'

'No, sir.'

'Well, I'm delighted to tell you that Miss Georgiana will join us before the year is out. Perhaps even before the monsoon breaks.'

Annie brightened the more. She'd taken to Georgiana at once when she'd visited Heston. 'I look forward very much to seeing Miss Georgiana, sir. And so, I'm sure, will Miss Allegra.'

He nodded, and with the satisfaction of recognizing that he need not fear at all for Georgiana's care. Annie had not the background of a regular governess, but she had a true character, which in the end, he'd always maintained, trumped breeding. But he'd not speak of it now.

He'd no wish to make her feel obliged just because he was returned from the field.

'Have you heard aught of your brother?'

He liked to bathe hot, even in the warmest weather. It seemed to help wash away all that had gone before. The air was still, now, but the windows – the louvred doors – were full open, and so he'd refused the punkah. He lay thinking of what had passed and what might come, but random thoughts, and to no particular purpose. A hoopoe began its call from below the window. Of all the birds, it was to him the most peaceful, and he closed his eyes to give thanks to his Maker for abundant blessings.

When he'd towelled himself dry and sat a while to savour a little more the joy of this place, he put on loose whites and brushed his hair. He thought perhaps he should send for the *nai*, for it was overlong, but there'd be time tomorrow before parade.

Coming up the stairs as he left his dressing room was Ayah Aaby, Sarah's help, with a tray of tea. She looked confused on seeing him.

He stood aside, smiling, and beckoning her to pass. '*Matiya vanakkam, ayah.*'

She bowed rather anxiously. '*Vanakkam, sahib.*'

'I come with you, ayah.'

She looked uncertain, but he took the tray and bid her lead on.

Kezia didn't at first wake when they entered. He put down the tray as Aaby pulled back the gauze curtains and pushed wide the louvres.

Then her eyes opened.

Aaby lowered hers as she left.

It was an hour before they went to the nursery together. Master Hervey was not only in good health but in good voice, and his ayah evidently had the measure of both mother and child. After a while Allegra joined them. 'His name is "Eyre",' she said – for Hervey was a stranger again

– bringing mildly rebuking words of explanation from both Kezia and Annie; but he himself thought it amusing, for it was said kindly, and he could judge these things.

Afterwards they strolled in the gardens, then sat for an hour talking before it was time to dress. When he told Kezia that Major Garratt and the adjutant were to call, she said they must stay to dine: 'Poor Edwin will have an empty homecoming otherwise, for he's too senior to throw himself on the officers' house, and without many acquaintances in the garrison yet, I doubt he can invite any to his own table.'

Her generosity warmed him the more.

It was true, he told her, and strange, also, how much he'd come to rely so surely on a man he'd never known before. Fortune, indeed, smiled on him very liberally now. Except, of course, he would soon lose St Alban, and there was no knowing if, or when, he could get Pearce to return.

'And there's another letter, which I didn't mention,' he said, and somewhat hesitantly. 'Captain Fairbrother writes that he will come to Madras.'

Kezia put her hand on his. 'That is the best of news. I think he must be the truest of companions.'

Her good opinion in that pleased him more than he could say. He could never have imagined it before. 'And he's of no little account in the field. I would have had great use for him in Coorg.'

'There will be other occasions, I imagine.'

No doubt there would be. The Company did not keep an army in India to no purpose. Now, indeed, Fort St George – Fort William even – would have him leading every expedition there was against whatever nabob or dacoit had the effrontery to challenge their dominion.

The adjutant came carefully upon his hour, as an adjutant must (the major, he knew, would be a courteous quarter of an hour late). They went to the further end of the garden and sat in the bamboo chairs next to the rockery that Kezia had made in his absence, now the home of butterflies, which he'd not thought to see in Madras, believing it somehow too hot. The heat of the day had become the pleasant warmth of evening, however, so that the ice in their glasses – American ice, brought but an hour ago by a specially got-up *tanga* (and at a woeful price) – chilled the hock rather than just diluted it.

'Now, Edward, you were minded to tell me something, and I put you off telling me. I confess I was somewhat preoccupied. Not displeasing news, I trust?'

'I trust not, Colonel.'

'Proceed.'

'Well, I don't know quite how to say this, Colonel – and perhaps I ought to have put it in writing . . .'

'Good heavens, man, you're not seeking redress of grievance, are you?'

St Alban looked rather abashed, joke that it was. 'No, Colonel. Not at all. Not in the least. Quite the contrary.'

'Well then, do not suspend the pleasure!'

'I wish to beg leave to withdraw my resignation.'

With effort, Hervey managed to keep his countenance. There was no better thing he could have wished to hear, but . . . 'Why? Upon what grounds?'

'On the grounds, Colonel, that my earlier decision was based on poor judgement.'

'Indeed? Explain.'

'I had formed the view that our presence in India was inherently unjust, that we exploited the country solely for our own gain, and to its detriment, and—'

'Wait. You have objection to the principle of trade?'

'No, of course not, Colonel. Free and fair trade, that is.'

'Then the new Act will be to your liking.'

The new Charter Act turned India into a colony and the Company from one of merchants into one of administrators.

'It is one of the reasons I wish to retrieve my papers. If the Company no longer has a monopoly of trade, there is every reason to suppose any present ills may be cured. But I confess I see now, as I didn't before, that we do good here, even if it is merely consequential on the Company's trade. Now that it is to be a true administration, I think it will be wholly admirable, and I would be part of it.'

He did not say also, for he could not without breach of all propriety, that he'd formed such a regard for his commanding officer that he wished to serve here as long as may be.

Kezia came.

'My dear, Mr St Alban is to stay with us after all. I confess to being a little pleased.'

Kezia expressed herself even more pleased. 'I have seen little enough of my husband since we came here, Edward, and I would not wish him to spend a moment longer at office than need be.'

St Alban returned the smile. 'I am doubly honoured, then, ma'am.'

When Somervile came, towards eight, the khitmagar brought a third bottle of champagne, since Major Garratt had arrived not long after St Alban's *vin d'honneur* (Kezia had laid in a basket of Monsieur Moët's best for Hervey's return) and had found the ice, in his words, a blessed relief, no matter what its provenance.

'St Alban is to remain with the regiment, Sir Eyre,' explained Hervey.

'Capital!' replied Somervile, beginning on a long encomium to the Sixth.

Hervey's thoughts, however, were with the Preacher once more, the son of David, king in Jerusalem: *To every thing there is a season, and a time to every purpose under the heaven.* There was for him, the soldier, in the end just the two: time of war, and time of peace. He'd seen much of war, and now he hoped to see something of peace – true peace. His wife was restored to him; he had a son; his daughter would join them soon, and his good friend likewise; he had command of that which had been his world for twenty-five years; the people about him were of his choosing, and he had friends close at hand and in London too. He had tasted generalship, and there was the promise of more – and honours. His world was complete.

It was the time to dance.

HISTORICAL AFTERNOTE

ESTIMATES PUT THE NUMBER of those involved in the disturbances in Bristol at between 5,000 and 10,000, though perhaps 'only' a thousand were active in Queen Square. The city's infirmary recorded that twelve were killed during the rioting, ostensibly by the military, and 86 wounded. This is generally thought to be well short of the total, however, for many perished in the fires, while others crawled home to die of their wounds. The Bristol coroner's records for the period are missing.

Once the authorities had re-established control, whole areas of the city were searched for stolen goods. In the subsequent trials, presided over by Sir Nicholas Tindal, Chief Justice of Common Pleas, 114 were indicted for riot, arson or theft. The death sentence was passed on 31, though this was commuted in all but four cases. The population of Australia received a boost.

All the silver at the Mansion House was recovered, with the exception of a large salver. An old woman, confined in the New Gaol on a charge of receiving plunder, hanged herself.

A Special Commission tried Mayor Pinney for negligence, and exonerated him. He seems to have acted with commendable resolve in what were probably the worst civil disturbances in modern history.

Captain Warrington was court-martialled and sentenced to be cashiered. He was, however, allowed to sell his commission instead.

After Colonel Brereton's suicide, his daughters, Catherine and Mary, were brought up by a great-uncle. Catherine died aged 11 in England;

Mary, it seems, travelled to the Cape, whence her mother's family came, and in 1847 married a cousin.

On 7 May 1834, Coorg was formally annexed to the East India Company's territory. Nevertheless, there were misgivings in London, and the rajah was subsequently treated with no little consideration, being allowed to live in comfort in Benares. In 1852 he was permitted to come to England to argue for the return of his wealth. He was accompanied by his 11-year-old daughter Gouramma (spelled Gauromma in British newspapers at the time), and both were received by Queen Victoria. Indeed, in July Gouramma was baptized at Buckingham Palace by the Archbishop of Canterbury, with the Queen as one of her godparents. Known subsequently as Princess Victoria Gouramma, she was painted (beautifully as always) by Franz Winterhalter, and later photographed by Roger Fenton.

In 1860 she married a British officer, Colonel John Campbell, a widower with several sons, and in 1861 they had a daughter, Edith Victoria Gouramma Campbell. Princess Victoria Gouramma died in 1864, however, just a year after her father. She is buried at Brompton Cemetery, and he, the last Rajah of Coorg, at Kensal Green.

The officers of the 55th Regiment erected a memorial tablet to Lieutenant-Colonel Charles Mill in St Mary's Church, Madras, where it remains today.

In the aftermath of the Indian Mutiny (1857), by the provisions of the Government of India Act 1858, the East India Company was nationalized and the Crown took over its Indian possessions, its administrative powers and its army and navy. Now began the period of the so-called British Raj.

MATTHEW PAULINUS HERVEY

BORN: 1791, second son of the Reverend Thomas Hervey, Vicar of Horningsham in Wiltshire, and of Mrs Hervey; one sister, Elizabeth.

EDUCATED: Shrewsbury School (praepostor)

MARRIED: 1817 to Lady Henrietta Lindsay, ward of the Marquess of Bath (deceased 1818). 1828 to Lady Lankester, widow of Lieutenant–Colonel Sir Ivo Lankester, Bart, lately commanding 6th Light Dragoons.

CHILDREN: a daughter, Georgiana, born 1818.

··························RECORD OF SERVICE··························

1808: commissioned cornet by purchase in His Majesty's 6th Light Dragoons (Princess Caroline's Own).

1809–14: served Portugal and Spain; evacuated with army at ✕ Corunna, 1809, returned with regiment to Lisbon that year; present at numerous battles and actions including ✕ Talavera, ✕ Badajoz, ✕ Salamanca, ✕ Vitoria.

1814: present at ✕ Toulouse; wounded Lieutenant.

1814–15: served Ireland, present at ✕ Waterloo, and in Paris with army of occupation.

1815: Additional ADC to the Duke of Wellington (acting captain); despatched for special duty in Bengal.

1816: saw service against Pindarees and Nizam of Hyderabad's forces; returned to regimental duty. Brevet captain; brevet major.

1818: saw service in Canada; briefly seconded to US forces, Michigan Territory; resigned commission.

1819: reinstated, 6th Light Dragoons; captain.

1820–26: served Bengal; saw active service in ✕ Ava (wounded severely); present at ✕ Siege of Bhurtpore; brevet major.

1826–27: detached service in Portugal.

1827: in temporary command of 6th Light Dragoons, major; in command of detachment of 6th Light Dragoons at the Cape Colony; seconded to raise Corps of Cape Mounted Rifles; acting lieutenant–colonel; ✕ Umtata River; wounded.

1828: home leave.

1828: service in Natal and Zululand.

1829: attached to Russian army in the Balkans for observation in the war with Turkey.

1830: assumes command 6th Light Dragoons (Princess Augusta's Own) in substantive rank of lieutenant–colonel, Hounslow.